REDEEM

Redeem

Wanda -
Thanks for buying my
inappropriate book! :)
Best wishes

Patrick E. Douglas

Library of Congress Control Number:		2010918206
ISBN:	Hardcover	978-1-4568-2874-5
	Softcover	978-1-4568-2873-8
	Ebook	978-1-4568-2875-2

This book was printed in the United States of America.

To order additional copies of this book, contact:
Xlibris Corporation
1-888-795-4274
www.Xlibris.com
Orders@Xlibris.com
90837

For my Dad and Justin
Gone too soon.

re•deem (ri dem) 1. to get back; recover 2. to set free 3. to carry out or fulfill 4. to make up for

1

Friday, October 4, 1983

The star-filled Colorado sky seemed like an eternity away. Like staring down the edge of a cliff leading nowhere. The abyss hovered aimlessly over the peaks of pine trees that rose to greet the blackness of that night, Andrea on her back, looking up at distant stars like a curious child. For a second, she thought she was safe and back in some forgotten memory. Waves of nausea flowed through her brain as the pain quickly returned with her consciousness. You can't imagine even for a moment, what it must feel like to be lost, at least lost in the way Andrea was. The stream of blood cascaded from her nose down the side of her face and into her ear, reminding her that her nightmare was far from over. If only she could just stand up and leave.

A spider crawled over her bare leg and she shivered as the tiny legs tickled her skin. She didn't even think about her fear of spiders, nor did she comprehend that one had in fact touched her. It was getting colder.

Another shiver revived her soul as a frigid breeze blew through the forest. Feeling more alert, Andrea mustered up enough strength to prop herself up. Someone was coming. The crackling of branches and brush did nothing more than charge her already speeding heartbeat. But it was so dark.

She could feel the steady dripping of blood onto her bare leg as she sat in a semi cross-legged style. The warmth of her blood was easily recognizable on her cold skin. Taking her mud-covered hand, she wiped across her face realizing that her nose was split open. Oddly enough, it didn't hurt that much. It was just annoying, like the few times she accidentally got water up her nose while swimming. She was too scared to feel the extent of the pain. Groggy and fading, her memory slowly began to return as she recalled running into a tree in her haste to get away from the madness. *The madness!*

Her breath became a fog when she hopped back to her feet and thrust herself into the cool air all around her. The visions in her mind were just as cloudy and quick to disappear. What had just happened? Innocence gone and never again a part of her life, the wave of panic came back like a tidal wave.

The sounds of young men screaming filled the darkness of forest around her and she saw a faint light in the distance. Nowhere to go, she aimlessly charged through the black in hope of just getting as far away from everyone as she could.

As was the case moments before, *she was running for her life.*

"Andrea!" a voice echoed through the trees. "Andrea, get back here! Please stop. No one is gonna hurt you. Come back!"

Stop? She didn't start anything. Why was this person telling her to stop running? There was no way in hell that she was going back to that campsite, not as long as Richard Tark remained there. She wondered where Alexis was. Why wasn't she out there looking for her? Andrea thought about their friendship, and aided by her head wound, conjured up a scenario that had Alexis laughing back at the campsite at the expense of her friend's fear. This was no joke. She had to get away.

Andrea had no idea what nightmare Alexis had gone through. She didn't know that her blood had been spilled into the dirt and had no idea she was already dead.

The campsite was now a chaotic collection of regretful witnesses and guilty perpetrators. As the flames tickled the night air, the only person left calm was Richard. He didn't seem to realize anything. He just stared blankly at the fire with a dumb grin on his face. It's like he knew that they were all finally equals. In a matter of minutes things went from a normal camping trip, to a bunch of teens succumbing to their sexual inhibitions and finally to a crime scene. The realization that you are a murderer and a rapist hits like a ton of bricks, and it isn't the thought of jail time that suddenly points your mind towards right and wrong. These young men were all battling their own demons and mixed with alcohol, those demons can get pretty loud.

"Andrea!"

"Where'd she run?" Seth asked Willie. "She can't get out of this forest. If she gets away, we're all fucked."

Willie seemed to understand that sentiment. They needed to find her and keep her from going to the police. They needed to keep her from verifying the truth that they were horrible people. She was the one witness that could not be trusted and rightfully so. It wasn't like they wanted her back because they were worried about her or because they felt bad for what had happened to her. The guys didn't want her to talk. No one knew for sure what they were going to do or say to sway her from turning them all in, but they had to get her back first and foremost.

And they had to do something about Alexis.

Willie pointed to the spot where he saw Andrea disappear into the darkness and Seth pushed him to find her.

"Hurry," Seth said.

Willie quietly jogged into the brush with his flashlight lit and held firmly in one hand, a Swiss Army knife in the other. He didn't know what was out there and was honestly a little scared of the creatures that may or may not want to eat him.

"Andrea!" he yelled. "C'mon out."

No response.

"Alexis is hurt bad and we need to get her out of here," he said. "C'mon Andrea. Everything is okay."

He slowed to a walk and followed a path of trampled grass obviously cut by Andrea's fleeing feet. Every noise startled him and his nervous reactions were triggered by sheer adrenaline. Partially scared of what could be stalking him and partially hoping beyond hope to find Andrea sitting on a rock, Willie was a wreck.

Eventually, Andrea's path faded and Willie found himself following his instincts, rewarded with absolutely no luck at all. In the background he could hear Seth yelling at the other guys. The camp was getting farther away as was Willie's conscience. His pace slowed to a crawl as his knees felt like they were going to give out. Sprawled out on the forest floor was a rotting trunk from a long forgotten tree that had fallen years before. Willie sat down for a rest, already trying to come up with an alibi for what he and his friends had just done.

"Please come out Andrea," he said just before he broke down in tears. He cupped his face in his hands and wept out loud, something that he hadn't done in years. The night was a disaster and he was stuck trying to find someone in the dark that didn't want to be found. His guilt was even more powerful since it was he who convinced the guys to take both girls to the mountains. It was he who brought Richard along.

"She's fuckin' dead ya'll!" Charles yelled back at the camp sight. Willie heard that. "Muthafucka!"

The boys all gathered around Alexis' body and looked at the disgusting site. Her clothes were ripped and covered in mud, dirt and semen. Reggie knelt down and closed her legs, tugging her skirt down over her exposed crotch as if he wanted her to have a dignity in death that she obviously didn't have in life. Worst of all were her eyes. Both were open, gazing at the boys in a cryptic, final gesture of finger-pointing. They were the ones who had left her in that state. Reggie then slid her eyelids down with his fingertips just like he had seen in movies. It felt like the right thing to do.

"So, what the fuck we gonna do?" Charles asked in panic, more agitated than anything else. "I don't have time for this dead bitch. If this shit gets out, they sure as fuck won't let me play ball this year." He pounded his leg on the ground like a little boy having a tantrum. "Fuck this shit, man!"

"Ball?" Seth yelled, bumping chests with the much larger Charles. "Ball? Dude, if this gets *out*, your ass is going to the electric chair. No, no, no. You're ass is going to be fucking strung up. Now, shut the fuck up so I can think here." Seth put his hands over his temples and rubbed them, thinking hard about a solution. "Jesus. I was just trying to get laid."

"You the reason she dead!" yelled Reggie. "Ain't 'cause of me. Ain't 'cause of Charles. Ain't 'cause of this sad sack of shit." Reggie pointed to Richard. "You the one that was so fuckin' rough. What'd you do to her anyway?"

Seth charged at Reggie.

"I fucked her same as you!" he yelled. "What makes you think I killed her?"

"Uh, she sure as hell wasn't movin' when I was on her," Reggie replied.

"So, what does that make you?" Seth accused. No one spoke for quite awhile after that question was asked.

Seth was the fearless quarterback. He always came up with the right answers at the right time. This was when they needed him the most. He had to come up with the right play for this particular game. Charles recognized Seth's outburst as a serious threat and remained quiet for the rest of the night. He had to think about it pretty hard. Could he trust Seth? Reggie stood over Alexis' cold body. Tears streamed down his cheeks for the better part of ten minutes and as was the case with the other guys, he thought of his role in the murder. Looking back, he felt like maybe he did know she wasn't alive when he came inside of her. So what did that make him? The worst nightmares of humankind were all being played out live and in person. The spine of a young man who would rape and murder a young girl is nothing more than a piece of black licorice. There's nothing sweet about it.

As if he had to make amends to her lifeless body, Seth gently lifted Alexis off of the ground and carried her to the fire pit cautiously setting her on Richard's blanket. Now the boys were acting like civilized human beings. Now they were concerned about the well being of this girl as if she'd jump up at any minute and shake off the dirt and have a few beers and a laugh over it all. Everyone involved in the crime paced around her, nervous about what had happened, and curious as to the whereabouts of Andrea.

The wind got fierce and whipped through the trees, creating a sound reminiscent of someone screaming far away. The boys all jumped, all except Richard. He continued to stare at the flickering flames as he had done since he chased Andrea to the edge of the forest. Paranoia set in as it began to feel like thousands of eyes were fixated on the boys, witnesses to their terrible crime.

"What the fuck was that?" Reggie asked. Again the noise echoed through the trees with a strong gust of wind aiding it. Worse than the noise was the silence that followed. No wind. No sound. All four boys could hear nothing but their breathing.

"It's just the wind," Reggie calmly said to himself. "God damn, I'm gonna have a heart attack."

"Hey, get her off of my bed!" Richard yelled, diverting the others from their anxiety over the wind and the surrounding darkness. In a flash, he sprung from his seat in front of the fire, and pulled his blanket from under Alexis, tossing her body around like a rag doll.

"Whoa. What the fuck? What do you think you're doing?" Seth screamed, his face turning dark red. He wanted to punch Richard. The next person that got in his way was going to end up with a fat lip. "Here's the deal you guys. We need to get rid of what happened tonight. Forget about the fucking wind," he said, waving his hands around at the trees. "Forget about your fucking blankie," he said, pointing at Richard. "Let's figure this out. No one can know what happened tonight."

The guys continued to stare at her dead body. The world as they knew it was through. Life could not, and would not, ever be the same. Reggie stared at her chest, naively hoping that it would move as she took in air. It never happened.

"This fuckin' sucks," Charles said.

The tears all faded.

The screams were all silenced.

It was time to repair the situation.

2

Six Weeks Earlier

Waves of steam hovered at chest level just as the shower was turned off. Lingering with the fog was the smell of steamed outhouse shit from a morning dump that still floated in the bowl. For some reason he had a phobia of flushing the toilet before taking a shower. Something about how he felt it would magically make its way into the clean water and spray right back on him. A towel was raised and used to clear the condensation from the mirror. Reflecting back was the tortured face of Richard Tark. His features were flush because he had stood in the shower for nearly forty-five minutes and emptied the hot water tank completely. Scowling at his reflection, Richard was well aware of his being up so early.

All the water in the world couldn't wash away his dire feelings. The lump in his throat first appeared as he opened his eyes to start the day, and was getting bigger by the minute. If anything, he wanted to cry and get it over with.

Summer was over.

Life was to continue as planned.

This sucks, he thought as the image in the mirror again began to fade from the steam. He wiped it clean again and clenched his jaw. If a foggy mirror was irritating him, it was surely going to be a long day. The radio was loud, as usual, and was belting out the latest tune from Men At Work. Taking into consideration the fact that Richard absolutely despised Men At Work, you can see how his concentration was focused on something other than the music. He didn't have a clue. Thoughts of Geoff surfaced and the lump in his throat grew more irritating.

All summer long he had tromped around with Geoff, the one true friend that he had during his rocky pre-high school years. The one friend that didn't stab him in the back. The one friend that stayed by his side when his parents split up. Now Geoff was gone.

The summer had been an extended going away party that made the rest of his life seem somewhat meaningless and anticlimactic.

Geoff's family, more specifically his father, decided to move to California at the end of the summer, all in the name of public education and the opportunities which were presented in other parts of the country. You see, Geoff's father was a high school teacher and had taken a job in Salinas. Sometimes it's not fair how little say children have in the affairs of their families.

Richard and Geoff made the most of their time and did everything from water skiing to watching porn together, the latter a preference for Richard. The water skiing trip was courtesy of Geoff's father, as he felt somewhat guilty for tearing his son away from such a good friend. The porn was also courtesy of Geoff's father, although he was oblivious to it.

It had been more than two weeks since Geoff took off, and Richard hadn't heard a peep from his old friend. It didn't matter anyway. Richard knew the drill and said his goodbyes to Geoff with the full intention of never seeing or hearing from him again. In Richard's experience, people didn't leave and then come back. In fact, they didn't seem to even look in the rearview mirror on the way out of town.

Again, Richard cleared a circle on the glass in front of him. Why bother? It would just fog up again thirty seconds later. He didn't feel like a freshman. All of the years prior, he had visions of how high school was going to be and what he was going to feel like once he got there. The butterflies that engulfed his mid section were fierce, yet he continued to stare at himself as if a solution to the problem would jump out and present itself. Was he different? Could he handle the tortures and pressure that came with the final stretch of public education? Should he even bother? That was just a microcosm of the bulk of thoughts and questions that raged in his troubled mind.

"Fuck it," he said as he turned to leave the bathroom, picking his clothes off the floor on his way out. "Stop worrying about it," he said, coaching himself to forget about what lay ahead. He knew that no matter what he tried nothing would work.

Richard made his way into his bedroom and locked the door behind him. His room was a complete disgust. Clothes, shoes, empty pop cans, even some pizza boxes lined the floor, hiding a carpet that was too disguised to even divulge what color it was. He threw the clothes that were in his hands and walked to the corner of his room, looking out of his window.

He sighed.

The world outside seemed like it was being viewed through different eyes. In the summer, everything looked better. The people, the trees, the animals. Starting on that first morning of school, things looked gray. It was like having the perfect peach and forgetting about it, realizing its existence only after it has started to stink. Nothing was real. He couldn't wait to grow up and move out on his own. Then he wouldn't have to get up at all. He could lie in bed all day, jerking off, watching television and eating Ramen noodles.

Speaking of jerking off.

For a normal teen, a glance is all it takes sometimes. Richard was certainly not normal and he knew from the moment his eyes met his closet door what he was going to do next. It had gotten to the point where it was almost a scheduled exercise. There was no real physical or mental trigger. It was just that time of day. Quietly and somewhat anxiously, he walked to the closet and opened it. He looked around suspiciously, like someone was going to catch him in the act. Who would see? Reaching up over the top shelf, he pulled down the tattered remains of a Hustler magazine that had been his soulmate since he found it discarded in a ditch a few years before. He didn't need it for help but had an inkling that it might make it a better experience. He knew what page to go to as it was dog-eared and pretty roughed up. In a male teenage minute he had his hand down his underwear, rubbing himself in a rhythmic dance that led to the ultimate stain in his BVD's. As usual, he felt a wave of pain and regret once the act was over. It didn't make sense that something that felt so good couldn't satisfy him once it was complete. It just left him feeling hollow and humiliated. Still, there was nothing that could take the place of a good spanking first thing in the morning.

Standing in the middle of the rubble, feeling like he had just wet his pants, Richard surveyed his room for a pair of reasonably clean jeans. There was one positive to having just jerked off, he didn't feel as tense as before. It was almost as if he was on his way to being ready to take on another day.

KNOCK! KNOCK!

His mother was banging on his bedroom door, and knowing what he had just done startled him completely. What if she had done that two minutes earlier?

"What!" he snapped.

"Honey, open the door," the muffled voice of his mother said. He could see that she was trying to turn the handle, and he lifted his head in a sigh of relief at the fact that he had indeed locked it. He walked to the door and turned the handle before cracking it just enough to peek his eyes around the corner. He still had a hard-on and wasn't about to give his mother something else to lecture him about.

"Son, I was talking to Mallory at work," she said before being interrupted.

"Who?" Richard barked. "What are you talking about?"

"Mallory. You know, she works with me. You've met her before," she continued. "Anyway, her niece just moved to town and is living with her."

Richard rolled his eyes. Here she was again, trying to set him up with one of her prissy, bitch acquaintances. He started to close the door in her face, prompting her to stick the front of her shoe in the way to jam it.

"Richard!" she said, scolding him. "Like I was saying, her niece is new to town and is going to Carver. I told her you would give her a ride to school." The two made eye contact and Richard knew his mother meant business. "I told her you'd do it."

"Jesus Christ!" Richard yelled, letting go of the door and walking deeper into the messy room. "Why are you always doing this to me? I can find a girl on my own."

"Son, it isn't going to kill you. She lives like three blocks from here and you can just swing by on your way to school." Inching her way into the wreck of his bedroom, she looked around disgusted, choosing not to say anything at first.

"Whatever," Richard said, his back still facing his mother.

"Here's her address," she said as she held up a piece of paper. Richard didn't turn to accept it. "I'll just put it here on your . . . um . . . how 'bout over here . . . or, maybe . . . Why don't you straighten this room up for once? It's a dang pigsty in here." She held her finger to her nose, pinching it shut. "And it smells horrible. Why do I smell piss, Richard?"

She didn't know it, but he had started pissing in the corner of his bedroom, feeling it was too much work to walk to the bathroom.

Richard finally turned to face her.

"You know what? It's the first day of school, in case you hadn't noticed, and I'm already late. Why don't you close the door and mind your own fucking business," Richard snapped, holding up his arm and pointing away. He had never before spoken to her using that word, the word that you just don't use around your own mother. Truth was, he was embarrassed and didn't want her to fight back. He just wanted her to leave.

A tear rolled down his mother's cheek and she placed the paper with the address on a pile of garbage that covered his nightstand. He had lost any kind of relationship with his mom the day his dad left. Not understanding why or having anything explained to him, the whole divorce just sort of happened. His mother became a shell of emotional breakdowns and was in no shape to be the strong figure he needed to steer him in the right direction. Richard, being a tiny and naturally lame individual, was the kind of kid you hear about every so often who requires a role model to succeed in life. His father left town and Richard never heard from him again. The Prick. That was the name used in reference to his father—The Prick.

The piece of paper with the address rested on a crusty pizza box. Richard picked it up and saw the location of some girl he was now obligated to transport. Next to it, the words "Love You," were written along with a crude drawing of a happy face. Even though the smiley face and words of endearment were shit to Richard, he still felt guilty and sad when he saw them knowing what he had just said to her. Unexplainable, for him that's just the way it was. It was too little, too late.

Richard's mom returned to the kitchen and stared out of the window. She was such a beautiful being at one point in her life but now was nothing more than a target of her son's aggression, a single parent and someone's ex. She did manage to salvage a rare, happy memory when Richard came downstairs and put his arms around her.

"Sorry I snapped at you," he said callously, as if forced to by a scolding voice of reason. Occasionally, although an extreme rarity, Richard showed signs of emotion and acted like a functional member of society. He didn't have the resources or knowledge that a lot of his peers did when it came to family values, but from time to time, he tried.

The two hugged and Richard grabbed a piece of cold toast from the table along with his house keys. He was the oldest freshman in his class at sixteen years of age and was the only one who had his driver's license, not that anyone cared. He had just earned it shortly before Geoff moved away and was still learning the basics so it wasn't a big deal to anyone but Richard.

"Thank you," Richard's mom yelled as he closed the front door behind him.

Resting in the driveway was the beat up remains of a vehicle that had its day and was far removed from it, an orange 1964 Volkswagen Bug. Equipped with all of the pleasantries associated with those fine automobiles, the car was certainly no sight for sore eyes. It had dented fenders, chipped paint, broken turn signals and who could forget the spot where someone had spray painted the words "FUCK ME" on the side in black? He had covered up the profane message with an orange spray paint similar to the color of the car, but a tad off. Anyone with a grade school education could still read the graffiti, even if it didn't stand out as much. Beggars can't be choosers and when you get your first car it doesn't matter if the thing looks good, it just has to run, regardless if it says "FUCK ME" on the side or not.

Richard never locked the thing since he had no key to unlock the doors. Who would want to break into it anyway? In any other circumstance he may have had to worry about someone driving off with it since it had a no key activated ignition switch. Without the use of or need for a key, the ignition switch dangled from the steering column and could be turned with any protruding object, ideally a flathead screwdriver. Richard knew this, thus he kept one handy on the passenger seat most of the time.

Angry and tired, the engine finally turned over and farted out its morning smoke after a few tense moments of wonder. Richard shook his head in embarrassment and slammed the stick in reverse.

Fort Collins was a pretty decent town to be raised in and go to school. Richard had his fair share of memorable times in the city but still wished on a daily basis that someday he could escape and see other parts of the country. Along the front range the hills still spewed forth lush green foliage even though it was nearing September. Soon enough, those hills would be covered with snow.

Richard didn't know what he was more nervous about, attending Carver High School for the first time, or picking up an actual female in his piece of shit car. He shook from the combination of chilly temperatures and his anxiety. A young woman would soon sit next to him. Would she be drop dead gorgeous? A complete monster? He had no clue.

"Lovely," he said as he pulled into the parking lot of her apartment. That parking lot would forever be cemented in Richard's memory like the steps of heaven. The complex itself looked about as crummy as his bedroom but he didn't mind at all.

A lot of people who fall madly in love with someone can tell you when and where they first saw their loved one. They might be able to tell you what the other was wearing, or something they said, or maybe even describe what it smelled like. Falling in love can be as easy as seeing someone that you want and knowing that you will die before that person walks the earth with someone else.

What stood before Richard was the ultimate in beauty, at least in his mind. A girl, standing about five-seven, sporting a perfect body and wearing a pair of tight jeans and a baggy blue sweater, stood at the bottom of a staircase with her books held tightly to her bosom. Her hair was so fluffed and heavily hair sprayed that it formed an impenetrable force field. Richard began to sweat as he pictured her beautiful body sitting in the crusty seat next to him. It had to be a dream. From Richard's point of view, she walked down the stairs in slow motion, her hair flowing in the breeze as she shook her head like a shampoo model. He imagined her smiling with a sensual look on her face. A look that said, "I'm ready when you are."

For anyone else viewing the scene, that was as far from reality as you could muster. As you'll see in this story, love does strange things to the mind of a confused and horny teenager.

She walked hesitantly towards the stranger's car, noticing the words "FUCK ME" covered up on the door with an orange three shades darker than the rest of the paint job. As he came to a stop, a wave of smoke caught up and engulfed her. She coughed. Richard pulled up along side of her and reached over to open the door.

"Are you . . ." he began, looking down at the piece of paper to find her name. "Andrea?"

She conjured a polite smile and nodded before climbing into his car, letting out a squeaky mouse cough as she tried not to embarrass him. Richard stared at her for a moment, breathing in her perfume as if it were the most heavenly aroma he had ever inhaled. He wanted to pounce on her like a wild animal. It was the first time he had ever driven the car without some foul odor taking over the air space and not only was it a pleasant smell, it was coming from a beautiful female.

"I'm Richard," he said. "Where you from?" He was desperately trying to strike up a conversation that would give him a cover just so he could look her over some more.

"A little town in Montana called Stanford," she said, offering a shy smile, praying that he would somehow drive away and get her to school as quickly as possible.

"Montana?" Richard belted. "Far out." He stared blankly at her. "I've heard of Stanford . . . John Elway played there, right?"

Silence filled the car, and yet he still hadn't started driving away from her apartment.

"Um, played where?" she said. "Stanford's not that big and I don't know who John Elway is."

"Why'd you move here?" he asked, still hoping he could strike an amazing conversation.

"My mom sent me to live with my aunt," she said, this time gesturing for Richard to at least begin driving. "What time is it? I don't want to be late on the first day."

Richard looked at his watch.

"Aww. We got plenty of time," he said, confident while stalling.

Eventually he slammed the gearshift into first and the two were on their way. Even though the conversation was thick in the beginning, the two didn't say much for about five minutes after he pulled away from her home. That was the recovery time Richard needed to assess the success or failure of his previous questions and begin anew. The gentle purr of the engine was actually calming for both of them. Andrea was beginning to fully wake up and was really enjoying the beauty that Colorado was famous for. Everything was so pure, yet seemingly fake and she hadn't allowed herself to really *look* at it since moving south.

"Hey, pull my finger," Richard said, pointing his finger at Andrea. She knew exactly where that joke was headed and immediately thought of Richard as a pig for even suggesting it. She hadn't experienced that since her uncle did it when she was a little girl. "C'mon, pull it."

Richard looked over to find Andrea puzzled and somewhat disgusted.

"Either way, it's gonna happen. Fine, I'll just have to do it myself," he said as he reached over and pulled on his right index finger, lifting his butt at the same time while releasing a sound reminiscent to an elephant's honk. The car soon filled with the aroma of shit. Richard laughed unmercifully to the point where tears streamed down his cheek. Geoff would've been crying along side him. That was their joke. If only Geoff could see Richard doing it with a girl. Classic.

Andrea breathed exclusively from her mouth and turned to look out of the passenger window, pressing her forehead against the glass. She still couldn't truly understand why her mother made her move to Colorado. It didn't make sense. This was not where she wanted to be. Back home, she was familiar with everything around her and actually liked Stanford. Now, she was riding to a strange school with a boy who just shit his pants and laughed about it as if it were the highlight of his day.

Most kids who grow up in a town like Stanford can't wait to get out. With just over 200 residents, there wasn't much incentive for youth to stick around. The world is just too big a rock for people to make that a first choice of a lifetime of residence. Andrea didn't really care for the mythological tales of big cities and fast food joints. She was one of the few her age content in po-dunk Montana. It wasn't a stretch for her to imagine staying there, meeting a man, having babies and living out her life on a ranch in the area. That's what you do if you stay.

The lonely dirt road that connected her family's humble home with the town itself was as familiar a sight as anything for Andrea, and she imagined her mother driving to work at the same moment she was going to school. Imaginative scenarios played out in her head over and over while Richard's smell intruded.

Negative memories of her childhood were erased and replaced by good thoughts, some of which didn't even happen in reality. It's strange when someone moves to a new town, they sometimes think of their former home as heaven on earth, even if it was far from it. Familiarity can be so comforting in the face of distress.

The biggest city Andrea had been in up until she moved to Fort Collins was a town called Great Falls, located just northwest of Stanford. With a population of merely 60,000 people, Great Falls wasn't what you would call a burgeoning metropolis. To Andrea, Great Falls was New York. The stores were bigger, the food was better, the streets were more crowded and the movies weren't black and white. It was her Disneyland. Great Falls had all of the major department stores, a large mall, and a seemingly infinite selection of restaurants to eat at. As sad as it may seem to those who have spent their lives in populated areas, Andrea was content with her Montana.

Make no mistake, Great Falls wasn't where her heart stayed. It was Stanford. Memories that stretched back to infinity in her mind all incorporated Stanford. The old fishing hole where she kissed a boy for the first time. The café where she did dishes for a first job. The lovely and boring lifestyle that came with the lovely and boring town. The place where she buried her father, and his father. It was all Stanford.

All of those things were now distant memories that seemed like ages ago. Walking to her aunt's car as it warmed up on that fateful day, Andrea felt like someone being led down death row. She didn't want this. If she could do anything in the world at that moment, it would be to turn around and go home. Her mother wouldn't have any of it. She was the warden leading Andrea to the electric chair. She wanted her daughter to go away and find a better life in what she thought was a better place.

The confusion and growing resentment was culminating with Richard's disgusting act of flatulence. Five minutes into the drive and the car still smelled like ass and gasoline. Richard could sense Andrea's revulsion in his display of jocularity and offered a half-hearted apology.

"Sorry about the whole fart thing," he said. "I thought it was kind of funny. It's something my friend and I used to do."

Andrea smiled and it was genuine. She hadn't actually done that in a while and even though the initial shock of having a stranger bust ass in front of her was hard to understand, it suddenly seemed kind of amusing. It wasn't that Richard was funny to her or that his act of uncanny rudeness was excusable, it was more like the scene itself was a joke that she was witnessing from afar. Like a giggling nut in an insane asylum, laughing at the absurd is sometimes the result of giving in to the world around you. His fart was her life now.

"What is that perfume you're wearing?" he asked. "It's pretty rad."

"Oh, it's nothing," she began. "I think it's called *Turquoise and Silver*. It's my aunt's."

Richard inhaled loudly, revealing his stuffy nose.

"It's not *nothing*, that's for sure," he said like an idiot. "I like it. It's cool."

Andrea didn't know what he was talking about since she still couldn't breathe through her nose without smelling his insides. The fact that he could enjoy her perfume through his own stench was amazing. "Thanks," she responded, not knowing what else to say.

Richard drove past the stadium where the local university played their home football games. It was the largest sports structure Andrea had ever seen.

"Geez, what's that for?" she asked.

Richard looked over with a puzzled expression. To him, it was just a stupid stadium where a collection of assholes would converge on random Saturdays during the fall.

"Have you ever heard of football?" he asked. "Or do they play that in Montana?"

Andrea turned to give Richard a dirty look. She was already sick of the Montana jokes, not realizing that by starting school, they were just beginning.

"Yes, I've heard of football," she said in a childish voice. "I was just asking *who* plays there."

"That's where the Rams play," he said, talking slowly as if Andrea was a special ed student.

"The who?" she asked.

"Never mind," he giggled.

The rest of the drive to Carver was quiet as the two battled their own thoughts of dread in anticipation for the day still to come. He had a good feeling about this girl and wanted to make all the right moves. In his mind, he was already on the right path. So what if he farted in front of her? That should've shown her how comfortable he was in her presence after just meeting her moments earlier. There were plenty of girls at school that he would never dream of farting in front of because it would just be too embarassing.

Andrea had no clue what to think of Richard. She was obviously disgusted by his lack of manners and most certainly turned off by him as a potential love interest. That wasn't even in the equation. If they really worked at it, she might learn to like him as a friend first and maybe look at him as a brother as a long shot. There was certainly no way in this reality that she could picture being his girlfriend or, god forbid, sleeping with him.

"I think I'm gonna barf," Richard joked as he pulled into the school parking lot. "This really sucks."

"What?" Andrea asked.

"Oh, just the fact that I am now at the bottom of the totem pole again," Richard said dryly.

"Totem pole?" Andrea said naively.

"You know, I'm a freshman," he responded. "I'm dirt. It was hard enough before but this is gonna be a nightmare."

Andrea somehow knew what Richard was talking about. She could relate. In Stanford, she attended a school that housed everyone from kindergarteners to seniors. The mere sight of Carver High gave her butterflies almost immediately. It was bigger than the mall in Great Falls and all of the students walking around outside its walls made her dizzy. Could this really be a school specifically designed for four grades?

Richard slammed the car into its spot and pulled on the emergency brake. He then let out a huge sigh.

"We're here, I guess," he said, looking as nervous as she had seen him that morning.

He looked around at the faces of his soon-to-be classmates, and studied for anyone whom he might recognize from junior high. All new. All different. Kids with gigantic hair. Kids with mullets. Kids hiding cigarettes in their jean jackets in between drags. But not one a familiar face. Everyone seemed happy and were already starting to form groups. Richard could see very few individuals walking around by themselves. Neither one of them wanted to get out of the car. It was as if they were having a duel, daring the other to open their door first. Truth be told, those thirty seconds would stand as the longest either one of them were joined together in agreement on something.

"You ready for this?" he asked Andrea as he opened his door and got out, pretending to be the strong one.

"Listen, Richard," she said as she exited the car, resting her books on the roof of the bug. "Thanks for the ride. That was really sweet of you." She had no one else to talk to and honestly felt sorry for Richard in a way she had never felt before. To her, he was like a lost dog wandering the edge of the highway. You know it's going to be squished at some point and deep inside you want to help it, but you also know there's nothing you can do to protect it from its own ignorance.

Richard smiled. She actually thought he did something sweet. She used the word *sweet*. His cheeks turned red as his face felt ten degrees warmer. No female had ever referred to him as sweet. *Sweet*. He had to thank his mother somehow for giving him this chance. A girl like Andrea didn't come around every day. She was special and he finally understood why people made such a big deal about falling in love. He was not only falling, but tripping, stumbling and bumbling his way into the abyss of lust, love and everything in between.

"Meet you back here after school?" he asked, thinking that he had in fact just asked her out on a date, not realizing that he was her only transportation. In reality, it was an affirmation that he could relive the experience again before the day ended.

"Sure. I'll need a ride back home," she said, offering a smile of her own. During the drive Richard managed to insult her, freak her out, make her gag, smile, blush, laugh and nearly cry. And, walking away from her experience with the freshman, she drew one conclusion—Richard was unique. Her instincts told her to keep a distance from the guy, after all, he did fart on her. Even her annoying redneck cousins in Montana weren't that piggish.

The two parted ways and walked to their respective entrances.

Richard glanced over at Andrea as she got farther away. She was perfect and she was at his mercy so long as he was her chauffer. Or was he at her mercy? Either way, he had different ideas about their experiences on the way to school. He thought his fart maneuver went over well, as he didn't walk away with a black eye and fat lip. To him, Andrea seemed like someone who was just as interested in him. Heck, she called him sweet. *Sweet.*

"Hey, it's Little Dick!"

Richard halted his gaze at Andrea and looked into the horizon not moving a muscle. He knew that name. That voice that so joyfully said it. He knew that behind him was trouble and most likely embarrassment. Moments passed and he continued to stare into the clouds that floated in the distance hoping beyond hope that the threat behind him had moved on. He turned to find the solid chest of Reggie Peterson staring him in the face.

"Whoa, watch where you walkin' holmes," Reggie said, grinning. His shiny white teeth stood out from his dark skin. Even when he was being a condescending asshole, he still managed to smile. Maybe that's where the condescending part came in. His pearly whites were as intimidating as his large frame. Reggie crossed his arms and let out a chuckle as he simultaneously thought about something to do to Richard in celebration of the first day of school.

Standing alongside Reggie were Seth Owens and Charles Manning. All three were seniors, stars on the football team, and all three lived in Richard's neighborhood. Even though Richard knew he would eventually bump into the Three Stooges—that's what he referred to them as in private—he managed to put it in the back of his brain. They weren't exactly kind to Richard, and took the time to play pranks on him as often as possible. His official nickname to the three athletes was Little Dick. They called it his "Indian name."

Richard Little Dick, the native butt jockey who was kicked out of his tribe for being such an impossible dork.

"You go here now Little Dick?" Charles asked. "Fuck, man, I thought you were still in grade school." Charles pounded his large hand on Richard's shoulder in a gesture of good fun.

Richard knew something was up and was extremely nervous. Even the thought of Andrea had evaporated from his immediate concern as he went over his internal fight or flight mechanism. He nodded yes without saying a word. Out of the three, he was scared of Charles the most. He stood about six foot, five inches and weighed around 225 pounds. Cut like a brick. He also had pearly white teeth to contrast his dark skin. Charles was easily the biggest dude on the team.

He wasn't quite as dark as Reggie, but still managed to sport a collection of perfect teeth. Unlike Reggie, he didn't show them often in the form of joy. Charles was more of a stoic person, without Reggie's sense of humor.

"Well, don't be shy lil' man," Reggie said as he put his arm around Richard. "We gonna show you around, this bein' your first day and all." Richard and Reggie began to walk, Seth and Charles close behind in the role of entourage. There was no doubt something was up but it was out of Richard's control. Without a real choice in the matter, he gingerly walked along side the three monsters. Reggie and Charles were the only two black people that Richard had ever met before. They seemed like honest-to-god brothers and were usually never apart. Richard felt a little intimidated by their color, although he couldn't explain why.

The school was set up in three separate buildings, all surrounding a beautifully landscaped courtyard. In the middle of that was a sculpture that adorned a fountain. The school's students were lucky to have a courtyard that resembled a Roman marketplace even if they didn't appreciate it at the time. Tiny trees lined the sidewalk and the grass looked and smelled as if it had just been mowed that morning. Richard began to sweat and his heart was racing with each step taken. He knew something bad was going to happen, it was just a matter of time.

"That buildin' is for us dumb folk," Reggie said, pointing to the smallest of the three buildings and holding his other hand to his chest. "That's where you'll find shop, the artsy-fartsy classes, and that shit you like . . . what is it again? Oh, yeah, sewin' and cookin' and shit." Richard was so scared he even laughed at the jokes that were targeted at him.

"Over there, my personal favorite, is the gym and cafeteria," Reggie continued, pointing at the largest of the three buildings. The four stopped strolling as they reached the water fountain. "Give me an indoor basketball court and I'm a happy mo-fucka."

Richard's heartbeat suggested that he was starting to calm down even though he still felt something bad was about to happen. They never treated Richard like a human being but, strangely enough, Reggie was actually helping introduce him to the school. It was a far cry from the things the Three Stooges did to Richard in the past.

Just a couple years prior, the three bullies got together and collected about ten pounds of dog shit from a neighbor's yard and mixed the feces in bags with water. Then they proceeded to pelt Richard with it as he rode his bike past Seth's house on a hot summer day. They all had rubber gloves on and as he rode by the house they burst from hiding spots behind a hedge, pulling mounds of crap from plastic grocery bags and covering him with it all. Richard was smeared head to toe with dog filth and dry heaved the entire trip home.

Now they were acting like his friends. Nothing was right about the situation.

"This sorry building is where most of the classrooms are," Reggie continued, referring to the third and final structure. "And this is you takin' a bath, asshole."

Reggie reached over, slamming his enormous palms against Richard's chest forcing him to stumble over Seth who was on all fours right behind him. Richard tumbled backwards into the fountain, and although the standing water wasn't more than two inches deep, he managed to get quite a soaking from the violent fall. In the process, he cracked his elbow against the concrete and landed square on his ass cheek, causing searing pain and an immediate bruise. The courtyard erupted with laughter and the three culprits slapped high fives. Richard couldn't decide what was worse; the embarrassment of the whole thing, the fact that he was soaking wet, or the pain from his ass and elbow.

Unbeknownst to Richard, and lucky for his psyche at the time, Andrea witnessed the whole fiasco from inside the building. She felt a wave of pity for the young lad who had helped her get to school. The weird little man was being ridiculed in front of everyone, and Andrea almost felt like crying for him.

Reggie offered Richard a hand.

"Sorry about that Little Dick," he said. "We had to do it. You understand? You a freshman and that's just how it goes."

Richard reluctantly accepted Reggie's hand and offered a fake smile. It was better to play the part of grateful loser than it would've been to show anger or hint at thoughts of revenge. He was a sucker when it came to those guys. Other than a girlfriend, Richard wanted nothing more than to be friends with the three. They were the ultimate in cool.

"Don't say a word about this, you hear?" Reggie whispered into Richard's ear as he helped him to his feet. "You don't want to get hurt for real."

Richard looked at the ground and nodded.

"Hey," Reggie said. "Look at me."

Richard looked up. His eyes met Reggie's and a fear of intimidation washed over his body. Water streamed down every square inch of his face and still he looked into the eyes of the man who did it, waiting for instructions on how to protect his attacker.

"You understand?" he asked, this time with a firm resolve.

Reggie was acting like a scolding father, and Richard felt as scared as a little boy.

What a way to start his first day of high school, soaked to the bone and humiliated in front of anyone who could've been fooled into thinking he was cool. Now, his reputation as a dolt and court jester was officially tagged as he entered the hallowed grounds of high school. In less than ten minutes on school grounds, his social fate for the next four years was sealed. He left his notebook and pen in the fountain. They were worthless.

"Look, don't rat on us, you hear?" Charles said to Richard, holding out his hand for a shake. "We just kiddin'. Coo'?"

Richard nodded and shook hands. Amazingly enough, he actually thought it was cool shaking hands with Charles like a good buddy.

"My man," Charles said as he joined Seth and Reggie who were already walking away laughing. To them it was the greatest start to senior year they could've imagined.

Richard stood in silence for a moment, thinking to himself. "My man," he repeated over and over in his head. "My man."

The bell rang and the people who were still slacking in the courtyard knew that meant they had one minute to get to class. In a flash the courtyard was hollow and quiet. Richard sat on the lip of the fountain and contemplated his next move. He was too wet to go inside, but couldn't just skip out on the first period of his first day of class. With a load of humility and an even heavier burden of shame, Richard reluctantly walked into the school and found his locker before heading to class. His shoes squeaked loudly as he walked the empty hallways, leaving a trail of wet footprints behind him.

Maybe it was all a dream. Like when you wake up in a cold sweat after having *the dream* where you are naked in school. Dreams of horrible experiences in school are common among students. Yeah, he was having a dream. He was so worked up about starting high school that he made himself conjure this horrible trip into the fountain. He smiled and took comfort in knowing that it was all just his imagination. Still wet, he entered the classroom late and sat down, greeted by stares and giggles.

It was his fate.

This was no dream.

In high school there are two categories, the winners and the losers. Period. You might think you're somewhere in between but, rest assured, there are those who have you tagged in one category or another. For most, those categories are picked from the day kindergarten begins, and the struggle lies in dealing with which side you were chosen to be on. Richard was a natural to be a loser, and would probably be voted the king if there were such an election. Sometimes it wasn't too bad a position to be in as long as he didn't end up with wet clothes.

As soon as the teacher caught a glimpse of Richard, she put a stop to his torture.

"Mr. . . . uh," she said, as she looked at her role sheet. "Is it Mr. Tark?"

Richard nodded.

"Why don't you go to the bathroom and get cleaned up?" she said. He couldn't figure out if she was mad at him or felt sorry for him. His shoes squeaked on the carpet too. Chuckles and smiles could be heard from all directions as he left the room, his head drooping to a new level. Just before he opened the door, he spotted something that made his misery go away, if only for a split second. Andrea was sitting in the front of the class.

She smiled at him in a gesture of pity. But, nevertheless, she smiled. Richard stopped to look at her and smiled back.

"Today, Mr. Tark," the teacher said.

He turned and left the classroom, releasing a pressure valve built up in the students, as they all erupted in laughter as soon as the door closed.

Not the day he expected.

But, nevertheless, she smiled.

3

Carver High School wasn't anything out of the ordinary. Pick any average high school in 1983 and Carver would probably be the same as any one of them. All of the typical cliques and categories were in full force, and most people stayed in their own bubbles. The school was reasonably modern, having been built less than ten years earlier, and the student population was comprised mainly of middle-class white kids.

Fort Collins High had been the main high school in town for a half a century and boasted one of the finest football programs in the entire state. That all changed two years prior in 1981 when Carver beat Fort Collins for the class 5A championship. The Carver Bulldogs repeated in 1982 and were the favorites going into the 1983 season. Not bad for a bunch of upstarts who hadn't won much of anything prior to their miraculous streak.

The success was mainly due to Seth's strong arm and Reggie's powerful running skills. It's amazing what a couple of blue chip athletes can do for a fledgling sports program. Let's not forget Charles and his efforts on defense either. The three young men had been All State performers during their championship runs and it was for good reason. It was like Carver's athletic department had somehow coaxed a few college stars to come back to high school and relive their glory days.

Hands down, they were the three most admired students at that school and were practically celebrities to everyone else in town.

"Would everyone be quiet? Please," the teacher pleaded, talking over the voices of her students. "I know everyone wants to blab about their summer vacations and whatnot, but I do have a class to teach."

The room was decorated like that of a first grade art class. The peg boards on the front wall were adorned with cardboard paper cutouts of stars and hearts with the names of each student written on them. Stars for guys, hearts for girls. Peppered amongst the cutouts were big primary colored letters stapled to the wall, spelling out cheesy phrases like "Have a Good Day," and "#1 Class." The teacher had written her name on the chalkboard in cursive. Mrs. Goldfinger. Every year, that warranted a chuckle from the male students. Goldfinger.

"What do you think that means?" Willie asked the girl sitting next to him. She responded with a puzzled expression that implied she didn't want to be talked to. She then turned back towards the teacher. "You know, what do you think that means, Goldfinger?" He knew exactly how much he was annoying the girl.

Again, she turned to give Willie a crusty look, adding fuel to his fire and encouraging him to continue. As she made eye contact with him, he lifted his hand up and formed a peace sign, bringing it to his mouth to lick the bottom of the V-shape. He provided a sinister smile and his right eyebrow rose an inch, like a young Jack Nicholson. "That's for you," he whispered.

"You pig!" the girl proclaimed, throwing her pencil at him in disgust.

"Mr. Becker, I presume," Mrs. Goldfinger said, staring directly at Willie. "Is there a problem, Mr. Becker?"

"No ma'am," he replied. "I was just asking my friend here for a pencil." He reached down on the floor and picked it up. "Here it is." He offered a coy smile.

"I won't put up with any shenanigans, Mr. Becker," Mrs. Goldfinger continued. "It's gonna be a long year for you if you think you're gonna disturb my class like this on a regular basis."

"Sure thing, boss," he said. "Not a problem."

Willie Becker may have seemed like an immature bastard to some, and you could argue a strong case that he was. Choosing to annoy particular underclassman was one of the only things that kept him interested in school. You wouldn't know it on this particular day, but it was a fact that Willie was one of the smartest students ever to attend Carver, and he's still referred to by some of the teachers that taught him back then as "the genius." His biggest problem was the fact that he didn't care about the classes he took and opted to concentrate more on his social skills. The courses were much too slow for him and it was a lot more exciting to chase girls and make people laugh. He found that hanging around with the jocks was more interesting than keeping company with the more intelligent kids, thus he had a substantial reputation as a meat head. For one thing, he didn't have the appearance most nerds sported so that wouldn't have worked out anyway. He dressed like a jock. He was extremely well cut and could've pursued sports had he showed any interest. His shoulder-length, curly, permed hair was a favorite with the ladies and he had no problem getting action when it was necessary. Another anti-nerd trait bestowed upon him.

His father was a surgeon at the local hospital, one of the best in the state, and his mother stayed at home as a homemaker. Neither one really knew how to handle Willie as a child. They knew he was smart, but they also knew he was a troublemaker at heart. His father expected perfection but only in a limited arena. The elder Becker demanded good grades and even better behavior so that his son could ultimately go to the family college in Boulder, the University of Colorado. The pressure of that fate was probably the ultimate reason why Willie chose to go down a different path.

Little did the family know at the time, Willie was never interested in attending college and was actually thinking about starting a band. Much to the chagrin of his father, he had played the guitar since he was eight years old and had become pretty good at it. Either way, he wasn't expecting to be in school ever again once he graduated.

As for girlfriends and future plans of marriage, it wasn't going to happen anytime soon. The girls found him extremely attractive, that is, until they got to know him. He wasn't exactly Romeo. Hell, he couldn't have even been mistaken as a distant cousin.

One story that made its way into legendary status among his classmates, and a story that is still told in the halls of Carver, occurred two summers before his senior year.

Willie brought a date to a friend's house party. It was a Friday night and a couple dozen people crammed into a three-bedroom home just off of Mulberry Avenue. Never being shy, or turning down a drink when offered, Willie was known for his public displays of drunkenness. He brought an excitement and life to any party and that's the biggest reason why he was always invited. He was the guy who would erratically pound his chest and hold his beer high and scream like a howling wolf just because everyone would laugh at him.

The night so often recounted in fable continued with Willie gulping down enough liquor to bring most mortals crashing to earth but he remained on his feet and fueled his insatiable appetite for women. He found an inebriated, yet conscious girl and convinced her to take a walk upstairs with him. The two barely made it into the room and soon Willie was getting head while standing against a wall. They didn't even bother to close the door, thus the show was on for anyone who walked by. On the verge of passing out, Willie began to sway unbeknownst to the mouth still attached to his waist. Incredible visions, mixed with a slow wave of nausea filled his head. The girl kept doing her thing even though he was past the point of knowing what continent he was even on. It was as if she was giving his dick CPR and he didn't even have the wherewithal to feel how good it was.

He tensed up and did the unthinkable.

She stopped giving *him* head when *her* head was engulfed in some of the foulest smelling vomit you will ever come across. A concoction of beer, tequila, vodka and a six-hour old tuna fish sandwich, this vomit was sent from the depths of hell. She backed away from him and let out a scream as the warm liquid ran through her hair, down her back and ultimately down both cheeks. Some even managed to stream onto the cracks of her mouth causing her to dry heave as she turned to vigorously wipe her lips and face off on the bed sheets behind her.

Just as she turned back to face him, Willie leaned forward and vomited again, this time landing his regurgitation on the back of her shirt. The poor girl screamed as she ran out of the room, splashing drops of vomit on anything and everything she passed. It was as if she was on fire and no one could offer her water. The people who were standing in the hallway moments before enjoying the voyeurism of watching someone getting their knob polished got an immediate whiff of the stench and the few with weak intestinal fortitude also began to throw up. In a matter of seconds, the entire upstairs of this house was cleared out as various souls emptied their systems wherever they stood.

Willie stood still, watching the chaos that he has caused. After triggering a chain reaction of barf and misery, he sat down on the carpet and looked around at the mess he made. He didn't even know whose room he was in much less whose house he had just completely destroyed. What he did know was; he felt a lot better. Smelly and disappointed, Willie got to his feet and pulled his pants up.

As the story goes, it took the owners of the house a full summer before the smell finally went away. That tale spread like herpes and it was referred to from that point on as the infamous "barf job." In fact, if you've heard that phrase in your town, they say that's where it originally started.

The stories of debauchery don't stop there.

None of his friends could forget the previous winter when he brought a girl skiing for the first time. She had never put on a pair of skis and knew nothing of the sport. Willie didn't know it when he first asked her, but this girl was annoying as all hell. Sporting one of the worst cases of dragon breath that Willie had ever encountered with a female, she did the worst thing you can do in that situation—she talked. She talked the whole way to the lodge. She talked the whole way up the lift. She talked while they were getting ready to go down the run. He smelled that wretched mouth for so long he found himself breathing exclusively through his own mouth even when she wasn't talking.

Midway through their first run on the hill, Willie darted off and left her behind. Once he hit the lodge, he packed his things and left. Since they were 200 miles from Fort Collins, it was pretty understandable how upset she was. He even left her with the bill for the hotel room. He didn't care. If it meant he could duck out of the situation with a free pass, that's what was going to happen.

She kicked him pretty good in the balls the next time they ran into each other.

Senior year was upon him, and he had another nine months to embarrass the females. The only questions were how would he do it and what new and improved disgusting story would come from it?

Willie squirmed his way through the next few periods, hoping that the day would finally end. It seemed like his classes were getting easier the higher he got in high school. Little did he know, his life was about to change forever. Sitting right in front of him was the same kid he had seen thrown into the fountain earlier in the day. It was Little Dick.

"Hey," Willie whispered, trying not to piss off another teacher.

Richard remained stationed forward.

"Hey, wet body," Willie said.

Richard turned around to find Willie staring right at him.

"What?" Richard asked.

"I saw you take a dive this morning," Willie said with a smile. "Good form."

"Yeah. You and the rest of the school," Richard replied as he turned back around. He thought Willie was just another heckler.

"I thought it was pretty cool the way you handled it," Willie said.

Richard turned.

"Cool? I was a pussy," he said. "I've never been cool in my life."

"Nah. You couldn't stand up to those guys if you gained two-hundred pounds, dude," Willie continued. "You did the right thing."

"Name's Willie."

"Richard."

The two shook hands and got back to their class work.

Richard stared at the clock and prayed for the time to go more quickly. Even after what happened to him, he could think of nothing more than Andrea. He knew that once the day was over, he was going to get in his car and smell her sweet perfume as she sat a mere foot from him. He was completely immersed in that beautifully dark zone of infatuation that comes with a full-on crush. Damn anything else in life, there's no way to shake that feeling other than the passing of time.

Richard snuck away from school at some point and returned home to change into dry clothes. He came back as quickly as he could, not even concerned about the hazing from earlier in the day. He thought about seeing Andrea in first period and how she smiled at him. He held on to that smile all morning.

Andrea sat in the back of the class, waiting for the teacher to do something. Anything. It was the first day of school and the so-called instructor just sat at his desk, reading from *People* magazine, occasionally looking up to make sure no one was on fire. Students took to doing their own thing, some reading or doing homework for other classes, while some took naps. No one seemed to care that nothing was happening. It was just another example of how different and weird things were compared to her former existence.

"You new here?" a voice asked.

Andrea turned to her right to find a girl adorned in the most ridiculous outfit, her leg propped up on the desk as she painted each toe lime green.

"Yeah," Andrea replied.

"I thought you looked new," the girl said, obnoxiously chomping on a piece of gum.

Andrea watched the girl paint her nails, completely enthralled by her appearance. Andrea couldn't remember ever painting her nails any color much less in the middle of a classroom on the first day of school.

"You can call me Alexis," the girl said.

Alexis definitely stood out. She wore a pair of black and white striped pants with the stripes going north to south. Her ankles were covered in red leg warmers, barely hiding a pair of blue canvas Converse. She had on a bright pink sweatshirt with giant shoulder pads and a baggy neckline. Her hair was as erect as a paper mache sculpture and she wore enough makeup to completely disguise her real appearance.

And one shoe was removed, revealing her pasty white foot.

"Where you from?" she asked Andrea, never once taking her eyes off of her handy work.

"Montana," Andrea said.

Andrea was very curious about this girl. It was as if she knew her from somewhere, or just had a connection. Either way, she liked her.

"Montana," Alexis began. "Where the sheep are scared and the men are why."

Andrea smiled. She was so tired of Montana jokes.

"What about you?" Andrea asked. "What's your story?"

"I'm from around here," Alexis said. "Born and raised in this boring ass town."

"Boring?" Andrea said. "I'd say it's far from that. You know what I saw the other day? I saw an ambulance, fire truck and two police cars racing down the street with their lights flashing and their horns blaring. They were going so fast, my aunt had to pull over. It was crazy. That's far from boring."

Alexis sat in silence for a moment, staring at Andrea with a stone cold look on her face before ultimately breaking out in a piercing laugh. The people in the room that were napping definitely got a charge from that sound. A geek sitting a few chairs in front of Andrea looked over at Alexis and scowled as if she'd interrupted his attempt to learn. She cocked her head to the side and flipped him off, slowly mouthing the words "Fuuuuccckkkk yoooooooouuu."

Going back to her business of painting her toenails, Alexis also returned to the conversation. "You saw an ambulance, huh?" she said mockingly. "That sounds really fucking exciting, Andrea. Jesus, where are you from again? Bum Fuck Egypt?"

Andrea blushed in embarrassment. Alexis reached over and put her hand on Andrea's wrist. "I'll take you out sometime, and show you something more exciting than a fire truck," she said. "You like to dance?"

Andrea shook her head yes.

"We used to line dance at the C.M. Russell Festival," Andrea started. "About twenty of us would get in pairs, and . . ."

She was interrupted.

"C.M. What? Stop right there before I totally get sick," Alexis blurted. "I'm talking real dancing. You know Devo right?"

Andrea shook her head no.

"They are totally awesome. I mean, to the max," Alexis said. "They wear these red cones on their heads. You just gotta see them sometime. Geez, I can't believe you've never heard of the greatest band on the planet. You must be from a small town."

"They sound . . . interesting," Andrea said with a sheepish grin, not knowing what she was talking about. Cones on their heads?

"Then it's a date," Alexis finished, asking a question and making a statement all at once. She liked Andrea and looked at her as not only a potential friend but someone who she could have some fun with. Someone who wasn't already stuck in a clique. Someone who was obviously in dire need of a music lesson.

Andrea turned back to her desk and continued staring into the abyss of the classroom. In a strange turn of events, her teacher had rested his head on his desk and fallen asleep. Two guys sitting in the front row were tearing pieces of paper to make spit wads and were launching them into the man's hair. After nearly five minutes, the teacher's head looked like a snow covered mountain range.

Twenty more minutes remained in her day and she wondered if Richard was still even at school. She felt horrible about what had happened to him earlier in the day and wanted to find out if he was okay. She had never witnessed someone being so humiliated in front of a crowd. He never returned to first period and she assumed that he must have gone home. Without a ride, she would just have to get some exercise.

The bell belched for the last time that day, signaling the final stage in a long day for most kids coming back to school from summer break. The hallways were instantly filled with jubilant voices and slamming lockers. One day down, the rest of the year to go.

Andrea made her way out to the parking lot and saw that the orange bug was parked in the same spot they had left it earlier in the day. She sighed in relief, knowing that if Richard had left her there, she'd have a long walk home. Fort Collins was still a strange city, and she wasn't even sure she could find her way home on foot.

She waited about five minutes before Richard appeared from the sea of humanity.

"Sorry you had to wait," he said, fumbling through his pockets for his keys.

"No problem," she responded, going out of her way to be extra nice to him. She wasn't sure whether or not to bring up the fountain incident. She wanted to let him know that she was sorry it happened, but on the other hand, she figured he probably didn't want to be reminded. Richard put the screwdriver in the ignition switch and turned the tired car over. As usual, a giant cloud of noxious smoke billowed from the tailpipe, and disappeared as quickly as it arrived.

He stared into the distance for a moment, knowing that Andrea was looking over at him. "What?" he said, almost irritated by her gaze. "What is it?" His day was a complete failure. His humiliation mixed with his hatred for school and classwork turned him into a grouchy son of a bitch. Puzzled at first by his harsh reaction, Andrea spoke up.

"Um. Nothing. I . . . I . . . I saw what happened this morning," she said, a concerned look on her face. "I'm sorry you had to go through that Richard. Those guys are jerks."

Richard was angry. It was enough that so many people saw it happen, but to know that Andrea witnessed it also—well that was just too much. Not even a day had gone by since she met him and already she knew he was a miserable dork just like everyone else.

"You saw it?" he asked, still not making eye contact with her.

"Yeah," she said.

He lowered his head in shame. "It's all right," he said, admitting his role as a loser. "It was kind of funny, I guess."

"Funny?" Andrea belted. "It was completely lame, Richard. I should've stormed into the principal's office and ratted those guys out for you."

"Don't do that," Richard snapped. "I don't mind. It's okay. No one got hurt."

He turned to look at her. "Please don't start trouble," he said. "Those guys were just havin' fun."

His attitude quickly changed and he appeared nervous at Andrea's proclamation for justice.

"Let's just go home," he said.

Andrea shrugged her shoulders, confused by Richard's sudden changes in attitude and his relentless requests for her to drop the incident. *Why wouldn't he want those assholes to get in trouble?* she thought.

"Whatever," she said, turning away from him to look out of the passenger window. "I think it's bull, that's all. But, do what you want."

Richard wanted to start the day all over again. He'd have Andrea pull his finger and the two would laugh and have fun. He would park on the other side of the school and wouldn't have even seen the Three Stooges, nor would he have taken a bath in the fountain.

Andrea noticed his clothes were different.

"Did you go home to change?" she asked. "You weren't wearing that get up this morning."

Richard looked over at her and put his finger to his lips, not saying a word, motioning not so bluntly that she needed to shut her mouth. Then he slammed the gearshift in reverse and slowly backed away. The car jumped a bit when in reverse and the transmission was surely on the verge of dropping out all together. Richard drove her back to her apartment and the two didn't speak a word the entire trip. He stopped and waited for her to exit the vehicle, wanting to smile and wish her a good evening, but opting not to. He was still embarrassed that Andrea had witnessed him being abused. It was as hurtful on his pride as it was on his sore elbow.

She waited for a few seconds before getting out. Richard looked rejected and horribly confused and she wanted to comfort him. After all, this was the guy who took the time to make sure she made it to school and back. Other than the infamous fart, he didn't seem so bad to her. At least not bad enough to warrant such misery.

"Well, goodbye," she said, pulling on the tired door handle. "See you in the morning?" she asked, hoping that the rides would continue. She surely didn't want to walk.

Richard turned to look at her.

"I'll be here," he said, realizing moments later that he was committing to the second day of rides. Hell, he was close to having a girlfriend by his standards. One ride was lucky. Two rides was getting pretty close. Three, four, five and so on—the more rides, the nearer he got to nabbing his first girlfriend.

She put her first leg out of the door and was about to lift herself out of the car.

"Andrea," he said.

She turned.

"Thanks."

"For what?" she asked.

"For not laughing," he said, turning away so that she wouldn't see the tears that were welling in his eyes.

"You're welcome," she said before climbing out and shutting the door behind her.

He watched her walk up the stairs to her apartment before driving off.

Football practice had started two weeks before school began, so suiting up for another two hours under the sun wasn't something that was alien to the guys in the locker room. Still, they weren't big fans of it. Practice was the worst thing about being on the football team and once school started, it became even more cumbersome.

Reggie, Charles and Seth sat on the bench in front of their lockers, pulling on their practice pants while the rest of the team were dressed and ready to hit the field. It was just like them to be late, after all, it's not like the rest of the team mattered.

"We're waiting on you three jokers," Coach Bruce barked as he peeked into the locker room to find stragglers. "We'd like to practice sometime today, ladies."

Even though he made wise cracks, the coach was always at the mercy of the three stars. Why else would he make the entire team wait for them? He knew who his stud horses were and he didn't want to sacrifice them for any reason and would go to great lengths to make the three happy. Even if it meant alienating the rest of the team.

Eventually, and without giving too much credit to Coach's attempts at motivation, the three were ready to go.

Seth was your typical All-State quarterback. He had led the team to an undefeated record the season before and passed for a state record 2,330 yards. His strong arm was an asset to the football team and his looks were the reason he had his own cheering section of females that would do just about anything to get in his pants. He was your typical golden boy star quarterback.

Reggie carried the football for the Bulldogs and did an outstanding job in the process. He earned his All-State status by rushing for nearly 1,500 yards, a big feat when you consider the fact that they were a primarily passing offense. His loud, thunderous voice and large presence made him the captain of the team. In many ways, he was looked at in the same light in which quarterbacks become famous. He was looked at as the general.

Charles was the biggest player on the squad. He was the core of the defensive line and chalked up 13 sacks on his way to his second straight All-State title. The guys referred to him as "Brick Jaw" because of his tendency to rush the lineman using not only his hands, but his helmet.

Most of the time, the three were never seen apart. Other than the fact that they had to go to different classrooms, that was the honest-to-god truth. People moved out of the way when those guys walked by. They were like the school's very own version of the mafia. The only thing you needed to know to be a "made man" in the Carver High Football Mafia was how to use a football.

The clacking of cleats on cement echoed into the distance as the team headed for the practice field. A handful of clingy girlfriends waited outside the locker room to flirt with their boyfriends. The Three Stooges weren't interested in those girls because they were focused on the one that was getting into a car across the parking lot.

"Check it out, yo," Charles said as he tapped Reggie on the shoulder. "Look who got a girl."

Charles pointed at Richard at the same time he was getting in his car with Andrea to leave school after the first day.

"She don't look too thrilled to be getting a ride from Little Dick," Seth chuckled, pointing out Andrea's concerned expression.

"She pretty hot, in a *Little House on the Prairie* sort of way," Reggie said.

"I'd fuck her," Seth chimed in.

The three slapped high fives and laughed hysterically.

"You'd fuck an elephant," Reggie said in between laughs. "If you had a ladder."

"How'd you know I fucked your mom?" Seth said. "She tell ya or were you peeking?"

Reggie stopped laughing and stared into Seth's eyes.

"Oh shit. No one told you did they?" Reggie started to say. "That weren't my mom, that was yo's. Whoa, I thought you knew. That's fucked up, man."

Charles got in the middle of the two. The boisterous trio was at their best when "mama jokes" came into the fold but they could get a little out of control.

"I fucked both yo mom's . . . at the same time," Charles contributed. "So shut the fuck up. Both ya'll. Let's go. Forget about that dumb mo'fucker and his bitch."

The three continued walking to the practice field, laughing at their stupidity.

4

The music softly spewed forth from Richard's alarm clock and the darkness filled his room. It was nearing midnight and he was just getting to bed. His mother worked the late shift at a nearby restaurant and usually didn't come home until one or two in the morning, so he virtually had the house to himself all night. The darkness seemed to sooth his constant feelings of anxiety that came with each morning. The knowledge that he was all by himself in the house also comforted him because he knew no one was there to judge.

His mother just aggravated the situation by coddling him and choosing to ignore his obvious mental disorder. You could probably put some of the blame on the system, since not one of his teachers or mentors ever suggested medication. They just accused him of being too shy or harmlessly antisocial. Honestly, they mostly dismissed him as being a bit creepy. Thinking back to his first day of school, he found it difficult to fathom the fact that he had four entire years left at that hellhole. Something was going to have to happen to get him through the torture alive. There was no way he would make it to senior year, or beyond for that matter, unless he found a way to cope with his problems.

His hand was hard at work under the covers as he thought of Andrea. It was strange actually thinking of an acquaintance during masturbation. Usually, it was one of the girls in his Hustler magazine, or someone that he may have seen walking down the street. He didn't actually know many girls at school so this was indeed a special occasion. He wanted Andrea more than anything, and he honestly thought that he could get her. She was vulnerable having just moved to town, and more importantly, needed someone to be her friend. Richard knew that he could play the friend role perfectly and would end up moving in for the kill at a later date once he established trust and worked a little on his obvious lack in social skills with the ladies.

Faster and faster he danced with himself, Andrea's image dancing along with him.

Unaware that his mother had come home early because of a headache, he continued his pace. Had he had his eyes open, he may have seen the light from the hall shining under his door, just after his mom flicked it on. A gentle knock on his door, un-audible to the horny teen's mind, was all the warning he was afforded.

"Richard," she said as she opened the door slowly. "Are you awake?"

Richard quickly flipped over on top of his boner.

"Richard, what's going on?" she asked, noticing his acrobatics, oblivious to what could possibly be happening or what she had just interrupted.

"Nothing, mom," he said, irritated, embarrassed and pissed beyond belief. "I'm trying to sleep."

"Oh," she said. "I guess I'll talk to you in the morning. I love you."

"Yeah. Love you too."

His mind turned full circle. Moments earlier, he was jerking off and finding pleasure in something, no, rather someone, if only for a brief moment. Since his mother crashed head-on into his fantasy, he found it difficult to think about anything. In fact, he was growing angrier as his hard-on subsided and eventually he rolled over to punch his pillow. Anger brewed from somewhere deep inside. It didn't take much to trigger a mood swing and that's what made them so frustrating. He couldn't control his anger and usually got even more pissed off when he tried.

All she had to do was knock louder. All he had to do was lock the door. Why did he forget? Perhaps because he thought she was going to be at work all night. Regardless of the reasons behind the intrusion, he felt completely embarrassed. To him it was as if he were sitting naked on the couch covered in baby oil, going to town on himself as his mother watched from across the room.

Truth be told, she had no idea what he was doing, and frankly didn't give a shit. She had her own problems.

Four blocks away, Andrea was finally asleep.

She had been up crying off and on for two hours after first crawling into bed. She missed Montana and it broke her heart to be so far away from it. She constantly had spells where she could do nothing more than cry. Strange that two people with two completely different days together were left in misery that evening, yet they were as far apart as any two souls could possibly be.

As Richard was doing the same thing, Andrea lay on her back in bed staring at the black ceiling, thinking about her future and how miserable she was. The only thing she had to look forward to was her scheduled trip back home for Christmas. There was no way she would have agreed to move to Fort Collins if she had to give up Christmas in Stanford. That was one of the things her mother actually compromised on. If anything, Andrea had Christmas.

The only way to defeat such dark thoughts is through optimism, even if it's not reality. She convinced herself that she had met a pretty nice guy in Richard.

So what if he introduced himself by farting? She had plenty of cousins and relatives in Montana who did that sort of thing every day. What about Alexis? She had the potential to be one of those friends you keep around for life.

It actually wasn't bad for her first day out. School went okay for the most part. As well as could be expected. It's the first day that is so hard to wake up for. She convinced herself that the reason she was so lonely for Montana on this night was because she had been so worried about the first day of school on previous evenings, there just wasn't enough energy to really think about what she had left behind. Now, it was catching up with her all at once, she thought.

Losing the familiarity of daily life, even if it is for the better, can be devastating, especially for a young child. A person can wake up every day and feel like they have nothing to live for, but change their daily routine, or remove someone close and watch them turn to into zombies. Her mother knew that Andrea needed to move to another town to grow as a person. No one becomes successful by staying in a small town their whole life. Andrea's mother recognized her daughter's importance in the world and felt that Stanford was too small for her little girl.

Tough love is a bitch. Andrea fought the idea and even contemplated running away, but seriously, where would she go? With prairie and mountain ranges peppered across the landscape for miles in any direction, it's not the best place to run from. Anyone who knew Andrea would tell you that she was much too passive to run away and fend for herself at that age. She had no choice and she knew it. Andrea's aunt was an obvious choice as guardian and so Fort Collins was her destiny. That didn't mean she had to like it.

Unbeknownst to each of them, Andrea and Richard individually battled inner demons that night and occasionally thought about one another.

Richard however, had much bigger problems.

The morning came like a lion. A misty fog rolled in over the town and the air was much cooler than the day before. Andrea stood outside her apartment waiting for Richard and got an opportunity to look at the mountains that lined the front range. They were even more beautiful when the fog softened the colors that were waiting to burst forth. Birds chirped nearby and to Andrea the world was beginning to look different. Crisp mountain air filled her lungs and she knew that things were going to get better. All she needed was a little time to see the big picture.

Richard seemed like a completely different person when he arrived to pick her up. He sped into her parking lot ten minutes late and slammed on his brakes, causing a squeal and cloud of smoke from the tires. Andrea cautiously walked towards the car wondering what the story was behind his grand entrance.

Unlike the day before, Richard didn't lean over to let her in. In fact, he didn't even look at her. He stared straight ahead like a robot.

She got in and buckled her seatbelt, hesitant to talk to the creep sitting next to her. This was a stranger compared to the person from the previous day. It felt as if she were hitchhiking and picked the wrong car.

Richard's face was cold and emotionless and he hit the gas as soon as she got in. She noticed the muscles in his cheeks as they flexed from his clenching jaw.

No *hello*. No *how are you*. No words at all.

"What's up with this fog?" she asked, trying to make conversation.

"I couldn't give a shit," he said, still not looking at her.

Andrea was stunned.

"What's up with you? Did you have a bad night or something?" she asked.

"You know what," he said. "I don't want to talk about it."

He was still pissed about his mother, but for the life of him couldn't remember why. What did she do again?

Andrea was horribly uncomfortable with Richard. She thought about how much she'd rather be around the guy who farted and at least acted like he was happy to share her company. This was a totally different person.

Nothing more was said between the two the entire way to school, and once they got there, Richard got out of the car and walked towards the school before Andrea had even unbuckled her seatbelt.

That afternoon, she walked out to the parking lot to find Richard already gone.

You could justifiably accuse Andrea of being a naïve person and that's why she found herself waiting in front of her apartment building the next day, books in hand. Perhaps Richard was just having a bad day and didn't have time to consider her feelings. Hell, she wasn't his girlfriend or anything. Maybe he would pull up and have a perfectly good explanation for his behavior the day before.

Again, Richard sped into the parking lot slightly late.

Andrea watched his actions carefully while the vehicle came to a stop. A pause then and slight movement. Yes, his hand was moving over to the passenger side. Yes, he pulled the knob, unlocking the door. Yes, he yanked the handle allowing her to get in.

Still, he was acting like a complete asshole.

"Hi, Richard," she said, holding back the urge to slap him for ditching her at school the day before. Did she have feelings for this guy? Why would she care enough about him to want to hurt him?

He turned to her, something she didn't see the day before. "*Good, he's not being a dick*," she thought. She sighed and waited for his response.

He shook his head and slammed the car in drive. Like an ogre, he hacked and snorted, clearing his sinuses and throat of phlegm before swallowing whatever mucus concoction he had just created. He repeated the process, this time rolling down the window to spit out of the car.

In Andrea's opinion, that was one of the most horrible noises a human could make.

The engine of the bug vibrated the seats and made Andrea even more nervous and anxious about the things she wanted to say to Richard. How dare he be so rude? She did nothing to deserve this treatment. She could play the game too. If he wasn't going to be nice or even talk, she wouldn't either. He would provide a free ride to school and she would provide, well, nothing. Not even a dime for gas.

Furthermore, if he forgot to pick her up one more time, she was going to tell him where to fuck himself and go about her business. If people really wanted to see the Montana girl come out of her, they could just keep pushing like Richard was doing. If he kept it up, she would take out every bit of her frustrations on him and he would bear the load of everything she ever wanted to say to her antagonists but never had the courage to.

If he really pissed her off, she could easily handle his skinny frame and would drop his ass in one punch. Or so she thought as her anger invaded a daydream.

Acquaintances of Richard could honestly say that they dealt with *one* of his mood swings, but no more. Once friends witnessed one, they were pretty much comfortable with ditching Richard as a friend or companion. It was almost a relief.

So why did Andrea still cling to him? She couldn't shake the feeling she had when they first hung out together. It wasn't love per se, but more like a feeling of comfort. There's a lot to be said of the way a girl feels when someone shows that much interest. She wanted it to be that way again, so much in fact that she was embellishing that first car ride in her mind to justify those feelings.

The two pulled into the school parking lot and Richard put the car in park. Andrea reached over and placed her hand on his forearm.

"Are you okay?" she asked, genuinely concerned about him. "You're freaking me out."

Richard reacted as if someone was pouring acid on his skin. The pressure of her hand on his arm was enough to make him explode and he swiped his arm away from her grasp.

"Don't touch me!" he barked.

Andrea stared at him with sad eyes and gently opened her door before walking away from the car. She would return to his car later in the afternoon and even the next morning, but felt different. From the moment he snapped at her, she knew that the two would never have a future, even as friends. They were barely carpooling acquaintances.

His attitude continued for the rest of the week.

Each day he picked her up in the same mood. Each day he brought her home in the same mood. It had to stop, and Andrea had to find someone else to get a ride from.

Richard sat in his room, tired and weary having finished his first full week of high school. Other than the dunking he took on the first day, he managed to stay far away from the Three Stooges and any other kind of trouble. Thinking of Andrea he felt no remorse or regret. In fact, he didn't even remember being such a dick to her. Regardless, he didn't just alienate Andrea during his first week of school. He was notorious with his teachers as being a bad student. Richard didn't quite have the same mentality as his classmates. He couldn't concentrate long enough to take in information provided by the teachers, and he couldn't stay focused enough to learn much from reading. Starting at a new school, he had a chance to change that reputation, but ended up screwing himself in the first week alone. He was already a loser.

His grades were consistently average, hovering around C-level his entire academic life. That didn't bother his mother since it was good enough to pass her son through from grade to grade. As long as he wasn't failing and being threatened with repeating a grade it was all good. Sometimes it bothered Richard to know that here he was, older than every one of his freshman peers, yet one of the worst students. Was he that stupid? It really didn't matter in the long run, he just wanted to get the hell out of that building and get on with life. His future wasn't going to involve college or a high paying job and he knew it. So, why bother trying? Burger King doesn't care if you passed all of your math tests in the ninth grade when you're being hired. In fact, they kind of prefer that you not be a Rhodes Scholar.

As Andrea was finding out, he had a serious problem and was in obvious need of help although no one seemed to offer it. He could go from an innocent, charming young man to a quiet, withdrawn bastard in a heartbeat. Sometimes his mood swings would last a couple of hours, sometimes a couple of weeks, depending on the trigger. Everybody goes through such changes—it's unavoidable in our species—but this was a unique and ugly transformation of both body and mind and it could happen in a flash.

Richard's mother had tried to get him into therapy, but he didn't last long. They couldn't figure out what sorts of triggers were causing the mood swings and tried to treat him with hypnosis and aspirin. An obvious failure of the system.

As volatile as he seemed during his anger streaks, he was just as normal and sweet on the other side. It was sometime Saturday night when his attitude inexplicably shifted back to pleasant Richard. Physically, he felt it when things got better. It was as if his muscles were tense and sore the entire time he was angry and finally cutting loose from the spell relaxed his entire body giving him reason to smile. It was almost orgasmic. He thought about Andrea again, something that he hadn't done most of the week, and went back to being excited to see her Monday morning. Emotionally, he thought she'd be there, brand new like the first day they met. Strange that he didn't even realize how shitty he'd been to her the week prior. It was as if he turned into the Incredible Hulk and had no recollection of what he'd done or destroyed while in that state. He just woke up somewhere with ripped clothes and sore muscles.

He lifted his nose in the air and inhaled hard, remembering her luscious perfume and perfect legs. He couldn't wait for Monday to come and he owed it all to Andrea. Sweet, perfect Andrea. It was as if he had been in a coma all week long. Had he even gone to school?

Looking around the disaster area he called home, he lifted his mattress, pulling a small, tattered notebook from under it. Its red cover creased, missing a corner, the notebook had surely seen a better day. He opened it to a page that was dog eared and pulled an old pencil out of the tired binding. It was time for another entry.

Before he started seeing a shrink, Richard looked at journals and diaries as something middle school girls wrote in at pajama parties. The doctor recommended he keep one as part of his therapy and although he'd never admit it to his mother, he found it very relaxing and comforting. It was like talking to a close friend. He didn't make entries in it on a nightly basis, nor did he visit it weekly. There was no rhyme or reason to it, he just wrote in it when he felt the urge.

The impression he had of Andrea and feelings he felt towards her had to be put down on paper. There was no emotional reaction in his memory that compared to the one that he experienced when she was near. Treating her like shit the whole week didn't seem to matter at all to him. Like it never happened. He wrote like a love struck child. He wrote of her beautiful legs and gorgeous hair and oh, how he yearned for her perfume. It was the most amazing scent he could imagine.

Monday morning arrived and Richard piled into his car, anxious to see his love. He didn't even really remember picking her up most of the prior week and felt like it was the day after he first met her. He thought about his finger fart trick the first morning and laughed out loud when he remembered her facial expression. Did she really make that face as he so vividly remembered? Probably not, but you couldn't tell him that.

He pulled into her parking lot and noticed something different right away. Andrea wasn't there. Not knowing which apartment was hers, he parked the car and waited. Tense, he bounced his leg in a rhythmic pace and chewed bits of fingernail from one of his sorry fingers. Why wasn't she out there waiting? Andrea watched from her window and saw Richard pull up. She wanted so badly to just skip school and ditch him but knew that she had to go out and face him. After all, it was a free ride and wasn't so bad that she would prefer walking the whole way to and from school every day. She just needed to bide her time and find someone else who would be willing to pick her up.

She reluctantly grabbed her bag and walked outside. Richard showed all teeth the few times you could catch him smiling and he did just that when he saw her beautiful body walking towards his car. He thought of her dallying as being fashionably late. He finally knew what that phrase meant. Like a gentleman, he reached over and opened the door for her.

She noticed.

He hadn't done that since the first day of school. That had to be a sign that he wasn't being a jerk.

Andrea got in the car, studying Richard the whole way. He waited for her to buckle her seatbelt and inhaled loudly.

"God damn I love your perfume," he said. "What is it anyway?"

Andrea wondered if this was even the same guy. They had already had this conversation the week before. Where was the guy that clenched his jaw so hard that it looked like he had a piece of licorice stuck in his cheek? Where was the jerk that treated her like his enemy?

"Uh, *Turquoise and Silver* . . . remember?" she sassed, adding a little prissy tone to her answer.

"Oh, yeah, that's right. I don't remember if we talked about this or not. How'd school go for you last week?" he inquired, obviously not choosing to recall the four days in which he completely ignored her. He didn't even remember how school went for himself and felt a wave of anxiety wash over when he suddenly thought of the fountain incident. Did that really happen?

Andrea didn't respond. She pressed her forehead against the glass and stared at the mountains as she did the first day they met.

"What's wrong?" he asked. "Why aren't you talking to me?"

Richard began to sweat. Why was she acting like that? He had been looking forward to picking her up most of the weekend. In fact, that's all he was able to think about. Was it something he said? Could she still be mad at his fart joke?

"Did something happen to you?" Richard asked. "Are you homesick or something? Please tell me."

Andrea turned to him, extremely concerned about the way he was acting. He was truly coming unglued, and was actually starting to frighten her. Obsession can lead to disturbing actions.

"Richard, just drive," she said, realizing that something had changed in him since the week before. He must have been crazy. "I just don't feel good." Regardless of his behavior, she knew it was over between the two. No more rides. No more communication. He had to go.

She lied.

Richard continued to drive, wanting to talk to her but holding it in. Occasionally, at red lights, he would glance over at her legs. He thought it was so cute how she would cross them and gently bounce the one that remained in the air. What he didn't realize was that she was bouncing her leg because she was nervous and didn't want to end up dead in a ditch somewhere.

When the two reached the school parking lot, Andrea was the first to get out. She was headed up the sidewalk before he even had a chance to turn the engine off.

"Andrea, wait!" he yelled, stumbling over the curb in his haste to catch up.

She reluctantly slowed down, although she never turned to look at him.

"You wanna do something after school?" he asked. It may have seemed like something trivial to most people, but asking a girl to do something, anything, had never happened with Richard Tark. She had to know that fact, respect it, and agree. She just had to.

"I don't think so," she said, and continued walking. She wanted to tell him right there, whatever the reason for his mood, the rides were over. In time she would.

Richard stood in place, rejected and embarrassed. He watched her disappear into the building and began to cry. Nothing worked out for him. He wondered why she was so distant. Even though she was holding back her feelings and wanted to truly deck him, he realized it was serious. Her silence spoke to him louder than a fist to the jaw and the jubilation that he felt earlier in the morning was ripped from his mind.

Richard walked into the building and soon was engulfed in the sea of students struggling to get to their lockers and ultimately their classes. Flashes of silence and chaos overlapped each other as he stared at the ground. One minute, he heard all of the people around him and was deafened by their chatter. The next, he was alone in the hall, not a sound. Two seconds later, the chatter and crush of humanity returned. He felt like he had just gotten off of the Zipper at the fair and was ready to vomit.

Clutching his books he made his way down the hall towards his first class of the day, trying his best to forget about Andrea and the way she treated him. At the same time he knew she would be in the classroom.

He strolled around the corner and ran directly into a stone wall made up of his favorite seniors. It figured that on this—such a stressful day—he would run into those fucks. At first he didn't acknowledge them, hoping that it was all a dream and they would disappear all together.

Things never worked out the way he wanted.

Reggie, Seth and Charles were waiting for him and formed an impenetrable barrier. It was time to take his medicine.

"What's up guys?" Richard asked nervously, walking backwards in a feeble attempt to avoid the inevitable prank. "I was just . . . um . . . I was just . . . just going this way," he said, stumbling over his words while pointing towards the door that led out to the courtyard and that horrible fountain.

All three bullies smirked and smiled. Something was up and just like before, Richard wasn't going to get out of it. Like a child who knows he's gettin' a whoopin', Richard eventually calmed down and prepared for whatever punishment deemed necessary.

Andrea was sitting in one of the restroom stalls taking a leak. She sat deep in thought, listening to the crowds of people that were collecting just outside of the main bathroom door. It wasn't looking like a good day up to that point and she hoped for a pleasant afternoon. Either way, she knew she would be walking home after school.

A burst of noise and clatter flooded the bathroom along with the sounds of someone pleading to be released. Shortly after the initial explosion of chaos, a muffled thud filled the room, followed by the sounds of booming laughter and guys slapping fives. Just as quickly everything went silent. Andrea wiped clean and hesitantly walked out of her stall. Just around the corner, a large black trash can rested in front of the entrance to the restroom. Two legs were sticking out and kicking back and forth. The person wrestled himself out of the can and looked up at Andrea.

It was Richard.

A ribbon of blood streamed across his forehead and he looked thoroughly defeated. For a few seconds he stared at Andrea, breathing in and out like a scared puppy, not making a sound. He glanced over at a mirror and in a flash he was above the sink, vigorously brushing the blood from his face. It wasn't his but he'd wished it was. It would've been better than knowing it came from a soaked tampon housed in the garbage can somewhere.

Andrea continued to watch him, half disgusted, half mortified by what was happening. She wished she'd never had met this guy and was thoroughly confused by his presence in her life. Even though a tiny part of her continued to feel sorry for the fool and what he went through, most of the time she was scared of him.

"Uh," he started. "I was just leaving. Sorry."

Andrea shook her head and walked out of the bathroom. She was embarrassed for the both of them.

"Wait, Andrea," he said, following her.

The crowd of people waiting outside of the restroom not only laughed at Richard for being thrown in there, but at Andrea for being the girl who saw him. Mortified and confused, she ran down the hall in terror, leaving Richard far behind. It was bad enough that he was picked on all the time but she certainly didn't need him to get her involved.

"Andrea!" he yelled.

She didn't know how to feel about Richard. How could someone allow themselves to be abused to such an extent? No wonder the guy was a modern day Jeckyl and Hyde.

Alexis noticed Andrea's uncomfortable appearance when she first entered the room. Again, the class was filled with people not knowing why they were even there. The room was already filled with quiet banter between students and there was obviously no *teaching* and certainly no *learning* going on.

The teacher, or Mr. Chode as the male students had cheerfully started calling him, sat at his desk and filed paperwork. It was a change from the previous days when he spent the hour looking over magazines, and picking his nose. This was the first person Andrea had ever seen who could pick his nose with his thumb. Andrea stared at Mr. Chode as he struggled to deal with an unholy quest. His thumb was lodged in his nostril all the way to the first digit. He was digging and concentrating on the task while half of the class watched in horror. Eventually, he pulled out a crusty specimen and proceeded to shake it off onto the carpet.

At one point, Andrea thought he was actually going to do something productive when he got up to write on the chalkboard. First, he had to pull his pants up and yawn. Her wildest dreams could not have conjured up such a character. How could a teacher in an established high school manage to do nothing for more than a week?

He drew a circle and sat back down.

"What is that?" she turned and asked Alexis. She was overwhelmed with amazement and kind of freaked out by his gesture.

"Um, it looks like a circle," Alexis said, mockingly. "You know what a circle is, don't you? Do they have those in Montana?"

Andrea looked really confused.

"I know what it is . . . but, this is Anthropology isn't it?" Andrea said, holding up her unused and still sparkling new textbook. Other students were looking at each other with similar looks of confusion.

"Technically? Yes," Alexis responded.

"So what's with the circle?" Andrea asked.

Alexis shrugged her shoulders.

"Are you okay?" Alexis asked. "You seem really, well, you seem like a real bitch today."

Andrea looked down at her books and sighed. If she didn't talk to someone soon, she was going to lose it. Living life in the "Twilight Zone," isn't healthy and eventually everyone needs a friend. Andrea had found a stalker in Richard and needed to somehow get away from the guy. Alexis was the perfect solution. She was just the kind of person that Andrea wanted to be around and could possibly, eventually, confide in.

"Do you have a car?" she asked Alexis.

"What? Yeah. Who doesn't?"

"Nevermind," Andrea said, a little nervous and embarrassed about what she needed to ask. She didn't know Alexis enough to impose like that.

"Why?" Alexis inquired.

"Nothing. Just forget it."

"Why?" Alexis formed a sly smile and knew that Andrea needed a favor. Even though she seemed like a real bitch, Alexis had a soft spot for Andrea and was really growing fond of her.

"I need a ride to and from school everyday, and this guy that's been taking me is a psycho. Every day I see him, I don't know if he's going to hate me, or smother me, I wish I would've never met him . . ." Andrea started. "I mean, just last week . . ."

"Whoa, girl. You're totally wiggin' out," Alexis chimed in. "I can give you rides. It's no biggie. You don't have to tell me your life story for a ticket to ride. Just follow me to my locker after class and we'll go."

"Thanks," Andrea said before turning back to watch the teacher.

He was gone.

The same two students who had shot spit wads in the teacher's hair the week before were up at the chalkboard, drawing stick figures in sexual positions. One of them had drawn an equal sized circle next to the one Mr. Chode had made, and followed it with a couple of nipples, producing the largest image of breasts any of them would see in a lifetime. Andrea and Alexis were the only two that didn't laugh at the gesture. Andrea thought it was somewhat embarrassing, while Alexis thought they could've been drawn so much better.

"These guys don't have a fuckin' clue about what tits really look like," Alexis said, leaning towards Andrea's ear. "Have you ever seen 'em that perfectly round?" As she said that, she grabbed one of her breasts and squeezed. "He wishes."

Alexis leaned back in her chair, noticing a boy sitting a few chairs over. He was staring at her like a kid that had just peeked at his Christmas gifts.

"What?" she said, returning the stare, grabbing her other breast. "You want some of this? You wouldn't know what to do with 'em anyway."

The kid's face turned two shades of red and he averted his eyes to another part of the room.

"Fuckin' perv," she finished. "What's with this guy?"

Class ended and the two girls left the room. Andrea was depressed and Alexis was just downright irritated. It was going to be a long year if that class continued in such a manner and the question was—how were the students even being graded?

In a matter of seconds, Richard was in Andrea's face. He had left class early and waited outside Andrea's classroom. No way could he allow her to walk out of his life. He was just as stupid as he was ignorant when it came to girls.

"Are you ready to go, Andrea?" he asked, conjuring up a coy smile, coming off as a stalker.

"No, Richard. I'm going to get a ride from Alexis, here," she said, pointing to her flashy friend. Alexis stared at Richard with a smug look on her face, magnified by the obnoxious chomping of gum.

Richard looked at Alexis with anger and hatred.

"What do you mean? I . . . I . . . I'm giving you a ride, right?" he asked, lowering his voice as he got closer to Andrea's ear. He reached over and slowly, but firmly, grabbed her by the arm as if she were a pet on the loose.

"Richard, go home," Andrea said, pulling away from him.

"Yeah, Richard. Go home before you get hurt," Alexis said, raising her fist and pumping it in his face.

"I'll meet you out front," he said. It was as if he didn't understand a word the girls were saying. "I . . . I . . . I'll meet you out front. Please."

"That's the guy you got a ride from?" Alexis asked as the two walked away. "He's a real winner. Fuckin' go for it, girl. That's classic." Andrea just closed her eyes and tried to ignore the teasing.

The girls made their way through the madness of people and eventually drove away in Alexis' Honda Civic. Andrea felt a little bad for ditching Richard but only because of her morals. She knew he had problems that were out of his control but she also knew that she didn't have time to deal with his horrible attitude. She had her own shit to deal with.

Richard sat in the courtyard for nearly two hours, waiting for Andrea to come out, not fully coming to grips with the fact that she left right after school. The trickling of water from the fountain was relaxing. Something inside told him that she would be there. Eventually he lost hope, picked up his books and walked to his car just as the evening sun was headed for the mountains. The football players had all gone to practice, finished and left for the day, so his car was the only one in the lot.

He was hurt more than anything and felt his own brain had betrayed him because he was convinced Andrea was still there and would come out of the building expecting a ride. If he just left, he would be abandoning her there, or so he convinced himself.

Despite his shortcomings, Richard was able to comprehend the real world from time to time and thought intensely about Alexis pumping her fist in his face. He remembered Andrea's sudden change in personality. Her demeanor had turned from shy and loving to crass and volatile and he had no idea he was the cause of it all.

Richard stopped thinking about Andrea when he noticed a dog strolling down the parking lot towards the Volkswagen he was sitting on. It was a large German Shepard, and didn't look threatening at first. As it got closer, Richard hopped onto his feet. Finally, the dog reached his car and sniffed his tire before it lifted its leg and pissed on his fender. Richard flew towards the dog and reared back his leg, connecting with the animal's abdomen full-force with the tip of his shoe.

"Aaarrrfff!" the dog yelped, crashing into the fender in which it had just pissed on.

"How dare you piss on my car, motherfucker!" Richard screamed as he kept kicking the animal over and over again. Finally, he lifted his leg in the air and landed it on side of the injured dog's head.

CRUNCH!

The German Shepard's skull caved in and except for the occasional twitch, the dog stopped moving. Richard had blood all over his shoe and a trail of the red liquid streamed down the asphalt. For a moment Richard stood above the dead dog pumping with adrenaline and anger. He looked around to see if anyone witnessed the beating. He wished the entire school had been there. Maybe people would stop fucking with him if they knew how tough he was. Who else could beat a dog to death? And, not just any dog—a German Fucking Shepard.

The dog should never have picked his car to piss on. If it had just walked by and pissed on a flagpole, it would still be alive. Richard knelt down and touched the still-warm animal smiling at what he had accomplished. People were going to have to start treating him better, or they would end up like the dog.

For that one moment, he was king.

Slowly he stood back up and again surveyed the area around him, taking in a deep breath and smiling for the world to see. He couldn't remember ever feeling so happy. The stress and anger that had built up inside the previous ten days all came flooding out with each swing of his foot. The dog wasn't the source of his problems; it just helped him relieve stress.

Still, the dog shouldn't have pissed on his car.

The next morning Richard arrived at Andrea's house to pick her up just as he had done every day before since school started. He waited outside her apartment until eight o'clock, the time the bell rang at Carver. The rage he felt as he sat alone in the parking lot was confusing. He had been betrayed again and this time by someone he loved. Someone else spent time with her that morning and even if it was just a girl, he felt jealousy akin to someone who pictures their loved one having sex with someone else.

As expected, he showed up late to class and was embarrassed by the teacher when he walked in right in the middle of a lecture. Andrea was stationed in her usual spot in the room and Richard glared at her. She refused to look at him, which pissed him off even more.

The entire hour passed and you'd swear Richard never blinked. He didn't hear a word the teacher said. He did manage to scare the shit out of Andrea, who noticed his intense behavior. At that point in Richard's life, she was just another person on a long list of people who eventually shit on his parade. And yet he still wanted her. The more she pushed him away, the more he wanted to be with her. The obsession was growing by the day.

And, he would have her.

5

"Here we sit again," Gabe said. "I seem to recall having this same conversation last year and where has it gotten you?" The room was silent. No TV. No radio. No ticking clocks. That's when it got tense in the Becker household. When it was quiet.

Willie and Gabe sat across from each other in the dimly lit confines of their dining room. The man-to-man conversations were beginning to wear thin for Willie.

"You know, each year I think that you are going to break out of this little . . . rebellious stage and each year I find that I have wasted my time with you young man," Gabe continued. "I don't have a single colleague that shares this problem. Their sons and daughters are all well behaved and striving for better lives. You just seem to go at your own pace. Hell, no one can touch big, bad Willie Becker."

It was another lecture for Willie. Throughout his schooling, he had found ways of getting into trouble and quite frankly it was all intended to piss off his pops. Willie was somewhat proud considering that school had just begun and it only took two weeks for trouble to come calling.

This talk was the direct result of Susie Fargas and her "accidental" fall. Well, "accidental" meaning Willie had taken a socket wrench and unscrewed the four bolts that held her chair together. Susie was a perpetual loser that followed Willie through the ranks of school. The two were actually friends in the second grade.

She'd turned into a real peach, sporting a huge set of braces in her mouth while battling the fiercest case of constant acne anyone had ever seen before. Her skin was severely pocked and blistered from the zits.

The year prior, she had confessed a crush to Willie and that was enough to warrant a "dick stage." Willie was usually a decent guy to most people but there were a few who received the brunt of his shenanigans. He wanted everyone to know he didn't share her sentiment and the only way to do that was by being brutal. Since her confession, he had managed to ignore and sneer her every move. The chair incident was just the topping.

When he saw her stand up, her hair a mess and tears streaming down her face, he felt sorrow for what he had done. He still managed to put up a front and smile as the class erupted and she ran from the room, crying hysterically and holding her side.

"You keep hanging around those losers and you'll find yourself without an education or worse yet, rotting down there in Cripple Creek." It wasn't the first time Gabe had brought up prison. Willie had never broken the law; at least he'd never gotten caught. Sometimes he thought Gabe threw the prison references into his lectures because he secretly wanted to see his son there. His dad was convinced that Willie was hanging with "losers," because that's just what parents do when their kids begin acting like complete morons and do things like that in school. Willie was his own person and didn't need anyone else to help him get in trouble. He did his occasional dirty work as a solo artist and was pretty proud of that.

Willie sat still, staring at the floor, wishing that he was anywhere else. He was speechless. There was no one on the planet he'd rather impress than Gabe. Willie wanted to be the man Gabe envisioned. He wanted to graduate from high school and become someone famous, but on his own terms. Not Gabe's. It just wasn't in the cards. Willie wasn't destined to be a doctor or even a good student. The only thing that ever interested him was writing. He had written a short story in some long forgotten class early in high school and that really got his attention. Even that was a stretch, considering he hadn't really written anything since.

The lecture continued for another 15 minutes, Gabe doing all of the talking and Willie doing all of the staring. That's the way all of their discussions went. Strangely enough, Gabe taught Willie to sit up straight and keep his mouth shut when the two talked. However, Gabe always managed to get mad when Willie didn't speak. It was a Catch-22 clusterfuck.

There was one rule that couldn't be negotiated. Willie knew it. Gabe knew it. The conversation was going fine until Willie did what he does best and messed everything up. He broke one of the cardinal rules in the Becker household. A sin that he was taught not to attempt from the day he was born. You never, under any circumstances, roll your eyes at Gabe. He had instilled that rule in Willie from an early age and was certainly not above kicking some ass when it happened.

"Look at me when I'm talking to you," he snapped at Willie. Willie's eyes met Gabe's. "You need to focus your energy on school. Time to stop messing around, young man."

Gabe was barking out one cliché after another, just as he always did. Willie was frustrated and tired from the same old conversation and soon the two sat silent, staring into each other's eyes for a good minute without saying a word.

"You don't seem to understand what I'm saying," Gabe barked. "How would you like me to spell it out? You . . . will . . . show . . . some . . . discipline." He talked slowly as if he were directing his words to an infant.

Willie sat back in his chair, and took a deep breath and without thinking about it, perhaps doing it to spite his father, rolled his eyes. *He rolled his eyes!*

"Oh, that's it!" Gabe screamed. He stood up and grabbed his coffee mug, leaning over the table towards the still sitting Willie. His arm flew in a roundhouse motion, and the coffee mug clanked off of Willie's skull, instantly breaking the skin, releasing a sea of blood that streamed down the left side of his face.

You don't roll your eyes at Gabe.

Willie fell to the ground in a blur. Seconds later he sat up and felt a searing pain in his head just before the blood blinded his left eye. He saw his father standing above him with the still intact coffee cup in his hand. His vision wobbled as he tried to gain some composure.

Gabe stood above his injured son and knew that the cut was serious. It wasn't enough that he had caused the gash, but he walked away. He left the house, got in his car, and drove away. He wasn't going for help, nor was he concerned with his son's well being. All Gabe knew was that it wouldn't be much of a lesson if he stayed to sew up the wound. Even though he'd never admit it to Willie, he felt bad for what he had done and ran because it was easier to ignore.

Willie's mother, Joan, heard the commotion and sprinted into the room just as Gabe was peeling out of the driveway.

"Oh my god!" she screamed. Head wounds are usually pretty messy and this one was no exception. Blood was smeared all over the white tiles of the kitchen floor, and Willie's face was caked in the liquid. His blonde hair was stained and he still hadn't gotten up for fear of falling from a lack of bearings.

Willie was a rather large individual for his age but genes don't fall far from the source and his father was just as big thus he had no trouble dropping the youngster. Using a coffee cup didn't hurt his power either.

"Willie," his mother pleaded. "Willie, speak to me. Oh Jesus, help me."

Joan cradled her son and clutched his soaked head to her bosom. Tears streamed down her cheeks. She had seen this before. Willie didn't fight back and the thought had never crossed his mind. It was his father and he knew better than to mess with blood. It was a fact of life and something that Willie knew as such. His father had a temper and Willie was well aware that he had become a disappointment. He shouldn't have hurt Susie Fargas and he finally realized why.

Joan composed herself and managed to help Willie to his feet, walking him to a chair at the dining room table.

"Sit here and be calm," she said. "I'll be right back."

Willie was dazed and was having trouble staying conscious. He had lost a lot of blood and could barely remember what had happened.

Joan returned with a wet towel, jar of pickles, a needle and some medical thread. She had learned how to sew up a wound years before Willie was even born and knew she had to get his scalp sealed. As quickly as possible, she wiped the blood from his face and around the wound.

"Now, this is going to hurt a bit," she said, twisting the metal lid from the jar of pickles. "Just think of something nice. Think of the Lord." As she said that she stared up at the ceiling and closed her eyes.

Joan poured pickle juice on the wound. Willie screamed in pain and kicked his feet. She used vinegar on open sores due to its acidity. The pickle juice had the vinegar but also had salt and she thought of it as an added bonus. She got to work on Willie's scalp and soon had the two-inch gash sealed. She even managed to wash most of the blood from his hair and face.

The two made their way to the living room and sat down. Willie's head was throbbing and Joan provided a couple of aspirins for the pain.

"You make me proud," she started.

Willie just stared at the floor. He didn't want his mother's approval. What he had done was wrong, just as what his father had done was wrong.

"Regardless of what that man says," she added, referring to his father. "*you* are a wonderful person and will become a great man. You know what he's so angry about? He never had any friends. You have so much and you should be so happy the Lord has blessed you with the tools needed to be loved. I've seen it. You will never be lonely. And, you'll always have your mother."

Willie looked up to find her crying.

"Don't cry, mom," he said, trying not to speak too loudly. His own voice echoed through his brain to the cut. "Don't cry. That motherfucker is going to pay someday."

Joan paused. She was stunned by her son's language, but also a little invigorated. Hearing him speak that way about Gabe gave her a charge of emotion. Even if he was merely pissed, Willie was actually speaking of being accountable. An eye for an eye as they say.

That motherfucker is going to pay.

Joan invited Willie upstairs to the hall closet.

She pulled out a photo album, one that Willie had seen a hundred times. Willie sighed and thought about how comfortable he was going to be in bed. The pain he felt was tremendous, but nothing compared to his encounter with the pickle juice.

"Ma, I'm tired and I've seen these photos a million times," he started.

"You mind your mother," she snapped, gently slapping him on the wound. He winced. "God did not provide me with you so that I could be talked down to."

"I didn't mean . . ." he said before being interrupted.

"You didn't mean what?" she said. "You didn't mean to anger your father so that I had to rescue you again? You didn't mean to nearly bleed to death? Who saved you from that fate? Who sewed that little wound up?" She pounded her finger on his stitches when she said that. Willie buckled in pain.

"Okay, okay. I'm sorry," he said. "Show me the pictures."

Joan opened the photo album and turned to the back page. There she lifted the plastic and removed a photograph. It was a picture of Gabe, taken when he was a teenager, holding a line of fish at some forgotten lake.

She held it up.

"Yeah," Willie said. "Those are nice fish."

Joan flipped the photo over, revealing a tiny, yellowed newspaper clipping from the same time period as the photo.

The headline read: "Local teenager charged with theft."

Willie read the story.

"Your father was associating himself with the wrong people and got into a bit of trouble," she said. "It almost cost him his medical license when he got out of college."

Willie was confused and stunned.

"If this happened before high school, why would it affect him in college?"

"Because you can never escape your past," she said. "Who wants a doctor who robbed and beat a man?"

"Beat?" Willie asked. "It doesn't say anything in here about beating . . . oh, wait, here it is." He read about his father and how he had kicked a man to the ground before stealing his wallet. The man recovered, but managed to help catch his father. Surprisingly enough, Gabe only received probation.

"Why would he do that?" Willie asked.

"Like I said, your father was involved with the wrong people," she said. "That's why he's so paranoid."

"Luckily, most of the board members felt it had happened at too young an age to matter. Your father was grown up, had excelled in high school and done even better in college. Punks and thugs don't go to six years of college and become doctors. Gabe had a spark in him and they knew it."

"What about me?" Willie asked. "Do I have a spark?"

Joan paused. "I think so. You'll do just fine."

A lightning rod of pain shot through Willie's head.

"Oh fuck," he said, holding his hand up to the wound.

Joan slapped it away.

"Don't talk like that in front of your mother," she snapped. "You've said the f-word twice now and I won't have any more of it tonight. And, don't touch that wound, you'll infect it."

Willie waited patiently for his mother to make her point so that he could hit the hay. He was already in for a hard night of sleep.

"Your father is a bastard and pardon me for using such language" she said, making a cross over her chest, staring at the ceiling. "He made so many mistakes as a child and continues to make them to this day. Don't let him beat you down. Don't let him win. The almighty Lord hates a coward and your father will see that someday. And, if you continue with this apathy, he will conquer you too."

She sounded like an ancient prophet, but Willie listened.

"I love your father and will stay with him till death do us part," she said. "But, I don't condone what he did to you tonight."

"I'm not giving up my friends," Willie said. "And, I'm not going to be a doctor."

She smiled. If there was anything in the world that made her happy, it was knowing that Willie wasn't interested in following his father's footsteps.

"And, I'll apologize to Susie," he said.

"You be friends with whomever you wish," she said. "I trust you know who is evil and who is pure. Your father would be happy if you had no friends. What kind of man is that? Just remember, you have to be strong. No one can take care of you better than yourself."

Joan clutched Willie and pulled his head to her chest. Her shirt was already covered in his blood. Her fingers dug into his wound and he twitched in pain as she rocked back and forth, saying the words to the Lord's Prayer.

"Our father, who art in heaven," she began.

Willie broke free of her grasp and headed towards his bedroom. He hated when his mother smothered him in her overzealous religious beliefs.

"Willie," his mother beckoned. "Do not leave during the Lord's Prayer. Do not walk away from your savoir."

Willie turned around.

"I'm going to bed, ma," he said. In the back of his mind, he thought about his family and wondered how he had managed to stay sane. His parents were so fucked up and on such opposite ends of the psycho spectrum, he didn't know which one of them was worse. And, the wound was beginning to swell.

As he lay in bed, an unexpected and odd vision came to mind. He thought of the kid who was pushed into the fountain on the first day of school. Richard. Now that boy had problems. Perhaps Willie needed to step up and help him. It was obvious that Richard had a black mark at Carver and needed someone to come in and save him from a dire fate.

Willie smiled. Richard was just like Susie. He was going to be his project.

6

Three weeks had passed since Andrea stopped commuting to school with Richard. His grades were failing miserably and only one class had him down for anything better than an F and that was gym. All he had to do was show up for that class and he would get an A. Even that was a trying task as the jocks made it a daily effort to make him sorry he wasn't born a basketball player. In fact, he was still nursing a knot that had formed on his head after someone pelted him with a hockey puck three days earlier.

A reputation began to brew surrounding Little Dick. He was the kid that no one wanted to be associated with. The ultimate in geek-dom. His natural born quiet demeanor and withdrawn attitude merged with the constant hazing to fuel the fire that raged inside of him. It's hard to imagine the solitude people like Richard deal with yet we're surrounded by them everywhere we go. Maybe all it takes to save a person like Richard is another human being willing to sacrifice their time and show a little positive interest. One person in that entire school chose not to forget about him. It was the damndest thing too because that one person had no reason to give a shit. Sometimes all it takes is one person to break the barriers that children set.

"Here, I brought you this," Willie said to Richard, tapping him on the shoulder from the desk one spot behind him, holding something in his hand. "I don't need it anymore."

Richard turned out of curiosity, waiting for something bad to happen.

Willie was offering a closed fist to Richard and when the loser jutted out his palm in return, a beautiful class ring was dropped into his hand. Puzzled and expecting the punch line at any time, Richard shook his head and refused to take the ring. Willie persisted. What would Richard do with the damn thing? Wearing someone else's class ring is usually reserved for girlfriends.

"You know what?" Willie asked. "My father went out and bought me that fucking thing before I had even stepped one foot into this damn place. I hated it. I've always hated it. I never wanted to go to school here, you know. I wanted to go to Collins with my buddies."

Richard remained silent and perplexed.

"I figure I'm going to probably throw the damn thing away. So, you know, you might have more of a use for it since you're a freshman and all," Willie continued. "It doesn't have my initials on it or anything. It's just a generic ring."

"And hell, maybe you can give it to some dork freshman when you're a senior," Willie finished. Richard accepted the ring and paused. Was he just referred to as a dork freshman?

"Wait. That didn't come out right. I didn't mean to call you a . . ."

"Don't worry about it," Richard interrupted. "I've been called worse things than a dork."

Richard turned around and stared at the ring. It was amazing. It was the most glaring silver, accompanied by red jewels and the pewter inscription of Carver high's bulldog mascot shone right in the center. He had never received a gift from anyone who wasn't related to him. Regardless of the sentiment behind the gesture, Richard was honored to have something so precious. Willie had referred to it as nothing more than a possible addition to the landfill but to Richard, it was a treasure.

Other than the few bottom feeders who felt the wrath of Willie's occasional pranks, most knew him as the ultimate classmate. He was that one student that stood out as being popular among nearly all of the cliques that roamed the halls. Giving Richard that ring was just another example of why. He didn't even have to give Richard the time of day, but he did. He could've easily been one of the assholes who got their kicks out of dumping him in the girls' restroom trashcan had he been in the vicinity that day, but he wasn't. Just don't ask Susie Fargas for her opinion on the guy.

Richard slid the ring into his pocket.

"So, what's up?" Willie whispered.

"With what?" he responded.

"What's up with you?" Willie said. "You're weirder than usual."

Richard turned back around to face the front.

"What's up with your stitches?" Richard asked, his back facing Willie. "Did you finally get that lobotomy?" It had been a week since Willie was smacked by his father. He took the comment in stride and grew an enormous grin. The kid actually had potential.

"I know what's wrong with you. It's a chick isn't it?" Willie asked. "You've got a crush on someone, don't-cha? Is it that girl you we were with back in the first week of the year?"

Richard started to turn red and his face instantly percolated another 10 degrees even though he wasn't looking at Willie.

"It's not a crush," he said like a child being teased by an uncle.

"*It's not a crush*," Willie responded, mocking Richard. "Dude, who is it? Is she in this room? Give me something. Ha. This is great. Fuckin' freshman, man."

Richard turned around.

"Could you keep it down?" he asked. "You're going to get us in trouble."

The teacher noticed a commotion earlier when Willie handed over the ring and was getting quite agitated at the banter.

"Do you guys mind if I teach class?" he asked. "Am I bothering you by standing up here talking? If you two want, you can teach this class and I'll sit where you're at. How's that sound to you Mr. Tark?"

Richard nervously shook his head no.

"Mr. Becker?"

Willie smiled.

"Yoooou've gooooootttt a cruuuuuuush," he said one last time, singing his words like a little schoolgirl.

"Shut up," Richard said under his breath.

After class, Willie grabbed Richard by the arm.

"You know what?" he said. "I have a plan. I know something that will cheer your ass up. You're goin' to the football game Saturday."

Richard was seriously confused by Willie's straightforward manner.

"Don't argue with me either," Willie said in a matter-of-fact tone. "I'll call you. We'll go and have a good time, and pick up some chicks while we're at it. I haven't gotten laid in a loooong time. Something tells me you know the feeling."

Richard thought about how he had never gotten laid.

"I'll bring something good to drink too, if you catch my drift," Willie said diabolically, nudging Richard with his elbow. "Sound like a plan?"

Richard shrugged his shoulders.

"Good, it's a date." Willie smacked his hand on Richard's ass before leaving the room in a hurry. Richard cringed and rubbed the spot where Willie had just nailed him. The guy had power. Richard found himself extremely nervous and anxious. His instincts told him that he shouldn't trust Willie. He was a senior, and one of the most popular guys in school at that. Why would he have any interest in Richard other than for sport? He had seen "Carrie," before and didn't want to be the one standing under a bucket of pig's blood when the time came.

It didn't make sense. Maybe that's why he needed to just take a risk and go with it. What did he have to lose? It's not like he'd never been let down or humiliated. He felt the ring in his pocket. It could've been a trick, but why would he give up such a valuable item in the name of tom-foolery? Willie was the only friend Richard could claim and regardless of the motive, he had no choice but to accept it. A lonely person will go to great lengths to rid themselves of that feeling. Besides, Richard knew he was probably making too much out of the whole thing. It's not like Willie wanted to fuck him.

Richard slid the ring on his middle finger and stared at it for a moment. Its jewel glistened under the lights of the classroom and he smiled. It was beautiful. If only Andrea could see it.

Later that afternoon she skipped out on him again and he drove home alone. Not that he should've expected otherwise. Most normal people would've gotten the hint after a few days of waiting but he continued to hope against hope that she'd be at his car after school. He felt like he had been with Andrea for years, and the transition to single life was hard. The nausea that one feels when they lose a loved one is hard to overcome. It's even worse when someone falls in love and doesn't get the same sentiment in return. It tends to evolve into an emotion worse than anger or sadness or guilt. It's called *black love*. When you love something you can never have. It turns into living death.

Richard was swimming in *black love* and felt he was going to eventually drown in the thick, murky swamp. It made him physically ill, and that's why he had his mother call him in sick to school the next day. Something had to be done, and quickly, or he would end up in a mental hospital or worse yet—dead.

RIINNG!

Richard's phone was ringing again. It had been doing it all morning, a sign that his mother was either gone or hung over. Richard sat up in bed and dangled his feet over the side. His hair was ratted and he yawned at the same time he scratched his balls.

He didn't feel like answering the phone.

RIINNG!

It wouldn't stop. With each ring, he became more frustrated and eventually picked it up just before succumbing to the urge to kick something across the room.

"Hello?" he barked with the utmost agitation in his voice.

"Richard?" the voice on the other line asked. "That you Rich?"

"Yeah, who's this?"

"Rich, this is Willie. What's up? I didn't see you around yesterday. You sick or something?"

"No," Richard said in a grouchy voice.

"Okay. Anyway, I was calling to remind you about the game."

"Sure," Richard said. "When does it start?"

He rubbed the sleep from his eyes and let out another ferocious yawn.

"One o'clock," Willie said. "Don't worry about bringing any money either. *I've got everything covered, mang.*" He was using his best Pacino "Scarface" impression.

"Good, cause I'm broke anyway. Where should I meet you?" Richard asked.

"You know where the band hangs out before the game starts?"

"Yeah."

"Well, don't go near those faggots. They may try something on you and the next thing you know you'll be playing the skin flute."

Richard chuckled. This guy was weird. The sincerity behind Willie's jokes and jolly attitude was something that Richard had never seen in another person his age. No one acted the way Willie did.

A fly landed on Richard's arm.

"Ha. Ha. Seriously, where should we meet?" Richard asked.

"Meet me in front of the stadium ticket window about thirty minutes before kickoff," Willie said.

"When's kickoff?" Richard asked.

"I already told you, dork—one o'clock," Willie said. "Pay attention."

"Sorry. I'll be there. Thanks again, man," Richard said as he hung up the phone.

Richard looked at the mirror on the wall in front of him. This was his chance to have a friend again. Regardless of the fact that he simply didn't care for football, he was going to give it a shot anyway. After all, how could he say *no* to Willie when *no* just wasn't an answer.

He glanced up at the clock on the wall.

"Oh, shit!" he yelled.

It was already noon and he hadn't gotten dressed or eaten breakfast.

The next few moments Richard spent running the triathlon through his house. First, he ran to the bedroom and threw off his pajamas. Then he changed into a pair of sweats and a ratty t-shirt. Finally he ran to the kitchen, gulped a few drinks of milk straight out of the carton and grabbed an apple from the counter. He had to put something in his increasingly upset stomach. Such anxiety will have that effect on people.

Richard didn't live too far from the stadium and didn't wait for his car to warm up before peeling out of the driveway. As he drove into the stadium parking lot, the butterflies that had hassled him for the previous hour were beginning to run amok in the depths of his belly. He hadn't experienced nervousness that bad since the first day of school and now he was feeling it big time. He thought about all of the people that were probably going to be at the game, staring at his every move. Voices in his head tried to convince him that once he got there, he would be the butt of someone's joke and end up leaving to an eruption of laughter.

Nervousness goes a long way in life. Too bad it isn't really productive, or necessary. In fact, it is one of the most useless feelings that a person can experience. Richard experienced it tenfold on the way to the stadium, so bad at one point he ended up regurgitating part of his apple right back into his mouth. He had been driving too fast and was in too much of a hurry to pull over and puke on the side of the road. No, instead he allowed himself to puke what was in his belly into his mouth where he immediately sent it back to where it came from. It wasn't so much the apple that made it disgusting, but the milk.

It was the only thing he could do. He had never been to a football game as a student, much less with someone as highly regarded as Willie Becker.

He found a parking space and locked his car before he started running. His mouth tasted like apple-milk and stomach acid and he took the time to hack and spit the disgusting broth out while he ran. Glancing down at his watch he noticed the time—12:42. He was going to be late. Damn it, he should've told Willie that he was running behind.

The band was now marching towards the stadium as they always did before a home game. Richard smiled and thought of the term "skin flute." Why would Willie think the band members were all fags? They were just playing instruments, dressed up in some sort of uniform that resembled something from the Nutcracker.

"Skin flute?" Richard mumbled to himself as he let out a laugh.

Finally, the dork reached the ticket window. Out of breath, he grabbed his knees. He was tired and exhausted from the adventure to the stadium, but worse yet, he realized he was alone. Willie wasn't anywhere to be seen. Was this a joke? Was he coaxed into coming as part of a senior versus freshman hazing thing? All of those images raced through Richard's mind as he began to sweat. Thinking of being the fool made his blood boil and his brain hurt. He was instantly pissed and thought of grabbing one of the instruments from the band and beating a random pansy to death. They say smokers lose 14-minutes of their lives with each cigarette they smoke. I'd wager a guy like Richard lost months on his lifespan with each incident like this. It was certainly harsh on his body.

"BOOO!" He was startled as someone grabbed him from behind.

Richard turned to find Willie standing there with a huge grin on his face.

"Kid, let me tell you something about punctuality. When someone tells you to be somewhere at a specific time . . ."

"I'm sorry, my car gave me trouble, and . . ." Richard said as he interrupted Willie.

Willie returned the favor and interrupted Richard right back.

"Let me finish," he said, holding up a finger. "When someone tells you to be somewhere at a specific time—you tell them to go fuck themselves. Punctuality is for sissies."

"Well. Do you think we should go in and find our seats?" Willie finished.

Richard nodded.

"Follow my lead," Willie said as he walked towards the band. For some reason, he seemed really suspicious, his head swiveling in both directions, looking for something or someone. The two walked swiftly until they were behind the band members. The line was mostly comprised of nerds with instruments, Willie and Richard. Eventually Willie broke from the pack and began to shout.

"Okay, people!" he yelled, putting his arms up before clapping loudly. "Listen up. I need all of you to stand single-file and walk through gate number two." Willie looked over at Richard and winked. He clapped his hands together again and made a motion to lead the pack. "Okay, let's get a move on. We don't have all day."

The band members scrambled and made their way towards gate two like a herd of elephants. They acted as if Willie was in charge and followed him blindly. He led the way up until they actually reached the gate where he managed to fall back in line, still acting like the leader of the group.

"All right, let's not push," he said, motioning each member forward. "C'mon people."

Richard stopped when he reached Willie, who resembled a traffic cop waving cars through an intersection.

"What are you doing?" Richard asked under his breath. "You're gonna get busted."

"Shut up and watch," Willie said. "You might learn a thing or two."

The ticket attendants were overwhelmed with the band and backed off, letting everyone through. The idea was ingenious. Willie and Richard managed to walk into the stadium without anyone noticing or asking questions. Hell, they stood out like sore thumbs without instruments or uniforms. Willie's act as some sort of band leader had fooled even the ticket takers.

The two slapped high fives when they got in and laughed like a couple of giddy schoolgirls.

"Man, that was amazing!" Richard yelled, his familiar anxiety replaced by the much more intoxicating adrenaline. "You're like Superman." Willie pumped his chest out as he walked, acting like the Man of Steel. "No, I'm not Superman," he said jokingly. "I'm Batman."

They giggled and walked around the concourse.

Bicklesford Stadium wasn't your average high school field. It rivaled the size of the college venue across town and sat more if you counted the removable bleachers that were placed by the north end zone. All three local high schools shared the stadium, thus the logic behind its enormous size. It was built by a local millionaire named James Bicklesford a few years earlier and was easily the largest high school stadium in Colorado at the time. Richard had never stepped foot in it and was easily awed by the size and magnitude of game day. He stopped during their walk around the concourse and stared at the field.

"C'mon," Willie said, grabbing Richard by the arm. "I want to show you something. We have to hurry."

The two walked fast around the ring of the stadium until they reached the bleachers on the north side.

"Is this where we're sitting?" Richard asked, somewhat disappointed.

"Yeah dude, just keep walking," Willie snapped.

They walked under a massive section of bleachers and found a twisted labyrinth of metal rods meant for holding the structure above. The bleachers were nearly full to capacity as was the rest of the stadium. The game featured one of Carver's bitter rivals in Loveland High School.

"Why are we down here?" Richard asked, looking around at all of the broken bottles and garbage already being tossed below by people sitting above. Willie's face changed. He smiled and scoffed at Richard. Curious, Richard noticed Willie's gaze and felt slightly uncomfortable. Was this where the joke was meant to be sprung?

"What is it?" Richard asked.

Willie reached into his pocket and pulled out something that looked like a cigarette. It was a joint.

"Ever smoked one of these?" he asked.

Richard felt a wave of excitement. He knew exactly what it was, although he'd never tried it before. He had dreamed of the day when someone would offer him a beer or some pot. The cure for severe teen angst always seems to resonate around booze, boobs and dope at some point in a young person's life. Willie put the joint in his mouth, lit a match and cupped his hands over his face, lighting the reefer. He inhaled and squinted as the smoke billowed into his eyes. Before he exhaled, he reached out with the joint in his hand.

"Here," he said, obviously trying to keep his breath in.

Richard anxiously grabbed the joint and put it in his mouth before inhaling. He instantly started coughing and dropped the smoke on the ground. Willie finally exhaled.

"Man, don't drop the damn thing," he said, bending down to pick it up. It had dirt caked on it where Richard had managed to spit halfway up the shaft before pitching it.

"Fuck," Willie said, wiping it off on his shirt.

Willie didn't want Richard to feel like an idiot, nor did he want to alienate him, but God damn that was a good joint. He pretended nothing was wrong and took his second hit and so did Richard. With his third try, Richard finally managed to keep some of the drug in and started to reach the pay off. Both of them sat down on a cement pillar and relaxed. Richard couldn't remember being more happy or relaxed in his entire life.

"This girl," Willie started. "What's she like?"

Richard took another hit and stared up at the bleachers above. Now he was really getting the hang of it.

"She's fucking amazing," he said. "You know how a girl can walk by and you know by her smell whether or not she's the right one? I knew the second I smelled her that she was the one for me."

Willie looked over at Richard and grabbed the joint.

"Uh, that's kind of fucked up," he said. "So what did she smell like, dude?"

"Like heaven," he said. "She smelled like heaven."

Willie let out a boisterous laugh and nearly choked. Tears began to stream down his cheeks and he needed more than a minute to compose himself.

"Oh Jesus," Willie said. "Do you realize how incredibly lame that sounded?"

Richard frowned in disappointment.

"*She smelled like heaven*," Willie said in a mocking fashion, still laughing. "Listen, I'll give you all the advice you need to know when it comes to chicks. You need to master five basic body parts and you'll have the girls screaming for more. You'll never be alone again."

"Five basic whats?" Richard asked, thoroughly confused and very interested.

"The five basic body parts," Willie said. "Okay, you got the obvious one downstairs." Willie pointed at his crotch. "Without that, you have a serious problem. Chicks dig the cock first and foremost. Very important that you remember to bring it when you go on a date."

"Second," he started, flicking his tongue out of his mouth. Richard's expression changed to disgust. "The tongue. It doesn't matter how big your dick is, or what you can do with it, the real challenge comes when you use this bad boy." Again, he stuck his tongue out and fiddled it around.

"Third," he held up his index finger. "Fourth," he held up his middle finger next to his index finger. "And, fifth," the ring finger followed. "You get a girl who can deal with these three bad boys and you may have found your future ex-wife."

Richard didn't understand.

"What do you do with those?" he asked.

Willie burst out laughing again.

"Man, you really are something. You got a lot to learn my young friend. Okay, you do know where you're supposed to put your dick right? I mean, I don't have to explain that part do I?" Willie asked. Richard nodded that he understood. "You know where you put your tongue right?" Richard nodded again, although he'd never imagined in his wildest dreams that he would have that opportunity with a girl. "Well, you put the three digits in the same spot."

"Okay, but why would I put my fingers in her mouth?" Richard asked.

Willie just closed his eyes and shook his head.

"They all go in the pussy, you retard," he said. "Not the mouth. The pussy."

Richard's face puckered and he looked like he'd sucked on a lemon. Feeling the effect of the marijuana he held up his three fingers and looked carefully at his hand, imagining the act.

"My god," he said.

Willie smiled and leaned back against a metal pole.

"Fuck an A," he said.

"Oh, I almost forgot." Willie reached into his inside jacket pocket and pulled out a flask-shaped bottle of liquor. "Now it's a party."

Richard was already falling asleep.

Willie twisted the metal cap off and took a deep drink, smacking his lips and grunting right after he swallowed.

"Here," he said, offering the bottle to the excited freshman.

Richard held the bottle to his nose and sniffed, pulling it away as his eyes began to water. Feeling like a bad ass, he tipped the bottle and took a gulp like someone finishing off a Pepsi. Willie wasn't too happy when Richard spit tequila all over his new shirt.

"Give me that fuckin' bottle!" he said, swiping it from Richard's hand before taking another drink. "You want to try that again greenhorn?"

Richard nodded and again took a drink, this time limiting the amount. Thirty minutes went by and the two continued to drink until the bottle was empty. The joint was long gone and Richard felt so good.

Then Willie got an idea. He knew that Richard was like a little boy. He had never sipped alcohol. Never smoked the ganja. Never gotten laid. And, looking at the scrawny bastard, probably never kicked someone's ass. The idea entered his mind when he saw an equally scrawny fellow walking towards them from the other end of the bleachers. It wasn't a public walkway and Willie felt a bit threatened, like someone was sent down there to spy on the two. They were there first and shouldn't have to explain anything to anyone. Willie was also extremely appalled by the way in which this person was dressed. Sporting a hot pink t-shirt and a pair of stone washed jeans, this young *man* also had the brightest blue hair Willie or Richard had ever seen. As the kid in the blue hair neared, Willie tapped Richard on the arm and motioned for him to stand. Reluctantly, Richard got to his feet, feeling the effects of the smoke and booze. The boy nodded and looked a bit nervous, speeding his pace up to walk by the two, not making eye contact. It wasn't going to do any good.

"Hey Blue Hair," Willie yelled. "Hold on a second."

Blue Hair stopped and waited for Willie to walk closer. Smelling the pot and liquor, Blue Hair's heart began to race.

"Yeah?" he asked. "I . . . I . . . I don't want any trouble."

Willie scratched his head.

"What are you trying to say?" Willie asked. "You think me and my friend here are asking for trouble? You know, I'm offended that you would say that. In fact, I demand an apology."

"I . . . I . . . I'm sorry," Blue Hair mumbled.

"What?" Willie screamed.

"I . . . I . . . I'm sorry."

"I can't hear you, what?"

Blue Hair stepped back.

"Speak up, you faggot!" As he finished his sentence, Willie connected on a powerful punch to Blue Hair's stomach. The freakishly dressed boy crumbled to his knees and winced in pain. Before he even hit the ground, Willie swung his foot up, connecting with the guy's face. A stream of blood flew through the air and landed on Richard's shoe. He was equal parts scared and invigorated.

"C'mon Richard," Willie yelled. "Show this fucker what we do to people with blue hair. Show this fucker what *you* can do."

Richard looked around and found the empty tequila bottle and walked over to Blue Hair who was beginning to sit up, holding his nose. It was apparently broken and the blood that streamed from it was intense.

"C'mon!"

Richard took a deep breath and reared back his arm. The sound of the crowd above erupted in response to something happening on the field. Blue Hair yelled and cringed before Richard connected the bottle to the back of his ducking head. The glass shattered and Blue Hair slumped to the ground, unconscious. The sound of the bottle hitting his head was surreal. Like someone pounding a fist on a watermelon.

Richard climbed over the limp body and flipped him over, exposing his defenseless face. The one thing he wanted to do, the one thing he had never experienced in his life, he finally had a chance. He pulled back his fist and brought it down, connecting with Blue Hair's mouth. Richard had been on the receiving end of many a punch, but had never connected one himself. The thing he realized right away was the pain that the attacker sometimes feels when his fist connects with bone of ones face. He held his hand up and looked as a couple of cuts now graced his skin. They must have been caused by Blue Hair's teeth.

"Holy shit," Willie yelled. "Would you look at that? You busted his fuckin' teeth. God damn Richard, you are an animal! I've never seen someone punch out teeth like that."

Truth was, he'd seen someone get a tooth or two knocked out. He just wanted Richard to feel like a beast. Willie again rolled Blue Hair over and picked up two teeth off of the dirt.

"Here," Willie said, handing one of the teeth to Richard. "Put this in your pocket and set it somewhere safe when you get home. You're going to remember this day as long as you live. This will be a trophy you look at twenty years from now."

Richard leaned over and played with one of Blue Hair's earrings. He had two gold loops that dangled about a half-inch below each lobe. Faux pearls were skewered onto each ring. Richard put his finger through one of the earrings and pulled, ripping it from the skin. He wiped the blood from it and placed it in his pocket with the tooth. Out cold, Blue Hair didn't even wince.

The two stood over Blue Hair as he sat motionless. Neither one of them felt much remorse.

"Is he dead?" Richard asked. His tone almost implied that he was hoping the answer was "yes."

"Oh, hell no," Willie said. "You'd be surprised how much the human body can take before it gives in. No, this cat's still alive, and he'll be fine. He'll just be a little sore tomorrow."

"Why do you think he painted his hair that way?" Richard asked. "It's stupid."

"Fuck if I know," Willie said. "This dude was screaming for someone to kick his ass. You don't walk around in a get-up like that and expect people to leave you alone."

Willie quickly looked in all directions, wondering if anyone could've seen the attack. It was all clear.

"We better get out of here before someone finds this dolt," Willie said. Richard agreed and they walked around the rim of the bleachers, looking for a way out. He patted Richard on the back like an accepting father on the way.

"You did good, man," he said. "It felt good didn't it?"

Richard nodded.

"I can't believe we just did that," Richard added. The two burst out in uncontrollable laughter. You know the kind of laughter you get when you've had too much to drink? It doesn't take much to trigger and it lasts forever.

The two drunks managed to stumble out into the main concourse and made their way up the bleachers. An open spot waited for them towards the top of the row and the two carefully made their way up so they could sit.

"Damn, it's already the third quarter," Willie said, pointing to the scoreboard.

Richard looked at Willie and shrugged as if he didn't give a damn about the game anyway and the two burst out in snickers and laughter again.

"You said turd," Richard said, laughing.

Willie smiled.

"No, dude, I said thhhiirrd. Clean out your fuckin' ears."

As was the case with the giggles and joy, the feeling of regret and pain arrived just as quickly. Richard suddenly thought about what hell was going on below them. Some poor soul was lying unconscious in the dirt below the bleachers, possibly dying. Possibly already dead. That's when he heard a familiar name over the loudspeaker to take his mind off of it. Seth Owens was in the game at quarterback.

The Three Stooges were performing for everyone again.

Richard fantasized that those three guys were the ones getting their teeth knocked in. He thought about them all sitting on the ground in pools of their own blood, looking up at Richard with tears in their eyes, pleading for mercy. He fingered the broken tooth in his pocket and pretended it came from Charles.

Unable to really focus on any one particular subject for longer than a minute or two, his attention quickly shifted to another interest.

Sitting two rows down from him, he spotted a girl that he had been gawking at in one of his classes. Although most of his sexual attention was devoted to Andrea at the time, he noticed this girl as well and was extremely attracted to her if for no other reason than she had the best body at Carver. When he wanted to mentally cheat on the image of his nonexistent girlfriend Andrea, the person sitting down from him was the subject.

Her hair was blowing in the wind and she was wearing a busty tank top reserved exclusively for girls with skinny bodies and big boobs. His view from two rows back was perfect for anyone in the mood to gawk at cleavage.

The worst thing about high school for Richard was the constant barrage of beautiful girls he could never have. He hadn't been laid before and seeing the pretty girls all around him just frustrated him more and more. These were girls that actually had breasts and weren't stuffing bras or trying to hide them.

Here he was, forced to fake enthusiasm for a meaningless game with one of his addictions sitting right in front of him. Life was certainly not fair.

His mind started racing.

Not now, he thought as he looked towards the scoreboard.

Faster and faster he swam into a sea of dirty images.

I'm serious, he said to himself as he scolded his brain one more time. The alcohol was too much and he couldn't control himself if he tried. Sexual thoughts filled his sexually deprived mind. He couldn't stop thinking of the girl in front of him and images of her naked, crawling on top of him in a meeting of passion right there in front of everyone in the stadium. A bulge began to appear in his sweat pants and he knew that he was seriously in trouble. It wasn't just a chance bulge, but a hard-as-a-rock bulge. The kind that don't just go away.

"Shit," he mumbled to himself. It was bad enough that he spent his days pining for Andrea, now he had to deal with this. He had pitched a tent right there in his pants. Figures that on this day he wore sweats. You can't hide a boner in sweats no matter how hard you try.

Willie glanced over at Richard and noticed him sitting with his legs crossed like a woman. "Don't sit like that, dude. Guys don't sit like that."

Richard moved his legs, revealing his hard on.

"Oh Jesus," Willie said, trying not to laugh. "Where'd that come from?" He looked around to see what Richard was looking at and eventually saw the girl. "Oh, I see. She's definitely worth a teepee but you've gotta control yourself, man. Right now? C'mon, we're at a football game."

"Excuse me . . . sorry . . . pardon me," a large man carrying a couple of hot dogs was squeezing his way down the row, trying to get back to his seat. "Comin' through."

The entire row was standing up, moving out of the way to let the man pass.

Willie stood.

Richard didn't want to move. He couldn't.

"Excuse me," the man said, slightly aggravated that Richard was the only one sitting down. "Exxxcccuuusee me."

Richard looked up in embarrassment and stood up straight. The man walked by and Richard's boner rubbed against the big fellas leg. The man stopped and stared at Richard before looking down at his pants.

"What the fuck?" the man was perplexed. "Kid, you need to watch where you're pointing that thing. Someone might come along and break it off. Geez. Kids these days."

Soon the entire row was alerted to the fact that the dork in the sweatpants had a hard-on. And, the ironic thing was—Richard didn't really care. Even though Willie brought him to the game to help make him a man, Richard's peers still found a way to ridicule him. But he didn't care. The drugs and alcohol in his system helped relieve any kind of stress or self-consciousness.

Richard looked the man in the eyes. "What are you jealous?" he asked.

The man stormed to his seat and Willie sat down with Richard.

"Oh my god," Willie said. "I can't believe you said that to him. Jesus, you are going to be just fine. I thought you were in sad shape, but I think there's hope."

Maybe this was the first step in Richard's transformation into manhood. That quite possibly could've been the greatest boner he had ever produced.

Carver had a 21-14 lead and had the ball. With less than half of the third quarter remaining, the game was nearly over with. Not that Richard was disappointed. Just seeing the Three Stooges on the field was enough to remind him why he wasn't a huge fan of football.

Seth had thrown two interceptions by the middle of the third quarter and Reggie had rushed 12 times for a mere 35 yards. Both superstars weren't effective at all, which always meant the team was going to suffer.

With a minute left in the third quarter, the Carver Bulldogs found themselves pinned on their own 22-yard-line. Seth hadn't had much luck handing the ball off to Reggie, so they decided to pull him out of the game for a moment for the backup running back Eddie Billups. He hadn't had much experience, but Coach Bruce needed a spark to ignite his team.

Richard smiled when he realized that Reggie was unhappy with the decision to be benched. The running back threw down his helmet in disgust.

Serves you right, asshole, Richard thought to himself.

Seth pulled in the next snap and scrambled to his left. Billups was wide open in the flat and Seth dumped it off to him.

Now, you know the old saying, "*When it rains, it pours?*" That goes well in more references than just in regards to the weather. Carver was having one of their worst games since Seth took over at quarterback years before and it was about to get worse.

Billups raced down the sideline with the ball tucked under his arm with nary a defender in sight. Unfortunately, he was pumping his knees a little too high off of the ground and eventually booted the football from his own grasp with his thigh. The ball squirted out of his hands and bounced towards the hashmark where a Loveland defender pounced on it.

Loveland's star quarterback was an Indian named Eddie Broadus. He had played well most of the game but still had his hands full if they expected to win. His jersey was stained with blood from an earlier hit and his finger was taped up because of a sprain.

At the risk of sounding cliché, he definitely had the heart of a warrior.

Neither team was doing well throwing the ball but no one was giving up on the air attack.

Broadus dropped back to pass with four receivers and a tight end all running routes. As before, he didn't want to just dump it off, but rather hit the home run with a streaking wide receiver. The first man he spotted was covered like a blanket, but the second man, burning down the right sideline was as open as he could be with a coverage man on him.

Richard wasn't even paying attention. His attention had returned to the guy under the bleachers and he nervously looked around for the cops, expecting them to start after him at any minute. He looked down at his hand, feeling the pain from the two deep cuts on his knuckle. Teeth marks. He clenched his fist over and over again, watching the blood pool and the skin pull.

Pulling back his arm in preparation for his catapult release, Broadus hurled the football as far as he could muster. The receiver continued to run as fast as possible with the defender, knowing that the football was grossly underthrown. Faking out the defender doesn't go any better than this as the receiver stopped in mid stride and jumped to the ball. While the defender was trying to compensate for stopping so quickly, the receiver was starting up again, this time running untouched into the end zone. With the extra point, Loveland had tied the score.

Richard looked over and saw the man with the hot dogs, glaring at him like a scolding father. Richard just smiled. He was drunk. Glancing over at Willie, Richard chuckled when he saw his friend sleeping. He was still sitting up, his head slumped over. Was there even a game going on?

Without fail, Richard didn't feel good for much longer. His belly rumbled and he began to burp up the sour and spicy juices that raged in his stomach. He tried not to think of the taste that he had in his mouth from the apple-milk barf incident but it seemed like his mind was working against him. His brain wanted him to throw up. It was an unavoidable event in his future.

Carver received the kickoff and made it all the way to midfield.

The liquid fire burps kept coming. One after another. Tequila tastes like battery acid when regurgitated and he could sense the mess he was about to create.

"Willie," he said, elbowing his friend. Willie shook and snorted like an old man getting charged from a nap. "Willie," Richard said again, poking him in the side.

"I . . . I . . . I think, I'm going to be sick," Richard said.

Willie burped.

"No. No onions," Willie said.

"Willie, I'm going to throw up," Richard said. "I need to get out of here."

"I can roll my eyes whenever I feel like it," Willie said, drunk and dazed.

Richard couldn't wait any longer. He stood to his feet just as Seth had completed a pass to a wide-open receiver. Carver was within ten yards of another score and the crowd got to their feet and cheered.

Richard nearly lost it right then and there. He tried to maneuver himself down the row, getting some help from the people who were already standing. The countdown was on and when his body finally gave out, there was certainly going to be a stinking mess.

"Richard wait," he heard Willie say. "Where are you going?"

Eventually, he knew it was time. You know when you are going to vomit and there is nothing you can do about it. There isn't time to run to the bathroom, or look for a garbage can, you are just going to lose it wherever you stand. It doesn't matter if you are already clutching the toilet, or sitting in a classroom.

It's time.

Richard was standing next to the surly hot dog man who felt his boner. He was standing up, waiting for Richard to pass so that he could go back to the game, still angry at being violated earlier. Richard turned and barfed right on the guy's shirt. The vomit streamed down his pants and onto the ground below. The apple milk finally won.

Standing in shock, Willie knew that Richard was in trouble as soon as the hot dog man recovered from the initial shock. Willie pushed his way through the people and snagged Richard just as he was done with a second wave of vomit. The two began to laugh as they shoved a path to the stairs, the crowd in close vicinity of the barf growing increasingly aware of the mess. Willie clutched Richard's arm and they scrambled to get away from the hot dog man who was swiping at them. The boys ran down the stairs with the barf-covered man close behind. If you can picture the most pissed off person you have ever seen, this guy would've certainly replaced that memory and taken the top prize.

"Get back here motherfucker!" the man screamed.

The crowd erupted in celebration as the Bulldogs scored the go-ahead touchdown. Willie and Richard stopped on the stairway and clapped, pretending like they gave a shit about the score. The man was just about to reach them when they disappeared into a crowd of people celebrating in the aisle.

Richard and Willie slowed to a walk once they reached the parking lot. Willie was already starting to feel sober. The small amount of liquor wasn't really enough to get him sloppy drunk and the five-minute nap helped him recover.

Richard wasn't so lucky.

"How you feelin' kid?" Willie asked, quickly rubbing his fingers through Richard's hair like a feisty grandpa. "You ready for another round of . . ."

Richard stopped and puked on the asphalt.

"Never mind," Willie said.

The two continued to stroll, getting close to Richard's car. Richard dug deep into his pocket and pulled out the tooth. Willie saw this and did the same. They stared at their respective prizes without saying a word. That is until Richard spoke up.

"I can't believe we did that," he said.

"Like I said, the guy probably deserved it," Willie responded.

"No, I can't believe we kept his teeth. I'm holding that dude's tooth."

Willie shoved his back in his pants.

"It's not like he was going to jam 'em back into the socket. He's going to have to get that shit fixed regardless of whether he has these or not. Consider it a trophy."

"Kid, you beat the shit out of someone at least three years older than you today. You should feel like a monster." Willie reached over and grabbed Richard's bicep with both hands. "Damn, you're stronger than I thought."

Richard was embarrassed.

"And you puked on that fat bastard."

7

The curtains in the room were flapping from the cool breeze blowing through the window. It was obvious that fall was upon the front range of the Rockies and winter was just around the corner.

"Bbbburrrr," Alexis said as she rubbed her hands over her arms. "It's gettin' chilly out there." She got up and closed the window. The crackling of leaves blowing off to their ultimate and unknown destinations was also a reminder of the changing seasons.

"Say, Alex?" Andrea asked as she sat cross-legged on Alexis' bed. "You think I did the right thing with Richard don't you? This isn't going to scar him for life or anything is it? I mean, I didn't know what else to do."

"Andy, from the sounds of it, the creep was a psycho," Alexis said. "Why are you worried about it, anyway?"

"I don't know," Andrea said. "Sometimes I catch him staring over at me in class. It's like he's lost his mind or something. I don't know, maybe he never had one. He kind of scares me."

"Sounds to me like he's got a serious crush," Alexis said. "Those are the ones you need to stay far away from. Tell him that if he comes near you again, you'll kick him in the balls. That'll keep him away. He'll get over it and move on to his next stalk."

Andrea had known Alexis for only a month, but felt like she had found someone who could be a friend for life. The two seemed to always have something to talk about. Plus, Andrea couldn't think of anyone cooler than Alexis. She just had an attitude that Andrea was drawn to.

They couldn't have been more opposite either.

Andrea was an innocent girl in most every sense of the word. The furthest she ever got with a member of the opposite sex was the French kiss stage, and that made her uncomfortable and embarrassed.

Alexis on the other hand, she probably had more experience in bed than Andrea's mother. You wouldn't technically call her a whore, though. High school whores are the girls that the guys will even point at and laugh, after they hook up of course. The whores of the school usually consisted of low esteemed garbage that had nothing to look forward to in life. With absolutely no self-respect, the whores will always bounce around and tend to deflower as many boys as possible. Understandably, they're also the ones who end up with children before they reach their junior years.

Alexis was a different.

She was attractive and looked at as a definite score whenever a guy was lucky enough to get that far. She didn't give a fuck about her reputation either. If you were a girl, and you didn't like the fact that she got more intimate with your boyfriend than you were willing, that was just tough shit. And if you wanted to confront her about it, you had better be ready to rumble. Underneath her flashy clothes and valley girl style, she was one tough bitch.

Her family wasn't anything out of the ordinary. She had a reasonably normal mother and father, plus an older brother who had moved out two years earlier. They lived in a middle-class neighborhood and lived middle-class lives.

"What was it like in Montana?" Alexis asked, resting on her bed with her back against the wall.

"It was a different world," Andrea replied, dreaming of a far away place that somehow seemed like heaven. The more time she spent away from Montana, the more she regretted leaving it and the more she wished she could go back. "I can't believe how much I miss it."

"Just think," Alexis started. "If you hadn't moved, you would totally have missed out on meeting me."

Andrea burst out laughing and Alexis jumped on her, forcing out a high-pitched scream. The two wrestled around on the bed for a while and eventually calmed down. In an uncomfortable yet seemingly natural position, the two laid side-by-side, staring into each other's eyes.

"So, you gonna tell me about her," Willie started.

Richard sat across him at a table in the lunchroom. Crowds of people lined the walkways between tables, and you could definitely tell that the masses were hungry.

"About who?" Richard asked, trying to avoid eye contact and the subject.

Willie looked at him in disappointment.

"Are we gonna play games?" Willie asked. "Are we back in fuckin' third grade?"

Richard knew what he was talking about.

"She's just a girl," he said as he took a bite out of a hamburger. "There's nothing to tell."

"*Just a girl?* Did you know that most people who use that phrase fantasize about the person they are talking about?" Willie said, sipping a drink of soda from his straw. "It's true. What's her name?"

Richard paused.

"Andrea."

"That's good. That's good. She's got a nice name. That's a starter," Willie said. "Does she have big, beefy tits? That's also a good starter. Very good." Willie held his hands up to his chest to emulate a set of large breasts.

Richard shook his head no.

"I'd say she has . . . average boobs," Richard said shyly. "What am I talking about? They are beautiful. They are perfect. I think about them all day long. They're way better than average."

Willie formed an enormous grin.

"You said 'boobs'. Fuckin' freshman."

The two continued to eat.

"So why don't you ask her out?" Willie asked.

"She fuckin' hates me," Richard said. "I don't know why. I gave her a ride to school the first, like, couple weeks. After that, she found another ride and now won't even talk to me."

"What did you do?" Willie said, sternly. "You made a move didn't you? You tried to jump her."

Richard shook his head no.

"I didn't even get a chance to make a move," Richard said, eating a French fry. "She wouldn't even pull my finger."

Willie's jaw dropped. The building could've exploded and Willie wouldn't have cared or even noticed. He just stared into the eyes of dumbest person he'd ever met.

"When exactly, and I want the truth, did you ask her to pull your finger?" Willie said, sounding like a scolding father.

"Shit, like five minutes after I first met her," Richard said with a giggle. He was starting to realize how insanely immature it was. Willie just buried his face in his hands. He shook his head and let out a sarcastic whimper.

"Christ. Did she pull it?" Willie asked.

"No . . . I pulled it myself."

"Please tell me you're kidding," Willie said. "Please tell me you didn't bust ass right there in front of the girl of your dreams right after meeting her for the first time. Please tell me you didn't fart in her face in that already smelly car of yours. Please."

Richard again looked puzzled.

"What's wrong with that?" he asked.

"What . . . what's wrong?" Willie said, stuttering over his words. He nearly choked on the mouthful of French fries he was eating. "You don't fucking fart in front of the ladies, man. What's wrong with you? And you pulled your own finger? Who does that? What are you, in fifth grade?"

"I thought it would show her how comfortable I was with her," Richard said.

"Yeah. You could've gone a step further and sniffed her ass and wagged your tail, too, but you didn't," Willie said, raising his voice. "Jesus, you're amazing. You're sure you're not fucking with me? I can't even imagine what that poor chick thought of you when you lifted a cheek and farted!"

Then Willie burst out in laughter. Richard smiled and soon joined him.

"That is pretty funny though," Willie conceded. He got close to Richard and whispered. "You know what's worse?" Willie said. "Puking on a bitch while you're gettin' head. I don't suggest that on a first date."

This time Richard's jaw dropped. Willie nodded and backed away.

"That's right. Picture it," said Willie.

There was a long pause as the two thought about the images they had just shared.

"I think I'm gonna to help you," Willie said. "We're gonna get you that chick. Yeah. This'll be fun."

Both of them got to their feet and dumped their garbage, headed for another boring class. The wind in the courtyard was merciless and not many people were outside during their lunch break.

"I know some guys who can help you out," Willie said. "They're my buddies. Together we'll get this girl. I promise. By the time we're done, she'll be asking you to pull her finger."

Richard stood stunned. He felt good, if even for a moment. Earlier in the week, he wanted to kill himself. In and out of such horrible bouts of anger, he wondered if he could make it through another day. Then Willie came along and showed him there was at least one more person in the world he would be willing to trust that could potentially build his hopes for the inevitable disappointment. It didn't matter, though. He would let it happen again. He needed a friend that much.

They both stared out of one of the large cafeteria bay windows and watched helpless people struggle through the wind, trying desperately to get from one building to another.

"That was pretty funny at the game the other day," Richard said softly. "I wonder if that guy finished his hot dog."

Willie chuckled.

"Yeah," Willie responded. "That was fuckin' gross."

"Dude, I'm bored," Seth said to Reggie as the two walked through the school parking lot after practice. The wind had blown hard all afternoon and no one who was out on that field was happy. "You wanna do something tonight?"

"Like what?" Reggie asked, agitated and tired.

At that very moment, Richard drove by, accompanied by the unmistakable sound of his VW beetle. He didn't see Reggie or Seth standing there. The two athletes turned to look at each other. Both were sporting the most evil grins imaginable. They each had their own plan that instantly popped up in their respective brains. Only one was chosen among the two, however. Although each idea involved the orange bug, Reggie's idea was the clear winner.

"We should slash his tires tonight," Seth said.

Reggie smiled. "No, I got a better idea."

Darkness fell quickly and Reggie rode in the passenger seat of Seth's car. Just as they figured, Richard's vehicle sat by itself in the dark driveway. Since the garage had room for just one car, Richard's was the one left out in the cold.

Reggie crept in the lead, trying not to make much noise.

"You got the grips?" he whispered back to Seth. Seth nodded and held up the tool along with a large flashlight. Seth hummed the "Mission Impossible" theme song as the two crept along in the darkness.

"Yo, shut the fuck up?" Reggie snapped.

"You got the minerals?" Seth asked Reggie, who promptly turned around and held them up so that Seth could see. Two stones.

Remaining as quiet as a couple of monks, they reached the car and got to work. Seth held up the flashlight, looking around the neighboring houses to see if anyone was looking. Reggie jammed a rock into each tailpipe. They fit perfectly, albeit a little tight, and he used his finger to jam them into the pipes about four inches deep.

"Give me the grips," he said, turning to Seth, who handed him the next part of the prank. Reggie clamped the vice grip onto the first tailpipe and squeezed with all of his might. More and more he clamped the grip, then opened to reset the depth. The pipe was eventually sealed shut before he went to work on the second one. Seth could barely contain his laughter, and settled for the occasional burst through his nostrils. Snickering.

"Shhhh," Reggie motioned, maintaining a whisper. He clamped and sealed the final pipe. "Let's get the hell out of here."

Without saying a word, they reached their car and slowly drove away. Both erupted in laughter immediately, releasing the tension that was building.

"Man, this is gonna be awesome!" Reggie said.

"Dude, what do you think'll happen?" Seth asked Reggie. "I mean, what's that going to do to his car?"

Reggie looked over with the biggest smile.

"I don't have a fuckin' clue," he admitted. "I saw it in a movie once."

Seth's face dropped.

"What movie?" he asked.

"I don't remember," Reggie said.

"Do you remember what happened to the car after it was plugged?" Seth asked, this time showing some concern.

"Ummm . . ." Reggie started as he tried to think back. "I think it exploded."

"What?" Seth said in a fit of emotion. "We gotta go back and fix it. Dude, this isn't what I was thinking it was."

Reggie started to laugh.

"Man, I got you goin'," Reggie started. "I don't remember what happened in the movie. All I know is, it was coo'. Little Dick's gonna shit."

Seth didn't know whether to believe Reggie but had no choice. Either way he was unexpectedly nervous for the rest of the night on into the next school day. He agreed to mess with Richard but certainly didn't want to kill him. Out of the three thugs, Seth was the one who actually had the capacity to feel remorse for their actions towards Richard, although it didn't happen very often. Charles and Reggie absolutely thought of Richard as the shit on their shoes and would never see him as their equal.

The very next morning Richard woke to feelings of numbness. Thoughts of Andrea were mixed anymore. One day, he couldn't eat because he wanted her so bad. The next, he didn't think about anything other than dying. Willie was helping to quiet the demons in his head, but couldn't get rid of them completely. This mood was somewhere in between. He was quiet and withdrawn, and as was the case so many mornings before, refused to talk to his mother before leaving for school.

"Have a good day, Richard," she said as he hurriedly walked out through the door, slamming it behind him.

What had been a stiff breeze the day before, was now a bitter chill. The clouds above suggested that it could snow any day. Richard wasn't ready for the change of seasons, adding to his misery. He absolutely despised snow.

He got into his car and waited to start it. With the screwdriver that he used to ignite his vehicle gripped firmly in his hand, he stared blankly at the garage door. Frozen in thought, he worried about the surprises that inevitably hid around every corner. At least ten minutes went by and Richard's mom noticed he was still waiting in the driveway. She walked outside, her feet cold from the chilly cement pushing against her bare skin. Although she yelled Richard's name three or four times, he didn't turn to look at her. Worried, but oblivious to the gesture, she figured he was listening to a song and the volume prevented him from hearing her. Her feet were freezing and she turned around and bounced back into the house.

Richard stared at the garage door.

He lifted the screwdriver and turned the car over. It hesitated at first, but roared to life for a brief second before it sputtered and shook. The final deathblow came with the thunderous sound of metal thrusting against metal. His car filled with exhaust and the engine violently erupted before resting in an eerie silence. The brief disruption in the combustion cycle caused the engine to lose a valve, which exploded, sending thousands of tiny metal particles through the circulation of the engine. It seized in a matter of seconds, and Richard didn't even blink. The only thing that woke him from the slumber that had engulfed his mind was the dizziness and coughing that occurred when his lungs began to fill with emissions. He got out, walked back to the rear of the car, and popped the hood. A smoldering eruption of smoke and fumes came wafting from the compartment. Richard looked even further down and noticed the crushed tailpipes. A tiny ribbon of smoke trickled from them.

Richard sat down behind his car and leaned against the oily, recently deceased engine compartment. Although his body was cold, he felt numb. He knew who had done such a horrible thing, and in a way, he wasn't mad at them. After all the years of torture and pain, he realized that he was a loser. He was sent into the world to deal with the winners and to give them the ammunition to continue through their winning ways.

He missed school that day and again the next. Combined with the weekend, he didn't really leave his room for four straight days. His mother was concerned to the extent that she pretended like he was sick and showed up at his door with soup or a sandwich every once in awhile. It was the only way she knew how to handle his mood swings. She didn't even know about his car until he asked her for a ride to school the following Monday. He had lost his right to drive himself.

Monday afternoon Willie sat in the cafeteria, waiting for Richard to show up. He had seen the freshman in class earlier in the day but couldn't get his attention. Richard ignored him.

Richard didn't skip lunch this time. He got his meal and just like he had done so many days before, he walked towards the table where Willie sat alone. Willie cleared his backpack from the space across the table, expecting Richard to park himself there. Richard walked by like he was the only one in the room.

"Hey, scrub," Willie said, as he picked his things up and followed Richard to another table. "Where you been? What's up? What's with the cold shoulder?"

Richard stared blankly out the window and ate a French fry.

"Hey!" Willie screamed just before he slammed his fist on the table. "Don't fucking ignore me. I hate when people ignore me."

Finally, Richard snapped out of it. He rolled his eyes at Willie.

"And, don't fucking roll your eyes at me," Willie erupted.

"Hey, Willie," he said, smiling as if nothing happened. He ate another French fry and continued to look outside.

"What the fuck is wrong with you?" Willie asked. "Is this about your car?"

Richard smirked.

"They couldn't just leave me alone," he said. "How did you find out about it?"

Willie looked him right in the eyes and said; "The whole school knows about it."

"What no one seems to know is, who did it?" Willie said. "No one is taking credit for it, although someone sure as hell spread the news."

A tear streamed down Richard's expressionless face.

"You could've died," Willie continued.

"I'm not that lucky," Richard said.

"Dammit!" Willie barked angrily, once again slamming his fist on the table. "Enough with this pity-party bullshit. You need to learn how to get over these things. Life did not revolve around your fucking piece of shit car."

Richard looked up.

"This isn't about the car," he said, his eyes swollen with tears, his jaw beginning to quiver as he spoke.

"Then what is it about?" Willie asked, worked up from the anger that was building inside of him. He was truly starting to care about Richard.

Richard raised another fry to his mouth.

Willie smacked his hand away from his face, sending the fry onto someone's plate at the table next to them.

"Hey," said the kid who had just inherited the French fry.

Willie turned to him.

"Go fuck yourself!" he said before turning back to Richard. "Look, stop ignoring me."

"You wanna know what's bothering me?" Richard asked, this time weeping more than before. "You really wanna know?"

Willie was silent and attentive.

"I have no place in this world. I have no one who even gives a shit whether I take my next breath or not," he began. "You . . . you . . . you can have any chick you want. You can get any friend you want. Hell, you even know that if anyone in this school messed with you, you could kick the shit out of 'em."

"What does that feel like?" Richard finished. "What does it feel like to live?"

Willie looked around and noticed more than a few people staring at their table.

"Piss off!" he barked, causing the crowds to immediately go about their business. "I know what this is about," he said, a smirk appearing on his face. "This is about that chick. Buddy, I've been there. It'll get better."

Richard shook his head no.

"You just don't get it," he muttered. "This isn't just about Andrea."

A long pause followed Richard's remark and Willie just stared at his young friend. Richard was the exact opposite of Willie. They couldn't have been further from each other, yet they were friends.

Now Willie wanted to help Richard more than anything. He didn't know if he was truly starting to like him as a friend or looked at him as a project, but he knew things had to change for Richard.

"We're going to get you that girl," he continued.

"And, you know what? We might even get you laid too. I'll come pick you up tonight at around . . . seven," Willie said. "I got somebody I want you to meet. That cool?"

Richard nodded. It was obvious that Willie couldn't understand what was going on. He didn't really care about meeting Willie's friend, but he was tired of arguing.

He was numb.

8

"Man, gimme that controller, punk," Reggie barked as he swiped the joystick from Charles' hands. "Let me show you how it's done."

The flashing lights and neon colors propelled from the television screen as Seth, Charles and Reggie sat around playing *Missile Command* on Reggie's Atari 2600. The three had mastered video game trash talk and were again competing for the high score. Since it was his game and his house, Reggie was by far the best player and he made sure everyone in the room knew about it.

"Man, I wish I could've been there with you guys," Charles said, referring to the prank on Richard's car. "Shit, that would've been cool. That kid is such a waste."

Seth's face turned serious.

"Well, it wasn't cool," he said. "That car hasn't moved from his driveway since we did that, and I heard that his engine was torn to shreds."

Reggie laughed.

"That's his own damn fault. He should've got a better car," Reggie said. "Instead of that piece of shit German wind-up toy. Hell, we could've ruined that engine just by taking a piss on it."

Seth shook his head. Regardless of what Reggie said, it was too far to be a prank. He didn't mind giving the kid a good soaking or hitting his books out of his hands on the way by, but ruining his ride was bad.

"C'mon you piece of shit!" Reggie yelled as he hurriedly tried to blast the missiles that converged towards his bases. "Dammit, I lost one!"

"Seth, don't worry about it, bro," Reggie barked, still staring intensely at the television. "Honestly, I feel a little bad about the whole thing too. But, we didn't mean for it to happen the way it did. We just wanted to play a joke."

Not once did Reggie take his eyes away from the television as he attempted to console Seth.

KNOCK! KNOCK!

"Can someone get that?" Reggie asked, wildly swinging his joystick around.

Seth got up and walked to the door.

"These guys will help you out," Willie promised, standing at the door with Richard. "They're a good group of fellas."

He reached over and knocked again.

Seth opened the door. His eyes met Richard's and the two froze. Richard felt a wave of sickness that consumed his body. He looked at Seth and then Willie and waited for the bucket of pig's blood to fall on his head. He saw Reggie and Charles in the background, huddled around the television. He couldn't hear anything and began to panic, looking all around as the inevitable prank was sure to hit.

"What's wrong Richard?" Willie asked.

Seth looked at the ground in shame, thinking for certain it was about the car. As he did that, Richard turned and ran off into the darkness.

"Richard!" Willie yelled, chasing him until he got to the end of the driveway.

Richard's one true friend was one of *them*. He was one of the winners. Richard should've known all along but couldn't help but like Willie. He ran until his legs were rubber and then walked the rest of the way home. It was only a few blocks, but seemed like miles. He wondered what joke they were planning on pulling.

"What just happened here?" Willie asked Seth. "Do you know Richard or something? Because he sure as fuck seems to know you."

Seth was ashamed. Willie upped the volume of his voice.

"Seriously, what's going on?" he yelled.

Seth finally spoke.

"Yeah, we know Richard," he said. "We've known him for a few years."

"So what's the problem?" Willie asked. Then he saw the two guys in the back, looking over at the door, agitated and curious about the noise.

"Oh, I get it," Willie said with a chuckle. "You're the three guys that pick on him. He never told me your names. In fact, he won't even really talk about you motherfuckers. What's he done to you?"

Seth walked out on the porch and closed the door behind him.

"Willie, the real question here is why are *you* hanging around that kid?" Seth asked. "He's just a dorky freshman. This is ridiculous. You're getting all huffy about this guy like he's your damn girlfriend or something."

"Well, at least he's not an asshole," Willie chimed, jamming his finger in Seth's chest. "Did you guys seriously throw dog shit at him?"

"Dude, you better cool off," Seth said. The two young men were roughly the same build and would've made for an excellent fight. "I feel like shit for what we did to his car."

"That was you too, huh?" Willie said. He scoffed and shook his head. "Well, I need a favor, and I think you owe it to that kid."

"Hey, before you start pointing the finger," Seth started. "Remember the bacon cat?"

"Oh my God," Willie said. "That was Richard's? Tell me that wasn't Richard's."

Two years before, the group got together and snuck into Richard's garage, coating his cat top to bottom with bacon grease. The initial prank didn't physically hurt the animal, but after being harassed by every dog in the neighborhood, numerous washings and a shaving, the cat realized what it meant to be the butt of someone's joke.

"That poor guy," Willie said. "Let's talk."

The two walked back into the house.

Richard slammed the front door and stomped upstairs.

"Richard!" he heard his mother yell.

He didn't care. He marched directly to his room and slammed the door behind him. As usual, his floor was hidden under the piles of junk and debris. He kicked a flattened basketball across the room, knocking his closet door off the hinge. His mother gently knocked at his door.

"Richard?" she asked, slowly opening it, slightly concerned about what she would find on the other side. "Richard, are you okay? Do you want some milk?"

He turned to her and stared with the most sinister look in his eyes. The edge of his lips rose and he smiled like a madman.

"Go away," he slowly ordered.

Outside, Willie was walking up the Tark driveway, staring at the deceased Volkswagen. It was hard to imagine such destruction for a simple prank.

"Amateurs," he muttered.

He walked up to the door and knocked.

"Yes?" Richard's mother said.

"Is Richard here?" Willie asked.

"He's sleeping," she said in an obvious lie.

"Tell him it's Willie," he said. "He'll get up."

"I'm sorry, Willie," she continued.

"It's okay, let him in," Richard said from behind the door. He wanted to know what Willie had to say about his plans. What were they going to do to him?

"Richard, I'm sorry," Willie said. "I didn't know about those guys. You never told me they were the ones."

Richard looked puzzled. He didn't tell him?

"If you're their friend then they had to have talked about me," Richard said.

Willie shook his head no.

"They never said a word about you. But, I got some good news," Willie continued. "Seth is going to help us."

"Help with what? Andrea?" Richard barked. "What can *Seth* do about Andrea? He's just a big asshole."

"Oh, he has his ways," Willie said. "You know *star quarterback* has a nice ring to it."

"Are you going to make me play football or something?" Richard asked. "This is ridiculous. Besides, she doesn't give a shit about football. Honestly, I don't give a shit about football."

"I'm not talking about fucking football, dude. He'll come up with something," Willie said. "We'll talk more about it tomorrow at lunch."

With little options remaining, Richard decided to think about it. Willie seemed sincere. Maybe there wasn't a punch line to this joke.

"I'll talk to you tomorrow," Richard said as he closed the door in Willie's face. He waited a few moments and then swung the door open. "Can I get a ride to school?"

Willie turned and gave a thumb's up as he opened his car door.

"Sure thing," he said.

"Do you ever think about it?" Andrea asked.

Not caring about the cool temperatures or the fact that it was nearly midnight on a school night, the two girls lay in the grass that was slowly dying in Alexis' backyard. Bundled up and staring at the stars, they sometimes talked for hours like that.

"Think about what?" Alexis asked.

"You know," Andrea started. "Do you ever think about your future husband, or what your life is going to be like five years from now?"

Alexis looked over at Andrea.

"You're totally freaking me out," Alexis said.

Silence. Then, Alexis actually opened up a little.

"Well, sure I think about it sometimes," Alexis continued. "Who doesn't?"

"How do you see yourself?" Andrea asked.

"Five years from now?" Alexis said.

"Yep," replied Andrea.

"I see myself with a large man. He's a professional athlete. He's had his share of bad relationships and found me just as he was giving up all hope in women. We'll have a couple of kids right away while he brings home a bitchin' paycheck. Eventually, we'll settle in a three bedroom home overlooking the valley," Alexis said.

Andrea turned over.

"*Geez*, Alex, have you been thinking about this for awhile?" she asked.

Alexis chuckled. "No. I just came up with all that on a whim. What about you?"

Andrea lay back down and looked up.

"I don't know. I just want someone who's nice and loves me," she said.

Alexis burst out in laughter.

"Do you actually know any guys?" she said. "I mean, what ever gave you the idea that a man like that even exists? If you know something I don't, please tell me."

Andrea shook her head.

"I don't think it's that crazy."

Peering at the girls through his bedroom window in a curious, yet concerned manner was Alexis' father, Butch. He had noticed the girls spending an abnormal amount of time together and was starting to worry about their friendship. He spied on them for a good 20 minutes, listening to their conversation, hoping to catch them doing something that could warrant an immediate termination of their friendship.

"Girls, you need to come inside," he said behind the darkness of his bedroom curtain.

They looked up and saw him move the drapes, revealing his ghostly image.

"Jesus," Alexis said. "You scared me. How long have you been standing there?"

"It doesn't matter," Butch replied. "Just get inside. It's too late and too damn cold for you girls to be playing around in the backyard. Don't you have school in the morning?"

"Yeeeesss, dad," Alexis said in a mocking voice.

They skipped towards the door in a friendly race, as one of them shrieked upon winning the contest. Butch shook his head when he heard the noise and walked away from the window.

"Come to bed Butch," his wife said, half awake from her slumber. "Leave the girls alone."

"I really don't like their relationship," he said as he crawled under the covers. "I think they're too close. I've never known a couple of girls who were as attached at the hip as those two. Have you noticed that Andrea practically lives here now?"

"Butch, she doesn't have anyone else," Jill started. "Other than her aunt, she has no family here, and just one friend. Give 'em a break. And close your eyes and go to sleep."

Butch took off his glasses and rolled over.

"Jerk," Jill muttered.

Downstairs, Andrea and Alexis were crawling under the covers together. They shared Alexis' full size bed, which had plenty of room for the two.

"You know Alex," Andrea started. "I think I'm going to talk to Richard tomorrow. I don't think I was fair to him, and I really believe he's got problems. Maybe I can help him."

"You just feel sorry for the dweeb, that's all," Alexis said. "You said it yourself, the guy is a helpless jerk and you need to forget about him."

"I don't know," Andrea said. "Maybe he's just confused. I mean, it's not like he did anything to hurt me. He was just really weird, that's all. I just don't know."

Alexis reached her hand across the bed and placed it over Andrea's mouth.

"Goodnight," Alexis said.

Andrea pushed her hand away and rolled over.

"He *is* kind of cute," Andrea whispered to herself.

The next morning the girls woke to the alarm clock and both swore that it was the last time they stayed up late on a school night. They both had bags under their burning eyes and neither one could muster the strength to shut off the alarm.

"Shit, this sucks," Alexis said as she initiated the exodus from the warm and comfortable confines of the bed. "I call shower."

Andrea stayed in bed for a while, drifting in and out of consciousness. She wanted so badly to have a few more hours of sleep. Maybe she could just nap until noon and miss the first half of the day. As good as that idea sounded, it just wouldn't work since she wasn't the type to call in sick to anything. She waited fifteen minutes and was eventually pushed out of bed by Alexis who had just gotten out of the shower. Alexis moved into her brother's room when he left, allowing her to have the bigger space, and her own private bathroom.

"Get up girl," she said.

Andrea climbed to her feet with the help of Alexis and the two stood close for a split second, giggling. That's when Butch walked in the room. He knocked, but did so as he opened the door. He saw what appeared to be his wet daughter dressed in a towel, embracing Andrea.

"What's going on here?" he asked, paranoid as usual. "What are you two doing?"

"Don't you knock?" Alexis asked, angry and embarrassed. She walked towards the door and pushed her dad back into the hallway. "What do you want?"

He stood silent in the hall of his home.

"Um . . ." he stuttered. "I just wanted to make sure you were awake. I know you stayed up late last night."

"Daddy, I need my privacy and I don't appreciate you barging in the room like that," she snapped at him. Just as quickly she turned and shut the door in his face.

Feeling emotions that ranged from embarrassed to angry to confused, Butch walked back to the kitchen and sat at the table.

"What's wrong?" Jill asked.

"I just saw our daughter half naked dancing with Andrea," he said, not blinking.

"What?" Jill replied. "Butch, you're seeing things. You need to leave those girls alone."

Jill was just playing "devil's advocate." Part of her believed Butch and was feeling the same as he. The girls were getting really close, but Jill believed that in order to avoid a conflict, she needed to be on her daughter's side. Alexis had just told her a few mornings prior that the two were planning on moving away together once they finished school. They were talking about heading to Florida to become lifeguards. Jill thought it was an innocent gesture of a child who was talking about what they were going to do when they grew up. All kids do that, and they change their minds constantly. The worrisome part was, Alexis wasn't really a *kid* anymore and was just a couple of years away from growing up.

Jill didn't tell Butch about her daughter's future plans. That would surely cause trouble and could tear their modest family apart. As the mother, she had a duty to keep everyone together and she would do just that.

"Don't worry about it, Butch," Jill said. "They're just kids. Realize that and stop being so paranoid. I'm sure what you saw upstairs was innocent."

"They're even calling each other Alex and Andy," he said before he got up and left the room, headed for work. He didn't say goodbye to anyone, but just got in his car and sped away.

Alexis eventually hopped down the stairs with Andrea.

"What was that all about?" Jill asked.

"Oh, you mean your Peeping Tom spy for a husband?" Alexis snapped.

Jill's mouth dropped.

"Don't you dare talk about your father like that," Jill replied.

"Mom, he burst into my room without even knocking," she said. "He shouldn't do that when I have a guest over. What if Andrea was buck naked in there?"

Buck naked? Were the girls showering together too? Now Jill was really starting to believe her husband. She decided to end the conversation and worry about the solution later.

"You girls need to hurry up and get to school," Jill said. "You only have twenty minutes."

Problems seem easier to deal with when ignored. Just ask Richard or Willie's mothers.

Andrea looked back at Jill as the two girls were leaving the house. She noticed Jill had started to cry and was wiping a tear from her cheek as she stared at the kitchen floor.

"Why was your mom crying in there Alex?" Andrea asked once the girls were in the car headed for school.

Alexis turned puzzled. "What?"

"She was crying when we left." Andrea continued.

"Oh man. My dad must have gotten her worked up," Alexis started. "He's always gotten involved in my life and done everything he could to fuck it up. Did he do that with Danny? No. He let my brother get away with whatever he wanted."

"Bastard."

"But, why would he be talking about you to your mom?" Andrea asked. "What did you do that would make your mom cry?"

"Nothing," Alexis said. "I don't know what his friggin' problem is. Maybe they were talking about our trip."

Despite being completely terrified of him and reluctant to trust that there could possibly be a shred of decency about him, Richard was somewhat excited to meet with Seth. All he really ever knew about him was that he could throw a football and that he was one of the three people that Richard wished he could be friends with instead of just a target of. It was definitely a love-hate thing. With the looming possibility that the whole meeting could be another prank, Richard shrugged off the demons in his head that were trying to convince him of that scenario.

Time came and the lunchroom was as packed as always. Richard got there early and sat at a table, too anxious to even stand in line for food. He waited nearly ten minutes and still no one sat next to him. He looked around the cafeteria from where he sat and saw no sign of either Seth or Willie. Bad thoughts were beginning to win the battle for his attention. He slowly started to panic. Was he set up? Was Willie involved? He neurotically looked over both shoulders, waiting for something to come flying out of nowhere, targeted at his head. Nothing came.

"BOO!" a voice blasted as a pair of strong hands grabbed Richard by the shoulders from behind.

It's a no brainer to say that Richard jumped. The funny part came with the feminine-like shriek he let out. Immediately he turned to find Willie and Seth hovering above him, carrying trays of food.

"Mind if we sit here?" Willie asked.

Richard nervously cleared his backpack and books from the table.

"I believe you two know each other," Willie started as he opened his chocolate milk, hoping that Richard and Seth would at least speak. Richard stared at the table, nervous and shy. All of his inner feelings of hatred and anger towards Seth were now replaced by admiration and a hope that they could be friends. Seth initiated the conversation.

"What's up, Rich?" he said. "How ya been?"

Richard looked up at the football star.

"Good, I guess," he said.

Silence and an uncomfortable pause filled the air around the small table.

"Guys, we're here for a reason," Willie said as he pounded a hamburger into his mouth. "We need to get Richard laid."

Richard turned red and shook his head no. The prospects of getting laid weren't enough to warrant the embarrassment that he felt at that moment.

Seth saw this and looked over at Willie puzzled. He was wondering what the fuck he was doing in that position. It was like trying to help the Elephant Man with his complexion. You might as well have asked Seth to lend Richard his dick for a few weeks.

The three sat at the table for another fifteen minutes, not really speaking as Richard watched the two large young men pack away their food like cattle. Just as Seth was thinking of leaving, Richard chimed in.

"There she is," he said excitedly, pointing out Andrea to Seth and Willie. "There's Andrea."

They all looked over at her as she walked towards the trash can with her tray of garbage.

"She's pretty cute for a freshman," Willie said. Truth was, he actually found her extremely attractive and stared intensely at her as she walked. She had an innocent farm girl kind of look to her and wasn't at all like most of the girls at Carver. In an appearance sense, Andrea was more frumpy than dolled up, but she was the kind of girl that didn't need all the accoutrements of beauty.

"She's alright in a Brady Bunch kind of way," Seth added, just trying to be polite.

"I want to fuck her," Richard said.

Seth and Willie both turned to look at Richard, who glanced up at Willie like a five-year-old who just said a bad word in front of dad.

"And, she's a sophomore thank you very much," Richard finished.

"Damn, kid," Seth said. "I like it. Goin' for the older chicks."

Seth raised his hand for a high five. One that Richard gladly provided. What Richard didn't expect was Andrea walking towards their table. Alexis was walking behind her as the two got closer to the table with each step. Richard also got more nervous the closer they got.

Finally, Andrea got to the table.

"Hey Richard," she said. "Sorry about your car."

Richard nodded like a dumbfounded child.

And just like that she was gone.

Andrea turned to Alexis as they walked away and whispered in her ear.

"Who was that guy sitting next to Richard?"

"Which one? The hunk on the left?"

Andrea nodded.

"That's Willie Becker. He's a senior."

"I kind of like him," Andrea said. "I wonder what he's doing with Richard."

Seth meanwhile, was making eyes with Alexis, who had noticed him sitting at the table next to Richard. Seth was a prize for most of the girls at the school, even the ones who didn't care for jocks. It's no secret that the quarterback of a high school football team has no problems finding a date.

"Who's that?" Seth asked.

"You don't know who that is?" Willie said. "What school have you gone to the past four years?"

"I don't know, man," Seth said. "I don't pay any attention to their damn names."

"Well, haven't you at least seen her around before?" Willie continued.

"What's with all the fuckin' questions?" Seth asked. "I just want to know her name."

Richard turned to both of them.

"Uh, hey fellas, remember me?" he said. "That's the girl. That's the one that I've been dreaming about since the first day of school. That's the reason we're all sitting here together."

"You're welcome," Seth said.

Richard lifted his eyebrow.

"Um . . . ok. For what?" Richard asked.

"She wouldn't have come over here to apologize for your car if Reggie and I hadn't fucked it up for you," Seth said, realizing how stupid a comment it was just as he finished making the statement. Richard looked disappointed. Deep down he knew who did it from the moment it happened. It just felt weird sitting across a table from the culprit.

"Yeah. Thanks a lot," Richard said sarcastically. "I guess I owe you one."

"I've got an idea," Seth said.

The three of them huddled together and hashed out a plan. It was one way Richard could get to know Andrea away from all of the hustle and bustle of school. He had a second chance awaiting him. It was Richard's chance to get marooned on a desert island with his dream girl. Imagine what Gilligan could've done with Mary Ann if he'd just tried harder.

"Did you see who was sitting with Richard," Alexis giggled, excitedly.

Andrea shook her head yes, thinking about Willie.

"Seth Owens," Alexis continued. "Only the finest man at Carver High. Oh, what I wouldn't do to that man."

Andrea looked over at Alexis with disgust.

"Stop it, you're totally grossing me out," Andrea said, picking up the local lingo quite nicely. "He wasn't that hot."

Alexis stopped walking and grabbed Andrea by the crook of her elbow, swinging her around.

"Girl, you have got to be joking," she said. "I mean, you just said that because you know you'll never have him, right? Because if you truly mean what you just said, I'd have to, like, not be your friend anymore."

They both laughed and continued on their way.

"Fine . . . he's hot," Andrea admitted.

The plan was simple other than the fact that they had to somehow convince Reggie and Charles to participate. The girls were a shoe-in. In fact, the only problem involved in the whole issue was whether or not they were willing to put aside their feelings about Richard in the name of a good time.

Seth, Willie and Richard arrived at Reggie's place later that evening. Seth and Willie walked in like it was their own home. Richard hid in the shadows, hoping that the night would soon be over.

"What up, Willie?" Reggie yelled as he got off the couch and gave Willie five. They shook hands and soon Charles was on his feet, greeting Willie in his own way. Things got real quiet when Reggie and Charles simultaneously discovered Richard standing just inside the doorway, hidden by Reggie's mother's coat rack.

"What the fuck is he doin' here?" Reggie asked. "Is this about the damn car? Because I ain't payin' nothin'.' It was a fuckin' joke. Deal with it."

Seth grabbed Richard and pulled him to the front, like he was his child.

"Guys, Richard needs our help," Seth said. "And we're going to help him."

Charles looked around the room.

"I don't see any bitches here, so don't act like you're talkin' to one," he blurted. "Now, repeat what you just said. We're gonna help this little shit?"

Seth nodded.

"Yep," he said.

"And why?" Reggie asked.

"Because if you don't, folks might just find out how the Windsor mascot got run over before our game last year," Seth said. "You don't want that do you?"

Reggie and Charles both looked at Seth in pure disgust. He was blackmailing them. The two had played one of their pranks on the Windsor football team the year before, taking their bobcat from its cage and releasing it on a busy stretch of road. It was crushed by a bus carrying elementary students to the game.

"You motherless cracker," Charles said. It looked like the man wanted to beat the hell out of Seth.

"Cool it Charles," Reggie said. "What the hell do we have to do to help this sad sack?"

The five sat down and talked about the plan. It involved both Andrea and Alexis and had to include those two or the deal was off.

Seth, Reggie, Charles and Willie were planning to head for the hills for a weekend of camping the first week of October. They had been talking about it since the year before when they were all juniors. It was going to be the first in a long line of senior farewell parties for the foursome.

Thirty miles west of Fort Collins was smack in the middle of the Rocky Mountains, right were the peaks touch the clouds. Reggie knew of a spot where a tributary fed melting snow water into the Poudre River. The area was well secluded, found only by following a logging route and was as perfect a place as any to guarantee privacy. By October the trees would be turning yellow, and the creek would be dried up, allowing them to avoid animals and the accompanying hunters that roamed through the area from time to time.

Seth came up with an idea that involved that exact camping trip. He was treading into dangerous waters, messing with something that was held so sacred to the other guys. He was asking them to invite others. He was asking them to invite freshman. He was asking them to invite females. He was asking them to put aside their disdain and invite Richard Tark.

Seth figured that if they took Richard, Alexis and Andrea with them, Richard could hook up with Andrea and he could hook up with Alexis. Problem solved. Everyone's happy. Willie just wanted to have a good time and didn't care who came with. So what was in it for Reggie and Charles?

"If we get her drunk enough, she might fuck us all," Seth said, referring to Alexis. He had asked around about the girl, and was told stories about her willingness to do things that the other girls weren't into yet. "This girl has done some crazy shit, my friends. She'll be easy as sliding on a pair of cleats."

"It would be kind of cool to have some pussy around," Reggie conceded. "What do you think?"

Charles nodded in agreement.

"Yeah. You say she gives?" Charles asked Seth.

"That's the rumor," he said. "She gives like the fuckin' Jerry Lewis Telathon."

Reggie and Charles looked at each other and then Richard.

"A'ight, we in," Reggie said. "But I'm only doin' this 'cause I feel bad about your car and shit."

They all knew that wasn't true.

The camping trip was to take place the following weekend, and the guys didn't have much time to convince the girls to go along with it. They needed a foolproof plan to lure the flies into the web.

They needed an edge.

Seth approached Alexis the next day. Strangely enough, Andrea wasn't around her. The two seemed to be recently separated Siamese twins and having Seth simply talk with Alexis was the best thing that could've happened. She had to have been the leader of that duo. The decision maker.

Alexis saw him coming and actually felt her cheeks as she began to blush. She actually blushed at this guy. Watching him walk down the hall, life seemed to slow to a crawl. The bright yellow lockers all turned gray. The students jamming the hallway all stopped and lost their colors as well. The only thing she could focus on was Seth as he continued walking. He was the quarterback.

"Hey Alexis," he said, as if he had known her his whole life.

She turned and smiled.

"Say, I was wondering if you wanted to do something next weekend," he started. The gesture was completely unexpected and she reacted with curiosity.

"Uh . . . sure," she replied. "You mean, like a date?"

"If you want to call it that," he said. "You see, a few of my buddies and I are going to this place just north of the Poudre Canyon, you know, to camp . . ."

Her face wrinkled and she appeared confused. That was the last thing she expected him to say.

"Camp?" she interrupted.

"Yeah, me and a few other seniors are going to camp for a night, and I was wondering if you'd like to go," he said. "And, actually, you could bring your friend Andrea."

Alexis turned and closed her locker.

"Camp?" she said again. "I don't really do camping, bud."

She wanted so badly to hang out with Seth and was willing to camp. She just needed a second to realize that he wasn't joking. Who asks a girl to go camping with a bunch of other guys on a first date? Especially someone who doesn't really know anything about that person.

"So what do you say?" Seth asked. "Bring Andrea."

"Why do you want us to go with you?" Alexis asked, sensing something fishy. Twice he had mentioned Andrea. Maybe he was interested in her. Seth looked around and brought his face towards hers.

"'Cause I got something I want to show you," he whispered, pointing down to his pants. Alexis blushed even more.

"Oh you do, huh?" she said, turning to shut her locker. It was already closed. "Okay. Sounds like fun," she lied. Camping most certainly didn't sound like fun.

"And Andrea?" Seth replied.

That was three times.

"I'm sure she'll be thrilled," Alexis said, throwing in a small serving of sarcasm. "She'll be there."

The two stood around talking about the trip as Seth tried to make it sound better than she was imagining. He arranged to pick her up Friday evening as the plan was to have everyone camp Friday night and possibly Saturday night, depending on the weather and everyone's spirits. Beer supply was also a factor.

Seth ran into Willie later that day in the hall.

"She said no, dude," Seth said, looking as rejected as ever. "She said it would be a cold day in hell before she'd go camping with us. I don't know what I said, but she ended up taking a swing at me."

Willie shook his head and opened his mouth in amazement.

"That's it?" he said. "So, just like that, we got nothing? I knew I should've talked to her. Why'd she try to hit you?"

Seth cracked a smile.

"Who you talkin' to?" he said in a mobster's voice. "You know who you talkin' to? Ain't no girl goin' to deny me. I'm Seth Fuckin' Owens."

He held up his hand and smacked Willie's hand as the two shook each other. It was hard to believe they were so excited to get the girls involved.

"Better get your shit ready," Seth continued. "Both chicks are comin'."

Willie clapped his hands in a gesture of joy. He couldn't explain it, but he felt like he was a hero for Richard. If all went well, Richard was going to get the girl of his dreams, and it would all be because of Willie Becker. There was also the little voice in his head that told him he might have a chance with Andrea. That voice convinced him that if Richard didn't make a move, he should.

"Andrea, it'll be fun," Alexis pleaded. "C'mon. Seth is so cute and I think he likes me. I want to go."

"So go," Andrea said. "How am I stopping you?"

"He asked you to go too," Alexis said. "In fact, he seemed more interested in you than me. I'm not going if you won't. I'm not going up to the mountains with five guys all by myself. That's kind of creepy if you ask me. I don't wanna end up dead in a ditch somewhere, you know."

Alexis was practically crying she wanted Andrea to go so bad.

"And having me there is going to make it less creepy, how?" Andrea quizzed.

Alexis got on her knee and held Andrea's hand like a knight who has just found his princess.

"Please go," Alexis pleaded. "Please go, my prince."

Just then, her father walked around the corner into the kitchen where the girls were talking. He saw his daughter on her knee and dropped his glass of water on the floor where it shattered into a million pieces.

"Jesus, Dad," Alexis shouted as she leapt to her feet, trying to avoid shards of glass that flew through the air. "What's your problem?"

Butch just stared at Andrea, waiting for her to say something. Had his daughter just proposed to her friend? Was that even legal?

The girls left the kitchen, and Butch standing in silence with a glazed over glare of confusion. Alexis appeared in the kitchen again, this time by herself.

"You know what Daddy?" she started. "I can't wait until I graduate, because Andrea and I are moving to Florida and away from all of this." She made a gesture towards the glass and water that covered the kitchen floor.

"Florida?" he asked. "Both of you?"

"Yes!" Alexis barked. "Andrea is my friend. And you're weird."

She stormed out of the kitchen again. The girls walked through the next room and Andrea leaned her head over to whisper in Alexis' ear.

"I'll go," she said, reluctantly.

Alexis hopped with joy.

"Thank you," she said, kissing Andrea gently on the cheek before running back into the kitchen. "And another thing. I'm staying at Andrea's aunt's house this weekend."

Her father was still standing over his mess and didn't say a word.

The girls left the house and were walking to the car when Andrea stopped.

"Why did you tell him you're going to stay at my place this weekend?" Andrea asked.

"He's not going to let me go camping with a bunch of boys," Alexis said. "That I do know."

"Well, then you know he's going to call my aunt." Andrea said. "He's acting weird."

"How's he going to call, if he doesn't know the number?" Alexis said. "I haven't given it to him. Have you?"

Andrea shook her head no.

"Then, what's the problem?"

The girls got in the car and drove off.

Three days left in the week.

Three days left until Friday night.

9

"What should I do?" Richard asked Willie as the two looked down at Richard's sleeping bag. It was completely destroyed by mice. The cold and dark confines of the basement not only deterred Richard and his mom from ever going down there, but encouraged rodents and pests to set up shop.

Resting in the corner of an old walk-in closet across from the furnace was the shattered remains of the sleeping bag that Richard had since he was a boy. It looked like a firework had gone off inside of it, sending fragments of cotton and fleece all over the floor. Apparently the mice found a new home.

Willie rubbed the fuzz that was beginning to form on his chin.

"I don't have an extra bag," Willie said. "You got any heavy blankets?"

"Yeah," Richard said.

"Grab two."

Richard headed up the stairs and Willie trailed behind, cautiously pulling a flask out of his pants pocket. Earlier that evening he raided his father's Jim Beam bottle. He took a swig and hid the flask back in his pocket. Looking up at Richard as he walked up the stairs, he thought of the kid's knack for attracting bad luck. He couldn't explain why he entertained himself with Richard's life. The kid was a lost cause.

They grabbed a couple of blankets and raided the fridge for a few quick food items. Willie grabbed a package of hot dogs and Richard grabbed a soda.

"You want one?" Richard asked.

Willie shook his head no.

"That's baby stuff," he said.

"It's a Coke," Richard blurted. "Babies drink milk."

Willie chuckled and reached into his shirt pocket.

"Gotta second?" he asked. He was holding a joint just like the day they went to the football game. Richard smiled. The memories of that exhilarating day came flooding back into his thoughts. So many firsts. So many new things. He had thought about that joint and wondered if he'd ever get chance to smoke another one. They took a moment to medicate before heading back to the rig where Seth, Reggie and Charles were impatiently waiting.

"Let's ditch his sorry ass," Charles said, glaring at Richard's clumsy appearance as he almost tripped over an edge in the concrete walkway on the way to the rig.

"Where, in the fuckin' mountains?" Seth chimed.

"Nah, man. Let's just start the truck and leave both these crackas here," Charles responded. "We don't need neither of 'em."

"Dude, just shut up and drink another beer," Seth said, pointing to the cooler that rested between the two front seats. The guys had filled the cooler with many beers and had four twelve packs sitting in the back of the full-size Suburban.

Willie and Richard climbed in the truck and apologized for taking so long.

"We couldn't find him a sleeping bag, but he's going to be fine with these blankets," Willie said. It was as if he thought anyone in the car actually gave a shit about Richard's sleeping arrangements.

"Sure smells like it," Seth said, waving his hand back and forth in front of his face. The two reeked of weed.

"Alright. Let's get the chicas, mang?" Reggie said, using his best *Cheech and Chong* voice. "Where do these bitches live?"

A couple of the guys burst out laughing. Richard was just plain irritated. What was he getting Andrea into? Who talked him into this bullshit anyway?

"C'mon guys," Willie said. "We aren't bringing these girls along to treat them like shit. Hell, you aren't going to get any ass by being a bunch of butt pits."

Richard looked over at Willie, concerned about Andrea and happy that he had the balls to speak up to the Three Stooges. He thought about how strange it was to be in the same vehicle as his mortal enemies and how completely bizarre it would be if Willie weren't there to act as a buffer.

"Don't worry," Willie mouthed, trying to reassure the neurotic freshman.

Andrea and Alexis had been waiting on the corner in front of Andrea's apartment complex for more than an hour. Since everyone had to wait for the guys to get done with football practice, it was nearing six o'clock and the sun was nearly gone.

What about the football game? Well, Carver High had scheduled a week off as they did every year. Originally, it was a week set aside to honor the memory of the school's namesake, Henry Carver. He had died three years before, during a game, watching from the stands at the ripe old age of 103. Simply put, the school decided not to play any games the first weekend of October. That idea became a huge story and the school board figured they'd make it a unique and sappy way to bring pride to the school each fall. They would refuse to schedule a game that one week during the season. It is thought to be the inspiration for the bye week that the pro's get off these days.

That's also why the guys were camping in the cold. They couldn't get away any time before that because they played games each weekend. Any time after that, and, well, they'd be camping in snowdrifts. The cold wasn't a factor on this trip. It couldn't have been a more perfect night, temperature wise. The sky was crystal clear and other than a small, unnoticeable breeze, no signs of winter were present. Plus, the temperature was around 50 degrees during the day, sinking to just above 40 at night. Cold to some, comfortable to others.

The Suburban was soon filled with passengers as Andrea and Alexis climbed in, opting to sit in the back row of seats.

"What's up ladies?" Reggie belted, staring into the rearview mirror as he started to drive away. "Are you ready for a wild night?"

Shy and still unsure about what they were getting into, the girls didn't say much. In fact, they didn't say anything. They just smiled and nodded.

"I don't like this, Alex" Andrea whispered into her friend's ear. "What are we doing here? I want to go home."

"It'll be fun," Alexis said, lying through her teeth. She reached over and rubbed Andrea's leg for comfort. "There's your man," she said, pointing to Richard with a giggle. Andrea disapproved of the comment.

"Whatever," she mouthed.

Alexis elbowed her towards Richard, who was sitting in the row directly in front of the girls, facing forward. He was thinking about the fact that Andrea sat just behind him. He had closed his eyes the moment the girls took their seats, and proceeded to inhale the sweet smells of Andrea's perfume until he felt like he was going to pass out. He could hear them whisper and got goosebumps from the squeaking sounds of their voices. If only he could hear what they were saying, he'd be a happy man. Truthfully, he was better off not knowing.

The truck reached the edge of the foothills and although they had a 45-minute drive ahead of them, it seemed like they were almost there. Richard felt he didn't have much time to be this close to Andrea before they reached the campsite. He turned to say hi and just as he did it, he cracked his forehead against Andrea's. She had leaned forward to greet him.

"Ow," Andrea said as she sat back in her seat, rubbing the sore spot on the top of her head. She was smiling, embarrassed and surprised by the collision. It had been a while since she ditched Richard and it felt good to break the ice once again, even if it was at the expense of her skull. Richard also rubbed his head and made a face to make it seem like he was hurt. In all honesty, he barely felt it. He had a high threshold for pain.

"Hi," Richard said as the two eventually stopped acting.

"Hi," Andrea replied.

Richard continued to look at Andrea, staring at her with a dumb grin on his face. Andrea looked over at Alexis and giggled, uncomfortable to say the least. Why did he have to be so socially inept?

"What are you doing with these guys?" Andrea asked quietly, trying to keep their conversation as private as possible. She didn't know anyone other than Alexis and Richard and didn't want to share her thoughts with complete strangers. Frankly, she was shocked that Richard was associated with such notable people, not to mention the three guys known to abuse him.

"I'm with Willie," Richard whispered as he pointed to the guy sitting next to him. Willie was sandwiched between Seth and Richard and could hear the conversation, but pretended to be uninterested. He eventually turned to Seth and struck up a conversation with him so that Richard and Andrea could talk.

"You like camping?" Richard asked.

"Well, I don't know if this is camping?" Andrea said, referring to the fact that she didn't see much equipment in the car. "We used to camp all the time in Montana. I mean, my family and I practically grew up in the Little Belt Mountains."

"It'll still be fun," Richard said, bullshitting as much as possible. The fact was, he had no idea whether it would be fun or not. He was scared shitless. The only thing keeping him from having a panic attack was the aura that Andrea emanated.

Willie turned to Andrea and Richard and showed all teeth.

"You like booze?" he asked Andrea.

She frowned and shook her head no.

"I . . . I really don't drink much," she said.

"Here, take a chug of this," he said, offering her his flask. Richard was completely puzzled at Willie's interference, to which Willie responded with a wink and a nod. "You won't be nervous after a few drinks of that shit, I guarantee it."

Andrea reluctantly took a sip. She looked as if she had just tasted ass for the first time and immediately pushed the container back to Willie.

"Eww," she said. "That stuff is awful. What is it?"

Willie took a moment to look at his reflection in the flask, before chugging a shot. He cleaned his lips and stared into Andrea's eyes. She was frightened for a split second by the intensity of his glare.

"It's Jim," he said. "Beam."

Andrea turned to look out of the car, uncomfortable at best. How was it that she kept ending up in these situations?

The crew didn't really say much more to each other during the trip. The truck careened farther down the winding canyon road, nearly missing a direct hit with an enormous bull elk. No one actually counted the points on the antlers, but it certainly had more than any of them had ever seen.

The truck turned off the highway and began its trek up the logging road that would eventually lead to the campsite.

"No, keep going up this road," Charles said, bouncing around in the passenger seat.

Andrea looked over at Alexis and shook her head. What a miserable experience the trip had been so far, and they hadn't even gotten out of the car yet. Alexis was disappointed by Seth's lack of communication. He didn't say more than two words to her the entire drive up there.

"I know where we at," Reggie barked. "What I don't know is, where's that motherfuckin' turnoff? You know, where the . . ." he explained, moving his hand in a zig-zag motion as he tried to remember the words. "Where the . . . creek crosses the road and shit. We gotta turn on the creek and drive down it for awhile. Remember?"

Charles nodded. The two had scoped out the campsite before, but seemed to have trouble remembering where they had gone.

"I ain't seen no creek yet," Charles said.

"Right there, asshole," Reggie yelled as he pointed to the tiny stream that ran across the worthless ruts of the logging road. The creek consisted of a trickle of natural water, which formed a path of cobble stones through the trees. All they had to do was follow the water through the thick trees until they got to a small clearing and the eventual campsite.

Richard remained quiet for most of the ride and had even begun to sweat. He was nervous and touchy, wishing that he could keep talking to Andrea. There she sat, directly behind him, yet he didn't have the courage or balls to turn around and have a reasonable conversation like a normal human being. How many nights did he spend acting out the perfect conversation with her? When he had the chance, he chose to ignore her. He was thankful, however, that she wasn't being a bitch to him.

As the truck came to a stop in the abyss of trees and rock, Richard concluded one solid fact in his cluttered brain—he was going to have to make his move and quickly. In fact, he knew that his only chance to get Andrea to like him was going to be that very night. He thought more about her. Her smell, her laugh, her smile—those were the things he needed to hold onto to gain the confidence he needed.

Reggie and Charles turned to the rest of the crew and gave them the run down on what was going to happen.

"Alright, Chaz and I are gonna build us a fire," Reggie said. "Last time we were here, I put some firewood and shit over there under that tree. Everybody just chill for a few minutes while we take care of business."

"Man, you crazy," Charles belted. "We put the firewood under that tree." He pointed to the opposite side of the truck.

"I know where I put the God damn . . ." Reggie began to say, their voices fading as they slammed the doors shut and walked away.

The two athletes were armed with a flashlight, a few newspapers and a box of matches. Reggie managed to turn on the dome light in the truck before he walked off, which was a good thing for the girls. Sitting in a dark car, in the pitch black coffin of night with three guys that they hardly knew would've been a little too much to ask.

Seth finally turned to Alexis.

"Are you excited?" he asked, as he raised his eyebrows.

Alexis looked confused.

"Uh . . . yeah," she started, sarcastically. "This is really exciting. I can't think of a better way to spend my night."

She held up her thumb and gave a mocking smile. Seth had already managed to irritate her.

"Oh, sorry about all this," Seth said, referring to the fact that they were stuck in a Suburban in the middle of nowhere. It was as if they were playing out the opening of every horror movie they'd ever watched.

Richard never turned around to talk to Andrea.

Bored and having no clue as to when the guys were going to have the fire going, Seth came up with a plan.

"Well, let's get the lanterns and the tents," Seth said as he opened his door to get out. Willie got up to join him. "We should be able to have enough light with the lanterns to get the tents up. It's gonna be a bitch, though, with this dark."

Willie and Seth climbed out of the truck and began their chores.

Now Richard sat alone in the truck with the girls.

"You know, I'm sorry they did that to you Richard," Andrea said as she put her hand on his shoulder. "You don't deserve that."

"Did what?" he asked. "I don't deserve what?"

"You know, messed up your car," she continued.

"Oh well," Richard added. "Shit happens."

"That was a cute car," she said. "I liked it from the first time I got in it."

Richard smiled and thought back to that day. The feelings that he had sitting right there with her in that Suburban were the exact same as that day when he first laid eyes on her. This night was going to be great. She actually touched him. Not only that but she made an effort to speak to him. Shocked and a little nervous, Richard turned around to see Andrea looking at him with concern in her eyes. In an instant he felt comfortable and at ease with his situation.

"If it means anything to you Richard, I think what they did was mean and uncalled for," she said to him. "And I hope you fix your car and show them that it didn't hurt you one bit."

Alexis rolled her eyes. She knew that Richard was a dork, and she didn't like seeing her best friend talk to him like he was worth a minute of her time. Richard glared at Alexis every time he turned around. He disliked her for a totally different reason. She was the one who got all of Andrea's attention. He felt she didn't deserve her. He was jealous of her as if she were Andrea's current boyfriend.

Alexis wasn't going to put up with attitude from some scrawny freshman and eventually got sick of the dirty looks.

"Listen, Richard, here's a tip," Alexis said, leaning close to him. "Find a Kleenex."

Richard didn't know what she was talking about.

Andrea elbowed Alexis in the ribs.

"Ow," Alexis shouted. "Well?"

Andrea shook her head and looked genuinely pissed.

Alexis motioned towards her nose and Richard immediately grabbed his, discovering that he had a blood slowly leaking from it. He did nothing more than make things worse by grabbing himself, and soon the blood was trailing down his face like a waterpark ride.

"Shit," he said. "Do either of you have a tissue or something?" He tilted his head back and put his thumb in one nostril, and his index finger in the other.

They both shook their heads no. Alexis laughed.

Richard dug through the glove box for a clean napkin, finding nothing but papers and an instruction manual. Thinking nothing of it, Richard grabbed a sheet of paper and crumpled it up, cramming it up his bleeding nostril, making things worse. The sting felt from the paper cutting on his nose was something that he was prepared for so he didn't show any signs of being in pain.

Seth poked his head into the van.

"Are you going to sit in here with the girls and be a pussy?" he asked Richard. "We could use another hand out here putting together a tent that you're going to sleep in just like the rest of us."

"Actually, I think I'm going to just sleep in the truck tonight," Richard said.

Just as Seth turned to walk away, Reggie walked by and noticed Richard's clumsy attempt at stopping his nose bleed.

"What's that in your nose?" he asked. "What the fuck is that?"

Richard looked at him and pulled it out.

Now covered in blood and crumpled up, Richard knew as soon as he saw it that he was going to be in a little trouble. He had inadvertently used Reggie's vehicle registration to clean the blood out of his nostril.

"Get that out of your fuckin' nose," Reggie said, as he pointed into Richard's eyes. "That kid's a real waste of skin," Reggie said to Willie as the two walked over to the tent. "The motherfucker's using my fuckin' registration to wipe his nose."

"Well, you asked for it," Willie said.

"How so?"

"Well, you're the one who invited him."

Reggie stopped to look at Willie.

"Don't you toy with me, motherfucker," Reggie said, unappreciative of the jocular comment. "I will kick the shit out of that boy if he crosses the line. Belee-dat. Sheeit . . . you crazy if you think I invited that pussy. You fuckin' crazy."

Willie chuckled.

"Hey, both you guys. Shut the fuck up and help out here," Seth said as he bent down to put one of the tent stakes in the ground.

Thirty minutes later, the group was gathered around a crackling fire, faces glowing orange staring at the madness of the flames. Amazingly enough, the warmth of the fire, and the comfortable isolation felt by the campers allowed everyone to actually get along for a while.

Willie and Seth had completed the tent and were resting their tired bodies next to the fire. By that time, however, the cold beers were already starting to dwindle.

"I'm going to drag beers to the creek," Seth said as he got up and walked over to the truck. "Maybe that'll keep it cold until tomorrow."

"Thhheee gguyy wasss a . . . a . . .a flasss inn the paaan," said a drunk Charles, speaking of the Loveland quarterback who had gruesomely been taken out of the game a month earlier. "Hhhee wass justtt . . . a . . . puuttthhy fresssman."

Eddie Broadus broke his leg in five different places on a crushing low blow just moments after Richard and Willie ran from the puke-covered hot dog man.

"He was injured on purpose," Reggie confessed as he stared blankly into the fire. "The guy was taken out by that asshole."

The group collectively turned their attention towards Reggie except the only people in the whole bunch that weren't drunk—Richard and Andrea. They just couldn't be bothered by more football talk. Alexis was so blitzed, she would've pretended to listen to anything. For the rest, hearing Reggie make a statement like that was taken as serious as just about anything that comes out of the mouth of a drunk.

"He was fuckin' injured on purpose."

"What do you mean?" asked Willie. "How do you get injured on purpose?"

"Wasn't it obvious? Coach got together with Gibson just before the play. I saw it. I was only ten feet from the two of 'em," said Reggie. "Don't you find it strange that he talks to Gibson and the next play it's all over? We should've lost that game. You know, Coach Bruce is my . . . my mentor. And, he's the only person who ever cared about my future, but he can be a real piece of shit. Taking out that Indian kid was fucked up."

Charles remained silent for the most part, other than to say something nonsensical that no one could understand without a translator. Seth kept an eye on him most of the time to get an idea of when to try and cut him off. He wasn't just drinking beers, he was slamming them. One after another. He was definitely someone that acquaintances did not want to help get too drunk. He had a tendency to become violent.

Even Reggie had consumed enough alcohol to the point that he didn't give a rat's ass one way or another as to who was drinking too much or not. That was the point for bringing so much beer. No one was expected to wake the next morning and actually appreciate the beautiful scenery, smells and sounds of camping. In fact, it was an unannounced race to see who could pound the most beers and stay awake. No one cared that they were all qualifying for the worst of waking conditions—the campfire hangover. There aren't too many things worse than waking in the forest with lungs and sinuses raw from smoke, covered in your own vomit. It's not like you have a comfortable bed or couch to crash on or have access to a toothbrush either. It's lying on a tattered sleeping bag in the woods, smelling like three shades of ass, wishing that you would've just avoided getting drunk the night before. But you do it anyway, knowing that you'll regret it the next day.

Shortly after 11 o'clock, Seth and Alexis struck up a conversation that involved mostly whispers and nods. It would be a conversation that would determine the fate of everyone at the campsite.

"You look good in those pants," Seth said.

Alexis giggled. She was also feeling mighty toasted.

"Naw, I mean it," he continued. "I think the only thing that would make you look better, is if you were *out* of those pants. And, you should trust my opinion because I have an eye for fashion."

"That's so lame," Alexis said as they both laughed. They quickly met face-to-face and began embracing in a passionate kiss, only breaking their connection when they realized that others were staring.

Inebriation is the perfect excuse for making a mistake.

Eventually, the two got up and walked towards the truck. As Seth got to his feet, he almost fell into the fire, prompting a mixture of laughter and fear from his friends. No one made a big deal about them walking away because they knew what was going on. Alexis was brought along for one thing and one thing only—sex. As terrible as that sounds, it was true. She sure as hell wasn't brought along for company or to become one of the gang. Seth was just the first one who was willing to ask for it. Leave it to the confident QB to make the first move.

"You know, I've been looking at you all year," Seth said. He was spouting off a bold faced lie since it was only a couple of days earlier when he first saw her. He had no respect for Alexis, and with each step they took towards the inevitable, he respected her less. That didn't matter since he wasn't looking for marriage.

Alexis believed his lies and laughed.

"Then why'd it take you so long to ask me out?" she asked.

"I've been busy with football and just didn't have time," he said. "You know how it goes. Did I mention I'm All State?"

"Only about thirty times," she said, turning to him to put her arms around his head. Pulling closer, her lips met his and the two were soon engaged in a passionate kiss. This time, it was serious. This was the kiss that always led to greener pastures for both of them. They both knew it. Seth was given the green light when Alexis put her tongue in his mouth and reached down for his crotch with her hand, rubbing the growing bulge in his jeans.

Richard and Andrea had struck up a conversation of their own.

He wasn't about to let her walk away from the camping trip having not had the opportunity to get to know him. If he accomplished anything in his God forsaken and lonely life, it would be that one last push for Andrea's attention. The weeks prior to this encounter were spent with him wishing he had a second chance to have her alone. He wanted to say all the right things and make all the right moves.

"Sorry I was so weird when you first met me," Richard confessed. He knew he had problems and couldn't explain why he could be so happy one day and so pissed off the next. While his shame usually masked itself as introverted anger, there was no mistaking his true feelings. He knew his life was a lost cause.

Andrea on the other hand was pleasantly surprised to hear the words come from his mouth and smiled. The most volatile thing Richard had done to her occurred that first week when he changed personalities without warning. Apologizing to her at least acknowledged that he had some sense about the whole situation.

"Thanks," she said. "I wasn't trying to act like you were some bad guy or something. I just didn't feel comfortable around you, you know? You kind of freaked out on me."

She hadn't actually told Richard the truth until that moment. All along she beat around the bush, not wanting to tell him that she thought he was a weirdo. The fact that she finally told him the truth was a weight off of her shoulders. But with honesty like that, there's also a consequential guilt. Who was she to tell him he was weird?

"Does this remind you of home?" he asked, waving his arm around in reference to the serene beauty that engulfed them.

She looked around.

"I don't know," she said. "I can't see anything."

That's when she made eye contact with Willie. He was sitting across the fire, staring at the two as they spoke. Richard also glanced up at Willie and gave him a thumbs up and a smile. Willie smiled and turned his head, seemingly pissed off at the two.

"What was that all about," Andrea said.

"Nothing," Richard explained. "Nothing at all."

Seth and Alexis made their way just behind the truck. No one could see what the two were doing, and it was probably for the better. If someone sitting around the fire really wanted to, they could make out the appearance of silhouettes dancing behind the vehicle, but that was it.

Seth pushed Alexis against the truck. Still locked in their passionate kiss, Alexis propped her leg up on Seth's thigh and he gently rubbed her between the legs. Soon the two were tearing at each other's pants. Neither one of them could stand it any longer. They fell to the ground and Seth immediately penetrated her as the two began to fuck like wild dogs. Seth was grinding his hips into hers, causing her to moan in a mixture of pain and pleasure. It wasn't too comfortable for Alexis, having sex on the rocks and gravel that lined the earth, but she tried to ignore it at first.

The sounds of Alexis moaning could be heard by the group as the fire raged. The men that had just been involved in conversation with one another were now listening in on Seth's encounter with the female, growing aroused in the process.

It took less than a minute for Alexis to become unbearably uncomfortable as a rock began to dig into her lower back. She cringed in pain each time Seth thrust himself into her. Faster and faster he moved. Harder and harder the rock pushed against her back. She no longer felt good from the contact, she felt searing pain.

"Stop. Stop," she said when the pain became too much to bear. "Please."

The rock was sharp and had started to pierce her skin, pressing against the lower part of her spine. Seth continued as if she didn't say a word.

“Stop for a second, Seth. You’re hurting me!” she said as her voice got louder. She couldn’t move under his weight because she was just too little. He didn’t hesitate, instead placing his hand over her mouth as soon as she raised her voice. He didn’t want anyone to hear her complaints. That’s when she tried to scream. Now, he was truly distracted and couldn’t finish his act, which caused great discord in his mind. He pulled his hand off her mouth and she started struggling to get free.

“Let me go, you bastard,” she grumbled. “You’re fucking hurting me, you prick.”

The pain in her back was unbearable, but the fear from the attack was even worse. In a flash he reared back with his right arm, his golden throwing arm, and connected with a furious punch to her cheek. It sounded like a bat connecting with the ball just before a home run. Her head ricocheted off the ground and she was unconscious in the blink of an eye.

Charles heard the commotion and walked around the corner to find Seth still on top of her. Her struggles had ended, but Seth continued to go until he came inside of her. He was exhausted and drunk to boot. In fact, he didn’t even realize that what he did was wrong. Her presence at the camp seemed like an open agreement to deal with whatever the group deemed necessary. She couldn’t have possibly misunderstood the invitation as being anything more than a request for a live sex toy. At least that’s the way they all looked at it.

“Yoouu done yet, Superman?” Charles asked, barely able to stand, much less talk, much less construct an erection. It was implied, although not officially agreed upon, that the young men would take turns on Alexis. She had no say in the matter.

Seth, now feeling rejected and a little regretful for hitting her, pulled out and zipped himself up. He knew there wasn’t a problem. He’d gotten her so drunk, she couldn’t possibly remember the attack the next day.

“She’s all yours, dude,” he said as he wiped his face of her saliva and walked away. Hell, if the rest of the guys had at her, at least he wouldn’t be alone in his wrongdoing.

Charles climbed on top of her and went to work on the motionless body.

Seth went around the corner and made eye contact with both Reggie and Willie before he looked down at the ground in shame. All they knew was that Alexis was there to give them all some action and that she was doing that for someone. They didn’t judge Seth, but at that point, no one realized the magnitude of the situation. No one knew what he’d done to her.

Strangely enough, they did notice her sudden silence. She was obviously vocal during the early stages of her encounter with Seth, but not a peep was heard while she was with Charles. Now she wasn’t giving consensual sex to the men, she was being raped.

Charles finished his act and moved out of the way, nearly falling on top of her after he stood up. Reggie was next up and just as Charles had neglected to realize beforehand, he too didn't see that she was in a bad way. If he did, he sure didn't bother to help her. She was unconscious and bleeding from her ear due to a combination of the punch and her head ricocheting off of the hard ground.

Richard was as sober as he had ever been in his life. He hadn't had a single drink that night, a feat not even matched by the more innocent Andrea. Now they were both alone, next to the fire, talking to each other more than they had the entire time they had known one another.

Andrea wasn't stupid, and knew that Alexis was giving head to all of the guys behind the truck. The disappointment and embarrassment that Andrea felt for Alexis was enough to ruin any chance at making it a fun evening. She had put two-and-two together and finally realized what Alexis was all about. Alexis hadn't come right out and told her that she was a raging slut, but Andrea had picked up clues along the way. This night was just verifying her hunch. She knew that Alexis and Seth weren't an item or anything. She knew that earlier in the day Alexis had admitted that she wanted Seth but wasn't going to throw herself at his feet like all of the other girls. That was a lie.

Richard was well aware that his friends were getting some action and he could go over there as well. Put aside the fact that he was too much of a prude to participate in a gang bang, he felt in his mind that in essence, he was showing Andrea that he wasn't a pig like the rest of the guys. He was showing her that he was waiting for her.

He was the only guy in the group who wasn't cuddling up with her friend.

Andrea didn't see his act of chivalry as such but she did find him to be a good person to talk to while the whole thing took place. Being the only other female in a group of sexual predators in the middle of the woods was a dangerous position to be in. While Alexis was being brutally raped on the other side of the truck, Richard was making Andrea laugh, or at least trying to.

False signals can be bad when used on the wrong person, and Andrea was about to find out why. She was beginning to trust Richard, a mistake that she would soon regret. As soon as she let her guard down, sure enough, things went wrong. Like the flick of a switch, Richard's mind turned to darkness. He felt like Andrea didn't respect him enough. He was tired of having to work so hard for attention.

"I know why you came," Richard said with a different look in his eyes. He couldn't take the pain of knowing that his dream girl was right in front of him and he could have her at any time. Something in his brain told him that Andrea was the same kind of girl as Alexis, and that she was saving herself for him. Something evil was stirring in his mind.

In the whole scheme of things, he was a guy, she was a girl, and by nature's rule they fit together. The only thing keeping the two from making love was the love part, and Richard was tired of waiting for that to come into the picture. He would settle for a fuck. The more he listened to the guys have their way with Alexis, the more his sex-starved teenaged mind began to race. It was now or never.

Andrea noticed the now glazed look in his eyes. He wasn't the same guy that was talking to her about life and ambitions before. He was changing his mood all together. Terror revealed itself to Andrea in the form of Richard Tark. Frightened, confused and aware that there was nowhere to go, she became cautious. Even though she knew how bad his mood swings could get, he was still the least frightening person at the campsite at that moment. He would soon be worse than a nightmare.

"I know why you're here," he said.

Alarmed, she started to back away from Richard.

He made a motion towards the truck and what the guys were doing behind it. "You're playing hard to get, right? You really do like me. I remember sitting at home the day I met you, jerking off to the image of you in my mind. Doesn't it make you feel good to know that I've fucked myself over and over and thought about you the whole time? I had you on my mother's couch and you loved every minute of it."

"What?" she said. "Richard, what are you talking about you pig?"

Richard showcased a psychotic smile, apparently taking the pig comment as a compliment. Andrea jumped to her feet and ran towards the truck. She made it about 15 feet before Richard grabbed her from behind, wrapping his arms around her before turning her around to face him.

"C'mon," he said. "Don't play games anymore. I know you want to fuck me. Let's just do it."

Andrea reared back her knee and connected with the bulge in his crotch, turning around again in an effort to reach the truck. She had to get someone's attention.

"God damn it!" he yelled as he crumpled to the ground, clutching his groin. The pain shot through his body like he had just been struck by lightning. Andrea got to the truck and shook the handle to the passenger door.

Locked.

Right on the other side of the truck, hidden by the darkness of night, the other men were watching as Reggie finished up with Alexis.

Scared for her life Andrea turned to see where Richard was. She felt like she had entered a zombie movie.

Gone.

The spot where he had been moments earlier, hunched over, was now cleared.

Where did he go?

The men on the other side of the truck were now being as quiet as they could be. Without Alexis making any noise Andrea could hear only silence all around her. No one moved, and no one really knew why they were being quiet, they just were. The only sound that filled the air was the crackling of the fire.

SNAP!

Richard stepped on a tree limb just as he reached the back of Andrea, sparking fear in her and another run, this time she didn't know where she was headed. She screamed and began to cry hysterically. Around the truck she sprinted. Now she was screaming for help.

She was scared for her life.

"Help!" she yelped as she tried to lose her attacker.

The men behind the truck heard her yell, but didn't think anything of it. They all stood over Alexis, knowing deep inside that something was wrong, not caring what Andrea was screaming about.

Except for Willie.

He hadn't taken his turn on Alexis yet, and was concerned that Richard may be doing something bad to Andrea. It was obvious that her screams weren't from pleasure.

Just before Andrea could reach the beginnings of the forest that circled the camp sight, Richard finally caught up to her. This time he wasn't going to let her injure him as she had done before. He grabbed her and threw her to the ground some thirty feet from the truck and the crime that had occurred behind it.

Richard got on his knees and threw his arm back, connecting with Andrea's face. That got her to stop kicking and yelling. Then for good measure, he connected with the other side of her face, this time causing her body to go limp. He felt the same charge as he did the day Blue Hair lost his teeth. Such power.

He unbuckled her belt and unzipped her pants, pulling them from her legs along with her panties. He stared at her tiny patch of pubic hair and smiled. In a motion almost as fast, he yanked his belt away from his jeans and slid his pants off. His erection was still full, which was amazing considering the kick that he had just taken to his balls.

Just as he knelt down to penetrate her she lifted up her leg, connecting with his crotch for the second time in five minutes. The pain that shot through his system was unbearable as he fell to the ground and wept.

Andrea got on her feet quickly and sprinted into the darkness of the forest.

As frightening as the woods appeared, she could see no other choice. She obviously couldn't rely on the other men in the camp to protect her considering the situation at hand. With no shoes or pants on, she was unprotected from the environment that awaited her in the lush forest.

Richard stumbled back towards the truck. He could think of nothing more than his failure. In his mind, he had done nothing wrong other than fail to convince Andrea of his true love. He was already thinking of what he would say to her when she came back as if the past five minutes had never happened. As if he hadn't just violated another human being. There had to be a way she'd accept him. Willie ran over to Richard and grabbed him by the shirt collar.

"What the fuck did you do?" Willie yelled as he threw Richard to the ground. "What did you do to her?"

At the same moment, the men huddling around Alexis realized that she was in horrible shape. She seemed lifeless. Amazingly enough, they didn't seem to realize her vegetative state when they were having sex with her.

Andrea ran through the woods, cold and scared. Naked from the waist down. Her worst nightmares had just become reality. Nothing in this world could prepare a person for what she had just gone through or what she had in store. She didn't have time to think about it, she had to get away.

Get away from the demons.

"Where the fuck did she go?"

"Where the hell is she?"

"Andrea! Andrea come back here! Don't run!"

The star-filled Colorado sky seemed like an eternity away. Like staring down the edge of a cliff leading nowhere. The abyss hovered aimlessly over the peaks of pine trees that rose to greet the blackness of that night, Andrea on her back, looking up at distant stars like a curious child. For a second, she thought she was safe and back in some forgotten memory. Waves of nausea flowed through her brain as the pain quickly returned with her consciousness. You can't imagine even for a moment, what it must feel like to be lost, at least lost in the way Andrea was. The stream of blood cascaded from her nose down the side of her face and into her ear, reminding her that her nightmare was far from over. If only she could just stand up and leave.

A spider crawled over her bare leg and she shivered as the tiny legs tickled her skin. She didn't even think about her fear of spiders, nor did she comprehend that one had in fact touched her. It was getting colder.

Another shiver revived her soul as a frigid breeze blew through the forest. Feeling more alert, Andrea mustered up enough strength to prop herself up. Someone was coming. The crackling of branches and brush did nothing more than charge her already speeding heartbeat. But it was so dark.

She could feel the steady dripping of blood onto her bare leg as she sat in a semi cross-legged style. The warmth of her blood was easily recognizable on her cold skin. Taking her mud-covered hand, she wiped across her face realizing that her nose was split open. Oddly enough, it didn't hurt that much. It was just annoying, like the few times she accidentally got water up her nose while swimming. She was too scared to feel the extent of the pain. Groggy and fading, her memory slowly began to return as she recalled running into a tree in her haste to get away from the madness. *The madness!*

Her breath became a fog when she hopped back to her feet and thrust herself into the cool air all around her. The visions in her mind were just as cloudy and quick to disappear. What had just happened? Innocence gone and never again a part of her life, the wave of panic came back like a tidal wave.

The sounds of young men screaming filled the darkness of forest around her and she saw a faint light in the distance. Nowhere to go, she aimlessly charged through the black in hope of just getting as far away from everyone as she could.

As was the case moments before, *she was running for her life.*

"Andrea!" a voice echoed through the trees. "Andrea, get back here! Please stop. No one is gonna hurt you. Come back!"

Stop? She didn't start anything. Why was this person telling her to stop running? There was no way in hell that she was going back to that campsite, not as long as Richard Tark remained there. She wondered where Alexis was. Why wasn't she out there looking for her? Andrea thought about their friendship, and aided by her head wound, conjured up a scenario that had Alexis laughing back at the campsite at the expense of her friend's fear. This was no joke. She had to get away.

Andrea had no idea what nightmare Alexis had gone through. She didn't know that her blood had been spilled into the dirt and had no idea she was already dead.

The campsite was now a chaotic collection of regretful witnesses and guilty perpetrators. As the flames tickled the night air, the only person left calm was Richard. He didn't seem to realize anything. He just stared blankly at the fire with a dumb grin on his face. It's like he knew that they were all finally equals. In a matter of minutes things went from a normal camping trip, to a bunch of teens succumbing to their sexual inhibitions and finally to a crime scene. The realization that you are a murderer and a rapist hits like a ton of bricks, and it isn't the thought of jail time that suddenly points your mind towards right and wrong. These young men were all battling their own demons and mixed with alcohol, those demons can get pretty loud.

"Andrea!"

"Where'd she run?" Seth asked Willie. "She can't get out of this forest. If she gets away, we're all fucked."

Willie seemed to understand that sentiment. They needed to find her and keep her from going to the police. They needed to keep her from verifying the truth that they were horrible people. She was the one witness that could not be trusted and rightfully so. It wasn't like they wanted her back because they were worried about her or because they felt bad for what had happened to her. The guys didn't want her to talk. No one knew for sure what they were going to do or say to sway her from turning them all in, but they had to get her back first and foremost.

And they had to do something about Alexis.

Willie pointed to the spot where he saw Andrea disappear into the darkness and Seth pushed him to find her.

"Hurry," Seth said.

Willie quietly jogged into the brush with his flashlight lit and held firmly in one hand, a Swiss Army knife in the other. He didn't know what was out there and was honestly a little scared of the creatures that may or may not want to eat him.

"Andrea!" he yelled. "C'mon out."

No response.

"Alexis is hurt bad and we need to get her out of here," he said. "C'mon Andrea. Everything is okay."

He slowed to a walk and followed a path of trampled grass obviously cut by Andrea's fleeing feet. Every noise startled him and his nervous reactions were triggered by sheer adrenaline. Partially scared of what could be stalking him and partially hoping beyond hope to find Andrea sitting on a rock, Willie was a wreck.

Eventually, Andrea's path faded and Willie found himself following his instincts, rewarded with absolutely no luck at all. In the background he could hear Seth yelling at the other guys. The camp was getting farther away as was Willie's conscience. His pace slowed to a crawl as his knees felt like they were going to give out. Sprawled out on the forest floor was a rotting trunk from a long forgotten tree that had fallen years before. Willie sat down for a rest, already trying to come up with an alibi for what he and his friends had just done.

"Please come out Andrea," he said just before he broke down in tears. He cupped his face in his hands and wept out loud, something that he hadn't done in years. The night was a disaster and he was stuck trying to find someone in the dark that didn't want to be found. His guilt was even more powerful since it was he who convinced the guys to take both girls to the mountains. It was he who brought Richard along.

"She's fuckin' dead ya'll!" Charles yelled back at the camp sight. Willie heard that. "Muthafucka!"

The boys all gathered around Alexis' body and looked at the disgusting site. Her clothes were ripped and covered in mud, dirt and semen. Reggie knelt down and closed her legs, tugging her skirt down over her exposed crotch as if he wanted her to have a dignity in death that she obviously didn't have in life. Worst of all were her eyes. Both were open, gazing at the boys in a cryptic, final gesture of finger-pointing. They were the ones who had left her in that state. Reggie then slid her eyelids down with his fingertips just like he had seen in movies. It felt like the right thing to do.

"So, what the fuck we gonna do?" Charles asked in panic, more agitated than anything else. "I don't have time for this dead bitch. If this shit gets out, they sure as fuck won't let me play ball this year." He pounded his leg on the ground like a little boy having a tantrum. "Fuck this shit, man!"

"Ball?" Seth yelled, bumping chests with the much larger Charles. "Ball? Dude, if this gets *out*, your ass is going to the electric chair. No, no, no. You're ass is going to be fucking strung up. Now, shut the fuck up so I can think here." Seth put his hands over his temples and rubbed them, thinking hard about a solution. "Jesus. I was just trying to get laid."

"You the reason she dead!" yelled Reggie. "Ain't 'cause of me. Ain't 'cause of Charles. Ain't 'cause of this sad sack of shit." Reggie pointed to Richard. "You the one that was so fuckin' rough. What'd you do to her anyway?"

Seth charged at Reggie.

"I fucked her same as you!" he yelled. "What makes you think I killed her?"

"Uh, she sure as hell wasn't movin' when I was on her," Reggie replied.

"So, what does that make you?" Seth accused. No one spoke for quite awhile after that question was asked.

Seth was the fearless quarterback. He always came up with the right answers at the right time. This was when they needed him the most. He had to come up with the right play for this particular game. Charles recognized Seth's outburst as a serious threat and remained quiet for the rest of the night. He had to think about it pretty hard. Could he trust Seth? Reggie stood over Alexis' cold body. Tears streamed down his cheeks for the better part of ten minutes and as was the case with the other guys, he thought of his role in the murder. Looking back, he felt like maybe he did know she wasn't alive when he came inside of her. So what did that make him? The worst nightmares of humankind were all being played out live and in person. The spine of a young man who would rape and murder a young girl is nothing more than a piece of black licorice. There's nothing sweet about it.

As if he had to make amends to her lifeless body, Seth gently lifted Alexis off of the ground and carried her to the fire pit cautiously setting her on

Richard's blanket. Now the boys were acting like civilized human beings. Now they were concerned about the well being of this girl as if she'd jump up at any minute and shake off the dirt and have a few beers and a laugh over it all. Everyone involved in the crime paced around her, nervous about what had happened, and curious as to the whereabouts of Andrea.

The wind got fierce and whipped through the trees, creating a sound reminiscent of someone screaming far away. The boys all jumped, all except Richard. He continued to stare at the flickering flames as he had done since he chased Andrea to the edge of the forest. Paranoia set in as it began to feel like thousands of eyes were fixated on the boys, witnesses to their terrible crime.

"What the fuck was that?" Reggie asked. Again the noise echoed through the trees with a strong gust of wind aiding it. Worse than the noise was the silence that followed. No wind. No sound. All four boys could hear nothing but their breathing.

"It's just the wind," Reggie calmly said to himself. "God damn, I'm gonna have a heart attack."

"Hey, get her off of my bed!" Richard yelled, diverting the others from their anxiety over the wind and the surrounding darkness. In a flash, he sprung from his seat in front of the fire, and pulled his blanket from under Alexis, tossing her body around like a rag doll.

"Whoa. What the fuck? What do you think you're doing?" Seth screamed, his face turning dark red. He wanted to punch Richard. The next person that got in his way was going to end up with a fat lip. "Here's the deal you guys. We need to get rid of what happened tonight. Forget about the fucking wind," he said, waving his hands around at the trees. "Forget about your fucking blankie," he said, pointing at Richard. "Let's figure this out. No one can know what happened tonight."

The guys continued to stare at her dead body. The world as they knew it was through. Life could not, and would not, ever be the same. Reggie stared at her chest, naively hoping that it would move as she took in air. It never happened.

"This fuckin' sucks," Charles said.

The tears all faded.

The screams were all silenced.

It was time to repair the situation.

10

Eighteen Years Later

Friday, November 16, 2001

The human body takes an almost alien-like form when frozen for too long. If you remove most of the blood from the body before freezing it, you'll find the skin's pigment can turn a shade of white that rivals that of snow. It's actually quite fetching . . .

The wind on the snow covered prairie whipped around the white powder in a flurry of activity, piling up snowdrifts all along the landscape. The cattle that grazed the field were all confined to a section of land just over the hill to the north, closer to the landowner's home. Dark gray storm clouds hovered aimlessly over the valley most of the morning although not a fresh flake of snow had fallen as of noon. Like a godlike sneeze, the storm that had hit in the previous few days was horribly cold and had provided a surge of snow that the residents hadn't seen the likes of in quite some time. The winter had been especially brutal thus far. The first snowfall was in September and in the month and a half since, the area hadn't experienced a week without the white flakes.

A flap of frozen flesh blew in the breeze.

Standing less than three feet from it, a cow stared, grinding its mouth on a rare piece of straw, puzzled at the discovery it had made. Bitter cold accompanied each gust of wind and the cow continued its mindless gaze at a sight that would make any intelligent animal ill. The scene was proof enough that cows aren't very smart. Maybe it knew where the flesh originated and felt apathetic about the victim. After all, its flesh would soon be hung up to dry as well.

"There you are God dammit!" yelled a grizzled voice from behind the cow. "What the hell you doin' all the way over here? I almost gave myself a heart attack lookin' for you."

The rancher had gone out to count the head of cattle when he noticed that one was missing and a hole had been created in the temporary holding pen. The tracks led right to the spot where the cow was standing, about a mile from the homestead. Had the rancher waited to look, the cow would've frozen where it stood, buried in snow.

That's how Russell Meeder first got involved.

Thanks to the escape attempt of one cow.

"Are you sick?" the rancher rhetorically asked the animal after dismounting his horse. He walked slowly, wiping his runny nose off on his dirty duster. "What the heck are you lookin' at?"

Standing too far away, he couldn't see what the cow was fixated upon. It didn't take long to discover the truth about what had happened right there under his nose. Inch by inch, the nightmare that lay before him was painful to witness. Eventually he realized what it was and fell to his knees.

"Jesus-h-Christ," he muttered as he stared at the horrible scene. For ten minutes the rancher stayed on the ground, crying and staring. Staring at something he hadn't seen the likes of—even during the big war.

"Excuse me, sir," a woman whispered, leaning over to speak in Russell's ear. It was the reasonably stunning girl from the front desk at the Denver Public Library. Russell looked up from his reading and found his eyes fixated on her outfit. She was wearing a light turquoise summer dress that revealed her body as that of someone who worked out—a lot. Definitely not an outfit most girls wore in the winter.

He smiled. Beauty always seems to make one smile, more so in the midst of horror.

"This is totally embarrassing," she began. "I don't do this very often but I've noticed you come here a lot and I was wondering . . . well . . . would you like to go somewhere, sometime for some . . ."

At that moment, she looked down to see his book resting on the table in front of him. He was researching a case and had the book open to a page that showed the body of a man who had been butchered by his next door neighbor. The image was red with blood and the man's face was the center point of the photograph, bloated and disfigured from the stab wounds. Her jaw dropped and she let out a miniscule whimper. She immediately stood up straight, adjusted her dress and walked away, covering her mouth as if she was going to be sick.

Two angles of the photo showed the severity of the attack. The front view illustrated the amount of stab wounds, 20 to be exact. The side view showed the flatness of the man's head as the skull had been crushed by the force of the knife entering the face in so many different spots.

Russell cranked his head around, still curious about what she was going to ask him. Of course he'd be happy to go somewhere, sometime with someone like her. When he turned back to his book, he realized what she was so upset about and laughed. Maybe that's why he was still single. No one could ever understand what was involved in his job and that made for a rough and lonely career.

"Fuckin' Christ," he muttered. The only thing he could think about, other than the girl he'd just helped make sick, was a cigarette. If he had his way, smokers could go nuts in any public establishment, especially libraries.

Even though he rarely used the books at the library for reference, he tended to bring the ones from the crime lab, knowing that he could have an uninterrupted and quiet environment in which to read. No one at the office even knew where he was. He could just immerse himself in work and know that he wouldn't be distracted by every little detail. He'd give up smoking to have that feeling more often.

He wasn't actually reading the page that was open in front of him. He was just looking at the pictures. He probably should've been more sympathetic and courteous to the people around him when he brought the *University of Colorado Autopsy Reference Manual* with him.

In fact, the reason he had it this time was for an example that was found towards the rear of the book, in the children's section. He was investigating a case of a pregnant woman who had *accidentally* fallen on a knife, killing her unborn son and seriously injuring herself. The knife not only severed her son's torso, but her own kidney and a tract of intestine.

Once the investigation delved deeper into her situation, Russell began to entertain the notion that she may have done it on purpose to avoid the birth. He remembered an example of that in the back of the *Autopsy Reference Manual* and wanted to see if he had any basis for his hunch.

The trouble was he couldn't seem to find the energy to research the case that particular day. He was daydreaming and could do nothing more than flip through the pages. The grizzly images that were housed in the book were a reminder to Russell. He got into police work for a reason; to find the scum and toenail scrapings of society and bring them to justice.

Russell had moved to Colorado when he was 15 years old and had lived in the area the 21 years since. He was the kind of guy that you would consider as a possible link to Clark Kent. He had dark hair, done up like Elvis Presley, and a pair of dorky glasses. Nevertheless, his appearance remained handsome and his features somewhat defined.

Embracing law enforcement as a career was rewarding and challenging all at the same time. He didn't find it either at first. Having just graduated from college, Russell loved the idea of busting bad guys, but found the job to be far more boring than that. For the first two years of being an officer, Russell spent most of his time going to schools and helping with crowd control at sporting events around town.

It wasn't until he entered homicide for the Denver Police Department that he realized he had made the right choice. Many times he had the opportunity to bust murderers and lock them up. That's what made his job fun. Maybe too much fun. His fondest memory of being a rookie on the homicide beat was tying up a convicted wife beater. He hogtied the man and stuffed him in the back of a squad car after his wife was found bloodied. The whole drive to the precinct, Russell managed to whistle the theme song to *Andy Griffith* until the man was crying.

When he first joined, he was looked at as one of the finest and most promising officers on the force. In fact, he won the prestigious Rookie of the Year award at the annual Denver Police banquet in 1988.

Five years later, however, he was brought under investigation for two separate cases in which he had shot and killed robbery suspects. They were both legitimate cases of self-defense, but nevertheless had to be checked out as part of the department's policy. In February of 1993, he was found innocent of *Negligent Use of a Firearm in the Line Of Duty* on both counts, and returned to his job after being on paid leave for three weeks straight. That incident triggered feelings of irritation and bitterness towards the department. His burn to reach the status of detective was higher than ever during that time.

He yearned to be a detective for as long as he could remember but had to be put on a waiting list of recruits. Eventually he got the call and passed the required tests before gladly accepting the job. The fact that they wanted him, despite his past troubles, proved that he was meant to be a detective. He didn't miss much about working the police beat and quite honestly never looked back.

As a detective, he witnessed some prime examples of society's slugs at their best and still enjoyed and relished his job as if it were something wholesome and pride-inducing.

RING!

Russell turned to his jacket and reached in the pocket for his cell phone. People all around him lifted their heads in agitation from the sound that was violating their ears. In every direction, bookworms scowled and shook their heads as he pushed the send button. Talking on, or merely holding a cell phone in a public library is bad news.

"This is Detective Meeder," he said, noticing a college student still staring at him. Russell lifted his middle finger and directed it at the young man, who immediately turned back to his book.

"Russ," the voice on the other end said. It was Detective David Robinson, one of Russell's best friends and a fellow dick. "I've got a doozy for you."

Russell's facial expression relaxed itself until every muscle in his skull was loose. As David continued talking, Russell gathered his things and started for the door. What he was hearing couldn't have been true. If it was, it was certainly cause for alarm.

Maneuvering through traffic and battling icy roads, it took more than an hour to reach his destination twenty miles east of Denver. Once he arrived at the ranch, he had to wait for the Hummer police cruiser to drive from the scene of the crime all the way back to the rancher's house to pick him up. David was in the car and gave Russell the rundown on the way to the body.

"The rancher, a mister Roberts, John Roberts, found the body around ten thirty this morning," David began, "I gotta say Russ, this is the most horrible thing I've ever seen. Even worse than anything I've seen in movies. It's indescribable."

Russell turned and watched the arctic landscape around him as the car slowly trudged over the pasture. It was beginning to snow again, and the white peaks of hills went back as far as the eye could see. In the foreground, Russell noticed the large group of black cattle that were penned in together.

"The cow got out over in the far corner," David said as he pointed to the far end of the enclosure. "Roberts found it staring at the body. He said it wouldn't budge from its position, even when the horse made noise. It was zoned out on the body or something."

Russell wasn't interested in David's overly precise descriptions of the scene. What he had told him on the phone couldn't have been true. Sure, something strange was out there, waiting to be prodded, but not what he had described. Definitely not that. Not a human being.

"You know what sounds like fun?" Russell started.

David looked puzzled.

"Golf," Russell said before swinging his arms in a motion that insinuated he was chipping from about 50 feet from the green. "I could really go for some golf right now. Fuckin' snow. How many more months of this? Six? I wasn't ready for this cold shit."

David slowly shook his head yes. His eyes were wide open, staring at Russell like he was a raving lunatic.

"Russ, it's ten degrees out there," he said. "Let's just stick to our job."

The Hummer reached a spot where policeman and a few TV reporters were gathered and they passed a makeshift blockade to get down to the crime scene. On the fence was a yellow body blanket, draped over the barbed wire. Now Russell was puzzled. Why would a body be on a barbed wire fence?

Sensing Russell's confusion, David chimed in.

"Like I said, man, it doesn't make any sense," he told Russell. "I'll show you."

The two men got out of the vehicle and approached the body. Russell pulled the collar of his pea coat up to protect his neck from the cold wind. Making sure the reporters didn't get photos of the corpse, a few police officers walked over and lined up to form a human fence with their backs to the horrific leftovers.

David lifted the yellow blanket and tossed it on the ground.

Russell grimaced and turned away from the body for a split second, holding his hand over his mouth. It was certainly more horrible than anything he had ever seen, including the images in the autopsy book. A human life had been downsized to nothing more than a slab of meat in a freezer.

Regaining his composure, Russell turned back to the body and got back to his job. He had to collect evidence from it so that the police could remove it. With the TV reporters already in the area, word would soon get out to the general public and people would be coming out to catch a glimpse of the corpse. It happened every time.

There before Russell was the frozen-solid remains of a naked man. The man had his head removed at the neck and was hanging from the barbed wire like a pig that was being roasted over a fire. His innards were all missing as were his hands, feet and genitals. He had a cut from his anus all the way to where his genitals once were and the barbed wire entered through the wound and exited through the hole in his neck. The chest was facing the ground and the man's arms and legs were hanging and frozen in place.

The body truly resembled a pig that had been prepared for a pit rotisserie.

His skin was as white as a glass of milk.

"Have you ever seen skin that white?" David asked as he poked it with his finger.

"Fuckin' Christ," Russell said as he put on his rubber gloves. It didn't take long for him to discover a square patch of skin on the front of the victim that had been sewn back on. The victim was an overweight man and thanks to the laws of gravity, his belly had pulled itself towards the ground as the body slowly froze. On the front of the man's stomach, just above the belly button, was a square of skin about the size of a wallet. It had stitches all around it, suggesting that it had been removed and replaced just before the body froze. It is unclear whether it was done before or after the man died.

Russell got on his knees and took a few photos of the wound.

"What is it?" David asked, peeking over Russell's shoulder.

Russell reached up and touched one of the stitches, tickling it back and forth with his index finger.

"Do you think that's where his organs were removed?" David asked.

Russell shook his head no.

"No. There are no signs that the wound is deeper than the layer of fat," Russell started, pointing at the stitched area. "It almost looks like it doesn't even go deeper than the skin. I've never seen anything like this."

"Why would there be stitches then?" David asked.

Russell took a Swiss Army knife out of his pocket and sawed at the stitches that surrounded the square of skin. With each stitch, he pulled down on the frozen skin, tearing it away from the body. It was quickly apparent that his hunch was right on the money; the wound didn't go deeper than the top layer of skin. It was like peeling the skin off of a good roll of salami.

Just four stitches into the removal, Russell backed away. David looked over at the belly and then at Russell.

"What?" David asked. "What's wrong?"

Before continuing, Russell pulled a pack of cigarettes out of his coat pocket. In a flash he had one of the filter-less Camels hanging from his mouth. He patted himself down, looking for his lighter, realizing that he left it in his car.

"You gotta light?" he asked David. He shook his head no.

"Ah, fuck," Russell said, leaving the unlit cigarette in his mouth.

Russell shook his head as if he were getting rid of morning cobwebs and got back to removing the square of skin, the dry cigarette still dangling from his lips. He saw something under the patch and knew immediately what it was, but didn't tell David. He had to finish the job. The bitter cold wind froze the snot in Richard's nose and irritated his eyes, making it hard to see and forcing him to squint. Before even removing half of the stitches, Russell peeled back as much as he could and reached his knife up into the wound, digging an object from the frozen mass of skin. Finally, after a few tugs and some gentle prying, a plastic driver's license was pulled from the cavity.

"Holy shit," David said as he leaned towards Russell to catch a glimpse of the man on the license. "Who is this guy?"

"William Becker," Russell said as he grabbed the cigarette from his mouth, crushing it and dropping it on the ground.

"I need to know anything and everything about this guy," Russell said to David as the two briskly walked back to the Hummer. "I want to know where he hung out, where he lived, and who he associated with."

By late afternoon, the public had gotten word of the murder after local TV stations began airing the images of a yellow body bag covering something on a desolate country fence. It didn't take long for the murder to catch the national spotlight. No one had ever suffered such a fate.

Willie Becker had disappeared a week earlier but hadn't been reported as missing to the police. It wasn't abnormal for the man to vanish without a trace for weeks at a time. His mother hadn't heard from him in over two months, and without the fact that he missed his appointment with a court-ordered psychiatrist, no one would've known he was gone. He really didn't have any friends, and was unemployed.

Russell paid a visit to the shrink to get an idea of Willie's mindset. So far, no one was coming forward to claim Willie as a friend, making the case difficult.

"What can I do for you honey?" The secretary asked Russell, smiling at him like he was for sale. It couldn't be more obvious that she was interested in him. Russell leaned forward against her desk.

"Actually, I wanted to talk to Dr. Wangle," he said.

"And who may I say is here?" she asked.

"Tell him it's Detective Russell Meeder. I need to speak with him about a patient."

Her manners changed completely.

"Oh," she said. "You're a cop."

Even her sexy southern drawl changed. In fact, the new voice was awfully masculine. *She* was actually a *he*. Russell bit his lip and shook his head. After that, he couldn't even look at the she-male. It was getting more and more difficult to tell the difference with some trannies.

"Dr. Wangle there's a gentleman here to see you," the secretary said into a speaker.

"Send him in," the doctor replied.

As Russell walked towards the doctor's door, he turned to notice the secretary staring at his butt. He sped up and turned down the hallway.

"Did he say anything about someone wanting to kill him?" Russell asked the doctor.

"He never talked about anything of the sort," said Dr. Wangle. "He spent most of our sessions talking about God and his mother. There's really nothing I can tell you detective. This was a pretty standard patient."

"You do realize the man is dead?" Russell asked bluntly.

"Yes. Very unfortunate," Dr. Wangle replied. "I thought I was making progress."

Russell insisted on looking into Willie's psychological records, and had a court order to obtain copies to bring back to the station. On paper, Willie was listed as a pathological liar, was a schizophrenic and was agoraphobic, afraid of being surrounded by a lot of people in a closed environment. Other than that, he was physically clean and healthy.

Willie's mother was living on her own and had been for quite a few years. His father had died years before in a rock climbing accident just west of Boulder. She lived in a modest home, littered with piles of old newspapers that surrounded a grand and dusty organ.

When the police arrived to ask her questions, she did nothing but cry. Her son had been murdered and the fact that he was no longer living was almost more than she could bear. Shortly after hearing of her son's death, she pulled out a massive Bible and began to read passages out loud. Russell showed up late in the afternoon and could hear her sermon from the sidewalk in front of the family home when he first showed up to ask her questions.

"Jesus said to them, 'If you were blind, you would have no sin," she yelled. "But now you say 'We see.' Therefore, your sin remains."

Russell peeked into the home and saw Willie's mother pacing back and forth, holding the bible in her hand, waving her arms around like a televangelist on speed. He knocked, startling the woman.

"Who's there?" she barked. "What do you want?"

"I'm Detective Russell Meeder," he said. "I want to ask you a couple of questions about your son."

She came to the door and opened it, not asking him in, but letting him speak anyway.

"Yes?" she asked.

"I am one of the detectives that saw your son's body," he started. "I'm in charge of the investigation into his murder. I want you to know I am going to do my best to find the person or persons who did this, but I need your help."

Ms. Becker looked down.

"I didn't want to look at the body," she said. "It was horrible. Why did they have to take his head? My poor son will go through eternity without his heart. Where's his heart?"

"Why did you look at the body?" Russell asked, wondering why she was even given the option to view Willie's corpse. Not quite standard procedure in cases involving this much decomposition and mutilation.

"I wanted to make sure it was my baby," she said, breaking down in tears. "I didn't want to look, but I had to. I had to know for sure."

"Would you like to come inside?" Ms. Becker asked. "I'll make some coffee."

Russell agreed and walked into her home noticing the clutter of religious artifacts scattered throughout the living room. Her home smelled of dust and mold. It was hovering around 90 degrees and he immediately began to sweat. Going from freezing cold to blistering hot made him want to pass out.

"You keep it pretty warm in here Ms. Becker," he yelled.

"I don't like to be cold," she said as she poured his coffee in a plain cup.

"Thanks," he said as she returned from the kitchen with a hot cup of coffee. It didn't take more than a few seconds for Russell to get a whiff of the molten liquid. It smelled as if the coffee had been brewing for six months. It had a hickory-smoked scent to it. Like burnt popcorn.

"My Willie was a good boy," she started. "He had a troublesome time after high school and with my husband dying, he just lost it."

"What happened after high school?" Russell asked, pretending to take a sip, trying not to gag in the process. He quickly glanced down at the cup and noticed chunks of burnt coffee flakes floating on top.

"He changed his senior year," she started. "It was as if he became a totally different person. Before that year, he was always laughing and joking around. Shortly after he started that school year, he turned into a very angry boy. It wasn't his fault. Every boy goes through changes."

"Did he ever say why?" Russell asked.

"No. In fact, he would get so upset with me whenever I asked about his mood," she said. "I just backed away and let him be. His father wasn't as tolerant, though. The two got in many arguments . . ."

She stopped and began to tear up.

"What is it?" Russell asked.

"Nothing. It's just hard to talk about," she admitted. "When Willie dropped out, well, that was the end of their relationship. My husband couldn't believe that his own son wasn't going to graduate from high school, and the embarrassment turned into bitterness. They only spoke maybe a half a dozen times before my husband passed. Willie did show up for the funeral, but left before any of us could ask how he was doing."

"How long was it between your son's graduation and your husbands passing?" Russell asked.

"Two, maybe three years," she said.

Russell again lifted the coffee cup to his lips, trying to force himself to take a drink, hoping that he wouldn't dry heave in the process. The smell was awful, almost taking on the scent of burnt dog crap. He couldn't pretend any longer and set it down on a nearby table.

Ms. Becker continued to reminisce, not really helping with the investigation, but allowing Russell to bide his time. He hoped that something would come from her ramblings. Something that could help the case.

As she continued to spew worthless stories of her son's childhood, Russell glanced up at a photo on the wall. It was Willie's father, standing in a field, holding a dead pheasant in his hands. In the background stood a modest and old-fashioned barbed wire fence.

Russell stared at it and began to daydream.

How did the body end up on the barbed wire without having the skin ripped open? The wire traveled all the way through the body cavity, but went in through the rear and came out through the neck. Russell couldn't figure out how it ended up that way. The whole fence section would've had to have been restrung.

Russell spiraled deep into thought and stopped listening to Ms. Becker all together.

The whole case didn't make any sense.

11

Monday

Willie Becker was dead.

The newspaper headlines and saturated coverage by the networks combined to make the murder a media circus to say the least. His name was on the tip of everyone's tongue and seemingly came up every ten minutes in coffee houses all over Denver.

The man who was butchered like an animal.

If the murder wasn't newsworthy enough, the method in which the killing occurred was intriguing to say the least. No one in the public could've seen the photos of Willie's body, however a rough sketch drawn by someone who supposedly saw it in person ran all over the television. People couldn't believe it.

Local man butchered like a steakhouse prime rib, read the headline on Saturday's front page. The story was very descriptive and angered some in its frankness.

Sunday's paper was the keeper. The headline was a little more catching.

Man skewered on fence missing for two months.

Richard smiled when he read the name.

Make no bones about it, you couldn't find a soul on the planet that Richard wished death upon more than Willie. Many nights he fantasized about slitting Willie's throat or putting the barrel of a shotgun in his mouth and slowly squeezing the trigger. A couple of years before he had even attempted to find Mr. Becker in hopes of confronting him for all the pain he caused.

The dreadful scene everyone else remembered from Poudre Canyon couldn't have been more blank for Richard. He managed to block out everything bad that happened that night in regards to the two girls. However, life wasn't all peaches. Memories of that night were faded and pointless. He remembered Willie punching him in the face at some point and recalled the fearsome football players buckling near the campfire, crying like little babies. In hindsight, that part was amusing for Richard.

He didn't remember anything about what he did to Andrea, and had managed to erase her existence from his memory all together.

Willie showed up at Richard's house a week after the rape, drunk and wielding a butcher knife, yelling for Little Dick to come outside. The cops were called but he ran off before they arrived.

Losing Willie as a friend was the last straw for Richard and he fell into a deep state of psychosis that year, opting for Pine Meadows Institute for the Insane instead of a normal life. He was hospitalized for nearly five years, and was released soon after. Although he spent his time on heavy-duty drugs and had occasional hypnosis sessions with doctors, he never spilled the beans about what had happened that fateful night. How could he if he'd erased it all from his memory? The screams and horror all managed to simultaneously evaporate from his brain. The smell of burning flesh and hair didn't put a dent in his psyche.

He honestly couldn't remember what they did to those girls and that's why he was dangerous. Under close supervision by authorities and medical personnel, Richard was allowed to live in society and attempt a normal life. He had an apartment, albeit a run down dive, but didn't have the dependency of his mother anymore. He had no money other than the measly government disability check he received once a month. As was the case his entire life, he had no friends. That was probably best for all potentially involved.

Seeing Willie's name in the obituaries was something that Richard had dreamed about for a long time. He was just slightly bummed that he wasn't there to see him take his last breath. He clipped the obit and tacked it on his pegboard as a trophy of sorts. His nemesis was gone.

KNOCK!

Someone was knocking at his door.

Richard looked through the peephole to find an unfamiliar face standing on the other side. It was a Mormon missionary. Richard's favorite. The religious fanatics lined up in rows and used the shithole apartments as their staging grounds for any and all sales pitches. The poor are suckers when it comes to finding God. Look to them for self-pity and questions about man's existence, namely their own. Richard was too dumb to realize why they were always coming by the apartments but knew well enough that he didn't like them one bit.

He opened the door just the same.

"Hello, sir," the overexcited vermin said. "How are you today?"

Richard scratched his balls and peeked out of the door, looking to his right and left, seeing what else was happening in the hallways. The halls of Township Apartments were painted yellow, and the carpet was bright red and the ketchup and mustard clash always seemed to put Richard in a bad mood when he walked out of his home.

"Might I have a moment of your time?" the missionary asked. "You seem like a mmmpppf . . ."

Richard held his hand up to the man's mouth and covered it.

"Listen," he started. "I don't want to hear about your fucking God. I don't want to see your bullshit pamphlets, nor do I want to smell your anal scented cologne. Now walk back down this hall and forget about this door here because if I see you in front of it again, I am going to cut off your legs and beat you to death with them," he said. The man's eyes were wide and he continued to stand there with Richard's dirty hand on his mouth. "Then we'll see if your God exists."

The man slowly backed away.

Richard looked up with a menacing glare to his eyes. He cracked a smile and began to chuckle.

"Ruuunnnnn," he whispered.

A silent pause filled the corridor and the man was frozen in disbelief.

"Run motherfucker!" He screamed at the top of his lungs. The man dropped his briefcase and sprinted down the hall.

Richard again scratched his balls and walked back into his apartment. The mood swings he experienced as a child were still part of his personality although they were primarily on the grouchy and hateful side. There were no more moments of friendly banter or hope for a promising future. Now, he was either a bastard or a dangerous bastard. It didn't bother most others, though. How could it when he rarely left the house?

The situation with the Mormon was actually quite calm. He was in a good mood.

Willie Becker was dead.

"Seth Owens looks like he's ten years younger, Bob," said Chuck Rogers, the sportscaster for Denver. "He's already got 36 yards on the ground. I don't think he's scrambled with numbers like that for three years."

Seth was now in the waning years of his illustrious professional career.

Having spent seven seasons with Chicago before being traded to Kansas City in '94 where he put in six more, Seth was learning the offense of his third professional team—his hometown Denver Broncos. There was no question in the minds of NFL football fans and those around the sport that Seth was going to end up in the Hall of Fame when his magical career ended.

His numbers spoke volumes: more than 32,000 career yards through the air, 242 touchdowns and an NFL record 3,900 rushing yards all complimented his statistic of 12 consecutive Pro Bowl appearances. But, his crowning achievements were the three championships with two different teams. He brought the trophy to both Chicago and Kansas City prompting the question; which team would he be loyal to when it came down to Hall of Fame time?

The '99 season had brought him stellar numbers as usual, and he led Kansas City to the Divisional title game, but lost to Pittsburgh. His three interceptions in that game didn't do much to help land him an extension with the club as they were looking for a more youthful offense. Taking that into consideration, the team decided that they would do the unthinkable and trade him to division rival, Denver, for a number one and a number three draft pick in the 2001 draft. Denver gladly accepted the trade due to Seth's ties to the area and potential for a few more decent seasons. He could certainly boost ticket sales.

The season was half over, and San Francisco was in town for a battle with Denver on nationally televised Monday Night Football. The 49ers were the defending world champions, and the game was supposed to be a blowout in San Francisco's favor.

Denver took an early fourteen to nothing lead in the first quarter behind a bootleg touchdown pass from Seth to tight end Spencer Buckley.

With the pressure mounting from the weak side, Seth was forced to scramble early and often in the game, something that he hadn't done in years. What San Francisco was finding out, as well as Denver and their fans, was that Seth still had the ability to move in the pocket. It appeared as if his career had taken a positive turn after all.

Most quarterbacks who are traded that late in their career are left for dead, used primarily to pass on their knowledge to the younger understudy. Struggling between coaching and playing, the aging quarterbacks usually last one or two more seasons before throwing in the towel. Seth wasn't ready to do that yet.

The offense huddled up and Seth looked around at the young faces that greeted him. He was starting to feel like an old man.

"Okay fellas. I want to run a thirty . . . crosshair . . . split-forty-two . . . on two," he said with the utmost confidence. "If the backside pressure builds, I'm going to find either Jackson or Stuart deep."

He thought of Willie. His old friend was dead.

The other players looked to Seth as an idol. Some of them hadn't even been old enough to play football when Seth first donned a professional uniform. When he gave an order, they listened. That was something rare in the world of modern sports. Usually it was the old players who were ignored the most.

One problem Seth faced early on in the summer was the high altitude. It had been 15 years since he had to breathe such small amounts of oxygen while playing football. Now, he was a local legend who had returned to his home state of Colorado with the lungs of a gnat.

Seth was facing a tough third-and-ten situation from the 36-yard-line with under a minute left in the first half.

"Blue-forty two! Blue-forty two! Set. Hut! Hut!"

The ball was snapped into Seth's hands and he dropped back. His offensive line was doing an excellent job keeping the oncoming 49er defense at bay, but his receivers were blanketed. Deciding that waiting for the receivers to get open on their own was a futile endeavor, he did what he had done so many times before, he started running. Seeing this maneuver, the defense shifted. He had burned them enough with his feet.

The receivers were left open and Seth spotted Chip Jackson wide open down field. Hurling the ball through the air, the only thing between the ball and the end zone was the wide-open receiver. Simply having to open up his hands in full stride, Jackson caught the ball and glided into the end zone, putting Denver up 21-0. It was certainly a time to rejoice in the career of the great Seth Owens.

The team went into the locker room at the half with a huge lead and a newfound confidence in their offense. It had been awhile since Denver had a quarterback that could lead them on the field. Seth arrived at his locker to find a police officer standing by it.

"Mr. Owens?" the policeman said. "We're here about the package. Can we have it?"

"Now? I'm in the middle of a game," Seth said, slightly irritated.

"All due respect, this is a little more important, sir," said the policeman.

Seth let loose a timid sigh of relief. He had received a disturbing package in the mail and told the trainer about it. Due to the fact that he had an important game to play and the fact that he had received numerous strange items in the past, Seth didn't call the cops himself. The trainer knew better than to sweep it under the rug.

"It's right here," Seth said, handing the box to the officer.

The policeman lifted the box and opened the lid, revealing a jar that rested comfortably inside. He grabbed the metal lid of the jar and lifted it from the box. Inside, the jar was filled with a bright orange liquid. Three items tossed and turned with the waves of fluid.

"I don't even want to know what the hell that is in there," Seth said. "Whatever it is, I don't like it. In fact, I have a pretty good idea of what that is, I just don't want to open it to find out, you know? I just don't want to think of a reason why someone would send me a jar with shit in it. Maybe it's a metaphor for something else. Or, maybe I'm just lucky enough to have fans that care enough to send the very best. Could be a bitter Chiefs fan. You know how they are."

"I wouldn't worry about it. I'd say it's a Raiders fan. We'll be in touch with you," the cop said as he walked away. "Oh and Seth, good luck in the second half. I've got a few bucks on this game."

Seth sat by himself near his locker as the team buzzed around the coach. He didn't feel like a part of them when they weren't on the field. He was never a good locker room guy and didn't pretend to be. The only time he felt comfortable around the guys was when he was wearing his helmet, walking on the grass towards midfield.

He glanced up and remembered. Hanging from a nail was a necklace that was oh so familiar to his eyes. It was a reminder. The necklace had been with him everywhere he went as a professional football player, as a constant reminder that he could never be too happy. He had even carried the thing with him to the championship games. The necklace once graced the neck of Alexis Hall, until he pulled it off of her charred, dead remains.

The night of October 4th, 1983, still resonated in his mind and in a way he lost something that night.

Everyone lost something.

Alexis lost her life. Andrea's family lost a daughter and a sister. Seth and the crew all lost their innocence, or at least whatever innocence they had left.

Now one of the men who had carried out the crime was gone to meet his ultimate judge and jury. Seth hoped that Willie wasn't suffering in the depths of hell because eventually, he knew he would have to join him. He had been thinking about his fallen comrade quite a bit in the days leading up to the game. Never in his life had he felt as old as he did the day Willie died. He was too young.

The thought of him being butchered was frightening beyond belief. The two weren't really acquaintances anymore and Seth had no idea what kinds of people Willie chose to hang out with. He assumed Willie got caught up in a bad drug deal. That's the only way he could've ended up murdered and displayed in such a way. Whatever the reason, Seth thought of his former friend.

"Seth!" Coach Woody yelled after he asked the star quarterback a question, receiving silence as a response.

"You in there buddy?" Coach asked. "I asked you if you could come over here and participate in our game plan. You think you can handle that old man?"

Seth got up and snuck into the group of men. The quarterback wished that he would've gotten in touch with Willie before he had died. The two lived in the same city, yet not even a phone call was shared.

He was usually pretty withdrawn during the month of October for obvious reasons. In fact, he sometimes felt that his incredible career turned out the way it did because of his quiet, withdrawn personality during that time of year. He was able to concentrate on football more than off the field interests, like girls and partying. Seeing the leaves change colors would make his heart race as he always thought back to that night and what he'd done.

"We've got a comfortable lead," Coach started. "But, we need to find a way to keep our heads up. We need to continue to bury this team until they submit. Owens, I need you to keep playing like there's no fucking tomorrow. Don't get complacent. Don't get too comfortable with your performance. You are the reason why we are where we are and I'd like to keep it that way."

Seth nodded to the coach. He was trying his hardest to stay focused.

"You offensive lineman. Good job protecting Seth. Keep it up. Defensive lineman, you need to create the inside pressure. They are going to eventually find a way to pick us apart if you continue to give that quarterback so much time."

The group sat silent, listening to everything the coach had to say.

"Now let's get back out there and put those babies to bed," Coach finished. "Now gather round."

The group of highly paid men gathered in a circle, placing their hands in the middle.

"ONE, TWO, THREE, WIN!" they yelled.

The team again took the field, ready to finish the game and the defending champs. The contest was being played under the stars and the stadium lights in front of a national audience, something that rejuvenated Seth as he returned to the playing field. He was living a dream and had been for 15 years. His peers had all moved on to their careers, while he remained a kid playing a game for a living and getting paid a ton to do it.

The kickoff was booted sky high by the Denver kicker and the San Francisco return man knelt down in the end zone for a touchback.

Seth sat alone on the bench, waiting for his chance to get back out on the field to extend the already ridiculous lead.

Nothing bad entered his mind.

He was content.

For a moment.

Like a bolt of lightning sent from the depths of hell, a flash of light beamed into his eyes. Red and revolting, he thought for a moment that his life in the fast lane had come to an end and the devil was coming to claim his soul. It was a red laser, coming from the stands across the field.

Looking directly ahead of himself into the crowd, Seth spotted the origin of the beam, most likely coming from a laser pointer. A tool used primarily to irritate others, the laser pointer was soon becoming a hit with vigilant sports fans who felt the need to mess with opponents. If there was one thing Seth despised, it was those wretched things. He had been tormented by them before in recent seasons and was growing increasingly pissed off. The more aggressive he got, the more people wanted to fuck with him. The fact that it was happening at a home game was perplexing and even more disappointing.

Again the light flashed right in his eyes, this time irritating the local legend so badly, he pushed the water bucket over in a fit of rage.

"God damn it!" he yelled as he launched himself from his spot on the bench. Gesturing towards the other end of the stadium, he was letting the person know that he wasn't going to take their shit. He motioned for the culprit to come down on the field as if it was possible.

"What the fuck is going on with you?" asked Assistant Coach Gunther.

"Someone's got a fuckin' laser pointer and they are shining it right in my God damn face!" Seth yelled as he pointed to the other side of the field. The veins in his forehead were protruding and the sweat began to bead from his face. "I can't get away from the fuckin' thing."

The two men looked over towards the spot where the light had originated the first time.

Nothing.

Time ticked by and the action continued on the field, but the two men looked to the crowd for any sign of the laser pointer.

Nothing.

"Seth, I don't know what to tell you," Coach Gunther said. "It looks like whoever it was, they were just fucking with you. Try to calm down. We need you to stay focused. Don't worry about what the crowd is doing. Worry about this game. Stare at the ground if you have to."

Seth shook his head and returned to his seat, this time staring intensely at the crowd, waiting for his chance to see what section the light was going to come from the next time.

Nothing.

The laser pointer was about to be history as San Francisco got in formation to punt the ball back to Denver. Seth was going to take his place on the field again, primed and ready to score yet another touchdown.

Coach Woody was into trick plays and even with a commanding 21-0 lead he wanted to set the tempo again for the second half. He sent in a play that called for a bootleg shot to the end zone on first down. Seth welcomed the opportunity to show his stuff again.

"Okay, I need a belly-up . . . cross-seventy-one . . . boot toss . . . on two, ready break!"

The Denver offense took their spot on the line and got ready for another test against a reasonably good defense—so good in fact, they won the previous championship with those same eleven guys playing on the other side of the ball. It's rare to go into a consecutive season with no player turnover, especially if you just won the Super Bowl.

"Blue, forty-two. Blue, forty-two. Set. Hut. Hut." Seth yelled.

The offensive players scrambled to run their routes and do what was expected of them.

Seth? Well, he was brought in to win ball games and not screw up. That's exactly what was expected from him when he chucked the ball downfield into the arms of the again wide open Chip Jackson. This time the defender had fallen down during the route, leaving Jackson wide open for his second easy score of the game.

Denver was up by four touchdowns to start off the second half. Not bad for a team that was picked to lose by a dozen points by the bookies in Vegas. Seth had done his job for the day, and was pulled by Coach Woody for the rest of the game.

"Seth, I think you're done for tonight," the coach said as he patted Seth on the butt. "Go ahead and relax. You've earned it big fella."

Seth had mixed emotions about being taken out of the game. He felt that he should've been able to just stay in and keep pounding away at the defending champs. On the other hand, he was exhausted and his legs were about to give out. The game was ten times more physical than anything he had done over the previous months.

The bench was inviting and mostly empty, allowing Seth to pick just about any spot that he wanted to sit and look over some of the photos that were being taken of the game. He wanted to see what formation the 49ers had actually been in on the last touchdown. Jackson just seemed too wide open. Even though Seth had spotted the defender who had slipped and fallen to the ground, he couldn't understand why the safety wasn't in the picture.

If you poke a dog with a stick, it gets irritated and edgy. Take the stick and poke harder and it will attack. Once again, agitation replaced his joy.

As before, but with more annoyance behind it, the red dot wiggled its way back and forth on the photo in his hands. The source of the laser was behind him now. He turned himself around and looked towards the stands, hoping to catch the tiniest glimpse of the asshole.

Because the star quarterback showed interest in a section of the stadium, the sea of people were whipped into a frenzy trying to convince him to come over and sign autographs. Flashbulbs were popping off and he concentrated on trying to see among the madness.

Pop! Pop! The bulbs wouldn't stop flashing.

"Seth! Seth! Over here!" people yelled in a mass of chaos trying to get him to walk over.

The laser again went off from the middle of the masses, shining directly into his eyes, but from where? From whom? He didn't know what to do, or how to react. All he knew was that his blood was boiling and he was about to freak out. And, now to top the whole thing off, his eyes hurt from the direct blast that he had just taken from the asshole with the light.

In hindsight, what Seth did next was most definitely a bad idea, even considering what he was going through. It was what he thought was best at the time. Without thinking about the ramifications that would await him, he lifted his arm in the air and extended his middle finger, hoping that the man with the pointer would get the drift.

"Fuck you, you pussy!" he yelled with the gesture still pointing sky high.

Silence replaced cheers as the crowds of people that were excited to see him turning around, now saw him as the asshole that had just flipped them the bird. They hadn't done a thing to encourage this behavior and he was showing them that he was just a prick with a good arm.

He forgot a cardinal rule in sports—don't piss off the home crowd.

People started throwing their beers and cups at the Denver bench towards Seth. Even people who didn't witness the gesture got involved. Nothing attracts a crowd like a crowd. It doesn't take much to get a group of drunken football fans in the mood to kill someone on the team they are rooting for.

Coach Woody turned around when he heard the crowd's attitude shifting. He hadn't called a bad play or anything, which made it all the more strange that people were booing. What he saw was his star quarterback dodging a barrage of debris being thrown at him.

Beer cups.

Programs.

Hats.

Batteries.

"What the fuck?" Coach muttered to himself before handing his headset to the assistant coach. "Take over for me."

Coach Woody ran over to Seth, who was still staring into the crowd, hoping that the man with the laser pointer had one more in him. He was oblivious to the angry crowd. All he needed was a glimpse. This time he was going to spot him.

"Damn it son, what are you doing?" Coach said as he spun Seth around. "What the hell did you do to get them so riled up?"

"Someone has a fuckin' laser pointer!" Seth yelled, pointing to the unruly crowd. "They keep shining it in my face. I'm losing it, man."

"God damn it!" coach yelled. "Look, go ahead and get in the locker room and watch the game from there. If we need you to come back, I'll send someone for you. You had a good night, don't fuck it up."

It was a horrible way to represent himself in his first season back in Denver. Seth had managed to excite, piss off, and alienate the locals, all in one night. And it wasn't even his fault. All he wanted to do was find the person who was trying to blind him and get him to stop.

He ran to the locker room with a towel over his head, chased away by the boos of more than 75,000 fans. The last time he was covered in that much beer was back in college at a party in which he swam in a pool of it.

As he jogged off the field towards the locker room in the south stands, the crowd continued to boo him and yell things like "Go back to Kansas City, you punk!," and "I hear the Raiders are looking for help, you bum!" He didn't realize it at the time, but he was on the big screen at the moment he flipped everyone off. Seeing the crowd getting all excited prompted the Monday Night camera crew to focus on the quarterback to see what he was doing to get them so excited. The fans and the nation watching couldn't have gotten a better shot of him flipping off the people in the stands. It was an unfortunate situation for a person who was having such a great game. Just as unfortunate for the crew filming the live TV show.

Denver continued to play well without their star quarterback and won the game 35-3, owing most of it to Seth, their now controversial leader.

"There's no surprise as to who is getting my game ball," Coach Woody proclaimed to the room of sweaty, tired men. "Seth Owens has done a lot for the sport, and for the cities of Chicago and Kansas City. Now, it appears that he is on his way to helping out our team and our fine city."

The room was filled with applause and Seth reluctantly accepted the game ball from coach, his mind on so many other issues.

"And . . . and one more thing. Quiet down for a sec," Coach continued. "Seth experienced a situation with a fan that apparently had a laser pointer. If any of you experience that in the future, let me or one of the other coaches know right away. That is illegal as all hell, and I'm not going to allow it to continue. He almost got himself hurt tonight because of that shit. Next time, I'll let the ref know and we'll stop the damn game until the person is removed from the stadium."

The players all acknowledged the coach and went about their business of getting changed and ready to leave the ball park. Seth sensed some animosity from a few of his teammates because of the whole situation but could do nothing more than ignore it.

Seth wasn't your average quarterback. He had the clout to get the coach riled up enough to stick up for his actions. Hell, if Seth was unhappy, then the rest of the team was unhappy. He was the captain that everyone followed. It was truly odd to see a quarterback with such high regards actually hanging out in the weight room, let alone after a nationally televised game. Most QBs of his caliber avoided anything having to do with training or practice. They showed up when it mattered. He frequently stayed at least two hours after each home game to lift weights and soak in the hot tub. Since the team won easily and no one had suffered an injury, he was going to have the weight room all to himself.

No reporters, no fans, and no teammates.

"Hey, you comin' out tonight?" asked Jackson, Seth's apparent new go-to-guy. He had no urge to hit the town with the boys and didn't have time to anyway, relaying that fact to Jackson with a shake of his head.

"Naw. I got some things to do around here," he said. "I've got to do my workout."

Jackson gave Seth five and walked away.

As Seth worked out, he watched *SportsCenter*, hoping to see if he was given the credit he deserved. He got that and more. He was solely responsible for putting so many points on the board against the world champs. He was solely responsible for bringing together a team that would have been dreary otherwise. He was solely responsible for taking care of business in a fashion that warranted his paycheck.

He was solely responsible for looking like an arrogant asshole.

"Seth Owens seemed like a magician at times and a jackass at other times," the anchor said as they showed a clip of him passing for a touchdown before showing another clip of him flipping off the crowd, his fingers blurred out for TV.

Seth buried his head in his hands. He was already on people's bad sides. It was one thing to be ostracized in front of the home folks; it was another to be pointed out on national TV.

"How the hell did they film me flipping off the crowd?" he said to himself.

Seth wasn't concerned so much with the reputation that he was going to acquire after this event, rather what the children that followed him were going to think after seeing his irresponsible display.

For years he was in charge of leading various events that benefited the kids. Time and time again he witnessed other men in the same profession trip and fall in their personal lives. Teammates that drove drunk or did drugs, those were the guys that he was glad he wasn't. Although he was well aware that flipping off a crowd wasn't as bad as being caught driving drunk, it still didn't do him good in the minds of the children that idolized him. He also thought about his poor mother who was surely going to be disappointed as well.

Being a veteran of the game, Seth had been through ups and downs before and had come out on top each and every time and this circumstance would be no different. He would beat the reputation that he was surely going to be given.

Pumping his legs round and round, he rode the stationary bike like he was in the Tour de France. Nothing gets a person's mind off of something bothersome than a good workout. Sweat began to bead on his forehead which gave him the drive to go harder and faster. He was meticulous when it came to training and when it came to the way he took care of his body. Being 36 years old and starting at quarterback for a professional club required more attention to the body than it used to.

You didn't have to remind him of his age. He knew all too well. He wasn't your normal 36-year-old, having played football his entire life, but he still felt like he needed to put that extra time in the weight room. His legs ached a little more often, his back was sore a little longer into the week and his throwing arm was a little more tender as the seasons progressed.

He was getting old.

Peddling away, he glanced up at the clock. He had been working out for more than two hours. The locker room was still filled with the aroma of sweat and cologne. The once bustling room was empty and damp, but to Seth, it felt like home.

He took an extra long shower, since no one was waiting in line to use the stall. The water cascaded off of his back as he leaned against the wall deep in thought. All of the stress and workout that he had endured in the day was being released with the water that flowed down the drain.

Naked, he walked to the center of the room and stood on the Denver logo that decorated the carpet. Looking all around him, he smiled in a moment of reflection. He was the star that shone brightest over the city of Denver.

It had been the strangest feeling being back home, playing in front of the old fans that he knew and loved in college. Playing in Chicago and Kansas City brought him new experiences away from Colorado, but it never filled the void left when he had to leave the Rocky Mountains.

Of course, he had no choice but to try to leave the state. Too many flashbacks to that awful night of October fourth corrupted his brain. Too many images of the horror that ensued that fateful evening consumes his every thought in the months that followed. It was all *his* fault.

As was the case with every game he had played since killing Alexis, Seth spent his last moments in the locker room reflecting on what he had done. That was the only way he would accept it and move on. Like a confessional to himself, God and, hopefully, Alexis.

Thinking back to the camping trip brought regret and tears but it also brought the reminder of the terrible thing that he had done that night to another human being.

SLAP!

Seth hit himself in the face.

"Stop thinking about it you asshole," he thought to himself. "It's over."

Remembering that night was nothing more than a reminder of his weakest moment. He was a strong man, and a good one at that, but that one bout with temptation got him a life sentence of regret in his mind. Nothing could take away the pain that he felt. Nothing except for football and his inevitable date with death. It wasn't so much that he ended the life of another human being, or that he raped her in the process, it was that he put himself in a position to possibly ruin his own chances at success.

With football on his mind day in and day out since the attack, he had the perfect excuse to forget about Alexis and Andrea. The only person that he even remained in touch with every so often was Charles. All of the other guys that were there that evening didn't exist to Seth anymore.

He didn't want them to.

His presence in the locker room would've been God-like to an average football fan. He was a superstar in every sense of the word. He received hundreds of pieces of fan mail each week, all with autograph requests. But, he was merely a man, not some superhero like so many people had coined him. What would the world think of him had they known his past?

He patted himself dry and put some clothes on, ready to leave the stadium and head home for some well-needed rest. Knowing the media, he was going to have to explain his actions in the next couple of days, so he needed all the stamina he could muster to deal with those idiots.

On the way out of the stadium, he pitched the necklace into the garbage. It was time to move on and forget about the past. Alexis wasn't his problem anymore. Any trouble that he caused to her family was more than made up for by his inner anguish all those years, or so he convinced himself as he symbolically cut ties with his guilt.

The parking lot was bare, the concrete lit up by the seemingly endless number of street lights that resided in the gigantic lot. He stopped and gazed back at the stadium. The grounds crew was busy trying to finish up the garbage removal between seats. Seth never realized that so many people were employed to clean the trash up after the game, or that it took so long.

His eyes continued to wander and he looked up at the stars. It was a beautiful night with a calm breeze. The snow began to melt earlier in the day although it still covered the grass around the stadium. He was home. What had been an enjoyable moment of reflection turned upside down just as quickly as it arrived.

SCREECH!

A car that had been parked just outside of the main entrance sped out of the darkness and came to a screeching halt next to Seth.

"What the fuck is your problem?" he yelled as he walked closer to the driver's side door, ready to let his anger back out in the form of kicking someone's ass. The windows were tinted, making it difficult to see the person that had practically run over him.

"Get out of the car!" Seth yelled, smacking his fist on the window.

The vehicle stayed in place, the engine idling, but not a peep came from the driver.

Seth stared into the blackness of the car windows. This person was about to really piss him off.

"Get out of the . . ."

The window rolled down.

More and more the identity of the crazy driver became apparent to Seth.

"I'll be damned," he said as he dropped his bag to the ground.

There before him sat an old acquaintance. Someone whom he hadn't seen in years; not since his days in high school at least. For all he knew, this person that sat before him could've disappeared off the face of the planet eighteen years before and he wouldn't have been the wiser. The driver turned to look at Seth, staring into his brown eyes. Between those eyes glowed a shiny red dot from the laser sight of a pistol that rested in the hands of the familiar person and it was pointed directly at Seth's head.

"Get in," the driver said.

Seth was shocked. Was he being kidnapped?

"C'mon, you got to be kiddin'," he said, mustering a smug laugh. "Put that gun away. You only kiddin' right? Was that you in the stands tonight? You really pissed me off man, but that's cool."

Click.

Seth could see that the driver meant business when the hammer of the gun was pulled back. His only choice was to get in and hope that it was all a sadistic joke.

The car door slammed as the sports legend got in the car. The two drove off into the distance leaving nothing behind but Seth's brand new Lexus and a streak of burned rubber on the concrete.

The lights remained on all through the night.

And the Lexus remained safe.

12

Images of the frozen mess left on the Roberts Ranch were strewn out on Russell's desk. Earlier in the day a secretary had come in to offer a cup of coffee, saw the photos and hurried out of the room shaking her head. For some reason, women seemed to turn and run whenever they were exposed to his world.

Russell however, was enthralled by the images. He wanted to find the person who did such a horrible act and figure out how it could be possible. No one in their right mind, no sane human being with any shred of compassion or sense of right and wrong, could have done it.

The flesh was so white. Lifeblood missing. Seeing the remains of a human in such a state was a constant reminder of man's mortality. You might feel like you're on top of the world or even invincible because you're healthy and able to do anything you want, but at the end of the day, we're all just chunks of meat. Although the body was well frozen by the time Russell saw it, he knew it must have been an unspeakable mess when the man was gutted.

The hardest part of the case thus far had been the lack of acquaintances to Willie Becker. It seemed like the man just disappeared from society after high school. Even his mother was pretty useless for information. The guy was just an overweight bum who apparently ended up pissing off the wrong person.

Russell reached across his desk and grabbed a copy of the 1982 Carver High School yearbook. Willie's mother loaned it to him to help in the investigation. Just like everything else in his search, the book was of little help. Willie was a junior and only had two photos printed. His main photo was somewhat hard to see since someone had scratched out parts of his face years before. But, the other photo had Willie standing between two friends, their arms draped over his shoulders. All three of them making the same stupid faces most high schoolers make in candid yearbook shots.

It was the kind of photo that used to make Russell uncomfortable. Seeing someone in the prime of their youth, happy and care free, knowing what their fate had in store, was hard to look at in those early days of investigating murders. Willie was completely joyous in the photo with the other two guys. Now he was dead. When Russell was a young detective, he would get a little existential when it came to these types of cases. Now, it was just a matter of finding justice for the person who was wronged in such a horrible way.

A cigarette burned aimlessly, teetering on the lip of the ashtray that rested on the edge of Russell's desk. He took a drag when he first lit it, but forgot about it after that. The ashen tip was nearly as long as the original cigarette and the burning butt that remained eventually slid off the ashtray and rolled into a nearby trashcan. Seconds passed and a plume of smoke gently billowed from lit papers as the cigarette ignited the garbage.

"Shit," Russell said as he blew on the microscopic fire.

KNOCK! KNOCK!

"Fuckin' Christ," Russell said. "Hold o . . ."

Before he could even finish, the door opened and in walked an unfamiliar woman. She stood about five-nine and wore a man's sport coat. Her black hair was tied in a bun and a pair of thick black glasses adorned her face.

"Detective Meeder?" she asked.

"Yeah?" he responded, somewhat agitated at being interrupted, his heart still racing from the near fire in his garbage can.

She looked as if she was going to say something but stopped. Confused, she motioned towards his smoky trashcan.

"Do we need a fire extinguisher?" she asked, sarcastic tone included.

"No," he snapped. "I dropped my cigarette. What is it you wanted? I don't want any coffee."

She scoffed and her face turned serious.

"Actually, Detective, I'm here to introduce myself and discuss our working relationship," she started.

"What relationship?" he asked waving the charred papers in the air. Little specks of black flakes fluttered to the ground and the smoke continued to fill the air. "I don't even know who you are. And anyway, most relationships I've had start with a little foreplay and we haven't gotten that far sweetie. I don't even know your name."

"Okay, smart ass," she said. "I am here to let you know that I am going to be your new partner . . ."

"Alright, back to the whole relationship thing," he interrupted with a condescending snicker. "In order for you to be my partner, we have to get to know each other first, then foreplay, then relationship. You seem to be having trouble with that part, doll. You're jumping way too far ahead for me. You see, I'm really not that kind of clingy person who needs to hop from 'hello' straight to marriage, you know?"

The woman slammed her fist on his desk.

"Will you shut up? Detective Meeder, my name is Detective Wendy Valdez. I am a cop *just like you*. I have just as much experience doing this job as *you*. And, although I have tits, I don't feel like that should have any bearing on whether or not I'm qualified to, what is it you're doing again, eating Fritos and burning garbage?"

"Whoa, easy there sweet cheeks," he said. "Don't get your panties in a bunch now. Or do you wear panties? Perhaps boxers?" He was making a joke in reference to her man coat.

He still had no clue why she was standing in his office, talking down to him like an unapproving mother. Why did she barge into his office to begin with? Wendy turned red with anger.

"Okay you fuck," she said. "I could end you right now. I could easily press sexual harassment charges for what you're doing. No. Instead I'm going to stick with this '*marriage*' that I've been forced to participate in because I'm a professional, unlike you."

"Look, what are you talking about candy cane?" he asked. "I don't know you, and frankly, you're not my type anyway." At that point, Russell began to realize that she wasn't there to pick up on him. That didn't mean he would stop harassing her. It's the little things in life that made each day worth waking up for.

"Russell, we're partners," she said. "You know, cops that go to the same places together. Did you ever see '*48 Hours*?' Well, I'm Eddie Murphy and you're apparently Nick Nolte." She began to talk to him like he was a baby in a crib. "We get in the car and drive around and ask questions, *together*." She even made the motion of turning a steering wheel and driving.

"Sorry, honey buns," he started. "I don't have a partner and I don't need one."

This time Wendy laughed condescendingly as Russell lit up another cigarette.

"Call me one of those names again," she challenged. "I dare you. Just one more name and I'll shove this boot so far up your ass, you'll be tasting the shit from the last guy I kicked in the hole."

Russell leaned back in his chair, realizing the predicament he was facing. He took a deep drag on the cigarette and exhaled, the smoke causing his eyes to water a little.

"Why are we partners?" he asked, this time showing tiny signs of maturity.

"You ever heard of Seth Owens?" she asked.

"Sure, I guess," he replied. "Plays for Chicago right?"

"Uh, about ten years ago," she said. "No. He plays just a few miles from where we are standing, right here in Denver. How can you live in this city and act as a public servant and not know that he's the Broncos' quarterback? It is blatantly apparent that you have no clue about this guy or football. Regardless, he's missing. The man is missing."

"So, a lot of people are missing," Russell said. "How long has he been missing? And what the fuck does he have to do with me? And, more importantly, what the fuck does he have to do with you? And, why the fuck are we having this conversation? Get to the point, sister."

"Since Monday night," she said.

"Since Monday night what?" he asked.

"He's been missing since Monday night," she repeated with agitation. She paused to cool herself down a little bit now that she knew just how big of an asshole Russell really was. She'd been warned of his sometimes cantankerous attitude but was still having trouble getting past the first wave of it.

"So that would be what? Like six days ago?"

"Yes," she answered. "Good job."

"Big deal. That still doesn't answer my question as to why I now have to play babysitter. I can figure out these things on my own. I don't need some rookie brown nose to drag me into situations I don't want to be in. What can you do to help me on the case I'm working on now? What does it have to do with your case?" Russell snapped.

"Well, first off, it's right there in front of your face numb nuts," she said.

"Where?" he asked.

She reached over and pointed to the photo of Willie, Seth and Reggie in the Carver High School yearbook.

"Seth is the guy on the right. He's missing," she said. "You're boy Willie is in the middle, right? Is it a coincidence or actual news that these two guys were once close friends? Why was Willie carved up like an Easter ham, and why do I think Seth is getting there as we speak?"

Russell sat stunned.

"So that's Seth Owens, huh?" he muttered, looking at the photo. "Who's the guy next to him?"

CLICK.

"*Lose ten pounds in two days using the all new, Trojan Miracle Candy. Just eat a piece of candy when it's time to have a meal and . . .*"

CLICK.

"*You are the father . . .*"

CLICK.

"*Can I buy a vowel? . . .*"

CLICK.

"*In a bizarre twist of fate, NFL star and local sports legend Seth Owens has been reported missing by his family and friends, this after a nationally televised tirade on Monday that got the sports star fined fifteen thousand dollars by the league office. He hasn't been heard from in the six days since the game. Owens' brand new Lexus was discovered Tuesday morning, parked in front of the stadium, with no signs of a struggle present. The team and his family are asking anyone with information on his whereabouts to contact the police immediately."*

"Fuckin' Seth," Reggie said as he threw the remote down on his coffee table. "Always tryin' to be *the* news."

Reggie hadn't heard from the star quarterback in quite some time and was actually a little concerned when he first heard the story. After thinking about it, Reggie wasn't convinced that Seth was actually missing.

After the episode on *Monday Night Football*, Seth was probably hanging out with a friend or someone who wasn't telling anyone about his whereabouts. The guy wouldn't just disappear off the face of the earth. He was one of the most recognizable athletes in all of professional sports, and wouldn't be hard to spot anywhere in Denver.

Reggie got up and walked to the kitchen to grab another beer. Along the way, he scratched some lint out of his bellybutton and tossed it onto the floor, flicking his fingers to discard the useless fuzz. The three-time All State running back could've followed the same path as Seth, but chose to create his own instead. Who knew that giving up football would spell the end of Reggie's short climb to the top? The promise he had shown during his junior and senior years gave everyone around him the impression that he would go on to a huge school out of state and on to the pros.

He couldn't do that.

The past few days had been hard for Reggie, and had opened horrible memories that he had closed long ago. So many years had gone by and yet he still managed to think about it.

Haunting images of Alexis' deathly stare clouded his mind. Shortly after the murder, he found it impossible to think about schoolwork and playing football, and was soon out of school all together. In fact, out of the five guys that participated in the crime that night, only two graduated from high school—Seth and Charles. The others just dropped as time went by. Reggie and Willie were seniors and didn't last through the spring. Richard was pulled from school shortly after the attack and placed in a local psychiatric hospital. The men all remained in northern Colorado, but none of them kept in touch with each other. Seeing any of the five guys brought back memories that were so painful, they could trigger a confession, and they had all agreed not to say a word. They all swore on their lives. The best thing any of them could do was walk their own path alone. When any of the men would wake in the middle of the night to the horror of what they did, there would be no phone calls to the other guilty ones. It was a punishment of solitude. Any kind of friendship that they shared before the horror was gone and was put on the backburner. Friends aren't worth getting thrown in jail for life, or possibly executed. If you somehow manage to pretend like something horrible didn't happen, it can sometimes disappear from your guilty conscience.

After dropping out, Reggie thought that his clout in school would allow him to at least get a decent job. Who wouldn't hire a famous athlete from the city? He found out who wouldn't and that amounted to him eventually filtering through the system of fast food joints until he found a home with Denver Waste Management driving a garbage truck. It wasn't too bad a gig. After all, he started out as a garbage handler, hanging from the back of the truck, picking up and throwing filthy waste from the dumpsters of society. Staying with it and doing a good job along the way, earned him the coveted position of driver after just three years on the job. It takes most people at least five. There was still above average potential in the guy, it just didn't lead him where most people thought it would.

Standing in the dark kitchen, the light reflected onto his skin-tight dingy tank top. It stretched agonizingly across the girth that had accumulated on his midsection. Drops of food that didn't quite hit the floor peppered the upper part of the shirt but he stopped caring about stuff like that years ago. Grabbing his beverage, Reggie walked over to his sink and blew a load of snot out of his nostril, into the basin.

Outside the snow had begun to fall again. Just when he thought the weather was going to brighten up, shit hit the fan once more. He couldn't complain, at least he wasn't still throwing garbage.

On his table rested a newspaper from the week prior. The headline read: *Man skewered on fence missing for two months.*

It was good old Willie.

Here was another example of how someone had cut off all contact with Reggie to the point where he got updates on their life through the media.

Despite the not-so-happy split, he felt a wave of sadness and nausea as he read over the article again. Willie was a good friend at one point in his life and the two shared many great times together. Thankfully, Reggie didn't have to read the kinds of gory details Russell was working with or even the real condition in which the body was discovered. The article just said he was butchered and murdered.

Reggie was a lost soul. He had reached that age when you climb deep into your 30s and start to feel like you still know the people you went to school with as if you were all suddenly transported back to that time. Reading stories about them, he felt like he knew Willie and Seth in a way someone knows a person they just talked to the day before. Truth was, he knew nothing about them.

He decided to skip Willie's funeral, even though the thought of going did cross his mind. What would he say when he got there? Who would he talk to? Would the old gang be there, staring at him like a guilty jury of older and wiser killers? There was just no way of knowing what awaited him with such a morbid event. Besides, he had seen enough death in his life to last two lifetimes.

None of it mattered, because he didn't go. He didn't give them the satisfaction of pinning the murder on him. He didn't kill Alexis. She was dead when he climbed on top of her. At least that's what Seth said. Shortly after the rape, Seth confessed to the others that he had hit her and that she probably died within minutes. Reggie even managed, at times, to silence the voices in his head by convincing himself that he never actually raped her. You can't rape the dead, right? *Is necrophilia even a crime*? he'd ask himself.

"Hello?" a voice rang from the front door. "Dad are ya home?"

"Yeah. In the kitchen, son," Reggie barked.

The one thing that kept Reggie motivated and living was the existence of his 15-year-old son Jared. The two didn't really spend much time together in the years before Jared turned ten. All that was in the past.

Jared's mother wasn't what you would call, a "big fan," of Reggie's and tried to keep the father and son apart early on in the relationship. A court order initially opened up the gates of communication between the two and at that point both of them were ready to get to know each other. Since he lived a mere ten blocks away, Jared would occasionally ride his bike to visit his old man.

"Did you ride in this weather?" Reggie asked, scratching his ass cheek in the process. "Must have been real cold."

"What else is new?" Jared asked. "How you been pops?"

Reggie grabbed his lower back and grimaced.

"Well, other than this damn back pain, and my knee is startin' to go out, and I been havin' a terrible time with this diarrhea . . ."

"Ok, that's quite enough," Jared said, his face crunched up as if he'd just eaten a lime. "Go take a dump or somethin' . . . Jesus."

"That's the problem, little man," Reggie said. "My asshole is as raw as a fresh cut of chuck roast. I think I'm gettin' a hemorrhoid or somethin'. You wanna see?" Joking, Reggie turned around and began to pull his pants down.

"Um, yeah. I think I'm gonna go now," Jared responded. "Your raw ass is really the last thing I came here to see."

Jared looked over and saw the newspaper sitting on the table and picked it up for a closer look.

"Can you believe that, dad?" he said, referring to Willie's story. "I heard that guy had his dick cut off. Can you imagine that shit?"

Reggie jumped from his chair and raised his arm in a furious rage, ready to pummel the boy. He didn't touch him. Jared cringed then relaxed when Reggie backed off.

"What's yo problem?" Jared asked.

"Don't talk like that in front of me boy," Reggie said. "Okay? Just don't do it."

He didn't want to tell his son about Willie. It was best just to leave all of it in the past. Opening the door to stories of days of old could do nothing more than implicate the guys in the attack. Reggie had done exactly what they agreed on that night in the woods, he forgot about it. Sure, stinging reminders of the past always snuck up on him, but he managed to push everything behind.

One of the biggest punishments for their actions was the simple act of secrecy. As each year ticked by, and as each new memory was created, that awful event still rested firmly in the minds of the men who did it. The craziest thing about the murder was the way in which the investigation turned.

The girls were officially listed as missing runaways until their eighteenth birthdays. The family's certainly entertained the notion that the two ran off in love, vowing to get even with their insensitive parents. Alexis' father was the worst. He was the one that went to the papers and explained that his daughter was in fact a lesbian and she had fallen for Andrea. He also told the media about the situations when he caught the girls together, which gave him that inclination. Of course, the recollections were embellished and a little over the top. He also admitted that the two had threatened to move away together, making it obvious in his mind. If you were to talk to the families today, they'd probably back off of that stance knowing that their daughter wouldn't go nearly 20 years without so much as a phone call.

The threats of running away together gave the police no choice but to rule it a lost case. No one knew the girls were camping that night, thus the boys were home free as far as anyone outside of the secret was concerned. A search party was never organized because no one thought it was needed.

The five boys who burned Alexis' body that night knew that no one could possibly search the area unless tipped off and couldn't have been more relieved when the outside pressures never came. That meant Andrea never made it out of the woods alive to rat out the boys. They could trust each other. If the cops hadn't focused on the lovers run off theory, someone would've cracked and told the truth. And Reggie would be in jail.

He thought back to the horrible image of Alexis' body leaving the earth and grit his teeth together. He and Seth picked Alexis up and pitched her body into the flames of the fire. The two took turns stoking it to keep the flames going and the temperature high. They *had* to smell it.

"I think I'm going to be sick," Seth said as he put his hands over his mouth, turning to release the vomit that had been toying with him since the attack started.

"Jesus, that fuckin' smell is horrible," Reggie admitted, plugging his nose as the smoke billowed towards him. A constant popping sound emanated from the flames and Alexis' body. Her organs were exploding inside of her, and her skin was beginning to bubble and fry.

"Why is it doing that?" Seth asked, pointing to her arm which had began to boil and pop. The skin had amassed a huge blister the size of a football. It looked like someone took some gum, blew a bubble and placed it on her bicep. It eventually popped and burned away, but not before leaving an impression on the two boys. "It's like a god damn water balloon."

The two youngsters left the fire to get some fresh air. Everyone else had scattered to escape the smell and the images of death.

The burning of her hair and clothes was the worst of it. It seemed to violate their sinuses before finding a permanent home in their brain and memories. Shortly after that, the flesh began to melt away and burn into the fire. The oils from her body helped stoke the fire and the smell turned to that of familiarity. At that point, it was as if they were driving past Burger King on a hot summer evening. The smell of cooking flesh couldn't have been worse. They wished that it didn't smell so familiar, and some of the guys would've preferred it still reek as before when her hair was burning.

Nevertheless, she was starting to smell like barbecue although no one would admit it out loud.

"Why can't we go?" Richard asked, whining as usual. The freshman was starting to sound like one of the Brady kids. The rest of the guys ignored his question and continued to stare into the fire, drawn in by the work that they had created.

Her body was engulfed and had begun to crisp and become skeletal.

It took about four hours for the body to burn black. Her skeleton was eerie and horrible in the flames and the guys noticed its simplicity, cooking up another plan. They were going to dig a hole, throw in the bones and crush them with their feet and whatever else they could find. Then, they'd simply cover up the remains with dirt and go home. Reggie had come up with the plan, thinking that the skull and larger bones would crush easier after they had been burned to a crisp. What they didn't consider was; who was going to pick the bones from the smoldering fire pit and how? The area was dark and lit by the embers that remained in the hole. The eerie appearance of her skeleton was illuminated by the glowing orange streaks that lined the larger bones.

It would be light within the hour, but the boys didn't know whether that would be a good or bad thing.

"What about Andrea?" Seth asked Willie. "You seriously couldn't find her, dude?"

Willie nodded.

"If I found her, she'd be here, man," he said softly. He had been gone a long time, looking for Andrea in the blackness of night. He stared at the flames and didn't say another word. He felt responsible for bringing the girls.

"Oh well, this place is pretty secluded and she is probably resting in the belly of a mountain lion," Seth said, hoping that his vision was true. "But, if she gets away, we're all fuckin' dead."

"Hell, man, she probably watchin' us right now," Charles chimed in. "She jottin' down everything we're sayin'. You hear that bitch! I'm on to you!"

"That's enough!" Reggie barked. "Ain't no one out there writin' down what we're sayin'. The bitch is probably bear meat."

"Don't call her that," Richard muttered.

"What?" Reggie screamed. "What did you say to me you mothafuckin' waste?"

The football player lunged at Richard and punched him in the stomach, sending him to the ground almost as fast as Andrea had when she kicked him in the balls. With his foot, Reggie reared back and connected with Richard's chest.

At that point, Richard felt a little of what Blue Hair went through back at the game.

Seth and Willie pulled Reggie off the now coughing Richard. Charles laughed hysterically. Out of the five guys, he was the one still feeling the harshest effects of the beer. Even with the traumatic situation at hand, he was still drunk and feeling it hard.

"Shut the fuck up!" Seth said as he turned to Charles. "You guys need to stop arguing and help get these bones gathered."

"I can't," Willie said as he started to cry. "I can't touch those things, man. I just can't. I'm gonna be sick."

Seth knelt down and looked at his own hands.

"Fuck it, I'll do it," he said. Even though he felt like no one was working with him, he knew deep down that the whole thing was his fault. The only way to divert his guilt was to take the initiative.

Seth walked to the truck and returned with a tarp that was supposed to cover the tent. He fished through the fire, while Willie held a flashlight behind him. The skull and limb bones were easy to pull from the embers using a crooked stick. He smacked out larger pieces from the fire pit, grabbing occasional chunks of wood in the process. In the distance a wolf howled, a sound that sent goosebumps up the skin that lined everyone's backside.

As Seth continued excavating the remains from the fire, Willie backed off with the flashlight. They were finding out that collecting bones from a burned corpse in a fire pit was nearly impossible. Seth's fingers were getting burned, and the pain was starting to affect his anger.

"You guys just going to stand there looking stupid?" Seth yelled, directing his anger towards Reggie, Charles and Richard. "Go dig the hole."

"With what?" Reggie yelled back. "My fuckin' teeth? I'm sorry. I didn't bring my fuckin' shovel."

"Jesus," Seth growled as he stood to his feet. He turned and swiped the flashlight from Willie's hands. "I have to do everything myself. You guys are all fucking worthless. You know that, right?"

Seth stormed into the forest and returned with some large pieces of strong bark that were scattered on the ground.

"You think you can handle these?" he asked, returning to the fire pit to finish plucking the remains. "Dig with the wood."

Richard wouldn't accept his makeshift shovel, deciding to return to the Suburban. He climbed in and sat in the passenger seat. Reggie and Charles shook their heads and walked into the distance to find a spot for the grave. Both of them were ready to kick Richard's ass, and Reggie certainly would've killed him if Willie hadn't gotten involved.

"Fuck," Seth said.

"What?" asked Willie.

"Look at this."

Seth took his stick and lifted a charred necklace from the blackened wood, carefully rubbing it with his fingers. The gold had turned black from the flames, but went right back to shining beautiful wherever Seth's hands touched. He popped open the locket on the end, curious about the photo that she had in it.

Nothing.

Whatever picture she had in there must have burned away from the intense heat.

Seth picked up the flashlight again and searched closely through the rest of the pit. Nothing seemed to stick out. No garments. No bones. No jewelry.

He picked up the canvas tarp of smoking bones and carried it over to the spot where the guys were digging the hole. Seeing that it was deep enough, Seth immediately dumped the charred bones into the hole and told the guys to pound away on them with whatever they could find. Reggie lifted his foot and rested it on the skull, trying to break it with his weight.

"C'mon you damn thing," he said, not stopping to think for even a moment that he was standing on the head of a once living human being, one that he'd violated hours earlier. The shock of the attack left the men with little ability to rationalize or think logically. At that moment, none of them realized the severity of their actions that particular night. It was a fight or flight reaction where they could only think of themselves and covering up the crime that would certainly lead to a punishment of life in prison. It would be years later before they would all come to grips with what they did that evening and they would each do it on a personal level.

Looking like a bunch of guys crushing soda cans, the group jumped up and down on the bones. One by one, they took turns falling to the earth after sliding off her skull, or one of the limb bones. Each one of them hadn't factored in much in their hasteful plan to destroy the body. Reggie, Charles and Willie all had soot and black residue covering their shoes, and they weren't really crushing the bones all that well. They also hadn't factored in the strength of the human skeletal structure.

None of the bones really broke to tiny bits, and as far as crushing them into dust as they had envisioned, that wasn't happening. Her skull was broken, but only in two pieces. Seth walked by with a large rock and dropped it on her skull, breaking it up more.

"That's probably good enough," he said, trying not to breathe too heavily. "Let's cover her up and do a quick search of the woods for the other one."

Willie had already started kicking dirt on the torched body. He lifted his head.

"Um. I think that's a bad idea," he said. "I looked for her and those woods are too dark. Besides she wouldn't be anywhere near this campsite having disappeared hours ago. We need to stay together so that none of us get lost out there."

Seth nodded in agreement.

"Let's just go home," he said.

"Dad, what's wrong?" Jared asked.

Reggie had begun to cry. The flashbacks that he had started having in recent days were nearly as vivid and horrible as the ones that he had just days after the murder. That's exactly why the men all went their separate ways. Just seeing the name of Willie Becker was bringing back the demons to everyone who was there that night.

"You ever done anything that you just couldn't get away from?" Reggie asked his son. "I mean, have you ever done anything wrong and hidden behind the lie that stopped you from gettin' caught?"

Jared thought he knew what his dad was talking about.

"Yeah, man," he said.

Reggie wiped the tear streaks from his face, curious about what his son was going to say next.

"I can't believe I'm telling you this, but," Jared started. "You know how Mom's cat disappeared last year? Well, I sort of threw it in the dumpster behind the house."

Reggie shook his head, half shocked by the confession and half relieved that he still had time to reconsider his attempt at telling the secret.

"It sort of froze in there, I guess," Jared finished.

Reggie made a decision right then and there. A decision that was going to affect his life and the lives of those who were involved in the attack. He was going to confess his wrongdoings to an outsider.

"Son, I want to tell you about something," Reggie started. "Sit down."

Jared sat down at the kitchen table, excited and worried about what his father was going to say.

"Back in eighty-three," Reggie started. "Four friends and I . . ."

KNOCK! KNOCK!

Someone was frantically banging at the front door just as Reggie began his attempted confession. Jared was slightly annoyed since his father rarely spoke about his past. Reggie answered the door and to his surprise found nothing there but a package at his feet. He craned his head around each corner, hoping to find the courier who dropped off the box.

"Hmm," he muttered.

The box had an address label and was addressed to Reggie's home but didn't look like it was processed by any legit shipping business. It was slightly heavy and Reggie quickly brought it in the house, whipping out a small knife to aid in the removal of the tape.

"Who's it from?" Jared asked.

"I don't know. There's no return address."

He opened the lid and removed some packing popcorn. Encased in the box was a jar, filled with a bright orange liquid and what appeared to be chicken gizzards. Three fleshy items floated.

Reggie removed the lid and sniffed the contents. He quickly backed away mostly in self defense due to the potent mix, a smell akin to ammonia and rotten eggs, which emanated from the jar.

"What the hell is that?" Jared asked, holding his arm over his nose.

"Fuck if I know," Reggie replied.

He lifted the jar up to a light and shook it gently, bobbing the pieces of flesh around like a bunch of dead fish in an aquarium. He set the jar down and looked in the box for any kind of note explaining the package.

Nothing.

"We'll have to ask your mother about this," Reggie said. "Maybe this has something to do with her new diet."

13

"You really shouldn't do that," Wendy said.

Russell reluctantly took a break from reading the newspaper and peered over at her.

"I really shouldn't do what?" he said, mocking her in the process.

"You shouldn't smoke."

He buried his head back in the newspaper and began to laugh to himself. The fact that this woman was even sharing his office, if even for a tiny moment, was a joke to him. Add to that the fact that she felt the urge to tell him to quit smoking and you have a comedy in the works.

"Darlin', let me tell you something about *my* office," he started, twirling his fingers around as if he were giving her a tour of the room. "When I'm out there, I don't know what creep is going to be hiding in the bushes. I don't know what horrible crime scene awaits me. I just don't know. Have no clue. In here, in my office, I know exactly what is going on and I have complete control over my surroundings. Think of me as God."

Russell took a drag of his cigarette and blew it across his desk towards Wendy.

"And if you don't like my smoking, you know where the door is," he finished, pointing behind her before cracking the most sinister smile.

Wendy smiled back and fanned the clouded air around her.

"Actually, it doesn't bother me that much," she said. "I just thought you'd like to know how unsafe it is for yourself. There aren't that many offices anymore where smoking is even allowed."

Russell scoffed and returned to his newspaper.

"That's a damn shame," he said.

Wendy was as tolerant as anyone in law enforcement when it came to dealing with jerks. That's how she got to be in the position she found herself in, sitting across from one of the biggest assholes in the department. Being a female in any public servant position, whether it be firefighting or law enforcement always requires extra patience. She had to work a little harder than most to gain the respect she had. Everyone knew that putting her on the case with Russell could've been a huge disaster, but there was a chance that she could help. Perhaps balance things with his abrasive personality. There was a chance that she could push Detective Meeder like no one had ever done. She had a knack for finding the details in a case that others would overlook.

The two were going to make a great partnership and that was the reason they were stuck in the same room together.

"You like coffee?" she asked, flipping through the pages of a recent National Geographic, bored out of her mind.

Russell perked up from his laid back position once again and took his feet off of his desk. He was as excited as a school boy on Christmas morning.

"Are you serious?" he asked. "I have a secretary that does that from time to time but, between you and me, she's kind of an idiot. She usually brings me the overcooked shit that I hate. I'll take it black."

Wendy looked up and into Russell's eyes.

"You shouldn't drink that stuff either, it's bad for you," she said. "I've seen you slam the stuff pretty hard."

Russell's grin quickly melted into disappointment. It was going to be a long trek with this detective at his side. Next thing you know, she was going to tell him he needed to cut back on his drinking.

"Fuckin' Christ," he said, leaning back into his chair, propping his feet back on his desk. He made sure to make extra noise when he pulled the newspaper back in reading position. Glancing over the paper at the woman, he noticed her picking food out of her teeth.

"You shouldn't do that," he said.

"Why? Because it's *bad* for me?" she asked, mocking him and sounding like a bratty little girl in the process.

"No. Because it's fucking annoying."

RING!

Just as Russell turned and gazed angrily at an ignoring Wendy, his phone rang, startling him out of his hate-filled trance.

"Hello!" he yelled into the receiver.

"Is this the *great* Detective Russell Meeder? The awe-inspiring, master of criminology and murderer of two?" the person on the other end asked.

"Huh? Who is this?" Russell demanded.

"I was wondering, how do you plan on finding me? Better yet, I wonder what you'll do to stop me?" the voice said. "I think you know what's going on, but you don't quite know how to deal with it."

Russell propped himself up and snapped his fingers at Wendy. She immediately knew something was up and ran from the room, hoping to get a phone trace started.

"How do you know about me?" Russell asked.

"That isn't important," the voice said. "What's important is, you don't know me, at least not yet. And you won't know me, until I'm ready for you to. Is that understood?"

"Have you ever seen a deer gutted and hung from a tree?" the voice asked. The whispering monotone voice of person on the other end was almost synthetic, like the sounds of a robot.

Russell nodded. "Yes, I've seen pictures."

"Have you ever seen an asshole gutted and hung from a barbed wire fence?" the voice quizzed.

"I have now, thanks to you I presume," Russell responded.

"Now, Mr. Meeder, I have one more question for you. Have you ever seen a national icon hanging from a pillar of the very same voice communication infrastructure we're using right now? Did you know that multi-millionaire sports legends also bleed red? And, they also cry like babies when you pry out their eyes with a scalpel."

Russell grabbed a pen.

"What exactly are we talking about here?" he asked as he started jotting down the ramblings from the other end of the phone line. "Did you murder Seth Owens? Where is he?"

"Get in your car right now and drive north on I-25," the voice began. "Take exit two-forty and head east. About twenty miles later you'll take a right on a road with a yellow grain silo. You'll know if you've followed these directions." The voice burst into laughter. "Trust me, you'll know."

The line went silent following the gentle sounds of a click.

Wendy ran into the room.

"We almost had it," she said, trying to catch her breath. "It was from a cell phone, but we couldn't locate the source. Who was it? I hope that wasn't just a phone call from your mother or something. I mean, you signaled me as if it were an important call, so . . ."

"Would you shut up for a second," Russell said, interrupting her in mid sentence. "This guy wants us to go for a little ride. I think we're about to find out what happened to Seth Owens. I don't think he's going to be alive. I have a feeling you and I are about to become a footnote in the history books."

Wendy looked somewhat worried.

"Get your coat," Wendy said. "It's cold out."

Russell shook his head and ground his teeth. The working relationship that he was supposed to be building with this woman was as smooth as a sheet of 20-grain sandpaper.

"Excuse me," Russell said as he reached over and popped the glove box open. A white bottle of aspirin was the only thing in it. He grabbed the bottle and shook loose five or six of the pills into his mouth before he began to chew them. It wasn't the smartest thing he could've done since his stomach was already turning with each mile on the odometer. He had seen what this killer was capable of and feared the worst as they got closer to the secret. Russell wasn't the kind of detective you see on TV all the time who goes to crime scenes and acts like they're just doing a job. True, he was a professional and didn't allow himself to cry or vomit or anything that ridiculous. But, he never got to a point where he could look at the dead, or much worse, a butchered human being, and act like it was just another day. He had to stay focused at all times or face the possibility of a meltdown.

"How long have you been a cop?" he asked her, slamming the glove box shut. "I mean, they didn't send you here for your first assignment did they?"

"Russell, I am a detective. Just like you," she said. "In fact, I've been a detective for more than five years, and a cop for ten."

Russell was taken aback.

"Damn. How old are you then? Did you join up in grade school?" he asked, stunned. "You look like you're twenty."

"As if it's any of your business, but I am old enough," she said, not revealing her true age, but recognizing and appreciating his sentiment. "Thanks for the compliment, though. I still get carded when I go out for a drink, which isn't too bad a deal. I can remember a time when I would get upset by that, but you know, it makes me feel good now."

"Women," he muttered. "Why do you guys get so upset and 'hush hush' about your age? It's just a fucking number. I'm thirty-six years old, and it doesn't bother me one bit."

"Men," she responded. "Why do you refer to a group of ladies as *guys*? And, why do you insist on not following directions? I mean, chewing large amounts of aspirin instead of waiting until you can get a drink? Why don't you do what it tells you? It says . . ." she pulled the bottle out of the glove box "adults take two to three pills with a full glass of water."

Russell turned to the woman that was acting like his mother again and smiled, revealing chunks of the white powder still stuck in his gums.

"You are pretty much a pig," she said, turning away from his childish display.

"Yeah, but I'm good at it," he said, proudly. "Sweet cheeks."

Wendy turned to him and raised her hand.

"If you ever call me that, or anything remotely similar to it, I will punch you right in the face," she insisted. "You got that?"

Russell smiled condescendingly. He was beginning to like this woman. She wasn't your typical power-tripping cop, nor was she a weak do-as-I-say individual either. She seemed to care about him, while maintaining some self esteem in the process. He didn't see it but she managed to crack a tiny smile as a result of their play. It almost felt like she was in high school again.

"Sorry," he muttered.

"Okay, when I turn on this next road we are going to see what he wants us to see and it could get ugly," Russell warned. "I've seen this fuck's handy work and it's nothing like what you can imagine. Do you think you're prepared?"

Wendy looked over at him and gave a smug smile.

"Russell, I've seen lots of things that were pretty shocking," she said. "I didn't come to you from working at a daycare."

"Darlin', I've seen something in the past few days that would make most people cry for their mommies," he said. "Now, this same joker is leading us down this road for a reason, and I don't think it's to show us the beautiful snow-covered countryside."

"I saw the pictures of Willie," she said. "Sure it was bad but . . ."

"Fuckin' Christ," he said as the car began to slow down. Russell covered his mouth for a moment and actually felt ill for a split second. Emotions tend to overcome even the toughest of individuals, if given the right circumstances.

Rows of telephone poles lined the small county road like poorly sewn stitches on an uneven cut. As far as the eye could see, the poles lined up in a row of imperfection, rising and falling with the contours of the landscape that lined the ground.

Russell stopped the car and opened the door. Before getting out all of the way, he pulled out a cigarette and lit it, looking around at the cold scenery for a moment, hoping to forget about what dangled before them. He lifted the collar on his pea coat to protect himself from the cold wind. Years of training couldn't prepare someone for such a horrible sight.

Hanging from one of the telephone poles was the body of a man, crucified with his arms wide open and his legs together. It was Seth Owens. It had to be. Russell couldn't confirm it on a quick glance, but he knew what he was dealing with. It was safe to assume at that point. Thirty-two thousand yards passing and more than 240 touchdowns couldn't save him from the horrific fate that paraded itself in front of the detectives.

Russell looked over at Wendy and found her in shock. Tears were streaming down her cheeks and her face had turned white. She was staring at the body through the windshield and appeared in a trance. He kind of figured she'd have that reaction.

"Listen, if you don't think you can . . ." he started to say.

"Shut up," she barked, partially embarrassed by her show of emotions. She was just proving Russell right in his male chauvinistic perspective. "I can handle this just as well as you. Now let's get over there and take care of business."

Russell avoided the body for a few minutes, concentrating on fresh tire tracks or footprints that surrounded the area. He then got on the phone and called the police dispatch, ordering a few cars, but no ambulance. This wasn't the body of a man who could be saved.

"They'll be here in about fifteen minutes," he told Wendy, who was standing under the telephone pole, looking up at the body. It was nailed in at the very top and balanced roughly 25 feet above the ground.

Seth was completely naked. He wasn't in as bad of shape as the first body, but had just as horrible a display of injuries. Just like Willie, his genitals were removed, leaving behind a bloody patch of flesh and blood. They couldn't tell from the ground, but something had happened to his face, as it appeared soaked in blood. His feet were slit along the top, across the front of the ankle, and pulled flat against the pole, hammered in with a large utility nail.

"Is something written on his chest?" Wendy asked, pointing to a marking that appeared on the man's torso.

"Looks like it," Russell said, squinting in an effort to read it. "I think it says 'rapist' but I could be mistaken."

"Rapist?" Wendy asked.

The two stood silent, surrounded only by the sounds of wind blowing the snow, and the occasional car from the highway in the far horizon.

"Can you believe that we are looking at Seth Owens?" Wendy asked. "I mean, this is something we're going to talk about for years. We will be the creepy cops on those documentary shows that will come from all of this. We're the ones who found him. The whole world is going to know about this in less than an hour."

Russell again looked at her as if she were crazy.

"Documentaries?" he quizzed. "Jesus, this is serious shit. We aren't in a movie right now and we aren't looking at a famous football player. This is a fucking human being that was murdered and left as a martyr for some unapparent reason. He isn't throwing us a fucking touchdown and we aren't taking the fucking handoff. Christ!"

Wendy turned and looked Russell right in the eyes.

"Well we both know who seems to be buddy, buddy with the guy who did this," she said. "Why did he call you to tell you about this whole mess?"

"What are you trying to say?" Russell asked. "You think this murdering faggot is my friend? Listen. You were there. I didn't call this guy at home to chew the fat and talk about old times. He called me out of the blue and told us where to go. I don't have any control over that. It's not the first time a crook has called the police to find his dirty work."

Silence.

Just as Russell finished his tirade, the sounds of squad cars could be heard, blaring in the distance. Three cars came tearing down the road and just as Russell had moments earlier, all slammed to a stop when they realized what was hanging from the pole.

Murmurs of swear words and horrified responses could be heard from the officers that exited their vehicles. No one signed up to be a cop with the thought of this being part of the job.

"Are you Detective Meeder?" one of the officers said as they walked towards him.

"Yes sir, and you are?" Russell responded.

"I'm Officer Wayne Wang," he said, joining Russell in a puzzling look at the body. "You ever seen anything like this before?"

"I've seen worse," Russell said, distracted by the policeman. "You're name's Wayne Wang?"

The cop shook his head yes.

"Uh. That's cool," Russell said, repeating the name over and over again in his mind. What parents would do that to their child? "Say that ten times fast."

"Say what?" asked Wayne.

"Your name," replied Russell.

"Could we talk about the matter at hand?" Officer Wang asked.

"Oh. Sure. Sorry."

"I'm guessing this is Mr. Football, Seth Owens," Russell began as the two walked towards the pole. "He's been missing and . . ."

"And what?" Wayne asked.

"And, I got a call from what I believe is the suspect in the murders and he led me to this spot."

"He called you?"

"Look, let me do my investigation and you worry about getting this body down. Do your job and I'll do mine," Russell said, putting his hand on Wayne's shoulder. "What do you say, Wayne Wang?"

"You got it buddy," he reluctantly replied.

"Good. Now run along."

The cop looked rejected and a little pissed at Russell. None of it mattered so long as the body remained on the pole.

Two hours later, the corpse was finally removed from its crucified resting spot. It was discovered that Seth had his eyes and tongue gouged out and placed in the wound where his genitals once were, shaped like a penis and testicles. The carved letters in his chest did spell the word "rapist." And, perhaps worst of all were the injuries he suffered to his back.

When the authorities finally climbed up and removed the body, they discovered that his spine had been taken out. A groove was carved into his back from his pant line all the way to his neck, and the bone had been taken out.

The telephone pole acted like a giant backbone, keeping his body straight. As soon as he was unhooked by the arms, his body tumbled to the ground like a ragdoll.

A legend in the sports world was reduced to a piece of cutting-board meat. By no means was his image going to be released to the public, thus no photographs were taken of the body while it hung on the pole. It is policy in any jurisdiction in any town in the country to take photos of murder victims in the position where they were found, but no one was allowed to do it in this case as per Russell's orders. Reporters and media were kept off the road and weren't close enough to get photographs or interviews with the police officers.

As the body was being removed, Russell walked over towards the car.

"Russell," Wendy yelled. "Come here and look at this."

He walked over to her and looked at the ground.

"These tire tracks are awfully fresh and go down the road all by themselves. There aren't any other tracks. Do you think the killer may have gone that way to get out of here?" she asked.

"Let's check it out," he said.

The two carefully drove down the road, following the tracks and looking for any sign that someone may have left the road and walked through the snow. Since they were on a dirt road, the snow was still fresh and any kind of tracks would be easily spotted from the car.

About three miles into their drive, their excitement turned into disappointment as the road ahead merged onto an asphalt highway that was cleared of snow. They discovered something unusual in the dirt road just feet from the county highway. Russell stopped the car and got out to investigate.

Written in what appeared to be blood, the words: *DEAD END* were etched out in the snow.

"Fuckin' Christ," Russell said as he kicked the ground. He pulled a cigarette out of his pocket and lit it, taking a deep drag and closing his eyes in disbelief. The warm cigarette smoke felt good mixed with the bitter cold. "Let's go back and tell them about this shit and head back to the office. I've got someone I need to talk to."

14

"Sir, can I help you?"

The clerk's voice was getting louder with each attempt at the same question.

"Sir?"

"Sir, can I help you?"

"Could someone get his attention?"

A man who was waiting in line for beer and cigarettes elbowed Richard in the back. Richard snapped out of his trance and looked around the room like some lost child. He couldn't remember why he was where he was and didn't understand why he was holding a magazine. He flipped it over to see the cover. It was a copy of the latest *Beefy Tits*.

"Sir, you gonna buy that or what?" the clerk asked.

Richard set the magazine on the counter and walked towards the door. The ticking of the clock meant nothing to him, and he didn't know what the rest of his day would involve. At first, he saw the headline and thought nothing of it, pushing the door open and stepping a foot outside.

Then he moved back inside and stared at the paper.

Seth Owens crucified on rural road utility pole.

His dreams were all coming true. As excited as a little boy on his birthday, Richard grabbed the paper and walked back to the line where everyone had stopped to watch his every move. Without thinking, he strolled to the front of the line and flicked two quarters at the clerk before turning away with the paper.

"Sir, your change!" the clerk yelled as Richard walked through the front doors. "Ah hell."

"Forget him. It's just fifteen cents," said the man who had earlier elbowed Richard. "Consider it a retard tax."

Everyone burst into laughter.

Richard threw most of the newspaper on the sidewalk and quickly scanned through the article on Seth. It was like slow motion. For so many years he wished those guys would drop dead. Someone was carrying out that wish.

"Reggie Peterson," Russell said as he tapped his finger on the yearbook photograph of Seth, Willie and Reggie. "Wouldn't you think that it's a possibility that this guy would be next? I mean, it's a reasonable suspicion right?"

Wendy crossed her legs as she sat across from Russell.

"Uh, duh," she said, mockingly. "I've been saying that all along."

Russell ignored her self-glorifying statement and continued staring at the photograph.

"What is going on with you guys?" he quietly asked the images on the photo.

The office was dark with the shades always closed. Russell spent most of his days sitting at his desk, investigating his cases, and surfing the Internet for research. Occasionally he would venture out to the library for a quieter place to study. Having Wendy tag along made things even more difficult due to the fact that she had absolutely nothing to do while sitting in his office.

"Don't you have your own office?" he asked her. "Why do you always have to be here, staring at me, twiddling your thumbs?"

"Because I like you," she said before blowing him a kiss. "Yeah I have my own office, but it's just not as interesting as yours." She got up and walked over to one of his bookshelves, pulling a book from its resting place.

"'*Game Seven*'," she said, reading the title of the book.

"It's a book about a crazy, sexist office worker who goes off the deep end," he started. "It's standard reading in any college psych class. The guy who wrote it must have been a fuckin' looney."

"Oh, I know," she said. "I've read it. It's one of my favorites."

"Just, please leave my books alone. In fact, let's get out of here and pay a visit to our friend Reggie."

She slid the book back in place and followed him out of the room.

"After you, your highness," she said mockingly, patting him on the butt as he walked past.

"Uh, watch your hands," he said, appreciating the contact.

"Sorry, it slipped," she responded.

Reggie lived in a lower-middle-class part of Denver. He was spitting distance from Mile High Stadium, and could see the interstate from his bathroom window. His home wasn't exactly the best place to live, but did the job. On a positive note, he had never experienced crime, although a few of his neighbors had throughout the years. They had to get to Reggie before he found himself in danger.

"When did you first know you wanted to be a cop?" Wendy asked.

Russell took his eyes off the road and stared at Wendy.

"Why?" he asked.

"I'm just curious," she said.

"I don't know."

"C'mon, we all have stories about why it is we do what we do," she said, prodding for an answer. "I can tell you right now, I wanted to be a cop my whole life. And, my earliest memory was of me telling my dad that I was going to shoot bad guys."

Russell smiled.

"So," she said, waiting to ask again. "When?"

Russell took in a deep breath and sighed.

"When I was a kid," he began. "Senior in high school to be exact . . ."

"Wait, first, where did you go to high school?" she interrupted.

He looked over at her like a disappointed father who couldn't finish his old fishing story.

"Are you going to let me talk or what?" he asked.

"Sorry."

"Anyway, I went to Loveland High School, if that's what you want to know," he paused, not knowing where in his story he wanted to start. "So, there I was, your typical rebellious teenager, scared about what world awaited me beyond high school."

Russell stopped at a stoplight and got more involved in his story.

"I was going through this phase; you probably know what I'm talking about."

"What kind of phase?" she asked.

"I was just weird. I wanted to stand out and fit in at the same time, but didn't know how. And, needless to say, I got picked on quite a bit."

"Yeah? Who didn't?"

"Well, you're going to laugh, but . . . I had blue hair," he said. "Big, blue hair. Blue like Grover."

Wendy put her hand over her mouth as she let out a laugh.

"It's not funny," he said. "Besides, it was the '80s. We all did stupid shit back then."

"Oh. Sorry."

"It got me in some deep shit. I went to a football game one weekend and got jumped by two guys under the bleachers. It was the scariest and most fucked up thing I've ever gone through."

"Oh my god, did you get hurt?" Wendy asked, showing some concern.

Russell took his eyes off the road and looked at Wendy, pushing his two front teeth down with his tongue, revealing his denture-like artificial bridge.

"Jesus," she said.

"Yeah, it was pretty bad. I got knocked out quick, so I don't really remember a whole lot. I was told that I laid in the dirt unconscious for nearly three hours while the game was in progress. It wasn't until the game ended and everyone was leaving that I was discovered. Some kid cleaning up garbage spotted me and called an ambulance."

He pointed to the scar on his ear lobe.

"They also ripped one of my earrings out."

"Man, did they ever catch the guys?" she asked.

"How could they? I lay there for so long and with all of the people at the game, there was just no way the cops could even begin looking for the guys. I do remember there were two of them and one seemed a lot shorter than the other. I smelled alcohol and pot and knew they were wasted. There was nothing I could do. They didn't even give me a chance to run. I guess that's when I knew I wanted to be a cop."

Wendy sat stunned.

"Well, that beats the shit out of my story," she said.

Russell shook his head yes.

"From that point on, I wanted to do what I could to stop criminals from picking on the innocent."

Neither one of them spoke for the rest of the drive.

Russell pulled up to a spot in front of the house, right in front of a no-parking sign.

"Um, I don't think we can park here," Wendy said, pointing to the sign.

"I didn't see no sign, officer," Russell said, playing dumb with his best redneck voice. "You think someone is going to tow us in this neighborhood? They probably don't have any tow trucks for miles."

The two detectives got out and walked towards the house side-by-side. Truth be told, they were starting to enjoy each others dry jokes and cold shoulders. They were becoming true partners.

"Let me do the talking," he said under his breath as the two reached the doorway. "This guy has just lost two friends, and I don't want to piss him off, *or* upset him."

"Don't talk to me like I'm a child. You tell your idiot friends or children that you'll do the talking," she said, just as Russell rang the doorbell, ignoring her. "I know how to do my job and I'm not your damn . . ."

The door opened and a younger male answered it.

"Hello, I'm detective Russell Meeder and this is my partner, Detective Wendy Valdez. Can we speak to Reggie Peterson? Is he here?"

The kid at the door looked really confused.

"What do you mean you're Detective Meeder?" the boy asked. "Detective Meeder came about two hours ago and took my dad with him. Which one of you is Meeder?"

Russell's mouth dropped and he pulled his cell phone from his pocket. Wendy walked into the house and sat down with Jared to get more information. Confusion and a sense of urgency filled the room like acrid smoke.

"What was he driving?" Russell yelled from the porch.

"What?" Wendy yelled back, agitated by the fact that he wouldn't come in the house.

"What was he driving?" he repeated.

"Who?" Wendy again asked.

"What the fuck kind of car was the fucking guy who took Reggie driving in?" Russell said. "Jesus!"

Russell burst into the house.

"God dammit . . . you!" he shouted, pointing to Jared who was sitting on the couch. "What kind of car did they take off in?"

Jared shrugged his shoulders.

"I don't know, I think it was a blue pickup truck or something," he said.

"You *think* it was a . . . nevermind," Russell said, before relaying the information to the dispatcher on the other line.

"What's your name?" Wendy asked.

"My name's Jared."

"How do you know Reggie?" she said.

"I told you, he's my dad."

"Some horrible things have happened to a couple of your father's old friends in the past week and we are trying to protect your dad from possible danger," she said, hoping to be tactful, but honest in the process. "Did he say anything, or did anything strange happen before he left this morning?"

"He did get this in the mail yesterday," Jared said, grabbing over the couch for the cardboard box. "It's nasty though, and smells like shit too."

He handed the opened package to Wendy. She lifted the jar from the box and squinted to get a good look at the flesh that floated in the orange liquid.

"What is that?" she asked Jared.

"We couldn't figure it out," he said. "But it smells like shit."

"Yeah, you mentioned that," she said. "Could we try to avoid using that word? You shouldn't talk like that anyway."

"Lady, I'm fifteen years old, I can say what I want to," he insisted.

"Sorry kid, you're totally right. I'm not here to talk about your manners," she said apologetically. "Let's get back to your dad. Did he say anything strange? Did he talk about his friends?"

Jared got really quiet when asked those questions. He didn't want to answer either way and played with a loose string on his t-shirt.

"Jared, you've got to tell me everything you know so that we can find your dad," she said, putting a hand on one of his shoulders. "Now, did he say anything strange recently? Anything at all."

Jared began to tear up and shook his head no.

"I didn't believe him," he said, tears now streaking down his cheeks.

Wendy leaned over and pulled Jared towards her for a hug right as Russell walked in the room, having finished his conversation with the dispatcher.

"What the fuck is this?" he asked. "He's just a kid."

Wendy turned to Russell and leapt from her seat, getting right in his face.

"Listen here, asshole," she said. "I've got to talk to this witness about what happened today. If you are gonna be in the way, I'm going to have to ask you to step outside. However, if you want to sit quietly in this chair here, feel free."

Russell was stunned. Even Jared was stunned.

"Seriously, if I hear one fucking peep out of you, you're gone," she said.

Returning to her session with Jared, Wendy continued to sweet talk the lad, knowing that he had something to say. Russell found himself surprisingly turned on by her outburst.

"Alright, where were we?" she asked. "What didn't you believe?"

Jared looked over at Russell.

"Don't look at that asshole, look at me," she said, pulling his chin towards her. "What did he tell you, sweetie?"

"He told me that him and a few other guys did a bad thing in high school, and he thought they were being punished for it," Jared said. "That's all he said."

"Did he say what they did?" she asked.

"No."

Glancing to his right, Russell saw a book on the shelf and picked it up, flipping through the pages. His attention was averted when he looked up at the television and saw a story on Seth Owens. The volume on the set was on mute and he couldn't hear anything being said. Then a flash of white appeared on the screen as a reporter was live about a mile from the scene, right where the police had set up a media blockade.

Then they showed the footage.

A crusty, home movie quality video showed Seth hanging from the pole. It appeared to have been shot before even Russell and Wendy had arrived at the scene.

"Look at that," Russell yelled, interrupting Wendy's session with the kid.

Wendy instinctively turned around, wanting to smack Russell in the mouth. "Look at what?" she barked.

Russell pointed to the television and she turned just in time to find the footage of Seth being paraded on the set.

"Where'd they get the footage?" Wendy said.

Russell had already gotten on his feet and started dialing numbers on his phone as he walked outside.

"Who else was he friends with in high school? Did he mention other names?" she asked, pressuring Jared for more information.

"A guy named Willie Becker, a dude named Charles Manning, um . . . I think the other one was Richard Tark or something like that, and the fourth was actually Seth Owens," Jared continued before grinning wide. "My dad knew Seth Owens."

For a moment, Jared looked proud instead of sad. He couldn't believe that his father was once a teammate of such a huge star. He gazed that the television, looking at the horrible images, not putting together the fact that the dead body on the screen was Seth.

"But he didn't specify what they did that was so horrible?" Wendy pried.

"No," Jared said. "He just told me they did something bad and it was a secret."

"We don't have time for this shit, Wendy," Russell said from the porch, just on the other side of the screen door. "Hey kid, you got family?"

Jared nodded.

"Call 'em. I'll get a squad car down here to look after you until someone gets here. We're gotta go. Gotta find your father before he gets turned into bacon like the rest of his friends."

Wendy walked over to Russell and opened the door. He regretted what he'd said as soon as he finished speaking and knew he was in for trouble. It was like being married, only without the benefits. Maybe more like a kid who just screamed a bad word and just knew Mom was about to come around the corner with a bar of soap. As soon as she cracked open the screen door, Wendy raised her arm and slapped him across the face.

"This boy here just found out that his father has been kidnapped and you don't have the God damn common courtesy to use a little tact while talking in front of him?" Wendy screamed. "You are a disgusting bastard Russell Meeder."

Russell walked in, sat back down and pulled his phone from his pocket, calling for a police car.

"You didn't have to hit me," he mumbled, rubbing his cheek.

"Did you get the names that kid was rambling off?" Russell said as the two drove away from the home. Russell and Wendy both knew, however, that the next time Reggie Peterson would be seen, it wouldn't be pretty. They had no leads, and no possible way of finding where the killer was conducting business.

"Yes, I wrote them down, master detective," she said, mocking his lackluster display at the Peterson home.

"The TV station said that an anonymous viewer arrived at the station about fifteen minutes ago and gave them the tape," Russell said. "They told me that they were not going to show it again, due to the graphic nature. They were also worried that showing it in the first place was going to get them into trouble with the FCC. I can't believe they aired it to begin with, can you?"

Wendy shook her head no.

"You shouldn't have talked to the kid like that," she said.

"Like what?"

"You have to be more respectful and mindful about what you say in front of victims," she said. "That kid's dad is missing and we have to remember our jobs as well as our tongues."

Russell wasn't in the mood for a lecture.

"Whatever," he said. "Could we just get back to the job at hand? I'm sorry if I offended that kid. I was just excited."

Wendy pushed out a disgusted laugh.

"Oh yeah, I also grabbed this piece of evidence."

She held up the jar and showed it to Russell.

He slammed on the brakes in the car, coming to a dead stop on the inside lane of Federal Boulevard, one of the busiest arteries in Denver. Cars behind him honked, barely missing a huge pileup.

"Where did you get that?" he asked.

"Jared gave it to me. He said Reggie got it in the mail yesterday," she responded. "Why, you want a bite?"

She unscrewed the cap and waved the jar in his face, spilling some of the liquid on his shirt.

"Oh Jesus fuck!" he yelled, pushing her hands back "That smells like ass and gasoline. Close that shit. What the fuck's wrong with you?"

Wendy let out a laugh that could pierce the inner ear of any dog within two miles. She screwed the cap back on then brushed a tear from her cheek that had trickled down from her immense joy. Russell swiped the jar from her hands and shook it, mystified by its contents, pissed that he had to smell them still because it was on his clothes.

"This is like the jar that Seth Owens got the day he was kidnapped," he said, squinting at the jar as he held it to the light.

"Exactly," she said. "It's still back at the lab. What do you think it is?"

"That's what we're going to find out," he said as he slammed his foot down on the gas pedal, flipping a u-turn in the busy traffic. Cars avoided colliding with him in the other lane, but he didn't pay any attention to them. The two detectives made their way to the forensic lab and hurriedly burst into the main corridor.

"The contents of the jar recovered from Seth Owens were a set of human testicles and a human penis," said the lab tech as he walked over to Russell and Wendy with a zip-lock bag that contained the items from Seth's jar. "Pretty disgusting if you ask me."

Wendy pulled the jar from her purse and showed it to the tech.

"Jesus, there's more," he said as he held it to the light. "Yeah, see, that's the same deal there."

Russell turned to Wendy and shook his head.

"So, these guys are receiving someone else's dick in the mail the day they are to be kidnapped?" Russell inquired. "Is that what I'm to understand here?"

"Um, actually, sir, it appears they are receiving someone else's penis *and testicles*," the tech chimed in. "Don't forget the . . . um . . . testicles."

"Oh, I'm sorry, they are getting the *balls* too," Russell said, looking over at Wendy as if he'd just made a joke. She didn't laugh. "Don't want to forget the *balls*. That makes soooo much more sense to me. This guy's just sending out courtesy samples of frank and beans. What the fuck is going on around here?"

"Calm down drama queen," Wendy said as she took the jar over to the counter to discuss it with the tech.

Across town, Charles Manning was receiving a similar package, delivered to his front door in much the same way as Reggie's. The messenger knocked and ran, just like the previous deliveries. Charles wasn't home when the package was delivered, but found it on his doorstep when he returned from an afternoon jog.

Breathing hard from the jaunt, Charles took a moment to stand on his porch and wind down. He only glanced at the package and chose not to pick it up at first, opting to stare at the road instead.

"Hey Charles, how's your day?" asked a voice coming from the neighbor house.

Charles walked into the clearing on his patio and looked up. It was Mrs. Walker, a retired schoolteacher who lived next door. She was on the second floor of her home, talking to Charles through a screen window.

"Oh, hi Mrs. Walker," Charles said, trying to be polite. Truth be told, he really didn't like the old woman.

"I see you got a package today," she said, butting her nose into his business as usual.

"Don't you have anything better to do?" he asked.

"Ah, son, when you're my age, you'll wish you had someone to watch," she yelled down. "Watchin' folks is all I got."

"Well, if I ever get that desperate, please kill me," he finished, turning back to his porch and waving to her without looking. She smiled and watched.

Curious about the box, Charles lifted it and walked inside.

Charles ended up being the least concerned member of the group. It was probably due to the amount of liquor he had consumed that night and the fact that he didn't seem to care about what anyone thought of him. Waking up the next day, the whole thing seemed like a dream and he discarded it as such. He didn't care about Alexis or Andrea in the least so it was just a matter of sweeping it under the rug and going on with his life. He stayed in football his senior year and even went on to compete in track just before graduation. Once out of high school, he went to a community college in Fort Collins and majored in criminology of all things. He ended up choosing to be a prison guard and was pretty good at it, considering his athletic build and knack for sympathizing with criminals.

He sat down with his package and was stunned to read the return address. It just said "*Reggie*" on the upper left hand corner written in horrible cursive. He hadn't heard from his garbage-dumping friend in a long time. In fact, he hadn't even thought about him much until recent days as the bodies of Willie and Seth were discovered.

Charles opened the package to find what at least two others had discovered before their murders, a jar with human parts floating in it.

"What the hell?" he mouthed as he held the jar up to the light. He looked for a letter or accompanying message, but found nothing. Even though Russell and Wendy had the final say in whether or not the whole penis thing needed to be leaked to the public, they decided to hold off. It wasn't something they were prepared to see again.

Charles walked back outside and yelled at the neighbor's house.

"Mrs. Walker!" he barked.

After a minute or so, she appeared at her window.

"Well, look who's back," she said.

"Could you come down here for a minute?" Charles asked. "I wanna ask you 'bout somethin'."

"Sure thing, sonny. You'll have to wait a moment."

He walked to her porch and waited at her door. As the cold air whisked through his jacket, he rocked back and forth, trying to keep warm. The jar was most peculiar and had him really thinking about Reggie.

"What is it boy?" Mrs. Walker asked when she finally opened her front door.

Charles held the jar close to his jacket, trying to think of a way to explain the situation.

"Whatcha got there?" she asked, curious about what he held.

Charles continued rocking back and forth and she finally got the hint that he was cold. Jogging in the snow is one thing, but having to stand still is completely different.

"Oh. I'm sorry," she said. "Come inside."

Charles accepted her invitation and walked into her home. He held out the jar to show her.

"This was what was in the package," he said.

She took it from him and held it to the light.

"Curious. That looks an awful lot like . . ." she paused. "Yeah. I do believe that is . . ."

Grunting and grimacing, she tried in vain to open the jar, handing it to Charles.

"Open it, will ya?" she asked. "My grip isn't what it used to be."

As he twisted the lid off, he asked her again. "What do you think it is?"

Just as he asked, he pulled his head back, aghast from the smell.

"Jesus Christ that stinks," he said, handing the jar to Mrs. Walker before heading to an adjacent room. He felt dizzy from the wretched smell. Looking around the corner he watched as Mrs. Walker pulled one of the pieces of flesh from the liquid.

"It looks like pickled gizzards," she said. "That used to be my favorite. It must be some good imported stuff. Looks like it's almost gone too."

Then she took the squirrelly piece of flesh and bit a piece of it. Charles covered his mouth and walked back into the room. He couldn't stand seeing her put such an awful thing in her mouth. Midway through her small bite, she paused. Like a statue.

"Mrs. Walker?" Charles asked, reaching out to take the jar from her. Hesitantly he reached for her hand and helped her put the piece of flesh back in the jar before he sealed it up. "Mrs. Walker, are you ok?"

Her face sunk like someone who had just seen a ghost.

"Mrs. Walker?"

Then she slowly spit the chunk of fermented organ onto the carpet.

"That is the most awful tasting thing I've ever had in my mouth," she said as she walked into her kitchen for a glass of water. Charles stared at the carpet and the piled up slobbery piece that she had spit out.

"Um. I think I'm gonna go home and call the po-lice," he said.

Mrs. Walker didn't answer.

"Thanks for your help," Charles yelled. "I'm just gonna let myself out."

Wendy and the tech continued to talk as Russell thought about their next move. He walked around the lab, checking out the jars of human remains that lined the shelves along the wall. He saw brain. He saw liver. He saw eyes and tongue. Oh, and of course, he had already seen the penis and testicles. That's when it hit him.

"Wendy, I've got it!" he yelled, clapping his hands in a triumphant expression of victory.

"You've got what?" she asked. "An attitude. Yeah, we've known about that for quite some time"

"No," he said, ignoring her wisecrack. "These guys are getting their manhood removed, right? Well, that kid said they had done something horrible that none of them would talk about. Willie Becker's mother told me her son wasn't the same his senior year and that he dropped out of school. Seth had 'rapist' etched in his fuckin' body for Christ's sake. Some sick fuck out there is making a point to remove the twig and berries from all these dudes. Put all that together, wouldn't you say that it could've involved some sort of group crime in the past? Something these guys were really messed up by? Something that has caused overly hostile acts of revenge?"

"Sure, anything's possible," she said. "That could also be quite a reach. You're putting too much speculation in there with no real story to go off of. This isn't a movie. We need to find Charles and Richard and ask them to tell us before they end up dead as well. That's what we should be doing instead of hanging out here sounding like the gang on 'Scooby Doo,' trying to figure out a crime based on a hunch."

"A hunch, huh? I also did a little grabbing while we were at Reggie's place," Russell said.

The two walked out to his car and Russell reached into the back seat, pulling out a book. "I borrowed Reggie's senior yearbook."

"Why?" she asked. "Don't you already have one?"

"No, I have the junior yearbook," he said. "The kid said that they had done this horrible thing their senior year. Someone is getting these guys back for something they did that year. I just know it."

"What if it's just a guy who got picked on in school too much and is just now going after the guys on the shit list he's kept all these years?" Wendy asked.

"Now, who's reaching?" Russell replied. "There's no way that's the case. Why would this person be so hell bent on butchering the bodies and keeping us informed of what they're going to do next? Why would you want to meticulously cut the dick off of a guy for giving you a wedgie twenty years ago?"

"He's a whacko," she said. "There's no rhyme or reason. The guy's obviously not thinking logically."

It didn't take long to figure out that Seth and Charles were the only seniors to graduate out of the group. The only two even pictured in that edition. No Willie. No Reggie. No Richard. The yearbook was crisp, like new, as if it had never been opened before. The most perplexing thing was finding a senior yearbook in the living room of a man who didn't graduate high school and wasn't even pictured.

That wasn't what got Russell's attention. On the very last page, was a dedication and missing person's collage showing a few pictures of Andrea and Alexis. On each side of the top of the page were their school photos with a picture of the girls skipping hand in hand right in the center of it all. The text at the bottom of the page read:

Alexis and Andrea—1983 Missing but not forgotten.

"Looky here," he said, pointing to the images of Alexis and Andrea. "These two girls 'mysteriously' disappeared the same year all of these guys dropped out of school. This is big. This is something we need to look at. I don't know, girl. This seems pretty God damn obvious to me."

RING! RING!

"I hate this fucking phone," Russell said, pulling the cell phone from his jacket pocket. He was as hyper as a kid who just downed a box of candy. "This is Detective Meeder."

"I like it when you say your name," the voice on the other end said sadistically. "You wanna know what the worst thing about this whole process is?"

Russell perked up and again signaled to Wendy to stand by with a snap of his fingers.

"Do you or don't you wanna know?" the voice insisted.

"Sure, tell me," Russell said, playing along.

"I considered these guys to be friends at one point in my life," the voice said. "I trusted them. I believed that what we were doing was going to be fun. Well, I'm having fun now."

"Tell me about the girls," Russell said.

"You will find out on a 'need to know' basis, Detective," the voice said. "I'm no angel. I may seem like the innocent victim here, but I'm not. I have demons that no one could possibly understand."

He couldn't believe what he was hearing. The bodies he had seen were a testament to the evils of mankind, and this person was talking about being a victim. It always seems like society's afterbirth expects some kind of pity and reward for their heinous actions. Sure, Russell felt sorry. He felt sorry he ever came across the guy.

"Don't worry about that," Russell said. "I don't think anyone is going to accuse you of being neither innocent nor a victim you sick fuck."

"You have ten minutes to save a life," the voice said. "A life of a man who doesn't deserve to live. But, nevertheless, I give you one chance."

"In the darkness you will find a dying giant resting alongside its replacement," he started. "Alone in the moonlit shadows of darkness, you may be able to save the bastard."

The phone line went dead.

"What?" Wendy said, anxious. "Who was it? Was it him? What did he say?"

"He said we need to find a dying giant resting alongside its replacement," Russell repeated, completely flabbergasted. "What the hell?"

"Well, that's easy," Wendy chimed. "Mile High Stadium. The new stadium is done and the old one is being torn down. That's got to be it."

Russell perked up and walked over to Wendy, grabbing her on each cheek, pulling her face towards his for an unexpected kiss on the lips.

"You are a genius girl," he said. "We have ten minutes. How long you think it will take to drive there?"

"In this traffic?" she said wiping his kiss from her mouth, slightly turned on by the gesture. "At least a half hour."

"Fuckin' Christ," he muttered. "We gotta get someone over there now."

Russell got on the phone and ordered squad cars from the area to head to Mile High immediately. It was nearly 11 o'clock at night and the area around the stadium would be deserted. Four minutes and 35 seconds later the first of a dozen squad cars arrived at the stadium, as did a chopper with a spotlight. Chaos all around and only one vehicle rested in the parking lot, its back turned to the aging stadium, engine running. A seventies model Volkswagen beetle was parked in front of the old gift shop, its orange paint illuminating under the lights of the chopper. The gentle popping of the engine was off a bit, sounding as if it needed a tune up. The first response cops quickly converged on the vehicle, guns drawn, not knowing what craziness awaited them inside. They had all been briefed about the unpredictability and sick nature of this killer.

"*Holy shit, there's someone behind the car*," someone radioed from the helicopter. "*His hands are under the car, pointing directly at you fellas. Use extreme caution. I can't see a weapon. He's . . . he's also naked.*"

Spreading out, the officers moved slowly around the back.

"Freeze!" yelled the first officer as he swung around the rear of the car. "Holy Jesus! Shut this car off. Hurry!"

The naked body of Reggie Peterson was lying stiff as a board behind the car. He was on his stomach, his hands pulled forward and cuffed around the rear driver's side axle, his mouth wrapped firmly around the exhaust pipe. As the car continued to spit noxious carbon-laced fumes into his system, his body began to balloon and stiffen. He had died almost instantly when the car was turned on, but continued to take in the fumes like an air filter.

"Shut this car off, dammit!" yelled the officer. The doors were locked and they scrambled to bust the windows with the butts of their rifles. Glass flew in all directions and the car was finally penetrated.

"Sir, there's no ignition," one of the officers yelled.

The cop in the rear reached over to open the engine compartment above the body, finding it locked.

"There's got to be a way to stop this damn thing!" he barked before rearing his rifle back, smacking it down on the hood's handle. A few whacks and the handle broke loose. "Thank god for cheap ass German manufacturing!"

Reggie's body was building more and more pressure as the cop grabbed and pulled the distributor cap off, along with some spark plug wires, causing the engine to grind to a halt. The smell of burnt flesh, oil and gasoline emanated from the sight. The police officers stood over the body for a moment, watching it slowly sink as it released the gasses that had been pumped into it. One officer turned and puked on the cement, while a couple others walked away, fighting their own urge to vomit.

Russell and Wendy pulled into the parking lot and their car screeched to a halt. Police cruisers, flashing lights, a chopper and a couple dozen cops signaled something big and they were too late. Russell ran up to the car, pushing cops out of his way, Wendy trailing far behind with each step.

"What happened?" he yelled. "What the fuck happened here? You guys had ten minutes. Ten fucking minutes. I got here in . . ." he looked at his watch "Twelve."

Screams and yells erupted all around Russell. The cops that had shown up at the scene were subject to a horror that they assumed Russell didn't understand or respect. They were the ones who responded to the call and found the body and saved it from exploding. One especially furious cop had to be pulled away from Russell.

"You motherfucker!" the man yelled as he swung his fist around, connecting with Russell's cheek.

"Break it up! Break it up!" a voice yelled.

"You guys had ten minutes. He said ten minutes," Russell whimpered as he slid onto the ground next to the body.

Russell was helped to his feet just as the back tire was being removed. Reggie's arms had been handcuffed around the axle and were in full view. They were stretched to the point that one of his shoulders had come out of its socket. A pair of swimmer's noseplugs were on his nose, pinching off any chance of breathing in fresh air.

The skin around his wrists sat exposed and bleeding from what must have been a violent struggle to get free during those first few moments of being one with the VW. That suggested to everyone that he was alive when he was placed on the back of the car. His lips were charred and cooked onto the tailpipe and flesh remained when his head was pulled from the vehicle. The cuffs were removed and the body was dragged away from the car for further inspection of damage. Reggie's teeth were all chipped and broken from clamping down on the exhaust pipe. Trails of vomit that had already dried from the immense heat cascaded down his chin and chest into a pool of blood, sweat and piss that surrounded the spot where he died.

Russell put on rubber gloves and went to work, studying the body so that it could quickly be removed from the lot. He flipped Reggie onto his back and discovered a scene all too familiar. His genitals had been carefully cut from his body and the wound had been cauterized to prevent bleeding to death. The killer wanted Reggie to suffer on the tailpipe and had obviously kept him alive after castrating him.

Russell looked over at Wendy and the two instinctively knew at that exact moment, they were both thinking of Jared. His father was gone. Reggie's body was not only the most well preserved of the three victims, it was the closest they had come to finding someone alive. Someone who could give a clue as to what was happening. He was hot to the touch, whereas the other victims had frozen by the time they reached them.

"We've got to find those other two," Russell said, leaving the body to be taken away. "They link this whole thing together."

RING! RING!

Russell stopped dead in his tracks. Wendy looked over in fear.

His phone was ringing.

RING! RING!

"You gonna answer that?" Wendy asked.

Russell looked confused, like he didn't want to answer it.

"I'm tired," he confessed.

RING! RING!

"Tired?" she said. "Tired of what?"

"I'm tired of being involved in this shit. I'm tired of not knowing what person is going to die next. I'm tired of finding smelly, ripped all to shit bodies. I'm tired of it."

RING! RING!

"Don't be such a pussy! Just answer the phone," Wendy pleaded. "We need to keep communication open with this guy so that we can hopefully catch him."

"Yes?" Russell said into his phone.

"Did I catch you at a bad time?" the voice said. "I'm sorry you couldn't save our dear friend Reggie. He pleaded with me to extend my time limit, but I just couldn't. That would've made the game slightly boring, don't you think?"

"You didn't even give me five minutes," Russell said.

"Oh, I'm sorry, my watch is fast," the voice joked. "You know, I don't really want you to stop me and I absolutely don't want you to save these men. If you were to get too close, I might be forced to stop *you*."

"Tell me about the girls," Russell said.

"I miss Andrea," the voice said. "She should've never been there."

Silence.

"Tell me about Andrea," Russell pleaded. This validated his earlier hunch. "Where is she?"

"Don't talk about Andrea," the voice angrily quipped. "We're not speaking right now so that I can talk about Andrea Mitchell."

"You know what happened to Andrea and Alexis," Russell accused, hoping to get some information out of the creep. "Please tell me what happened."

"I'm going to tell you where you need to go next," the voice said. "And, you can decide whether or not you're up for it. However, if you stop, you may never know what you are chasing. You must follow directions."

"Ok," Russell said. "What do you got for me?"

"I'm going to tell you about Charles. This was a fun one," the voice said, followed by a chuckle. "Charles Manning wasn't exactly the nicest of men. He wasn't even that nice to me. He's sitting here with me right now, enjoying a cup of tea. You'll do well to forget about him as a living, breathing part of society. He'll soon be talked about on the news and read about in the obituaries like the rest of them. His legacy will be embellished and he'll be mourned in death as if he were a king in life just like the rest of these sad wastes of skin. I don't know what I'm going to do, but as always, you'll be the first to know Detective Meeder. How cute. He hears me saying all this and is struggling to get out of the chair. Don't worry, I've bound him pretty well and taped his mouth."

"I suppose it wouldn't do any good to scream in the phone and plead for you to let him go and end all this, would it?" Russell said, defeated.

"We both know the answer to that, Detective," the voice said. "He'll die like the rest of them."

"What is it about me?" Russell demanded. "Why are you calling me like I'm you're fucking shoulder to cry on?"

"Let's just say, you inspired me," the voice confessed.

"Inspired you?" Russell barked. "Inspired you to what, maim and murder? Huh?"

The phone line went dead.

"Fuckin' Christ!" Russell yelled, directing his anger at the night sky. He walked over to a light pole a few feet away and leaned against it, sliding to the ground. "What the fuck is going on?" He buried his head in his hands and began to weep. Russell Meeder actually cried.

"What did he say?" Wendy insisted. "Are you crying?"

"He told me to wait for his call," Russell said, wiping a tear from his face with a smug laugh. "He's got Charles already."

"Well, you know what that means?" Wendy asked.

Russell looked up at her, "What?"

"Richard's the only one left," she said. "He's the only one of the five left out there. Don't you see? We need to find this guy and at least bring him in for protection. Who knows, he might even be doing this shit."

"Jesus, you're so right," Russell said. "Let's go."

Russell and Wendy arrived back at the office and he flipped on the light switch, triggering the painful flickering of fluorescent lights.

"We have a lot of work to do," he said. "We need to find out all we can about Richard Tark, and find out where he lives and who he associates with. Who is his family and what connection did he have to Andrea Mitchell?"

"Why her?" Wendy asked.

"The man on the phone got really defensive when I brought up Andrea. I mean, *really* defensive. It's like he wanted to kill me just for mentioning her name. When I tried to get him to talk about the girls, he acted like he didn't hear the question. The key being that he knew her name."

In an hour's time they had managed to locate Richard's last known address, his mother's address and a work history for the man. Russell had a couple of cops go over to Richard's listed address but found that he had moved away four months before. The landlord didn't know where Richard went and hinted that the man might be homeless. He had no job and stopped paying his bills, thus the eviction.

"Tomorrow morning we need to pay a visit to his mother," Russell said.

"Where is Richard?" she asked. "We need to find him now. Why are you talking about tomorrow when all of this shit is happening today?"

"Hey, right now we have no clue where Richard is. She can tell us a little about him and she might even be able to help us understand what happened in 1983," Russell said.

"Let's go right now," she said, motioning towards the door. "Let's go talk to his mother right now. I don't want to wait until morning."

"I'll pick you up at your place tomorrow morning around seven thirty," Russell said, ignoring her plea. "Now shut the fuck up and go home."

Wendy grabbed her coat and stormed from the office, holding her middle finger up at Russell the whole time. He smiled and leaned in his chair. They were really starting to get along.

As she left the office, she too began to smile. It wasn't often that a sexist, machismo-laden asshole could sweep her off her feet, but Russell just had a way about him. She certainly wasn't going to let on that she liked that sort of thing, but nevertheless, she was beginning to like his attitude. She stopped and turned towards the end of the hall. Maybe if she walked back into that office and told him how she felt, things would be ok. Maybe if he knew that she liked his style and that she was finding him more and more attractive as the days went by, he'd admit the same.

Either way, it didn't matter.

She had to go.

15

The light rocked back and forth on the end of its electrical cord. The bulb was finally replaced after months of darkness in the bedroom behind the kitchen. The unusual presence of light in the room convinced Richard to keep it lit even when he wasn't in there. The window had been boarded up a couple years prior when a rock was thrown through it, but that was long before he moved in. Richard went through phases where he wanted everything dark and phases where he would actually let a little sunshine into his living space. He hadn't had a job in nearly seven and a half years and was done milking his mother for cash.

He walked into the kitchen, skillfully maneuvering around open boxes of generic toasted corn cereal that littered the ground. He didn't like milk and didn't really feel the urge to buy real food, so he lived on a staple of cereal in water. He ate two small bowls a day, one before he went to bed at night and one when he woke.

Looking at him, you'd know right away that the years had been hard on him.

Gently, he walked across the dirty floor and opened the refrigerator. The motor had burned out a long time ago and was merely acting as another cupboard. He kept his shoes and a pair of slippers on the racks in the fridge. He reached in and grabbed his slippers, holes gouged on the front of each foot and his big toes stuck out as soon as he slipped them on.

Richard's mother had spoken with him a few times in the previous six months, but had no real contact with the man. He had a tendency to black out and forget about long stretches of time. Sometimes days. Sometimes weeks. It got to a point in which his mother was fed up with having the same conversations with him and stopped putting forth any effort in communication. Although her love for her son was still admirable, she wasn't mentally capable of keeping a relationship with him. He was just too damaged upstairs.

He walked back into the living room and turned the paperclip knob on his 12-inch black and white television. It took about 20 seconds for it to burn to life, and he was sitting patiently by the time that happened. News of Seth's death was still a hot topic in Denver, more so than that of Willie and Reggie since the police were still keeping the details of a possible serial killer hidden from the public. Richard's yellowed teeth shined brighter with each death. He wanted them all to die, and expected the next one to happen very soon.

A pounding could be heard on the wall next to his chair, but he ignored it. He knew what it was and didn't really want to deal with it. Instead, he lifted his hand and stared at the Carver High School class ring that was cemented on his finger. He hadn't taken it off in nearly 20 years and planned on dying with it.

Still the banging continued.

KNOCK! KNOCK!

"C'mon girl," Russell yelled at the door. "We gotta get going. I'm sorry I was such a dick last night, but we have to go."

An old lady walked by him with her cane in one hand and a spray bottle in the other. She seemed to find joy in Russell's impatience.

"Banging on her door isn't going to make it better," she said. "You need to show her that you care."

Russell turned to the old lady, who was now past him, her back in full view.

"It's not what it looks like," he said. "We're partners."

The old lady didn't acknowledge him.

"Actually, that didn't sound right," he said. "We're partners at work. Oh never mind, you old bag. What would you know?"

Again, without turning to face him, the old lady spoke.

"I *know* that there's a note on the ground in front of your feet," she said, fading into the distance. "It's probably from her."

Russell looked down and sure enough, found a note sticking from beneath the mat. He picked it up read it.

Russell, go by yourself. I need to be alone.

Wendy

"Alone?" Russell said. "What the fuck?"

Not believing what he was reading, he knocked on the door again. Why would she bail on an investigation?

"Fuckin' Christ."

Walking back to his car, he tore the note up and discarded each piece as he made his way down the flight of stairs from her apartment balcony. Before getting in his car, he turned and looked back at her apartment, hoping to find her standing there, wishing it was all a joke.

Now, it really felt like he was married. No, better yet, he felt like he was a kid again, realizing that he had fallen head over heels for someone who he had treated like dirt, hoping to have another chance to tell her how he felt.

He hit the interstate, not quite ready to travel the 60 miles north to Fort Collins. Richard's mother was listed as living in the same home for the previous 20-plus years and Russell hoped that she could shed some light on what had happened while the boys were in high school. He also knew there wasn't much time. If the killer was telling the truth about Charles, only one person remained who could still be saved.

Fort Collins was bustling with activity when Russell arrived, and he took the long way to the Tark family homestead. Richard's mother lived in the shadows of Horsetooth, a key part of the foothills that started the Rocky Mountains. The neighborhood was quiet and well maintained. Children ran in the streets and played with the little snow that was left on the ground.

Russell thought of Wendy and felt a sense of emptiness for the first time in many years. He looked at her vacant seat beside him and realized how much he missed having a partner. More specifically her. Even if she did talk too much.

He pulled into the driveway at the Tark residence and walked up to the house, knocking instead of ringing the doorbell. He could hear rustling inside and turned to look around the neighborhood while waiting for her to answer.

Sitting in the driveway was a beat-up, half rotten Volkswagen beetle. Ages of oil trailed from its engine down the slope of the cement following a path of time that seemed to lead nowhere. Russell cringed when he first saw it. Visions of Reggie's mutilated mouth and the smell that came from it again flashed in Russell's memory. He noticed the tailpipes on the Tark-mobile were crushed and sealed. Interesting for a vehicle.

Finally, someone opened the door. A large man with a beard and long, brown hair appeared from behind it.

"Yeah?" he asked.

"I'm looking for a Mrs. Tark," Russell started, feeling like a British schoolboy standing next to such a large man. "Is she here?"

"Yep," the man said, before closing the door right back in his face.

Russell turned and faced the street again, not knowing if Richard's mother was going to come to the door or if he'd have to get tough. He walked over to the bug in the driveway and studied it. It was as if it hadn't moved in years. Russell bent down and grabbed one of the tailpipes. It looked like each one had been run over by a steamroller.

"It's not for sale," a voice said. Russell could see the shadow of a woman standing right behind him. It was as if she had fended off many prospective buyers for the car. "It's my boy's car and he don't want to sell it."

"I'm not interested in the car, but I am interested in what happened to the tailpipes," Russell said. "It seems like the car would have trouble running in that condition. It also seems like it has done very little of that in a long time."

"Some bad people did that to my boy when he was in school and ruined it for good," she said. "He won't let me move it, and I don't really feel the need to. It kind of reminds me of him sometimes."

"Doesn't he live in Denver?" Russell asked, whipping out a small notepad and pen from his pocket. "Why do you need a reminder for someone who lives an hour away?"

"Yes, he lives down there," she started. "I don't know why. It's too crowded. Too many people to have to live with. Anyways, I haven't seen him in a very long time. He doesn't really feel the need to visit me anymore." Her eyes began to well with tears. "If you aren't here for the car, then what are you here for? What's with the scribbling in that little book?"

"I'm a cop. I'm here to talk to *you* actually, Mrs. Tark," Russell said. "About Richard."

She closed her eyes and nodded.

"I was afraid of this," she said, turning to walk back to the porch.

"Wait, afraid? Afraid of what?" Russell insisted, running to catch up with her. "What do you mean?"

"Richard is a special boy," Mrs. Tark admitted. "He was a special boy in school and I had to keep a close eye on him, especially after his father left."

"Was Richard a troublemaker?" Russell asked.

The two sat down on a rickety porch swing. Richard's mother looked old and tired, like Mother Nature ran over her with a monster truck.

"Not really," Mrs. Tark said. "He had a tendency at an early age to get into trouble, but it was mostly because he didn't like to pay attention for too long. Plus, he was picked on unmercifully."

Picked on? Maybe Wendy's theory was right, Russell thought to himself.

Mrs. Tark rocked back and forth as if her memory was being restored. She seemed pleased to talk to someone about a child she obviously cared about long ago.

"Who are you?" she asked.

"My name is Russell Meeder and I'm a detective for the city of Denver," he said, showing her his I.D. "Your boy's not in any legal trouble per se, but I need to know a little about him to try to protect him. I think he might be in danger."

"You don't have to lie to me," she said. "He's probably up to something, right? Maybe he's robbed a liquor store, or started one of them crazy cults. What's he done?"

"There's no cult. Like I said, he hasn't been accused of doing anything, yet," Russell said. "I need to know a little about him, especially during high school. More specifically when he was a freshman."

Russell sat by, ready to write down every word she said.

"I need to ask you some questions about your son, like, what his current address is, phone, height, weight, you know that kind of stuff."

"You know when I dropped out of school?" Mrs. Tark asked Russell. Of course, he didn't know the answer. "I didn't. I stayed in school, even though I had to come home and take care of my younger brother and sister. I chose to tough it out."

Russell looked confused.

"When did he drop out?" Russell asked.

"When he was a freshman," she said, as tears began to fall from her eyes. "I thought he'd be the first from our family to attend college. He was so bright, but those boys drug him down."

"What boys?" Russell asked.

"There were some boys in this neighborhood, oh, I'd say a little shy of twenty years ago, that would tease my Richard to no end," she said. "He'd come home angry at the world, and it would be all due to those little hooligans. Do you realize my boy came home from school one day, covered in dog shit because those kids decided it would be funny to throw it at him? Dog shit, Mr. Meeder."

Russell shook his head no. As bad as it sounds, the thought did cross his mind that something like that might be somewhat funny, but it was immediately flushed away by his good conscience. Things were starting to really make sense although he still couldn't figure out where Andrea came into the picture, or Alexis for that matter.

"Who were these kids?" he asked.

"I don't know, just some kids," she admitted. "I remember the two black kids were unmerciful. I guess that's how they are, what being slaves at some point. I think years of picking cotton must've done that. Niggers made my son bad," she finished.

"Fuckin' Christ," he gently muttered to himself, wiping a bead of sweat from his forehead.

"What about Andrea?" he asked.

Mrs. Tark lit up and changed moods in a flash.

"She was beautiful," she said. "I introduced the two of 'em. My son was one of the first in Colorado to meet this lovely girl and gave her rides to school that same year she went missing. I introduced them you know. And between you, me and the rocks, I wanted them to get together."

Russell was beginning to see the whole picture.

The abuse at school.

The infatuation with the girl.

Richard needed to be stopped.

"What about her disappearance?" Russell asked. "Did anyone question your son?"

"No one knew they were even friends," she said. "They must have parted ways once they got to school, because no one ever talked to me, or my son, about the whole disappearance. Everyone just figured those two girls ran off together. Some lesbian thing."

Russell's phone beeped in his pocket.

"Excuse me," Russell said. "I have to answer this."

He got up and walked back towards the car, pressing the send button.

"This is Detective Meeder," he said.

The voice on the other end was the lab tech who was dealing with the jars of human parts.

"Detective Meeder," the voice said. "A fellow named Charles Manning received one of those jars with the penis and testicles yesterday. They brought it to me around noon. It's almost identical to the other ones, only this was from an African American."

Russell smacked the phone against his forehead.

"Yesterday?" he said, erupting in a temper tantrum. "Yesterday? If you had that jar at noon, you should've been speaking to me on the phone by twelve o'one. Now, that man is off somewhere getting turned into kung-pow while I'm in Fort Collins talking to the mother of the spawn whose doing it."

Russell turned to find Mrs. Tark running into her home crying.

"Mrs. Tark!" he yelled. "Ah, Fuck!"

Russell chased after her, but stopped immediately when the big fellow who answered the door stood in his way. Russell turned and walked back towards his car, stopping in the middle of the Tark front lawn to talk on his phone.

"If you get any more of those jars, you call me before you even set the thing down," Russell barked. "Is that fucking understood?"

"Yes sir," the beleaguered man said.

Russell put his phone away and chuckled to himself. In a flash he sprinted to his car to grab his camera. He ran back to the Tark home and took some photos of the tailpipes on the car, getting different angles. There wasn't much time as the big grumpy caveman burst through the front door with a metal baseball bat in his hand.

"Oh shit," Russell said, turning to run back to his car. His gun was in the glove box, and he didn't have time to mess with the psycho so he peeled out, waving at the man as he sped away.

On the way back to town, he thought again about Wendy and wondered why she would skip out on work. She wasn't really allowed to do that unless she was laying on her deathbed, which wouldn't be the case.

RING! RING!

Russell answered quickly, hoping Wendy was calling.

"Hello," he said.

"You're going to like this one," the voice said. "I had a hard time getting onto the football field, but once you get past the initial gate, you can go virtually anywhere you want in that stadium. The security definitely needs improvement before that place opens."

Russell's heart was racing.

"What did you do?" he said. "I talked to your mother today, you know."

"*My* mother?" the voice said. "Don't change the subject. *I* change the subject and *I* make the subject and *I* kill the subject. Understand? Don't talk to me about petty things when you have no clue. *I* am the master of this sport and you are a mere spectator. Don't talk to me about who *you* talked to because the only important person *you* can talk to at this particular moment in time is *me*. Don't piss me off again Mr. Meeder. Don't fuckin' push my buttons again!"

"I'm sorry," Russell said, completely at the mercy of the crazy bastard on the other end of the line. The only question remained—where was Charles and how badly was he tortured before he was ultimately put to death?

"You need to break into the stadium," the voice said. "Don't call for backup, and don't use your weapon. I will be watching you and I have something you may want back."

Russell was very curious.

"What could you possibly have that I want?" Russell asked.

"Russell?" another voice said into the phone. "Russell, it's Wendy. I'm sorry. I'm sorry I let him do this to me. Please . . ."

Russell's heart dropped to the floorboard and seemingly hit the gas pedal as the car flew down the interstate towards the football stadium.

"Don't hurt her," he instructed the killer. "We have done nothing to you."

"And you will continue to do nothing to me," the voice said. "Or, you will suffer. And so will she. I have a job to do, and nothing will stand in my way. That includes you."

"If you don't want me to stand in your way, why the fuck are you telling me where to find the bodies?" Russell asked. "Why are you teasing me with the possibility of saving lives? Why wouldn't you just do what you gotta do and then disappear?"

"I told you already, Detective Meeder. I'm not giving you the chance to save these lost souls," the voice said. "I am giving you a chance to play the game with me. You are my inspiration. You are the reason this is happening."

"Inspiration?" Russell barked. "Why do you keep saying that? Last I checked, I've never cut up another human being in my life."

"In time, you'll know," the voice said. "In time. Now, you have a stadium to break into, get breakin'. And remember, do *not* ask for help in breaking into the stadium and do *not* fire your gun for any reason."

Russell pulled into the parking lot at the new Denver football stadium. It was a beautiful testament to the money and popularity of the game. Like the thought of walking into a newly built Roman Coliseum, this was something meant to be exciting.

Breaking in was going to be a hard task.

Russell walked around the entire complex, looking for a passageway or entrance that he could cut with his standard issue bolt cutters. The killer said he couldn't discharge his weapon and he was going to follow that command. He found a door next to the ticket window and reared back his leg, hitting the glass full force. It took about a dozen kicks, but eventually the glass did break. Russell crept through the door and pulled his gun out, ready for anything.

He walked around the corridor, hoping to find someone at the stadium who could help him figure out what was going on.

There was no one in sight.

He found a gate that led to the lower level and eventually onto the playing field. Russell put his gun away and began to climb the bars, vaulting over the top on his way to the grass. Finally, he reached the entrance onto the field. The grass was void of snow. A new technology allowing the field to be heated at all times made it nearly impossible for snow to stick.

For a moment, Russell looked up and around at the beauty that was before him. The new stadium was truly magical. His vision of the new complex was about to change, and did when he looked down at the far goal post. Across the field, the horror of the situation again revealed itself.

There, hanging on the goal post in the end zone was the naked body of Charles Manning. Russell let out a sigh. He was again the first man on the scene.

As was the case with Seth, Charles' body was hanging in a crucified manner. His arms were outstretched on the yellow bars that would eventually see so many field goals and extra points pass through its space. Each wrist was held in place by handcuffs that were hooked on the post.

But, the thing keeping his weight hanging from the metal was the vice around his throat. An old Carver High football jersey was wrapped tightly around his neck and tied in a knot onto the yellow bar that rested behind his head. So tightly in fact, that blood trailed down from his neck to his abdomen.

His face was burned, but not to the point where it did any damage to his skull. The skin, however, was nearly burned to the bone and the hair was completely gone. Bruises adorned Charles' midsection. His ribs were smashed and shattered from the blows of something that must have been akin to a baseball bat or metal bar. Unlike Seth's body, Charles had his feet removed completely. Both of his bare feet were placed carefully below the body with a blood-stained football between the two.

As had been the case with everyone before him, the genitals were missing.

Glancing across the length of the yellow goal post, Russell saw words written in blood. To the right of Charles' arm it read "RAPIST" and to the left of his other arm, the word "MURDERER," was scribbled. The hole that was created by the removal of the penis was quite choppy. It wasn't as clean as the other victims and suggested more of a struggle occurred during this amputation. Charles was certainly the fighter of the group.

The smell of the corpse was nearly unbearable. It was a mix between rotting and burning flesh. Although he hadn't been dead for a terribly long time, he smelled as if he had.

Russell felt the need to remove the jersey and get a look at the body without the cloth. Apparently the killer also hoped Russell would feel that way, leaving behind the ladder that was used in the hanging.

He climbed the ladder and tried to pry the cloth from its knot. On a few occasions, Russell had to turn his head and cough from the horrible stench of the body. The sun beat down on it, making it so much more difficult. When he couldn't budge the jersey, he whipped out a pocketknife and began sawing. Minutes later the jersey was ripped away and Charles' head nearly came off of the body, only held on by a patch of skin.

His throat had been cut from ear to ear and his tongue was protruding from the wound. It appeared that his tongue had been yanked from the cut then nailed into the upper portion of his sternum with the same type of nail that had held Seth's body to the telephone pole.

Russell bounced off of the ladder and put distance between himself and the grizzly sight. It wasn't the kind of thing that he had signed up for when he trained to be in law enforcement.

It was quite a sight seeing a burned head with a perfectly ripe tongue sticking out of it. That was definitely a sign of a flash burn. The killer must had used a propane torch or something like it to fry the skin just enough to distort it.

Looking around Charles' backside, there didn't appear to be any markings, until Russell glanced at his buttocks. A shiny object barely protruded from the crack between his cheeks.

Having trouble standing the smell already, Russell knew that he had to go a step further and dig into Charles rectum to get the object out. It was a good thing he had a pair of rubber gloves in his back pants pocket.

Slowly he pried apart the former athletes cheeks, getting a better glimpse of what was protruding from it. It appeared to be a gold figurine of some kind. Pulling the figure from the orifice, Russell discovered it to be the top portion of a trophy. The little gold football player was covered in blood and shit, broken off of the base with such force that the metal was actually twisted.

"Fuckin' Christ," Russell muttered and with that the smell and horror that surrounded him forced a few bouts with dry heaves.

Russell shook his head, clearing out the cobwebs that were forcing his stomach to turn. He walked towards the barricade that separated the field from the stands and leaned against it, trying to get some fresh air.

He rested against the railing, looked at the body and wondered what his next move was going to be. He couldn't very well leave it there and not call the police. But, he was at the mercy of the killer. Hoping for a phone call he waited and bathed in the warm sun and smell of death. All around him was the final result of years of hard work in constructing a beautiful stadium. The plans that had been discussed in the media for nearly five years were all right there before him. He pulled out a cigarette and lit up, realizing two things. One—he hadn't smoked one in quite some time and two—he was masking the smell of rotting flesh with smoke. And who said cigarettes were unhealthy?

An hour past and Russell sat on the grass, looking at his cell phone, hoping for a ring. Strangely enough, he had seen a groundskeeper walking on the other end of the field, totally oblivious to Russell's presence, and even more disturbing, to the body that adorned the goal post.

The sun was beginning to fall behind the upper level of the stadium and Russell was out of cigarettes, butts surrounding him.

RING! RING!

"Hello! Hello!" Russell said, acting like a school girl who had been waiting all day for her boyfriend to call. "Hello!"

"Easy there, Detective," the voice said, mocking the now nervous man. "Do you like my handy work? I found a special pleasure in shoving that trophy up his ass. I was a bit disappointed when it broke. I thought it would be an artistic expression, having the whole trophy sticking out, tickling the people who walked past. Do you think I'm an artist?"

Russell was beat.

"What now?" he asked. "What about Wendy? Is she okay?"

"Don't worry, Detective," the voice said. "As long as you cooperate, and I don't see why you wouldn't, I won't hurt a hair on her head. I don't have a problem with her—yet. Now leave the stadium, the same way you came, and don't inform the police. I want him to hang there as long as possible. Go have dinner or something. I'll call you with my next instructions."

Russell flipped shut the phone without saying a word. He walked towards the exit, head down, eyes forward. He was done dealing with Richard Tark. The fact that one remained, and that one insisted on playing games, was a testament to the man's psyche.

RING! RING!

Russell raised the phone to his ear and pressed send, without saying a word.

"Don't get feisty," the voice said. "You don't want to lose your new partner."

Then the man hung up on Russell.

Racing through the streets of Denver is an art form, mastered by those who have lived and grown up on those very streets. People not as familiar with the pace tend to sit to the side, watching the whole world seemingly pass them by at lightning speed. Russell was driving on a mission. He didn't care how fast or how dangerous he was traveling, he had to get to Richard's latest shanty apartment. The address was scribbled in his notebook, courtesy of Richard's mother. At least she managed to do something right.

He shouldn't have let Wendy walk out of his office pissed at him. She was the only good thing on his mind.

The fact that a cop was trailing him for two miles with lights blaring was a testament to Russell's concentration on the mission at hand. He did pull over. After all, he was still a law-abiding detective.

"License and registration," the cop said.

"Sir, my name is Detective Russell Meeder," he said, holding his I.D. and wallet out for the cop. "I am on a case and need to go."

"Are you on duty, Detective?" the officer asked.

"Yes."

"Why aren't you driving your squad car?" the cop questioned.

"This is my squad car," Russell said. "I am an undercover detective. I don't have a fancy detective car with flashy lights and obnoxious whistles and horns. I investigate crime and to do that I need a normal car."

The cop stood confused. For a moment Russell actually thought the man was going to go through with his insistent ticket writing.

"Just be careful," the cop said, handing Russell back his wallet.

"Thanks," Russell said. "I know what I'm doing."

Before the cop could even get past his car, Russell gunned it and was back on the road, driving in and out of traffic like a madman. Richard lived on the edge of the city of Denver, but the traffic made it a chore to get to his apartment from the stadium.

Russell did nothing but sweat and stare. He stared at the other drivers, wondering if they realized that a whole world of shit was occurring all around them, and they were just as powerless as Russell in stopping it.

He pulled into the parking lot of Richard's apartment complex. It was a shamble of a building and looked like a haunted house. In a few years time it would no doubt be condemned and all the tenants removed, replaced by homeless meth heads and runaways. Without hesitation he flew up the stairs and raced towards the door. It was apartment 21-A, and had a do not disturb tag on the handle.

"Do not disturb," Russell read as he held the handle up, ripping it from the knob. He pulled his gun from its holster and braced for entry. He had no warrant and no reasonable search and seizure defense, but didn't care. Bracing for another beating to his foot, he reared back and kicked the door and to his surprise, it flew open on the first try due to the fact that it wasn't even latched much less locked. Russell nearly hit the ground when he gained such easy access.

Alert and ready for anything, he aimed his gun and cautiously walked around the living room, waiting for someone to jump out at him. The killer had told him not to do anything, but it didn't matter, he was going to stop the madness. He had the upper hand, not this nut job. Like a ninja, Russell tip-toed down the hall, gun held high.

The darkness of the house was nearly as frightening as the smell. It was as if the toilet was backed up and the family cat was rotting in the kitchen. Dirty clothes and used pizza boxes were strewn throughout the living room and hallway. It was like a frat house the day after a party when everyone was puking and ditching the house they just trashed.

The big break happened when Russell burst into the bedroom. Sitting on the bed, his back facing the angry detective, was Richard Tark. He seemed oblivious to the fact that someone was in his house, not to mention barging into his bedroom.

"Where is she?" Russell screamed, his gun pointed directly at the back of Richard's skull. "Where is she motherfucker? Where's Wendy?"

Richard didn't say a word.

Russell pounced on the man and threw him on the bed, flat on his belly. Richard moaned in discomfort, but didn't put up much of a struggle.

"You're going to find out how it feels to have something shoved up your ass, you raping, killing piece of shit," Russell said, jamming the barrel of his gun onto the crack of Richard rear. "I should shoot you right now and get it over with. Judge, jury, executioner. Right fucking now."

Richard didn't say a word. He just grumbled and moaned from the disturbance.

Russell frisked the man who was wearing a tattered and fuzzy pink robe over his clothes. He had a pair of dirty jeans on as well as an old, black, AC/DC t-shirt. It appeared as if his hair hadn't been cut or washed in a few months, and he smelled like shit.

"Jesus, don't you know what a shower is?" Russell asked, still patting down Richard's pants. "You seem awfully gamy for someone who was able to sneak up on so many people. In fact, you're pretty fucking small, how did you overpower the likes of Seth Owens and Charles Manning? Those guys are fucking monsters compared to you."

Russell pulled Richard's hands behind his back and cuffed him, lifting him from the bed by the chain that connected the cuffs.

"Nice fucking bathrobe, you moron," Russell said. "You thought I wasn't going to catch you, but you were sadly mistaken, bitch. Now, you're going to tell me where Wendy is and I may . . . I may let you live."

In the struggle, Russell managed to glance at Richard's broken down dresser drawer. Resting neatly on top was a tooth and an earring. His jaw dropped from the sight. He couldn't believe it. Russell slowly reached up and caressed his ear drum, playing with the scar that still lined his skin. He left Richard cuffed and laying on the bed and walked over to the dresser, picking up the tooth and earring. They were instantly familiar. He glanced back at Richard and for the first time since the attack, remembered his face. He was the smaller one. The pussy who beat on him after he was already down and out.

"Holy fuckin' shit," Russell murmured. "You're that little piece of garbage, aren't you? How is that even possible?"

Russell walked back over to Richard, not knowing if he could control his anger. Richard was still on his stomach and Russell pounced on his back again. The table next to the bed had a jar on it containing the sexual remains of Charles Manning. Russell saw the jar and let out a terrific laugh.

"Here, let's see how much fun it is to fuck with someone's cock," Russell barked, leaning over to grab the jar, twisting its lid off. "Whew, this shit is strong. You're going to love it."

Richard didn't budge.

Russell reached his hands into the liquid, gagging in the process, and pulled one of the fleshy items from the murky orange fluid. It was one of the testicles.

"Here, eat this, eat what's left of Charles!" Russell screamed, pressing the flesh against Richard's lips, crushing it against his teeth and rubbing it between the cracks like grout.

Richard looked over at Russell in a gaze of drunken stupidity, a string of drool hanging from his chin. He let loose a smile usually reserved for the mentally challenged and hopelessly retarded crowd. Obviously, Russell didn't understand.

"Oh, I see, you're going to play like you are too fucked up to stand trial," Russell said. "Either that or you're on something way too strong to be having a civilized conversation right now. Let's get you downtown and get all of the '*hi, nice to meet you'* bullshit out of the way. The media's going to love your dumb ass."

Russell walked out to his car, holding Richard up to prevent him from falling on his face. People from the apartment complex were coming out of their homes to see what the commotion was all about.

"Go back inside people," Russell said. "Nothing to see here. Just a man going to jail."

He placed Richard in the back seat of his car and began to drive away.

"Alright, motherfucker, where's Wendy?" Russell asked again. Richard didn't even blink. "I'm going to ask you one more time, and if you don't tell me where she is, we're going to take a drive down by the old paper factory where no one will hear you scream. Where is Wendy?"

Richard just smiled and drooled and turned to look out of the window. His head bobbed around like a newborn baby just learning how to sit up.

"All right," Russell said. "We'll get you settled."

Russell hit the gas then blasted the brake causing Richard to slam his head against the headboard behind the passenger seat.

"That's for knocking out my fucking teeth!" he barked. "Where's Wendy?"

Silence.

"Fine fucker, have it your way," Russell exclaimed.

Russell drove Richard to a part of town that had three abandoned warehouses and a factory. He had no intention of bringing him in for booking. Without any info on Wendy, Richard's life was most definitely in danger. The destination was a haven for gang members wanting to hone their tagging abilities and people who just wanted to break windows with rocks. A lot of homeless folks also made the area home. Russell got out of the car and opened the back door, dragging Richard out. He propped him up on the side of the vehicle and pulled his gun out, pressing the barrel against Richard's chin.

"Where's Wendy?" Russell insisted.

Richard just smiled.

"Where's Wendy?" Russell again asked, this time pulling back the hammer on the gun.

Richard started to play a game with his tongue and lips.

"Where the fuck is Wendy?" Russell insisted, now moving the gun up to Richard's forehead, pressing it so hard against his skin that Richard actually showed signs that he felt irritation. Most people in their right mind would be getting pissed off by that point but Richard showed great hesitation in displaying any type of anger.

Russell reared back his arm and punched Richard in the stomach, causing him to scream like a girl and act as if he'd been shot in the gut with a shotgun.

Russell felt something strange. Richard's stomach didn't feel like a stomach at all. With all of the abuse he had taken without so much as a blink, it was certainly odd that he would react in such a way from a simple punch to the abs. The detective pulled Richard back on his feet as he cried from the pain, pulling up his shirt in the process, revealing a disfigured torso. What he found were stitches, puss, a stream of blood and an awful stench. Stitches lined Richard's stomach, just as they had on Willie's belly, only this time the area in question was much bigger and the victim in question was alive. It looked as if a notebook had been attached to Richard's torso and sewn in.

Richard began to fade in and out of consciousness.

Russell also noticed something that he had either ignored earlier, or hadn't seen because of the robe. The clothing around Richard's crotch was completely soaked with blood.

"Oh my god," Russell said.

He grabbed Richard and walked him to a spot of dead grass, gently resting him on the ground. He uncuffed Richard's hands and rested his arms to the side. Gently and with extreme care, Russell unzipped Richard's pants, pulling his blood soaked underwear down in the process. Just as he feared, a fleshy patch of skin was all that remained of Richard's genitals.

RING! RING!

Russell jumped at the sounds of his phone ringing.

RING! RING!

He thought of Wendy and how she always pushed him to answer the phone. He wasn't going to let this call get away.

"What?" he answered.

"I see you've finally caught up with Richard," the voice said. "Wendy told me of your hunch about Mr. Tark, and I must say, I think I would've thought the same thing. Is he still alive? The medication I gave him should slowly be eating his stomach and digestive tract. Intense pain will be his accompaniment into the afterlife. Have you discovered the book I left you?"

Russell began to tear up as he tried to come to grips with what had just happened. Not only was he practically celebrating what he thought was the end of the drama and the final piece of the case, he had mercilessly beat an innocent man that he should've been protecting.

"Why are you doing this?" he asked.

"The book will tell you everything," the voice said.

Richard let out a yell and clutched his midsection.

"Oh, I hear him, such a sweet sound," the voice said. "I'm so glad I had a chance to hear the man die. Actually, he had it better than the others. He is on so much morphine and dope that he doesn't even know what planet he's on.

I had to do that to get the book inside of him without killing him from the shock. He screamed too much when I made the initial incision. Plus, I had to have him alive when you found him. It's definitely more fun when you do it that way."

Russell looked over at Richard and realized that the man had passed away. His eyes were wide open, staring into the sky like a gentle goodbye to a world that did nothing but bring him down. He was the latest victim.

"Detective," the voice said. "You're not saying much. Is he dead yet?"

"Yes," Russell said.

"Good," the voice responded. "Then you'll have an easier time getting that book from him. I want you to read it. It is my life's work. It's not very big, but it does have some important facts about what's going on. I respect your job and what you must do and I don't want to have to sit down and talk about things too much. You can tell the publisher that it is a true story about the lives of seven kids who followed each other to hell. I have taken to calling it '*RedeeM*' after you."

Russell didn't know what to think.

"After me?" he said. "What are you talking about? Why do you keep bringing me into this? I'm not like you!"

"Russell, you need to brush up on your reading. I will call you in a few days to see how you liked it. Be gentle."

The phone line went dead.

Russell sat on the ground next to Richard and cried. He didn't want to cut him open. This man was just in his care, and he abused him. He had punched and threatened Richard when all he was doing was dying, the next victim in the path of a madman. Oh God, he shoved that fermented testicle in his mouth too. The only way he could deal with and defend his actions—in his mind at least—was to think of Richard in high school, kicking out his teeth and saving them as a trophy.

Russell pulled his pocketknife from his pants and slowly began to pry each stitch from Richard's body. Warm pockets of blood and puss opened with each cut and Russell had to pause twice to dry heave.

A gang-banger walked by with a spray paint can and watched as Richard performed his own type of autopsy on the man. It was apparently such a horrible sight that the gang member whipped out his gun and immediately pointed it at Russell's head.

"Yo! What do you think you're doing?" the kid asked. "That's some sick shit, dog."

"Go away," Russell pleaded, not even looking up at the kid.

"Naw, you are going to jail, yo," the kid said.

Russell reached back and grabbed his badge.

"I'm a cop, now go the fuck away," he yelled, throwing his badge down before pulling his gun out and shooting a round into the air. The kid threw down his spray paint can and sprinted into the distance.

"Fuckin' punk!" Russell barked, getting back to his work.

Thirty minutes later, he was still nursing the patch of skin, trying not to hurt a man who was long dead. He could've just grabbed a piece and ripped it loose but that seemed so wrong considering the situation. The flap of skin was eventually and meticulously peeled back, revealing a stack of papers that were shrink-wrapped in plastic. A class ring was also shrink-wrapped. The killer had done an excellent job of hiding and storing the book under such a small layer of skin. Russell was eventually able to pry the book from the skin and removed the blood and puss stained plastic cover. A 40-page manuscript was revealed. Just as the killer had said, its title was "RedeeM." In the spot usually reserved for author credit, it simply said "The Reedemer."

Russell got to his feet and left Richard on the side of the road, got into his car and drove off. He didn't know whether to call the cops and report the body and didn't care to. An hour earlier, he was convinced he had solved the case when in reality, he did nothing more than cater once again to the puppet master who was controlling his every move. This had become much more than an investigation. It was survival.

He would follow instructions again and return to his office to catch up on some reading. Wendy was the only thing he needed to stay motivated and if reading that book was going to help him, then that's what he had to do.

16

My life has been a roller coaster ride of goods and bads. I started out on the wrong side of the LORD, but I have done my best to make it up. I have made sacrifices that no man should ever have to. I have done my best.

The words that you are reading are written not only to educate, but enlighten. I am a child of GOD and know no boundaries set by man.

Grab a cup of tea and something to snack on, because learning about the truth and the way in which it was laid out, might cause you to hunger.

Reggie Peterson.

Charles Manning.

Seth Owens.

Richard Tark.

And, perhaps you thought I too had fallen by the wayside. I was supposed to be the first victim, and in fact, I believe I was. It's amazing how easy it was to doctor a body with a simple driver's license. That's the ultimate in identity theft, don't you think?

No, that wasn't me strung up on the barbed wire. Killing Coach Bruce was the happiest moment of my life. He was the one who should've stepped forward and taken the initiative. He was a ruthless man. Probably more ruthless than I could have ever been. He was a child molester. He was a baby killer. He was the bringer of pain and suffering for many children who wanted nothing more than to play a game.

And he was the one adult who knew the secret and didn't tell. He helped us all to go on with our lives as if nothing had happened to those girls.

The football meatheads went to Coach Bruce, even after we all decided not to tell anyone. They said the guilt was too much to bear. He said, "tough shit" and helped them believe that those girls deserved to die.

He deserved to die.

I found it pleasing when I tied him up and began sawing away at his wrists. At first I couldn't decide which set of limbs would be more painful and challenging to remove. Hands? Feet? Hands? Feet? I finally made a decision and realized the hands would be missed greater. We all use our hands and we all use our feet, but I think we become more emotionally attached to our hands over time and forget about our lower limbs.

His hands were an easy choice to remove.

He pleaded with me to stop with each movement of the saw, but that just made me saw harder. I got a charge with the sounds of bone crunching beneath my tool. He cried out loud for quite some time, unable to move from my grasp.

I do believe he died before I even got through the second hand, which was probably a good thing because his persistent screams were starting to get annoying. I finished removing his hands and feet in a way so that identifying him would be difficult. I also removed his head, for the aforementioned reason. This you know. Or do you? Interesting question, isn't it? Considering you thought it was me based solely on a well-placed ID card. Hmm. Something to mull over, Detective Meeder.

Gutting him, well, that's a different matter all together. I had always wondered what a human would look like gutted like a fish. I didn't want to disturb his torso in any way, so that made it more challenging. I cut a large hole around his neck and removed the organs that way.

Kind of like a pumpkin.

Messy.

I wouldn't recommend that to someone who doesn't have the proper environment in which to do it. I chose to do it in my basement, and it made for an awful mess. I didn't even attempt to clean it.

I wasn't sure how easy it would be to pass my identity to someone else, but apparently didn't have too much trouble. I sewed my driver's license into his fat belly in the hopes that it couldn't be missed. Apparently, that was a good idea on my part. I wasn't quite sure how the police would handle the body. I had faith in law enforcement and thought they would figure it out for sure. What a surprise it was to find out just how ignorant the cops truly are.

I gave myself plenty of time to carry out my plans without the fear that the cops would come bursting through my door before I could finish. I believe you tried your hardest, Detective Meeder, but failed.

The most exciting thing about my experience with Coach Bruce was my display. I used to string up barbed wire with my dad on hunting trips when I was little. It seemed fitting to me that hanging him like a pig was appropriate.

As for the horrible things we, the proverbial we, the we of 1983, the we that I see as guilty, the we five of Carver High were guilty of? Once you know the whole story, you'll be thanking me for ridding the world of these monsters. None of them deserved to live after what happened that night. Especially Seth.

How could a man who took something so valuable go on to relish in the successes of life? I was glad to see him go. I don't even like football. The man was a menace to society. I remember seeing him on television, smiling, signing autographs, talking about his precious family. The man was a leech and a devil worshiper.

Let me go back and tell you a story. One of two girls, five bastards and the ultimate deception. This may shed some light on my duty and sacrifice.

The weather was somewhat chilly that night, certainly not a good temperature for a camping trip, but we insisted on going. Richard was the one who really wanted this thing to happen. He was interested in Andrea. The other fellas, well, they thought it would be a good excuse to get drunk and take advantage of the other girl—Alexis.

Richard was a funny little shit. I first saw him on the first day of school. He climbed out of that disgusting car with a girl, the likes I'll never forget. She was beautiful.

I ran into Richard in class some time after that and thought I'd offer my hand in friendship. He accepted it like I knew he would.

The thing with Richard and I was simple—we couldn't have been more opposite. He was a complete loser and I was not. I showed him how to stick up for himself. I showed him how to appreciate those who are more fortunate. And, I showed him how to get women.

Unfortunately, the more I got to know him, the more I got to know his infatuation with Andrea. I was soon overcome with the same emotions. DEVIL.

I had planned on getting Richard so drunk that night, he wouldn't have even known about Andrea and I. But, the guy just wouldn't take a drink.

Things were going so well until Seth and Alexis decided to fornicate in front of us all. That's not a good idea when you have a group of drunk and horny individuals trapped in the mountains. They should've waited, or run off into the woods, or used the tent, or even the truck. Then none of this would ever have happened.

I knew right away that something bad was happening when I saw the silhouette of Alexis struggling to get free. I think we all knew what was happening, but no one did anything to stop it. Moments later there was no movement at all. The other guys all disregarded her and climbed on for their turn. To understand these guys, I must go back and tell you a little about their pasts . . .

Russell turned the pages one by one, mortified by the story, enraptured by its sobering reality. He was the first one fooled by Willie's bait and switch maneuver. He should've realized that the man hanging from the barbed wire fence was too old to be Willie Becker. It was so obvious in hindsight.

The story sometimes read like that of a child writing a biography about their summer trip. Willie was very braggadocios in his descriptions, as proud as a father with successful children as he described how he managed to kill each one of his victims without anyone the wiser. Other times it was as smooth as a work of artistic genius. Russell was making mental images of what happened, trying to figure out the most important thing. He couldn't fathom how a normal boy, who admittedly stayed out of the rape, could end up being a monster.

Page after page, he skimmed through a madman's tale of rape and torture. Ramblings about school and how he met the people he would eventually murder peppered the manuscript. Unbelievable confessions that by today's standards could've been more than enough to convict someone.

Richard was the most disappointing person in the group. Those of us who knew him before that evening thought something was wrong in his mind, and afterwards, there was no doubt. He saw Alexis being raped and thought it was a green light to do the same to Andrea, a girl who had done nothing wrong in her life.

I loved Andrea. I found her to be an amazing person, but I never had a chance to prove to her how amazing I was. I saw her kick Richard, and I felt good for her. How dare he put his hands on such lovely skin?

I volunteered to find her in the woods. She was running blind with no one to help her and no clothes from the waist down. I saw her run into the forest naked. I saw her virgin skin, lit by the firelight, before it disappeared behind the trees.

Temptations are a part of our sick kind. I am guilty just like any other human scum. I am not immune to the horrors that we all face each day.

I chased after Andrea, hoping to find her and talk to her about the attack on Alexis. I hoped that she wasn't hurt or scared, but knew that she was both. I couldn't stop thinking about her naked body. It was as if I began to split in two—one half wanting to comfort, the other half wanting to sin.

"Andrea," I yelled in vain. "C'mon out." There was nothing I could do to coax her out of her hiding spot. I followed her trail as long as I could, until the grass was no longer flattened.

I didn't know where she went after that.

I walked until I could no longer sustain my own weight. Collapsing on a fallen tree trunk, I wept for the girl that got away. I could hear the guys back at the campsite. They were screaming and yelling about Alexis.

I didn't care about her, or them.

Then I heard the noise behind me.

I saw a silhouette of someone stumbling through the trees, disappearing down an embankment. I wiped the tears from my eyes and followed it down.

It was Andrea. She was walking like someone who didn't know what planet they were on. She was discombobulated and walking into trees. I yelled for her and ran down the hill to where she was standing.

"I hit a tree," she muttered, blood streaming down her face. "I, I ran into a tree. Please help me."

She stumbled backwards, landing on her back in a pile of brush. That's when the demons took over. I will never forget that moment, nor will I ever be forgiven. We've all had moments when we felt a presence of evil under our skin and that was certainly my undoing.

You know when you are at the grocery store and someone gives you back too much change? That voice that tells you it's okay also compels you to walk out without saying a word.

You know when you see that homeless man on the side of the road with a cardboard sign asking for a mere quarter? That voice tells you to look away and ignore him and he will go away.

Now, I realize those are trivial wrongdoings and not in the same ball park as what I did, but you understand the voice that pushed me. That little voice told me that this was my chance to have Andrea. No witnesses. No memory. No guilt. She wouldn't remember a thing, right? Her head was split open and she could barely walk.

Heck, I figured she wouldn't even be able to recall what happened to Alexis. We had an alibi sitting right there in front of me with her legs wide open.

The power of the LORD has convinced me that what I did was natural. I know that any young man my age would've done the same thing in my position. It's raw animal attraction in its purest form.

The other boys were the ones who committed the most heinous sin of all. They were the ones who took the life of another person. I was just going to commit the sin of rape.

At least that's what I told myself . . .

Russell was nearly finished with his reading. No phone calls from Willie. He thought about Wendy and how tough she was. Reading the text of a psycho was exhilarating and somewhat emotional. Russell thought about how unlikely it was to have such detailed information from a killer, before the person was actually caught.

Willie had accused Seth, Charles and Reggie of rape and murder, and Richard of attempted rape. However, Willie's sin was about to be revealed and it was the worst one of all.

> I quickly unzipped my pants and dropped my jeans to the ground before I climbed on her. I made sure to turn off my flashlight and found us to be in the most ideal spot.
>
> We couldn't have been found too easily, since the moonlight was hidden by the immense trees, and we were at the bottom of an embankment.
>
> I proceeded to fornicate with her and got a charge of excitement when she started to struggle. I didn't anticipate how exciting that would actually be.
>
> However, when she got too emotional, I had to put a stop to it. She screamed. In fact, she screamed so loud, I thought for sure someone was going to come down and catch me in the act.
>
> That never happened.
>
> She continued to struggle, and I finally put my hand over her mouth to prevent another vocal outburst. I didn't realize it at the time, but I was actually suffocating her. I don't know if I would've removed my hand had I known what I was doing.
>
> It was exciting feeling her writhe in pain under me as I grinded against her. She went limp before I did. As I filled her with life, hers ended.
>
> I left her body under some brush and branches, and convinced them not to search for her. The next day I drove out there and buried her where I killed her.

Today, I can write about killing Andrea Mitchell because I am saved. The person who committed that crime is dead now. I killed that part of me when I killed Coach Bruce.

Sawing off the hands of my decoy was like sawing off the hands that had suffocated Andrea. Taking out all of his organs was like releasing all of the pain and suffering I had gone through my whole life. Cutting off his head helped me forget what I did.

Killing Seth, Reggie, Charles and Richard just added to my spiritual cleansing. They had to die to make this right. Don't you agree?

And there was one person who helped me get through it all. She was the one who showed me the LORD and sheltered me from the bad people.

My mother helped me realize that I wasn't to blame for what happened. It was the devil. And the only way I could defeat the devil was by teaching the other guys a lesson in the name of GOD.

The more I tortured them. The more heinous things I did to them, the more I felt vindicated. The quicker Andrea's spirit would leave my body and go to her deserved resting place in heaven.

My inspiration for carrying out the torture was you Detective Meeder. You convinced me that it was okay.

I can remember coming home from the grocery store one night, throwing myself on the coffee table, lying on my back, watching the television upside down.

There before me was a detective, talking to the media about something no doubt important. That detective was Mr. Meeder. I sat in awe, staring at the screen, being forced by something more powerful than I could imagine. Then it hit me.

`I saw his name, and for whatever reason, I read it clearly as redeeM. I knew then what I had to do. I had to redeem myself for what had happened. I had to redeem the group for what they had done. And by a different definition, I had to redeem Andrea. The sign was too strong to ignore.`

`RedeeM.`

`Satan comes in many shapes and sizes, and I assure you that when you meet him, you won't know it. He arrives like a storm, comes into your life and destroys those around you, leaving just as quickly. It takes an immense amount of time to recover.`

`This letter is my final redemption. These aren't crimes that I want to cover up or escape from. I want people to know what we did to those girls and what I did to make it right.`

`The men who were there that night have all learned the consequences of their actions and are in a better place for it. I had to torture and mutilate them to release the demons. I had to remove their genitals to welcome the change. After all, it was that part of the body that caused all of this pain and misery. The more they suffered, the less the girls suffered in their deaths.`

`There is one more task that lies ahead for me. I must bear witness to my own immortality. I must remove the last surviving member of that fateful night.`

`RedeeM`

KNOCK! KNOCK!

Russell was startled out of a daze. The ramblings that he had just read seemed unreal. Willie Becker sounded like a deranged cult leader more than a serial killer. The two could probably be put in the same category. His beliefs on religion and the value of human life were frightening.

KNOCK! KNOCK!

"Fuckin' Christ, come in!" Russell barked.

"Sorry to bother you sir, but someone dropped this off for you," said one of the guys from the front desk. "He said you would want it right away."

Without saying a word, Russell burst from his chair and ran towards the man, swiping the package from his hands.

"Thanks, that'll be all," Russell said, motioning for him to leave. He walked back to his desk and stared at the cardboard box for what must have been fifteen minutes. He didn't move a muscle, just stared. Richard's manhood was sitting in front of him. It was the same kind of box that every victim had received at some point. He carefully reached forward and pried the top off the box, revealing the shiny, gold metal lid to the jar inside. He removed the glass jar and set it down next to his lamp. The reflection of light illuminated the sick delivery and made it appear like a broken lava lamp.

Attached to the bottom of the jar was a sticky note:

> Detective Russell—
>
> By now, you have probably read all about my so-called friends and I. You now know what I have done was not only essential, but heroic. I do, however, still have one more thing to take care of and I will need your assistance. Wendy needs your assistance as well.
>
> Enclosed you will find directions to a secluded campsite in the mountains. I expect you to be there by dawn tomorrow. No cops!
>
> RedeeM

Russell crumbled the note and grabbed the directions, running from his office in a hurry. He had to find the man who walked into his room with the package. He hadn't seen him in the office before. Racing down the hall, Russell nearly lost his footing on more than one occasion. The sun was already going down and he had to hurry.

"Hey," he yelled as he got close to the front desk. "Hey. Where's the man who brought the box to me? Where is he?"

The two girls sitting behind the counter looked confused.

"Where's the guy, about yay—tall," Russell said, holding his hand out at about eye level. "He had dark glasses and was wearing a black shirt."

"Detective, we haven't seen a package," one of the girls said. "No one's brought you anything as far as we know. At least they haven't checked it through us."

Russell went blank. The killer was there. Willie had walked right into his office and he didn't even know it. Maybe it was all the excitement from the story, or perhaps it was because he hadn't eaten much in the previous couple of days, but he didn't even look the man in the face when he walked in. He would've known.

"Detective Meeder," a voice bellowed from behind. "I need to talk to you."

It was Detective Wes Godnai. He had been Russell's supervisor for roughly six months, and had been a good one at that. The reason? He didn't bother Russell or interfere with the investigations that Russell worked on. That's the best kind of superior.

"The police found two more bodies today, mutilated just like the others," Wes began. "What I can't figure out is this; you are on the scene with the first three victims, and disappear for the last two? And where's detective Valdez? I haven't even seen her in the office for the past two days. We need to talk about what's going on. What have you found out?"

Russell, still breathing hard from the sprint and uninterested in the conversation, put his hand on Wes' shoulder.

"I didn't hear anything about bodies being found, or I would've gone out there," he started. "Honest to God. As for Wendy, she's not feeling well. She called me today and said she'll be back by Monday."

"This isn't a babysitting shift, detective Meeder," Wes barked. "If she feels like she needs to take large amounts of time off, she needs to find another job. I can't have my people sitting at home, when some fucking nut is out there cutting people's balls off."

"I agree and understand completely," Russell said, trying to get away. "I'll talk to her, and let her know how you feel."

He smacked Wes on the shoulder and turned to run back to his office.

"And stop running around here like a kid in gym class!" Wes yelled. "What the heck is wrong with you?"

"Okay," Russell said, continuing to sprint down the hall.

He had one stop to make before leaving town. Willie had mentioned the fact that his mother had supported him through the troubles. When he had gone to her home to question her about what he thought was her son's body, he found her to be quite cooperative. All of the religion that he felt when he walked into Willie's mother's home made him feel uncomfortable. He did remember that much. Hearing Willie talk of God and redemption did nothing more than set an example of how the apple doesn't always fall far from the tree. It all made sense.

As he drove up to the house that he had sipped stank coffee in just a little over a week earlier, he noticed that all of the lights were out and it definitely appeared like no one was home. Still he needed to knock and find out.

"Joan, are you here?" Russell yelled at the door, while pressing the doorbell over and over again. "Ms. Becker."

No answer.

Without much of a choice, Russell prepared to kick the door. "Here we go again," he muttered, growing increasingly tired of his new form of entry. His foot was beginning to raw from pounding down so many doors. He reared back his foot and connected with the door, sending it wide open, slamming against the wall on its way around.

The house was dark and dingy so he flipped on a light switch, illuminating the living room, surrounded by piles of newspapers and garbage.

"Hello?" he yelled, drawing his gun from its holster and cocking the trigger in place. "Is anyone home? Ms. Becker, are you here? This is Detective Meeder."

He carefully walked into the kitchen, finding nothing out of the ordinary. It was probably the most well kept room in the house, and looked like it was actually avoided. Apparently the Becker family didn't do much cooking.

"Hello?" he yelled again, hoping that if anyone were home, he wouldn't be sneaking up on them with his gun drawn. "Ms. Becker?"

He walked up the stairs and searched the bedrooms and the bathroom, again finding nothing out of the ordinary. It looked like the inside of any home belonging to a God-fearing single woman in her early sixties. Eventually, he relaxed his grip on the pistol thinking that if anyone were in the house, they would've already jumped him. Strangely, the only photos hanging from the walls were that of Jesus. No family. No scenery. Things had changed since he last visited.

The final place he had to check was not something he wanted to do. The house had an old basement like so many of the houses built in that era. The kind of basement that didn't have cement walls, just dirt. The kind that were originally meant for storing food in the heat of the summer. A tall crawlspace you could stand in. He specifically remembered Willie talking about a basement. Gingerly walking down the rickety old stairs, Russell cautiously pulled the cord on the light bulb, sending it in a swing. Back and forth the light rocked, illuminating the horror that Russell was about to be a part of.

The basement wasn't very big, only measuring about twelve by twelve, or roughly the size of a typical bathroom. Once the light was lit, he could see the spattering of blood that lined the dirt foundation. The ground was also covered in blood.

It's hard to clean up a mess like that when the ground is nothing but earth and dried soil. A table rested in the corner of the room surrounded by utensils consisting of various sized knives and a hand saw. An Exacto knife and a roll of surgical string were also present. Russell held his hand to his nose, trying to hold back the awful stench that emanated from all corners of the tiny room. Carefully and hesitantly, he walked over to the table and picked up the largest of the knives. The handle was sticky with dried blood and Russell immediately tossed it back onto the table when he realized the bottom of it was sticky. He wiped his hands on his jeans as if he had just spilled a canister of sulphuric acid on himself.

CLOP! CLOP!

The sounds of someone walking upstairs startled Russell. His heart began to race and he ran over to the light, pulling the cord and turning it off. He crouched down under the bloody table and lifted his gun, pointing it at the entry door. Waves of nausea and terror filled his cluttered mind. The footsteps got right above him, sprinkling the area with dust from the floorboards above. They stopped and for a moment the house was completely silent again. Whoever it was had to know someone had been there because the front door was kicked in. Russell slapped himself in the forehead when he realized that fact. It didn't matter, he told himself, he had the upper hand—a loaded pistol and the element of surprise in a dark basement.

CLOP! CLOP!

The footsteps continued until they got right up to the door leading to the basement. Russell shivered and shook as he held his gun firm, aiming it for the first motherfucker who dared to poke through. He sat in a semi-dried concoction of mud comprised of dirt and blood and pieces of rotting flesh and tried to avoid thinking about the horrible smell that was all around him.

He pulled the hammer.

All of his training couldn't have prepared him for the nightmare he faced. His heart raced and he couldn't breathe. The basement door creaked shut and a lock was sounded. As Russell scrambled back to his feet, trying to get to the door, the sounds of the footprints faded away. Whoever it was, they left in a hurry. Russell turned the light back on and tried to open the basement door to no avail. Nothing. Whoever it was had no problem leaving him down there and Russell kicked himself when he realized that he paid no attention to which side the lock was on.

"Fuckin' Christ!" he yelled at the top of his lungs. He didn't care who heard him. He was armed and pissed. Ready for anyone who walked through that door. Now, it's easy to feel that way, knowing that the person whom he feared just moments earlier, was gone.

Russell lifted his gun and aimed it for the spot next to the handle where the door actually locks into the wood. He turned his head to avoid shrapnel and let loose with two shots to the lock. With luck on his side, the door swung wide open and he burst from the basement. It was time to find Willie and figure out what the last thing was and why Russell had to be involved. More importantly, why Wendy had to be stuck in the middle.

On the way through the door and into the kitchen, he kicked something across the floor. Bending down to investigate, he had booted a Denver Police Detective badge belonging to Wendy Valdez.

"Bastard," he muttered, picking up his pace and running from the house. He got out into the yard and looked in all directions for someone, anyone who could've seen the person who had just been in the house. Nothing.

"Fuck!" he screamed, running for his car. He wanted to get to the mountains before Willie so he could avoid anymore surprises. It was extremely dark and looked as if the area was primed for a little snow or light rain. Still, he had no choice.

He had to finish it.

17

The drive to the secluded campsite was long and lonely for Russell. He couldn't get there quick enough and spent most of the time thinking of Wendy and how much he missed her. Funny how he couldn't stand her when she was around, but could think of no one else when she was gone.

Was he falling for this girl? Had he already fallen? Things couldn't have been more twisted in his mind. Russell Meeder wasn't the kind of guy who fell for women very easily. It was always the other way around. He was happy being single with the occasional fling. Nothing serious. It just complicated things. Simple as that. Now he was caught up in a triangle of hell involving his duty, his heart and quite possibly, his death. He grabbed his pack of cigarettes from the glove box and put one in his mouth before pushing in the lighter on his dashboard. Seconds later it popped out and he grabbed it, motioning towards his face to light the smoke. His face lit up from the orange glow.

He couldn't do it.

Wendy had scolded him for smoking on numerous occasions and wouldn't you know it, he had an urge to quit—for her. Never in his life could a woman convince him to give up a bad habit. What was going on? Frustrated with his tangled mind, Russell crushed the cigarette and threw it on the passenger seat floorboard.

It was past midnight as he drove through the quiet streets of Fort Collins just as he had earlier in the day. This time he was on his way to Poudre Canyon. Willie didn't want to see him until dawn, but Russell wanted to get there as soon as possible. No need in wasting time sleeping. His feelings were almost surreal, driving to the site of such a horrible crime that was still providing ramifications for its participants nearly 20 years later.

Russell looked over at the passenger seat and the jar that housed someone's penis and testicles. The grizzled flesh floated around in the putrid liquid like rotten ice cubes. It was hard, yet fascinating for Russell to look over and see something that at one time was probably the most important thing to Richard Tark. He assumed that the pattern remained true, and that the jar in his vehicle belonged to the last victim. It had to be Richard's.

He leaned over and grabbed the jar, holding it up in front of his face as he drove, illuminating the specimen with the city lights that surrounded the car.

HONK! HONK!

Russell swerved out of the oncoming traffic that he had wandered in front of as he gazed at the horrible display.

"Shit," he muttered, putting the jar back on the seat, not taking his eyes off the road for one second after that.

Eventually, he reached the point where he had to leave concrete. He wasn't driving a four-wheel drive, but knew things would be all right. Taking a 1974 Charger up a dirt embankment was no hard task.

Russell took his time, avoiding fallen branches and areas where the snow had drifted. A faint trickle of frozen rain began to pepper his windshield and soon he had his wipers going. Luckily for him, he had a spare pair of gloves in the trunk, along with a waterproof flashlight.

Looking at his directions, he realized that he would soon be coming across a stream that crossed the dirt road. He had to turn onto the stream and follow it. Russell crossed his fingers in the hopes that he could keep driving once he reached the stream. If the water was frozen or if there was too much snow, he would not only strand his car in the middle of nowhere, he'd be hoofing it for about a mile. Neither one of those scenarios waited him, as the area was dry of snow and the creek was flowing with water.

He turned his car towards the creek and began his trek through the wilderness. The one thing that stood out in his mind was the sheer isolation of the campsite. He pictured a KOA campground with hookups and an outhouse. This was nothing like that. It was as backwoods as you could get in a vehicle, which would explain how the boys got away with so much.

Russell pulled up to the open area that he assumed was the campsite. The eerie presence of ghosts circled his every move. He got out of his car, surrounded by darkness, not knowing if Willie was standing directly in front of him, or if he had driven right into a bear's den. Hell, he wasn't entirely sure he had even found the right spot.

Feeling his way to the rear of the car, he popped the trunk and got his flashlight, along with a Coleman lantern, a pair of warm gloves, and a parka to keep the frozen rain off of his dry clothes. He lit up the lantern and walked around the car, noticing that the ground was virtually rid of snow, although muddy in a lot of spots. It didn't appear that anyone was there yet and there were certainly no other cars around.

Russell pulled his notes from his pocket and looked for his work on Alexis' grave. He had studied the book that Willie had given him and wanted to find the pit where Alexis' burnt remains were located. That had to be done to verify the story in Russell's mind. He found the spot where the fire pit once was, unused for nearly 20 years, and walked north about 20 paces before finding a spot where some rocks seemed out of place. It was on top of a bulge in the soil, and didn't appear like it was placed there naturally.

Flipping it over, Russell pulled out his mini shovel and began to dig. Wet soil isn't very difficult to move, and Russell had no trouble digging the two-foot depth. Moments later, he discovered the soil had turned black. Carefully and quickly, he shoveled around the black soil, and found something that made his heart skip—a jaw bone. It was blackened and burned like a piece of chicken that had been forgotten on the grill, but was virtually untouched beyond that. Most of the teeth still remained in the bone and Russell picked it up, looking at it in the light.

Alexis Hall had been found.

Russell heard the popping sound of someone walking on twigs. He stood on his feet and placed his hand on his gun, ripping it from the holster, aiming it towards the darkness all around. The lantern was on the ground next to the grave and lit up a short area, most likely just illuminating Russell for anyone in the woods who wanted to shoot him. He waited as the sounds of rain and wind beating the trees around him took over. Again, the noise charged through the trees. It was impossible to figure out it was coming from. Was it from the front? Was it from behind? He couldn't tell. The sound ricocheted off of trees in all directions.

"Willie?" Russell yelled. "Willie Becker, is that you? Wendy?"

No response.

"Come out, or I'll open fire," Russell screamed, not meaning what he said. He knew better than to open fire into the darkness with the possibility that a fellow officer was out there.

No response.

Then an unexpected flash came from near the car. An animal burst out of the trees and ran past Russell towards the opposite end of the campsite. It was an immature deer, alone and probably separated from its herd. It was scared and hungry.

"Oh fuck me!" Russell said, trying to regain any composure he may have had. "I think I'm having a heart attack." He jokingly grabbed his chest and clasped his coat.

The hard task of finding the spot where Willie claimed to have buried Andrea was ahead for Russell. He didn't know where to start, but did have the testimony from Willie that he chased her east into the trees.

Russell carefully walked into the woods, hoping to catch a glimpse of anything that Willie had mentioned in his manifesto. The tree trunk, the embankment, the makeshift trail that Andrea had run down for a short time. Where would someone run if they were scared for their life?

He carried the lantern and led the way with the beam of the flashlight. He walked around for nearly an hour, without luck. He walked in circles. He walked in straight lines. He walked diagonally. Still nothing.

It wasn't until he did the most boneheaded thing he had ever done in his career. He wanted to check out a group of trees and was walking towards it when he heard a noise coming from behind him. He turned suddenly, accidentally swinging the lantern into a tree, breaking the glass and twisting it to the point where it was extinguished almost immediately. Walking backwards, trying to figure out what he was going to do for a light source more reliable than his flaky flashlight, he walked right into the embankment. He fell backwards and tumbled down the hill, barely missing contact with the few trees that grew on the side of it.

He fell all the way to the bottom, separated from his flashlight. Darkness all around, he shook his head, realizing at that point that the cold, frozen rain was coming down quite hard. Russell continued to sit on the ground, turning in all directions to see if he could spot his flashlight. A mere ten feet away, it rested on the ground, pointing its beam of light into oblivion. Russell got to his feet and looked up to where he had fallen down the hill. It was too dark for him to measure his slide, but he knew it must have been quite a sight.

Reaching down for the flashlight, he was startled into a false sense of reality. Seeing bodies was nothing new to the detective, and frankly after seeing some of the bodies that Willie had left, convinced Russell that he'd seen the worst. For some unexplained reason, seeing someone's skeleton was worse for Russell. The skeleton symbolizes the end of individuality and the beginning of anonymity. Seeing bodies disfigured and gushing with blood gave a corpse a uniqueness of a once vibrant life. Looking at a skeleton, the cold realization is that thin or fat, beautiful or ghastly, everyone looks the same eventually.

What he saw, in the beam of light that illuminated from his flashlight, was the forehead, brow and top of an eye socket of someone's skull, sticking out of the earth. On his knees, Russell slowly wiped the muddy dirt from around the skull, revealing it in all of its glory. It must have been Andrea Mitchell, a girl too young to die and too loved to be left to rot out in the middle of nowhere. Forever stuck on the same plot of land where she lost her life and her innocence, it was a miracle she was even found.

Russell continued to dig at the bones that were buried in the shallow grave, while the rain continued to fall from above. Mud and grass were caked under his fingernails and his clothes were completely covered in grime.

Time ticked by until Russell had retrieved not only the entire skull, but a few other large bones, probably from the arms. He didn't realize it, but the faint glow of cyan glistened on the horizon, symbolizing the start of yet another day and his date with Willie. He also didn't realize that someone had been watching him from the top of the embankment, laughing at how silly someone can look playing in the dirt.

"You realize that disturbing the bones of the dead is bad luck," Willie said, directing his statement to Russell, pacing back and forth from the hillside above. "She should stay right there, forever a reminder of what happened. Besides what more beautiful scenery can you ask for in your final resting place? She sure won't get that in a public cemetery."

Russell got to his feet and reached for his pistol. It was gone.

"Looking for this," Willie said, holding up Russell's weapon. "I think before you fall down a hill, you should make sure your holster is buckled and secured. I was going to take your gun from you, but you made it so I didn't have to."

Willie flipped the gun on his index finger like a cowboy, pointing it at Russell and making shooting noises with his lips like a five-year-old with a toy rifle. He started walking down the embankment.

"That's loaded," Russell said. "You shouldn't play with it like that."

Willie smiled.

"You're telling me how to properly handle a gun?" Willie said, walking closer to Russell, until he was right in the cop's face. "I know how to handle a weapon and quite frankly, I'm not the one who lost it, am I?"

Willie quickly raised the weapon next to Russell's head, pointing it into the distance, squeezing the trigger and firing off a round right next to Russell's ear. Russell screamed and buckled to his knees, cupping his hand over his ear. The ringing could not be avoided. It got louder with each sound that came from Russell's environment and for a moment it felt like his head was going to explode from the pressure.

"Sorry!" Willie screamed, bending over and yelling directly into the bad ear. "I guess it is loaded."

Russell got to his feet and rubbed his ear, pissed and ready to find the slightest wrinkle in Willie's movements.

"I need to tell you about a passage that might shed some light on what I have accomplished these past two weeks," Willie started. "It's Ezekiel seven-eleven. Look it up someday."

The rain continued to fall, adding to the ringing in Russell's head, and the mud that surrounded them both. Willie seemed happy, like someone who has just been reunited with a loved one after being apart for a long time.

The sky soon became illuminated by the morning sun and the two men were staring at each other face to face. Willie stood back and paced back and forth, tapping the loaded gun on his temple like a man deep in thought. Russell wished that he could reach over and pull the trigger.

In a moment's time, Russell's body went numb. A face that he tried to remember for so long suddenly appeared before him. He had seen photographs that triggered nothing. He had even seen him in person once and that didn't bring up the past. Standing before him was the man who had beat him down so many years ago in the dungeons of the bleachers. If he felt anger towards Richard, this was much deeper. This was the guy who attacked him, who initiated the contact and forced him to the ground. This was the man who started his path towards law enforcement in the first place. It wasn't until that night in the rain and darkness, his visions of the attacker became clear as crystal. Willie looked a little different, but for the most part remained the same. He didn't put on much weight at all, and kept the same hair style.

"Wendy told me about your problem," Willie said. "She told me *all* about it."

"What problem?" Russell demanded. "What the fuck are you talking about?"

"Oh c'mon," Willie said. "Don't play dumb with me. She told me how you are scared of being alone. She told me that you wanted to find the right girl and settle down. Why haven't you?"

Russell was growing increasingly angry. His private thoughts about women were of no concern to the psycho. Why had Wendy been talking to this asshole like he was her diary?

"You know what?" Russell asked. "It's losers like you who are always interested in the lives of others. You have no chance of getting laid and you insist on focusing on other people to hide from your own shortcomings. It's actually kind of sad."

"Tisk, tisk. Mr. Meeder," Willie said. "You have no idea what you're talking about do you? You *do* love that woman, and you're going to admit it to me right now."

"You're wrong. I don't love her," Russell said.

"Really?" Willie responded. "What if I were to take this little 'ol gun here and fire a couple rounds into her pretty little forehead? Would you change your mind then?"

"Where is she?" Russell yelled.

"You look very familiar to me," Willie said, scratching his scalp through his wet hair. "Have we met before?"

"Carver High School. 1983. Loveland. Blue hair," Russell said, somewhat relieved to get it off his chest and reveal who he was to his former attacker.

Willie smiled stunned. "That was you? I still have your tooth."

"Where's Wendy?" Russell insisted, changing the subject.

Willie put his fingers in his mouth and whistled loudly. The sound of the whistle could be heard for a few seconds as it bounced from tree to tree, echoing into infinity. Moments later, the muffled sounds of someone's voice, along with the rustling of branches and feet got louder as it reached the two men.

Russell looked behind Willie as the images of Ms. Becker and Wendy came into view.

"Wendy!" Russell said, motioning towards the two.

"Ah, ah," Willie said. "Don't make me shoot you Mr. Meeder."

Russell continued to stand in place. Wendy was being herded by Ms. Becker, a knife pushed against her throat. Ms. Becker was dressed in bundles of winter clothes and looked like a snowman, wearing pink winter wear. Wendy's mouth was covered in tape, and her hair was tied back in a braid. She looked cold and hungry and was too weak to get away from Ms. Becker.

"Okay," Willie said. "I want you to admit right now, that you're in love with this woman. Go ahead."

Russell looked over at Willie and clenched his jaw.

"Why are you doing this?" Russell said. "What does this have to do with anything? Seriously, this is so fucked. You're the one who needs to answer questions, asshole."

"Let's just say, I no longer have the ability to think sexually," Willie said. He reached into his coat pocket with his free hand, pulling a jar of human parts from it.

"Now, whose are those?" Russell asked.

"Say you love her," Willie demanded.

"You gave me Richard's balls last night," Russell said. "Now whose are those?"

"What makes you think those were Richard's testicles? What makes you think I gave you his penis?" Willie asked.

Russell was silent.

"I'm holding Richard's parts right now," Willie continued, shaking the jar and staring at its contents as they violently swirled around in the liquid. Then he grabbed his pants and pulled them down. He revealed the torturous carvings that graced the area that once housed his genitals. His mother smiled proudly.

"You have a part of me now," Willie said, referring to Russell's jar. "Someday, that will be worth some money."

"Why did you take Wendy?" Russell said. "She had nothing to do with your party. She wasn't here raping and murdering those girls. If you are so God damn remorseful over what you did to Andrea, why make it worse with Wendy? You're a fucking hypocrite."

"Russell, you know why I took her," Willie said. "The only way I could make sure you behaved was to take away someone you loved. I never intended on killing her unless you got in the way. You're right. This isn't about her or you for that matter. This was about me fulfilling my duty from God and taking care of this mess."

Wendy twisted her body, screaming from the mere shock of seeing Willie's disfigured lower half. The force of her movement allowed the knife to penetrate her skin, although not seriously. After that, she screamed from the pain.

"Take off her gag," Russell demanded. "She can't breathe. And take that fucking knife away from her throat. She has nothing to do with this!"

Willie walked over to his mother continuing to point the gun at Russell with his pants around his ankles. He quickly ripped the tape off of Wendy's mouth, taking skin from her face and lips, causing her to scream again. Tears rolled down her cheeks as she entered a world of fear and pain that she hadn't experienced in her days as a captive.

Willie turned back to face Russell.

"What do you want from us?" Russell said. "Why are we here?"

"I want you to tell her that you love her," Willie said, pulling the hammer back on the gun, lifting it up to point at Russell's head. "Tell her or your brains become part of this grave sight."

"This isn't about me, or Andrea or those other jerks that you've been chasing!" Russell yelled. He then turned to Wendy and quickly said, "I love you," the way a kid tells his grandmother while trying to get her to go away.

"Not like that," Willie said, shooting Russell in the leg.

"Ah fuck!" Russell yelled, falling to the earth as the pounding of his heart could be felt in his right knee.

"Tell her like you mean it. Here I'll show you."

Willie turned to face Wendy and cocked his head to the side, saying the words, "I love you," in a sensual manner. He continued to face her, repeating the words. In his mind, Wendy's face was transforming. Tears were streaming down her cheeks, reminding him of someone from his past. Russell rolled on the ground, holding his knee and grinding his teeth in pain. He put his hand down and reached his finger into the wound, trying to stop the bleeding.

"I love you," Willie repeated, now picturing Wendy as a completely different girl. In his mind, her face had changed into the face of Andrea. She continued to cry, and stare into Willie's eyes like someone who wished to be set free. Soon Willie saw the tears disappear and the old smile had returned to Andrea's face.

"I love you," Willie again said, this time tears dripping from *his* eyes. "I love you. I'm so sorry."

Ms. Becker poked the knife into Wendy's neck a little more, trying to get her son to snap out of his trance.

"Wake up, boy," she insisted. "You have a job to do."

In a flash, Willie held up his gun and pulled the trigger as both women fell to the ground. The chaos that surrounded the four individuals was matched only by that of the boys back in 1983.

Russell had no idea what had just happened and instinctively charged Willie, forcing the large man onto his back. With a loud snap, Willie grunted under Russell's bodyweight. His eyes were pointed to the stars and he blinked feverishly. Rain fell onto his face and cleaned off some of the mud that had splashed up on him.

Russell looked down and noticed a pool of blood accumulating from Willie's lower torso. He lifted his shirt and discovered that a sharp fragment of bone from Andrea's remains had been driven through Willie's lower midsection.

Willie gurgled and moaned in pain as Russell got off of him.

Behind Russell, Wendy was standing on her feet, rubbing her neck where the knife had been.

"You think that's poetic justice?" she asked.

Russell turned to Wendy.

"You're all right?" Russell said. "I didn't know if he had shot you just then. I . . . I just didn't know. I tackled him. I . . . I . . . Are you all right?"

Wendy smiled.

"I could eat," she said. "Those fuckers didn't feed me once, the whole time I was with them. I think that old bag was more messed up than this guy."

Wendy walked over to the body of Ms. Becker. She had been shot right between the eyes by her own son.

"She must have really pissed him off," Wendy said. "I wonder what happened there. He seemed like a different kind of psycho just before he shot her. Talk about a loser."

Russell pulled his phone from his jacket and called the police. His fingers were shaking as he tried to dial the numbers.

The two sat on a tree trunk that rested on the ground behind Willie. Neither one of them offered to remove the bone from his torso, but figured it didn't really matter.

"We're going to let you sit there and think about what you've done," Wendy said to Willie, speaking at a high volume, not knowing if he heard her or not. He was still blinking and wheezing for air. Then she turned to Russell and smiled. She was enjoying Willie's pain.

"Should we help him?" Russell asked. "I mean, he's still alive, isn't it our duty to help a man if we are able?"

"Ah, dammit," she said, leaning down in front of Willie. "It's your lucky day!" she yelled in Willie's face.

"Pull him up and I'll grab the bone."

With a yell and a pull, Willie was free of Andrea's grip. The detectives rolled him over and tied his jacket around his waist to stop the bleeding before placing him against the tree trunk on his back. He was breathing and awake. The muffled sounds of a chopper could be heard in the distance.

Russell turned to Wendy and grabbed her hand.

"Say," he started. "You know that whole scene back there? Well, I wanted to tell you something. I . . . I . . ."

She put her hand over his mouth.

"Don't you dare," she said. "I don't date coworkers, and I certainly don't date cops. You're kind of a dick, anyway."

Russell looked at the ground.

"Thanks for saving my life," she said, bringing herself up to his face, kissing him softly on the cheek. "I owe you one big fella. How's your leg?"

Russell put his hands on his swollen knee. The pain was so bad that it gave him goosebumps. He hadn't really even had a chance to think about his wound since tackling Willie.

"Fuckin' Christ," he said. "Fuckin' Christ."

"Why do you always say that?" she asked him. "It's so stupid."

"I don't know," he said. "What else should I say?"

"You could say something like '*oh well,*' or '*whatever*,' or '*dammit.*' Anything but that."

Russell shrugged.

"I don't think so."

Cops converged on the site and found the body of Ms. Becker along with the remains of Alexis Hall and Andrea Mitchell. Willie Becker wasn't as lucky as his mother and found himself alive and in dire need of psychological treatment and a doctor.

Russell was put on a stretcher and pulled up the hill. It was humiliating but sure beat having to attempt it on his own.

"Take my car back," he said, handing his keys to Wendy.

"This is strange," she said. "I'm the one who hasn't eaten in three days and just got saved from being held hostage, and you're the one being babied. Men."

Russell smiled and pulled a five dollar bill from his pocket.

"Get yourself a cheeseburger you skinny bitch," he said with a smile.

18

It had been two weeks since Willie Becker was arrested and Russell had managed to heal enough to use a crutch to help with a leg that housed a cast that spanned from above the knee down to his ankle. He had taken a much needed leave of absence from work and was coming down from the most emotional time of his life.

That's why he decided to take a trip to Montana.

Andrea Mitchell was being buried in Stanford and Russell felt it was necessary that he be there. Discovering her bones gave him the feeling that he, in some way, had played God. Giving Andrea back to her family was something that he felt responsible for.

He arrived in Great Falls by plane and was driven to Stanford by a Sheriff that lived in the area who volunteered to take him. The drive took less than an hour, allowing Russell to focus on some things that he hadn't had time to think about in some time. Along the way, he found himself mired in thought and overwhelmed by the beauty of the scenery.

Wendy didn't come with him on his trip to Montana because she was back on the job and couldn't take any time off. It was probably best anyway, since the two had felt somewhat uncomfortable around each other since that morning in the woods. It was almost as bad as the feeling you have after you sleep with someone you work with after a night out drinking. It's never the same after that.

"You been to Montana before?" the cop driving the car asked.

"No," Russell admitted. "This is my first time. I'm just here for the funeral."

The man looked in his rearview mirror.

"Trust me, I know why you're here," the man said. "And, I'm honored to drive you. I knew Andrea when she was just a little girl, and I always felt that she would be found someday. As hopeful as they were, I didn't believe the stories that she had run off with that other girl. That just wasn't Andrea. I know I speak for the whole town when I thank you for finding her."

Russell actually felt humbled by the sentiment and looked to the floorboard.

"Don't mention it," he said. "I was just doing my job."

He continued to look around at the beautiful landscape that encased him. The mountains were unmolested and the peaks had a dusting of snow. Being in the backseat of a squad car was new to Russell and he felt, for a moment, a peace in being transported that way.

Looking down to his left, he noticed a copy of the bible resting on the seat next to him. He tried to think back to the passage that Willie had referred him to. Ezekiel seven-eleven. Thumbing through the pages, he found what he was looking for.

Violence is risen up into a rod of wickedness: none of them shall remain . . .

"So, what are you up to these days?" the cop asked. "When do you think you'll be back in action? I mean, with your leg and all."

Russell put the bible down, and reflected on the passage he had just read.

"I haven't been back to work," he said, motioning towards his leg. "I'm kind of thinking of a career change. I've seen things that no man should have to see in a lifetime. I . . . I just don't know what I want to do."

"You want a cigarette?" the cop asked, offering his pack of smokes.

Russell shook his head no.

"Sorry, I gave it up," he said. "Haven't smoked in two weeks."

"Good for you," the cop said. "So, you're thinking of retiring?"

"Not retiring," Russell said. "I like to think of it as 'taking a break.' In fact, I think that's just what I need right now in my life. I just started working on a novel, actually."

"Novel?" the cop said. "You want to be a writer?"

"You bet," Russell said, looking at a herd of cattle walking in the breeze. He noticed the barbed wire fence and thought back to the nightmarish images that he had seen a month before. "I have a lot of up here that I could share." He tapped himself on the head.

"You got a name for your book yet?" the cop asked.

"Sort of," Russell said. He put his sunglasses on and leaned his head back against the headrest and looked at the ceiling. "I'm thinking of calling it . . .

. . . '*Redeem*.'"

Edwards Brothers,Inc!
Thorofare, NJ 08086
20 December, 2010
BA2010354